I0595665

Garrick David

The Dramatic Works of David Garrick

to which is prefixed a life of the author

Garrick David

The Dramatic Works of David Garrick
to which is prefixed a life of the author

ISBN/EAN: 9783337394950

Printed in Europe, USA, Canada, Australia, Japan

Cover: Foto ©Andreas Hilbeck / pixelio.de

More available books at **www.hansebooks.com**

THE
DRAMATIC WORKS

OF

DAVID GARRICK, Esq.

TO WHICH IS PREFIXED

A LIFE OF THE AUTHOR.

IN THREE VOLUMES.

VOL. I.

CONTAINING

LETHE.	EVERY MAN IN HIS HUMOUR.
The LYING VALET.	The FAIRIES.
MISS IN HER TEENS.	FLORIZEL and PERDITA.
ROMEO and JULIET.	CATHARINE and PETRUCHIO.

LONDON:

PRINTED FOR A. MILLAR, STRAND.

M,DCC,XCVIII.

Price bound *Ten Shillings* and *Sixpence*.

DAVID GARRICK, Esq.

D AVID GARRICK was born at *Hereford* in the year 1717. *His father followed the military profession and had at the time of his death been advanced to a Majority in the Army. Our Author received the first Rudiments of his Education at the Free School at Litchfield, which he afterwards compleated at Rochester, under the celebrated Mr Colson, since Mathematical Professor at Cambridge. On the 9th of March 1736, he was entered of the Honourable Society of Lincolns-Inn, being intended for the Bar: but whether he found the study of the Law too heavy, saturnine, and barren of amusement for his more active and lively disposition, or that a genius like his could not continue circumscribed within the limits of any profession, but that to which it was more particularly adapted; like the Magnetic needle pointed directly to its proper centre, or perhaps both, it is certain that he did not long pursue the Municipal Law; for in the year 1740, he quitted it entirely for the Stage. Having performed a noviciate at Ipswich, he made his appearance at Goodman's Fields; and October 19th 1741, acted Richard III. for the first time. His acting was attended with the loudest acclamations of applause; and his fame was so quickly propagated through the town, that the more established Theatres of Drury Lane, and Covent Garden, were deserted. These Patentees, alarmed at the great deficiency in the receipts of their houses, and at the crouds which constantly filled the Theatre of Goodman's Fields, united their efforts to destroy the new raised seat of Theatrical empire; in consequence of which, Garrick entered into an agreement with Fleetwood, Patentee of Drury Lane for £. 500 a-year. The fame of*

our

our English Roscius was now so extended, that an invitatio from Ireland, upon very profitable conditions, was sent him to act in Dublin, during the months of June, July, and August, 1742; which invitation he accepted. His success there exceeded all imagination; he was caressed by all ranks as a prodigy of Theatrical Accomplishment, and the play-house was so crowded during this hot season, that a very mortal Fever was produced, which was called Garrick's Fever. He returned to London before the winter, and now attended closely to his Theatrical professions, in which he was irrevocably fixed.—April 1747, he became joint Patentee of Drury Lane Theatre, with Mr Lacy; and in July 1749, married Mademoiselle Vilette.—In 1763 he undertook a journey into Italy for the benefit of his health; and during his travels gave frequent proofs of his Theatrical talents; for he could, without the least preparation, transform himself into any character, tragic or comic, and seize instantaneously upon any passion of the human mind. After he had been abroad about a year and an half, he turned his thoughts homewards, and arrived in London April 1765.— In 1769, he projected and conducted the memorable Jubilee, at Stratford, in honour of Shakespeare, so much admired by some, and so much ridiculed by others.—On the death of Mr Lacy in 1773, the whole management of the Theatre devolved on him; but being advanced in years, and much afflicted with chronical disorders, he finally left it in June 1776, and disposed of his moiety of the Patent to Messrs. Sheridan, Linley and Ford, for £.35,000. He died at his house in the Adelphi, Jan. 15th 1779. Notwithstanding his constant employ as both actor and manager, he was perpetually producing various little things in the dramatic way; some of which are originals; others translations or alterations from other authors, adopted to the state of the present times; besides which, he wrote innumerable prologues, epilogues, songs, &c.

DRAMATIS PERSONÆ.

Esop, *Mr* Bransby.	Frenchman, } *Mr* Blakes.
Mercury, *Mr* Beard.	Old Man. }
Charon, *Mr* W. Vaughan.	Mr Tatoo, *Mr* Marr.
	Po t, } Omitted in the re-
Lord Chalkstone, *Mr* Gar-rick.	Taylor, } presentation.
A Fine Gentleman, *Mr* Woodward.	Mrs Riot, *Mrs* Clive.
	Mrs Tatoo, *Miss* Minors.
Drunken Man, *Mr* Yates.	

S C E N E, a Grove.

With a View of the River LETHE.

CHARON *and* ESOP *discovered.*

CHARON.

PRITHEE, philosopher, what grand affair is transacting upon earth? There is something of importance going forward, I am sure; for Mercury flew over the Styx this morning, without paving me the usual compliments.

Esop. I'll tell thee, Charon; this is the anniversary of the rape of Proserpine: on which day, for the future, Pluto has permitted her to demand from him something for the benefit of mankind.

Char. I understand you;——His Maj sty's passion, by a long possession of the lady, is abated; and so, like a mere mortal, he must now flatter her vanity, and sacrifice his power, to atone for deficiences——But what has our royal mistress proposed in behalf of her favourite mortals?

Esop. As mankind, you know, are ever complaining of their cares, and dissatisfied with their conditions, the generous Proserpine has begg'd of Pluto, that they may have free access to the waters of Lethe, as a sovereign remedy for their complaints————Notice has been already given above, and proclamation made; Mercury is to conduct them to the Styx; you are to ferry 'em over to Elysium, and I am placed here to distribute the waters.

Char. A very pretty employment I shall have of it, truly! If her majesty has often these whims, I must petition the court either to build a bridge over the river, or let me resign my employment. Do their majesties know the difference of weight between souls and bodies? However, I'll obey their commands to the best of my power; I'll row my crazy boat over, and meet 'em; but many of them will be relieved from their cares before they reach Lethe.

Esop. How so Charon?

Char. Why, I shall leave half of 'em in the Styx; and any water is a specific against care, provided it be taken in quantity.

Enter MERCURY.

Mer. Away to your boat Charon; there are some mortals arriv'd; and the females among 'em will be very clamorous, if you make 'em wait.

Char. I'll make what haste I can, rather than give those fair creatures a topic for conversation. [*Noise within,* ˈbout, boat, boat!] Coming————coming————zounds, you are in a plaguy hurry, sure! no wonder these mortal folks have so many complaints, when there's no patience among 'em; if they were dead now, and to be settled here for ever; they'd be damn'd before they'd make such a rout to come over,————but Care, I suppose, is thirsty, and till they have drench'd themselves with Lethe, there will be no quiet among 'em; therefore I'll e'en to work; and so, friend Esop, and brother Mercury, good bye to 'ye.

[*Exit* Charon.

Esop. Now to my office of judge and examiner, in which to the best of my knowledge I will act with impartiality; for I will immediately relieve real objects, and only divert myself with pretenders.

Mer. Act as your wisdom directs, and conformable to your earthly character, and we shall have few murmurers.

Esop. I still retain my former sentiments, never to refuse advise or charity to those that want either; flattery

and

and rudeness should be equally avoided; folly and vice should never be spared: and tho' by acting thus, you may offend many, yet you will please the better few; and the approbation of one virtuous mind is more valuable than all the noisy applause, and uncertain favours of the great and guilty.

Mer. Incomparable Esop! both men and Gods admire thee! we must now prepare to receive these mortals; and lest the solemnity of the place should strike 'em with too much dread; I'll raise music shall dispel their fears, and embolden them to approach.

S O N G.

I.

Ye mortals whom fancies and troubles perplex,
Whom folly misguides, and infirmities vex;
Whose lives hardly know what it is to be blest,
Who rise without joy, and lie down without rest:
  Obey the glad summons, to Lethe repair,
  Drink deep of the stream, and forget all your care:

II.

Old maids shall forget what they wish for in vain,
And young ones the rover, they cannot regain;
The rake shall forget how last night he was cloy'd,
And Chloe again be with passion enjoy'd.
  Obey then the summons, to Lethe repair,
  And drink an oblivion to trouble and care.

III.

The wife at one draught may forget all her wants,
Or drench her fond fool to forget her gallants;
The troubled in mind shall go chearful away,
And yesterday's wretch, be quite happy to-day.
  Obey then the summons, to Lethe repair,
  Drink deep of the stream, and forget all your care.

Esop. Mercury, Charon has brought over one mortal already, conduct him hither.   [*Exit* Mercury.
Now for a large catalogue of complaints, without the

A 2   acknowledgment

acknwoledgement of one single vice;—here he comes—if
one may guess at his cares by his appearance, he really
wants the assistance of Lethe.

Enter POET.

Poet. Sir, your humble servant—your name is Esop—
I know your person intimately, tho' I never saw you before; and am well acquainted with you, tho' I never had
the honour of your conversation.

Esop. You are a dealer in paradoxes friend.

Poet. I am a dealer in all parts of speech, and in all the
figures of rhetoric— I am a poet, Sir—and to be a poet,
and not acquainted with the great Esop, is a greater para-
dox than—I honour you extremely, Sir; you certainly
of all the writers of antiquity, had the greatest, the sub-
limest genius, the——

Esop. Hold, friend, I hate flattery.

Poet. My own taste exactly, I assure you; Sir, no man
loves flattery less than myself.

Esop. So it appears, by your being so ready to give it
away.

Poet. You have hit it, Mr Esop, you have hit it——I
have given it away indeed. I did not receive one farthing
for my last dedication, and yet would you believe it?—I
absolutely gave all the virtues in heaven to one of the lowest reptiles upon earth.

Esop. 'Tis hard, indeed, to do dirty work for nothing.

Poet. Ay, Sir, to do dirty work, and still be dirty one-
self is the stone of Sysiphus, and the thirst of Tantalus—
You Greek writers, indeed, carried your point by truth
and simplicity,——they won't do now-adays——our pa-
trons must be tickled into generosity——you gain'd the
greatest favours, by shewing your own merits, we can only gain the smallest, by publishing those of other people
—You flourish'd by truth, we starve by fiction; *tempora
mutantur.*

Esop. Indeed, friend, if we may guess by your present
plight, you have prostituted your talents to very little purpose.

Poet. To very little upon my word——but they shall
find that I can open another vein——Satire is the fashion,
and satire they shall have—let 'em look to it, I can be sharp

as well as sweet—I can scourge as well as tickle, I can bite
as——

Esop. You can do any thing, no doubt; but to the business of this visit, for I expect a great deal of company—
what are your troubles, Sir?

Poet. Why, Mr Esop, I am troubled with an odd kind
of disorder—I have a sort of a whistling——a singing—
a whizzing as it were in my head, which I cannot get rid
of——

Esop. Our waters give no relief to bodily disorders, they
only affect the memory.

Poet. From whence all my disorder proceeds——I'l tell
you my case, Sir—You must know, I wrote a Play some
time ago, presented a dedication of it to a certain young
nobleman—he approv'd, and accepted of it; but before I
could taste his bounty, my piece was unfortunately damn'd;
—I lost my benefit, nor could I have recourse to my patron, for I was told that his lordship play'd the best cat-
call the first night, and was the merriest person in the
whole audience.

Esop. Pray what do you call damning a play?

Poet. You cannot possibly be ignorant, what it is to be
damn'd, Mr Esop?

Esop. Indeed I am, Sir,—we had no such thing among
the Greeks.

Poet. No, Sir!——No wonder then that you Greeks
were such fine writers——It is impossible to be described
or truly felt, but by the author himself——If you could
but get a leave of absence from this world for a few hours
you might perhaps have an opportunity of seeing it yourself——,—There is a sort of a new piece comes upon our
stage this very night, and I am pretty sure it will meet
with its deserts, at least it shall not want my helping hand,
rather than you should be disappointed of satisfying your
curiosity.

Esop. You are very obliging, sir;——but to your own
misfortunes if you please.

Poet. Envy, malice, and party destroy'd me—You must
know, Sir, I was a great damner myself, before I was
damn'd—So the frolicks of my youth were returned to me
with double interest, from my brother authors————But,
to say the truth my performance was terribly handled, before it appear'd in public.

A 3

Esop.

Esop. How so, pray?

Poet. Why, Sir, some sqeamish friends of mine prun'd it of all the bawdy and immorality, the actors did not speak a line of the sense or sentiment, and the manager (who writes himself) struck out all the wit and humour, in order to lower my performance to a level with his own.

Esop. Now, Sir, I am acquainted with your case, what have you to propose?

Poet. Notwithstanding the success of my first play, I am strongly persuaded that my next may defy the severity of critics, the sneer of wits, and the malice of authors.

Esop. What! have you been hardy enough to attempt another?

Poet. I must eat, Sir——I must live——but when I set down to write, and am glowing with the heat of my imagination, then——this damn'd whistling——or whizzing in my head, I told you of, so disorders me, that I grow giddy——In short, Sir, I am haunted as it were, with the ghost of my deceas'd play, and its dying groans are for ever in mine ears——Now, Sir, if you will but give me a draught of Lethe, to forget this unfortunate performance, it will be of more real service to me, than all the waters of Helicon.

Esop. I doubt friend you cannot possibly write better, by merely forgetting that you have written before; besides, if, when you drink to the forgetfulness of your own works, you should unluckily forget those of other people too, your next piece will certainly be the worse for it.

Poet. You are certainly in the right—What then would you advise me to?

Esop. Suppose you would prevail upon the audience to drink the water; the forgetting your former work might be of no small advantage to your future productions.

Poet. Ah, Sir! if I could but do that—but I'm afraid— Lethe will never go down with the audience.

Esop. Well, since you are bent upon it, I shall indulge you—If you please to walk in that grove, (which will afford you many subjects for your poetical contemplation) till I have examined the rest, I will dismiss you in your turn.

Poet. And I in return, Sir, will let the world know, in a preface to my next piece, that your politeness is equal in

you

your sagacity, and that you are as much the fine gentleman as the philosopher.   [*Exit* Poet.

Esop. Oh! your servant, Sir—In the name of misery and mortality what have we here!

Enter an OLD MAN, *supported by a* SERVANT.

Old Man. Oh! la! oh! bless me I shall never recover the fatigue—Ha! what are you friend? are you the famous Esop? and are you so kind, so very good to give people the waters of forgetfulness for nothing?

Esop. I am that person, Sir; but you seem to have no need of my water; for you must have already out-liv'd your memory.

Old Man. My memory is indeed impair'd, it is not so good as it was, but still it is better than I wish it, at least in regard to one circumstance; there is one thing which sits very heavy at my heart, and which I would willingly forget.

Esop. What is it pray?

Old Man. Oh la!—Oh!—I am horribly fatigued——I am an old man, Sir, turn'd of ninety——We are all mortal you know, so I would fain forget, if you please——that I am to die.

Esop. My good friend, you have mistaken the virtue of the waters; they can cause you to forget only what is past; but if this was in their power, you should surely be your own enemy, in desiring to forget what would be the only comfort of one, so poor and wretched as you seem. What! I suppose now, you have left some dear loving wife behind, that you can't bear to think of parting with.

Old Man. No, no, no; I have buried my wife and forgot her long ago.

Esop. What, you have children then, whom you are unwilling to leave behind you.

Old Man. No, no, no; I have no children at present—hugh——I don't know what I may have.

Esop. Is there any relation or friend, the loss of whom—

Old Man. No, no; I have out-liv'd all my relations; and as for friends, I have none to lose——

Esop. What can be the reason then, that in all this ap-

A 4

parent

parent misery you are so afraid of death, which would be your only cure.

Old Man. ——Oh, Lord! I have one friend, and a true friend indeed, the only friend in whom a wise man places any confidence—I have——get a little farther off, John—[*Servant retires.*] I have to say, the truth, a little money—it is that indeed, which causes all my uneasiness.

Esop. Thou never spok'st a truer word in thy life, old gentleman—[*Aside.*] But I can cure you of your uneasiness immediately..

Old Man. Shall I forget then that I am to die, and leave my money behind me?

Esop. No,– but you shall forget that you have it.——which will do altogether as well——One large draught of Lethe, to the forgetfulness of your money, will restore you to perfect ease of mind; and as for your bodily pains, no water can relieve them.

Old Man. What does he say, John——eh?—I am hard of hearing.

John. He advices your worship to drink to forget your money.

Old Man. What!—what!—will his drink get me money, does he say?

Esop. No, Sir, the waters are of a wholesome nature—for they'll teach you to forget your money.

Old Man. Will they so?—Come, come, John, we are got to the wrong place—The poor old fool here does not know what he says—Let us go back again, John——I'll drink none of your waters; not I——Forget my money! Come along, John.　　　　　　　　　　　[*Exeunt.*

Esop. Was there ever such a wretch! If these are the cares of mortals, the waters of oblivion cannot cure them.

Re-enter OLD MAN *and* SERVANT.

Old Man. Lookee, Sir, I am come a great way, and am loth to refuse favours that cost nothing——so I don't care if I drink a little of your waters——Let me see—ay—I'll drink to forget how I *got* my money——And my servant there, he shall drink a little, to forget that I have any money at all—and, d'ye hear, John——take a hearty draught. If my money must be forgot, why e'en let *him* forget it.

Esop. Well, friend, it shall be as you would have it——
　　　　　　　　　　　　　　　　　　　　You'll

You'll find a seat in that grove yonder, where you may rest yourself till the waters are distributed.

Old Man. I hope it won't be long, Sir, for thieves are busy now—and I have an iron chest in the other world, that I should be sorry any body peep'd into but myself— So pray be quick, Sir. [*Exeunt.*

Esop. Patience, patience, old gentleman.——But here comes something tripping this way, that seems so be neither man nor woman, and yet an odd mixture of both.

Enter a Fine Gentleman.

Fine Gent. Harkee, old friend, do you stand drawer here?

Esop. Drawer, young fop! do you know where you are, and who you talk to?

Fine Gent. Not I dem me! But 'tis a rule with me, wherever I am, or whosoever I am with, to be always easy and familiar.

Esop. Then let me advice you, young gentleman, to drink the waters, and forget that ease and familiarity.

Fine Gent. Why so, daddy? would you not have me well-bred?

Esop. Yes; but you may not always meet with people so polite as yourself, or so passive as I am; and if what you call breeding, should be constru'd impertinence, you may have a return of familiarity, may make you repent your education as long as you live.

Fine Gent. Well said, old dry-beard; egad you have a smattering of an odd kind of a sort of humour; but come, come, prithee give me a glass of your waters, and keep your advice to yourself.

Esop. I must first be inform'd, Sir, for what purpose you drink 'em.

Fine Gent. You must know, philosopher, I want to forget two qualities—My *modesty*, and my *good-nature*.

Esop. Your modesty and good-nature?

Fine Gent. Yes, Sir—I have such a consummate *modesty*, that when a fine woman (which is often the case) yields to my addresses, egad I run away from her: and am so very *good-natured*, that when a man affronts me, egad I run away too.

Esop. As for your modesty, Sir, I'm afraid you are come to the wrong waters—and if you would take a large cup to the forgetfulness of your fears, your good-nature, I believe, will trouble you no more.

Fine Gent. And this is your advice, my dear, eh.

Esop. My advice, Sir, would go a great deal farther——— I should advise you to drink to the forgetfulness of every thing you know.

Fine Gent. The devil you would; then I should have travell'd to a fine purpose truly; you don't imagine, perhaps, that I have been three years abroad, and have made the tour of Europe?

Esop. Yes, Sir, I guess'd you had travell'd by your dress and conversation: but, pray, (with submission) what valuable improvements have you made in these travels?

Fine Gent. Sir, I learnt drinking in Germany; music and painting in Italy; dancing, gaming, and some other amusements, at Paris; and in Holland—faith nothing at all: I brought over with me the best collection of Venetian ballads, two eunuchs, a French dancer, and a monkey, with tooth-picks, pictures and burlettas—In short, I have skimm'd the cream of every nation; and have the consolation to declare, I never was in any country in my life, but I had taste enough thoroughly to despise my own.

Esop. Your country is greatly obliged to you;—but if you are settled in it now, how can your taste and delicacy endure it?

Fine Gent. Faith, my existence is merely supported by amusements; I dress, visit, study taste, and write sonnets; by birth, travel, education, and natural abilities, I am entitled to lead the fashion; I am principal connoisseur at all auctions, chief arbiter at assemblies, profess'd critic at the theatres, and a fine gentleman———every where———

Esop. Critic, Sir, pray what's that?

Fine Gent. The delight of the ingenious, the terror of poets, the scourge of players, and the aversion of vulgar.

Esop. Pray, Sir, for I fancy your life must be somewhat particular) how do you pass your time; the day for instance?

Fine Gent. I lie in bed all day, Sir.

Esop. How do you spend your evenings then?

Fine Gent. I dress in the evening, and go generally behind the scenes of both Play-houses; not, you may imagine, to be diverted with the play, but to intrigue, and shew myself—I stand upon the stage, talk aloud, and stare about
—which

—which confounds the actors, and disturbs the audience; upon which the galleries who hate the appearance of one of us, begin to *biss*, and cry *off*, *off*, while I undaunted stamp my foot so——loll with my shoulder thus——take snuff with my right-hand, and smile scornfully——thus.—— This exasperates the savages, and they attack us with vollies of suck'd oranges, and half eaten pippens——

Esop. And you retire.

Fine Gent. Without doubt, if I am sober—for orange will stain silk, and an apple may disfigure a feature.

Esop. I am afraid, Sir, for all this, that you are oblig'd to your own imagination, for more than three fourths of your importance.

Fine Gent. Damn the old prig, I'll bully him—[*Aside.*] Lookee, old philosopher, I find you have pass'd your time so long in gloom and ignorance below here, that our notions above stairs are too refined for you; so we are not likely to agree, I shall cut matters very short with you— Bottle me off the waters I want, or you shall be convinc'd that I have courage in the drawing of a cork;——dispatch me instantly, or I shall make bold to throw you into the river, and help myself——What say you to that now? eh?

Esop. Very civil and concise! I have no great inclination to put your manhood to the trial: so if you will be pleas'd to walk in the grove there, 'till I have examined some I see coming, we'll compromise the affair between us.

Fine Gent. Yours, as you behave——*au Revior!*

[*Exit* Fine Gentleman.

Enter Mr Bowman *(bustily.)*

Bow. Is your name Esop.

Esop. It is, Sir.—Your commands with me?

Bow. My lord Chalkstone, to whom I have the honour to be a friend and companion, has sent me before, to know if you are at leisure to receive his lordship.

Esop. I am placed here on purpose to receive every mortal that attends our summons——

Bow. My lord is not of the common race of mortals, I assure you; and you must look upon this visit as a particular honour, for he is so much afflicted with the gout and rheumatism, that we had much ado to get him across the river.

Esop. His lordship has certainly some pressing occasion

for

for the waters, that he endures such inconveniences to get at them.

Bow. No occasion at all——His legs indeed fail him a little, but his heart is as sound as ever, nothing can hurt his spirits; ill or well, his lordship is always the best company, and the merriest in his family——

Esop. I have very little time for mirth and good company; but I'll lessen the fatigue of his journey, and meet him half way.

Bow. His lordship is here already——There's a spirit! Mr Esop—There's a great man!—See how superior he is to his infirmities; such a soul ought to have a better body.

Enter MERCURY *with* Lord CHALKSTONE.

Lord Chalk. Not so fast, monsieur Mercury—you are a little too nimble for me. Well, Bowman, have you found the philosopher?

Bow. This is he, my lord, and ready to receive your commands.

Lord Chalk. Ha! ha! ha! there he is, profecto!—*toujours le meme!* [*Looking at him through a glass*] I should have known him at a mile's distance—a noble personage indeed!—and truly Greek from top to toe.—Most venerable Esop, I am in this world and the other, above and below, yours most sincerely.

Esop. I am yours, my lord, *as* sincerily, and I wish it was in my power to relieve your misfortune.

Lord Chalk. Misfortune! what misfortune?—I am neither a porter nor a chairman, Mr Esop——My legs can bear my body to my friends and my bottle: I want no more with them; the gout is welcome to the rest——eh Bowman?

Bow. Your lordship is in fine spirits!

Esop. Does not your lordship go through a great deal of pain?

Lord Chalk. Pain? ay, and pleasure too, eh Bowman!——When I'm in pain, I curse and swear it away again, and the moment it is gone, I lose no time; I drink the same wines, eat the same dishes, keep the same hours, the same company; and, notwithstanding the gravity of my wise doctors, I would not abstain from French wines and French

cookery,

cookery, to save the souls and bodies of the whole college of physicians——

Esop. My lord has fine spirits indeed!   [*To Bowman.*

Lord Chalk You don't imagine, philosopher, that I have hobbled here with a bundle of complaints at my back. My legs, indeed, are something the worse for wear, but your waters, I suppose, can't change or make 'em better; for if they could, you certainly would have try'd the virtues of 'em upon your own—eh Bowman! ha, ha, ha.——

Bow. Bravo! my lord, bravo!

Esop. My imperfections are from head to foot, as well as your lordship's.

Lord Chalk. I beg your pardon there, Sir; though my body's impaired—my head is as good as ever it was; and as a proof of this I'll lay you a hundred guineas——

Esop. Does your lordship propose a wager as a proof of the goodness of your head?

Lord Chalk. And why not?—Wagers are now-a-days the only proofs and arguments that are made use of by people of fashion: all disputes and politics, operas, trade, gaming, horse-racing, or religion, are determin'd now, by *six to four*, and *two to one;* and persons of quality are by this method most agreeably releas'd from the hardship of thinking or reasoning upon any subject.

Esop. Very convenient truly!

Lord Chalk. Convenient, ay, and *moral* too.——This invention of betting, unknown to the Greeks, among many other virtues, prevents bloodshed, and preserves family affections——

Esop. Prevents bloodshed!

Lord Chalk. I'll tell ye how——When gentlemen quarrelled heretofore, what did they do?——they drew their *swords*——I have been run through the body myself, but no matter for that——what do they do now? they draw their *purses*—before the lie can be given, a wager is laid; and so, instead of resenting, we pocket our affronts.

Esop. Most casuistically argued, indeed, my lord; but how can it preserve family affections?

Lord Chalk. I'll tell you that too—An old woman, you'll allow, Mr Esop, at all times to be but a bad thing—What say you, Bowman?——

Bow. A very bad thing indeed, my lord.

Lord Chalk. Ergo, an old woman with a good constitution, and a damn'd large jointure upon your estate, is the devil—My mother was the very thing——and yet from the moment I *pitted* her, I never once wish'd dead, but was really uneasy when she tumbled down stairs, and did not speak a single word for a whole fortnight.

Esop. Affectionate indeed!—but what does your lordship mean by *pitted* her?

Lord Chalk. 'Tis a term of ours upon these occasions—I back'd her life against two old countesses, an aunt of Sir Harry Rattle's that was troubled with an asthma, my fat landlady at *Salt-hill*, and the mad-woman at *Tunbridge*, at five hundred each *per annum:* She outliv'd 'em all but the last, by which means, I hedg'd of a damn'd jointure, made her life an advantage to me, and so continued my filial affections to her last moments.

Esop. I am fully satisfied—and in return your lordship may command *me.*

Lord Chalk. None of your waters for me; damn 'em all; I never drink any but at Bath ——I came merely for a little conversation with you, and to see your Elysian fields here—[*Looking about thro' his glass.*] which, by the bye, Mr Esop, are laid out most detestably——No taste, no fancy in the whole world!——Your river there—— what d'ye call ——

Esop. Styx——

Lord Chalk. Ay, Styx—why, 'tis as strait as *Fleet-ditch* ——You should have given it a serpentine sweep, and slop the banks of it—The place, indeed, has very fine *capabilities ;* but you should clear the wood to the left, and clump the trees to the right: in short, the whole wants variety, extent, contrast, and inequality——[*Going towards the orchestra, stops suddenly, and looks into the pit.*] Upon my word, here's a very fine *hub-bab!* and a most curious collection of ever-greens and flow'ring-shrubs—

Esop. We let nature take her course ; our chief entertainment is contemplation, which I suppose is not allowed to interrupt your lordship's pleasures.

Lord Chalk. I beg your pardon there——No man has ever studied or drank harder than I have—except my chaplain ; and I'll match my library and cellar against any nobleman's in Christendom—shan't I, Bowman, eh?

Bow. That you may indeed, my lord ; and I'll go your lordship's halves, ha, ha, ha.

Esop.

Esop. If your lordship would apply more to the first, and drink our waters to forget the last——

Lord Chalk. What! relinquish my bottle! What the devil shall I do to kill time then?

Esop. Has your lordship no wife nor children to entertain you?

Lord Chalk. Children! Not I, faith—My wife has, for ought I know,—I have not seen her these seven years——

Esop. You surprize me!

Lord Chalk. 'Tis the way of the world, for all that—I married for a fortune; she for a title. When we both had got what we wanted, the sooner we parted the better—— We did so; and are now waiting for the happy moment, that will give to one of us the liberty of playing the same farce over again——Eh, Bowman!

Bow. Good, good; you have puzzled the philosopher.

Esop. The Greeks esteem'd matrimonial happiness their *summum bonum.*

Lord Chalk. More fools they! 'tis not the only thing they were mistaken in—My brother Dick, indeed, married for love; and he and his wife have been fattening these five and twenty years, upon their *summum bonum,* as you call it——They have a dozen and half children, and may have half a dozen more, if an apoplexy don't step in, and interrupt their *summum bonum*——Eh, Bowman? ha, ha, ha!

Bow. Your lordship never said a better thing in your life.

Lord Chalk. 'Tis lucky for the nation, to be sure, that there are people who breed, and are fond of one another ——one man of elegant notions is sufficient in a family; for which reason I have bred up Dick's eldest son myself; and a fine gentleman he is——is not he, Bowman?——

Bow. A fine gentleman, indeed, my lord.

Lord Chalk. And as for the rest of the littledo, they may fondle and fatten upon *summum bonum,* as their loving parents have done before 'em.

Bow. Look there! my lord—I'll be hang'd if that is not your lordship's nephew in the grove.

Esop. I dare swear it is. He has been here just now, and has entertained me with *his* elegant notions.

Lord Chalk. Let us go to him; I'll lay six to four that he has been gallanting with some of the beauties of antiquity

ty—Helen or Cleopatra, I warrant you;—egad, let Lu-
cretia take care of herself; she'll catch a Tarquin, I can
tell her that——He is his uncle's own nephew, ha, ha, ha,
——egad, I find myself in spirits: I'll go and coquet a
little myself with them——Bowman lend me your arm;
and you, William hold me up a little—[*William treads
upon his toes.*]—Ho—Damn the fellow, he always treads
upon my toes—eugh——I shan't be able to gallant it this
half hour—Well, dear philosopher, dispose of your water
to those that want it—There is no one action of my life, or
qualification of my mind and body, that is a burden to me:
and there is nothing in *your* world, or in ours, I have to
wish for, unless you could rid me of my wife, and furnish
me with a better pair of legs—Eh, Bowman—Come along,
come along.

  Bow. Game to the last! my lord.

           [*Exit* Lord Chalkstone *and* Bowman.

  Esop. How flattering is folly: his lordship here supported only by vanity, vivacity, and his friend Mr Bowman, can fancy himself the wisest, and is the happiest of
mortals.

Enter Mr *and* Mrs TATOO.

  Mrs *Tatoo.* Why don't you come along, Mr Tatoo?
what the deuce are you afraid of?

  Esop. Don't be angry, young lady; the gentleman is
your husband, I suppose.

  Mrs *Tatoo.* How do you know that, eh? what! you
an't all conjurers in this world, are you?

  Esop. Your behaviour to him is a sufficient proof of his
condition, without the gift of conjuration.

  Mrs *Tatoo.* Why I was as free with him before marriage, as I am now; I never was coy or prudish in my life.

  Esop. I believe you, madam; pray how long have you
been married? you seem to be very young, lady.

  Mrs *Tatoo.* I am old enough for a husband, and have
been married long enough to be tired of one.

  Esop. How long, pray?

  Mrs *Tatoo.* Why above three months; I married Mr
Tatoo without my guardians's consent.

  Esop. If you married him with your own consent, I
think you might continue your affection a little longer.

  Mrs *Tatoo.* What signifies what you think, if I don't

think

think so ?——We are quite tired of one another, and are come to drink some of your Le——Lethaly——Lethily, I think they call it, to forget one another, and be unmarried again.

Esop. The waters can't divorce you, madam; and you may easily forget him without the assistance of Lethe.

Mrs *Tatoo.* Ay, how so ?

Esop. By remembering continually he is your husband : there are several ladies have no other receipt——But what does the gentleman say to this?

Mrs *Tatoo.* What signifies what he says? I an't so young and so foolish as that comes to, to be directed by my husband or to care what either he says, or you say.

Mr *Tatoo.* Sir, I was a drummer in a marching regiment, when I ran away with that young lady——I immediately bought out of the corps, and thought myself made for ever; little imagining that a poor vain fellow was purchasing fortune, at the expence of his happiness.

Esop. 'Tis even so, friend ; fortune and felicity are as often at variance as man and wife.

Mr *Tatoo.* I found it so, Sir——This high life (as I thought it) did not agree with me; I have not laugh'd, and scarcely slept since my advancement; and unless your wisdom can alter her notions, I must e'en quit the blessings of a fine lady and her portion, and, for content, have recourse to eight-pence a day, and my drum again.

Esop. Pray who has advis'd you to a separation ?

Mrs *Tatoo.* Several young ladies of my acquaintance, who tell me they are not angry at me for marrying him ; but being fond of him now I have married him ; and they say I should be as compleat a fine lady as any of 'em, if I would but procure a *separate divorcement*.

Esop. Pray, madam, will you let me know what you call a fine lady ?

Mrs *Tatoo.* Why, a fine lady, and a fine gentleman, are two of the finest things upon earth.

Esop. I have just now had the honour of knowing what a fine gentleman is ; so pray confine yourself to the lady.

Mrs *Tatoo.* A fine lady, before marriage, lives with her pappa and mamma, who breed her up till she learns to despise 'em, and resolves to do nothing they bid her ; this makes her such a prodigious favourite, that she wants for nothing.

Esop.

Esop. So, lady.

Mrs *Tatoo.* When once she is her own mistress, then comes the pleasure !——

Esop. Pray let us here.

Mrs *Tatoo.* She lies in bed all morning, rattles about all day, and sits up all night; she goes every where, and sees every thing; knows every body, and loves no body; ridi- cules her friends, coquets with her lovers, sets 'em together by the ears, tells fibs, makes mischief, buys china, cheats at cards, keeps a pug-dog, and hates the parsons; she laughs much, talks aloud, never blushes, says what she will, does what she will, goes where she will, marries whom she plea- ses, hates her husband in a month, breaks his heart in four, becomes a widow, slips from her gallants, and begins the world again——There's a life for you; what do you think a fine lady now?

Esop. As I expected——you are very young, lady; and if you are not very careful, your natural propensity to noise and affectation will run you headlong into folly, ex- travagance, and repentance.

Mrs *Tatoo.* What would you have me do?

Esop. Drink a large quantity of Lethe to the lose of your acquaintance; and do you, Sir, drink another to for- get this false step of your wife; for whilst you remember her folly, you can never thoroughly regard her; and whilst you keep good company, lady, as you call it, and follow their example, you can never have a just regard for your husband; so both drink and be happy.

Mrs *Tatoo.* Well, give it me whilst I am in humour, or I shall certainly change my mind again.

Esop. Be patient, till the rest of the company drink, and divert yourself, in the mean time, with walking in the grove.

Mrs *Tatoo.* Well, come along, husband, and keep me in humour, or I shall beat you such an alarm as you never beat in all your life.   [*Exeunt* Mr *and* Mrs Tatoo.

Enter FRENCHMAN *singing.*

French. Monsieur, votre serviteur——pourquoi ne re- pondez vous pas?——Je dis que je suis votre serviteur——

Esop. I don't understand you, Sir——

French. Ah le barbare! ill ne parle pas *Francois*——Vat, Sir, you no speak de French tongue?

Esop.

Esop. No really, Sir, I am not so polite.

French. En verite, monsieur *Esop*, you have not much politesse, if one may be judge by your figure and appearance.

Esop. Nor you much wisdom, if one may be judge of your head, by the ornaments about it.

French. Qu'est cela donc? Vat you mean to front a man, Sir?

Esop. No, Sir, 'tis to you I am speaking.

French Vel, Sir, I not a man! vat is you take me for? vat I beast? vat I horse! parbleu!

Esop. If you insist upon it, Sir, I would advise you to lay aside your wings and tail, for they undoubtedly eclipse your manhood.

French. Upon my vard, Sir, if you treat a gentilhomme of my rank and qualitee comme ca, depen upon it, I shall be a littel en cavalier vit you.

Esop. Pray, Sir, of what rank and quality are you?

French. Sir, I am a marquis *Francois*, j'entents les beaux arts, Sir; I have been an advanturier all ove the varld, and am a present en *Angleterre*, in *Ingland*, vere I am more honore and caress den ever I vas in my own countrie, or inteed any vere else——

Esop. And pray, Sir, what is your business in England?

French. I am arrive dere, Sir, pour polir la nation—de *Inglis*, sir, have too much a lead in their heels, and too much a tought in deir head; so, Sir, if I can lighten bote, I shall make dem tout a fait *Francois*, and quite anoder ting.

Esop. And pray, Sir, in what particular accomplishments does your merit consist?

French. Sir, I speak de French, j'ai bonne addresse, I dance un minue, I sing des littel chansons, and I have —— une tolerable assurance; en fin, Sir, my merit consist in one vard—I am foreignere——and entre nous——vile de *Englis* be so great a fool to love de foreignere better dan deinselves, de foreignere vold still be more great a fool, did they not leave deir own countrie, vere dey have noting at all, and come to *Inglande*, very day want for noting at all, perdie——Cela n'est il pas vrai, monsieur Esop?

Esop. Well, Sir, what is your business with me?

French. Attendez un pue, you shall hear, Sir——I am in love vit de grande fortune of one *Englis* lady; and de lady, she be in love with my qualite and bagatelles. Now, Sir, me want twenty or thirty douzains of your vaters, for

fear

fear I be oblige to leave *Inglande*, before I have fini dis grande affaire.

Esop, Twenty or thirty dozen! for what?

French. For my crediteurs; to make em forget de vay to my logement, and no trouble me for de future.

Esop. What! have you so many creditors!

French. So many! begar I have 'em dans touts les quartiers de la ville, in all parts of de town, fait——

Esop. Wonderful and surprizing!

French. Vorderful! vat is vonderful——dat I should borrow money?

Esop. No, Sir, that any body should lend it you——

French En verite vous vous trompez; you do mistake it, mon ami: if fortune gives me no money, nature gives me des talens; j' ai des talens, monsieur Esop; vech are de same ting——par example; de *Englisman* have de money, I have de flatterie and bonne addresse; and a little of dat from a *French* tongue is very good credit and securite for tousand pound——eh! bien donc, sal I have dis twenty or tirty douzaines of your vater? ouy, ou non?

Esop. 'Tis impossible, Sir.

French. Impossible! pourquoi donc? vy not?

Esop. Because if every fine gentlemen, who owes money, should make the same demand, we should have no water left for our other customers.

French. Que voulez vous que je fasse donc? Vat most I do den, Sir?

Esop. Marry the lady as soon as you can, pay your debts with part of her portion, drink the water to forget your extravagance, retire with her to your own country, and be a better œconomist for the future.

French. Go to my own contre!——je vous demande pardon; I had much rather stay vere I am; I cannot go dere, upon my vard——

Esop. Why not, friend!

French. Entre nous, I had much rather pass for one French marquis in *Inglande*, keep bonne compagnie, manger des delicatesses, and do no ting at all; dan keep a shop en *Provence*, couper and frisser les cheveux, and live upon soupe and sallade de rest of my life——

Esop. I cannot blame you for your choise; and if other people are so blind not to distinguish the barber from the

fine

fine gentleman, their folly must be their punishment——
and you shall take the benefit of the water with them.

French. Monsieur Esop, sans flatterie ou compliments,
I am your very humble serviteur—*Jan Frisseron* en *Provence*, ou le marquis de *Pouville* en *Angleterre.*

[*Exit* Frenchman.

Esop. Shield me and defend me! another fine lady!

Enter Mrs RIOT.

Mrs *Riot.* A monster! a filthy brute! your watermen
are as unpolite upon the *Styx* as upon the Thames—Stow
a lady of fashion with tradesmen and mechanics——Ah!
what's this, *Serberus*, or *Plutus!* (*seeing* Esop.) am I to
be frighted with all the monsters of this *internal* world.

Esop. What is the matter, lady?

Mrs *Riot.* Every thing is the matter, my spirits are un-
compos'd, and every circumstance about me in a perfect di-
lemma.

Esop. What had disorder'd you thus?

Mrs *Riot.* Your filthy boatman, *Scurroon* there.

Esop. Charon, lady, you mean.

Mrs *Riot.* And who are you, you ugly creature you?
if I see any more of you I shall die with *temerity.*

Esop. The wise think me handsome, madam.

Mrs *Riot.* I hate the wise; but who are you?

Esop. I am Esop. madam, honour'd this day by Proserpine with the distribution of the waters of Lethe: command me.

Mrs *Riot.* Shew me to the pump-room then, fellow—
where's the company——I die in solitude.

Esop. What company?

Mrs *Riot.* The best company, people of fashion! the
beau monde! shew me to none of your gloomy souls, who
wander about in your groves and streams——shew me to
glittering balls, enchanting masquerades, ravishing operas,
and all the polite enjoyments of *Elysian.*

Esop. This is a language unknown to me, lady——No
such fine doings here, and very little good company (as
you call it) in Elysium——

Mrs *Riot.* What! no operas! eh! no *Elysian* then!
[*Sings fantastically in* Italian.] '*Sfortunato Monticelli!* banish'd *Elysian,* as well as the Hay-Market! Your taste
here, I suppose, rises no higher than your Shakespears and

you

your Johnsons: oh you *Goats and Vandils!* in the name of barbarity take 'em to yourselves, we are tir'd of 'em upon earth:——one goes indeed to a Play-house some-times, because one does not know how else one can kill one's time——ev'ry body goes, because—all the world's there——but for my part——call *Scurroon*, and let him take me back again, I'll stay no longer here——stupid im-mortals!

Esop. You are a happy woman, that have neither cares nor follies to disturb you.

Mrs *Riot.* Cares! ha! ha! ha! nay, now I must laugh in your ugly face, my dear; what cares, does your wisdom think, can enter into the circle of a fine lady's enjoy-ments?

Esop. By the account I have just hear'd of a fine lady's life, her very pleasures are both follies and cares; so drink the water, and forget them, madam.

Mrs *Riot.* Oh gad! that was so like my husband now—forget my follies! forget the fashion, forget my being, the very *quincettence* and *emptity* of a fine lady! the fel-low would make me as great a brute as my husband.

Esop. You have an husband then, madam?

Mrs *Riot.* Yes——I think so—an husband and no hus-band——Come, fetch me some of your water; if I must forget something, I had as good forget him, for he's grown insufferable o' late.

Esop. I thought, madam, you had nothing to complain of——

Mrs *Riot.* One's husband, you know, is almost next to nothing.

Esop. How has he offended you?

Mrs *Riot.* The man talks of nothing but his money, and my extravagance——won't remove out of the filthy city, tho' he knows I die for the other end of the town; nor leave off his nasty merchandizing, tho' I've laboured to con-vince him, he loses money by it. The man was once to-lerable enough, and let me have money when I wanted it; but now he's never out of a tavern, and is grown so va-liant, that, do you know——he has presum'd to contradict me, and refuse me money upon every occasion.

Esop. And all this without any provocation on your side?

Mrs *Riot.* Laud! how should I provoke him? I seldom

see

see him, very seldom speak to the creature, unless I want money; besides, he's out all day——

Esop. And you all night, madam: is it not so?

Mrs *Riot.* I keep the best company, sir, and day-light is no agreeable sight to a polite assembly; the sun is very well and comfortable, to be sure, for the lower part of the creation: but to ladies who have a true taste of pleasure, wax candles, or no candles, are preferable to all the sunbeams in the universe——

Esop. Preposterous fancy!

Mrs *Riot.* And so, most delicate sweet Sir, you don't approve my scheme! ha! ha! ha!——oh you ugly devil you! have you the vanity to imagine people of fashion will mind what you say? or that to learn politeness and breeding, it is necessary to take a lesson of morality out of Esop's Fables——ha! ha! ha!

Esop. It is necessary to get a little reflection somewhere; when these spirits leave you, and your senses are surfeited, what must be the consequence?——

Mrs *Riot.* Oh, a have the best receipt in the world for the vapours; and lest the poison of your receipts should taint my vivacity, I must beg leave to take it now, by way of anecdote.

Esop. Oh by all means—ignorance, and vanity!

Mrs *Riot.* (*Drawing out a card*) Lady Rantan's compliments to Mrs Riot.

S O N G.

I.

The card invites, in crowds we fly,
To join the jovial rout, full cry:
　What joy from cares and plagues all day,
To hie to the midnight hark-away.

II.

Nor want, nor pain, nor grief, nor care,
Nor dronish husbands enter there;
　The brisk, the bold, the young and gay,
All hie to the midnight hark-away.

III.

III.

Uncounted strikes the morning clock,
And drowsy watchman idly knock ;
Till day-light peeps, we sport and play,
And rour to the jolly hark-away.

IV.

When tir'd with sport, to bed we creep,
And kill the tedious day with sleep ;
To-morrow's welcome call obey,
And again to the midnight hark-away.

Mrs Riot. There's a life for you, you old fright! so trouble your head no more about your betters——I am so perfectly satisfied with myself, that I will not alter an atom of me, for all you can say ; so you may bottle up your philosophical waters for your own use, or for the fools that want 'em——Gad's my life ! there's Billy Butterfly in the grove——I must go to him——we shall so rally your wisdom between us—ha, ha, ha.

The brisk, the bold, the young, the gay,
All hie to the midnight hark-away.   *[Exit singing.*

Esop. Unhappy woman! nothing can retrieve her; when the head has once a wrong bias, 'tis ever obstinate, in proportion to its weakness: but here comes one who seems to have no occasion for Lethe to make him more happy, than he is.

Enter DRUNKEN MAN *and* TAYLOR.

Drunken Man. Come along, neighbour *Snip*, come along, taylor ; don't be afraid of hell before you die, you sniv'ling dog you.

Tayl. For heaven's sake, Mr Riot, don't be so boisterous with me, lest we should offend the powers below.

Esop. What in the name of ridicule have we here !—— So, Sir, what are you ?

Drunken Man. Drunk—very drunk at your service.

Esop. That's a piece of information I did not want.

Drunken Man. And yet it's all the information I can give you.

Esop. Pray, Sir, what brought you hither ?

Drunken Man. Curiosity, and a hackney coach.

Esop.

Esop. I mean, Sir, have you any occasion for my waters!

Drunken Man. Yes, great occasion, if you'll do me the favour to qualify them with some good arrack and orange juice.

Esop. Sir!

Drunken Man. Sir!—don't stare so, old gentleman—— let us have a little conversation with you.

Esop. I would know if you have any thing oppresses your mind, and makes you unhappy.

Drunken Man. You are certainly a very great fool, old gentleman; did you ever know a man drunk and unhappy at the same time.

Esop. Never otherwise, for a man who has lost his senses——

Drunken Man. Has lost the most troublesome companions in the world, next to wives and bum-bailiffs.

Esop. But pray, what is your business with me?

Drunken Man. Only to demonstrate to you that you are an ass——

Esop. Your humble servant.

Drunken Man. And to shew you, that whilst I can get such liquor as I have been drinking all night, I shall never come for your *water* specifics against care and tribulation: however, old gentleman, if you'll do one thing for me, I shan't think my time and conversation thrown away upon you.

Esop. Any thing in my power.

Drunken Man. Why, then, here's a small matter for you; and, do you hear me? get me one of the best whores in your territories.

Esop. What do you mean?

Drunken Man. To refresh myself in the shades here after my journey—Suppose now you introduce me to Proserpine, who knows how far my figure and address may tempt her; and if her majesty is over nice, shew me but her maids of honour, and I'll warrant you they'll snap at a bit of fresh mortality.

Esop. Monstrous!

Drunken Man. Well, well, if it is monstrous, I say no more;—if her majesty and retinue are so very virtuous—I say no more;—but I'll tell you what, old friend. if you'll lend me your wife for half an hour; when you make a visit above, you shall have mine as long as you please; and if upon trial you should like mine better than your own, you shall carry her away to the devil with you, and ten thousand thanks into the bargain.

Esop. This is not to be borne; either be silent, or you'll repent this drunken insolence.

Drunken Man. What a cross old fool it is!—I presume, Sir, from information of your hump, and your wisdom, that your name is——is——what the devil is it?

Esop. Esop, at your service——

Drunken Man. The same, the same—I knew you well enough, you old sensible pimp you—many a time has my flesh felt birch upon your account; prithee, what possess'd thee to write such foolish old stories of a cock and a bull, and I don't know what, to plague poor innocent lads with? it was damn'd cruel in you, let me tell you that.

Esop. I am now convinc'd, Sir, I have written 'em to very litttle purpose.

Drunken Man. To very little I assure you—But never mind it—Damn it, you are a fine old Grecian for all that, *(claps him on the back)* Come here, *Snip*—is not he a fine old Grecian?——And tho' he is not the handsomest, or best dress'd man in the world, he has ten times more sense than either you or I have——

Tayl. Pray, neighbour, introduce me.

Drunken Man. I'll do it—Mr Esop, this sneaking gentleman is my taylor, and an honest man he was, while he lov'd his bottle; but since he turn'd *Methodist*, and took to preaching, he has cabbag'd one yard in six from his customers; now you know him, here what he has to say, while I go and *pick up* in the wood here—Upon my soul, you are a fine old Grecian!   [*Exit* Drunken Man.

Esop. [*To* Taylor] Come, friend, don't be dejected; what is your business?

Tay. I am troubled in mind.

Esop. Is your case particular, friend?

Tay. No, indeed, I believe is is pretty general in our parish.

Esop. What is it? speak out, friend.——

Tay. It runs continually in my head, that I am——

Esop. What?

Tay. A cuckold——

Esop. Have a care, friend, jealousy is a rank weed, and chiefly takes root in a barren soil.

Tay.

Tay. I am sure my head is full of nothing see—

Esop. But how came you to a knowledge of your misfortune? has not your wife as much wit as you?

Tay. A great deal more, Sir; and that is one reason for my believing myself dishonoured—

Esop. Tho' your reason has some weight in it, yet it does not amount to a conviction.

Tay. I have more to say for myself, if your worship will but hear me.

Esop. I shall attend to you.

Tay. My wife has such very high blood in her, that she is lately turn'd Papist, and is always railing at me and the government—The priest and she are continually laying their heads together, and I am afraid he has persuaded her, that it will save her precious soul, if she cuckolds a heretic taylor——

Esop. Oh, don't think so hardly of 'em.

Tay. Lord, Sir, you don't know what tricks are going forward above! religion, indeed, is the outside stuff, but wickedness is the lining.

Esop. Why, you are in a passion, friend; if you would but exert yourself thus at a proper time, you might keep the fox from your poultry.

Tay. Lord, Sir, my wife has as much passion again as I have; and whenever she's up, I curb my temper, sit down and say nothing.

Esop. What remedy have you to propose for this misfortune?

Tay. I would propose to dip my head in the river, to wash away my fancies——and if you'll let me take a few bottles to my wife, if the water is of a cooling nature, I may perhaps be easy that way; but I shall do as your worship pleases.

Esop. I am afraid this method won't answer, friend; suppose therefore you drink to forget your suspicions, for they are nothing more, and let your wife drink to forget your uneasiness—A mutual confidence will succeed, and consequently mutual happiness.

Tay. I have such a spirit, I cannot bear to be dishonoured in my bed.

Esop. The water will cool your spirit, and if it can but lower your wife's, the business is done—Go for a moment to your companion, and you shall drink presently; but do nothing rashly.

Tay. I can't help it, rashness is my fault, Sir; but age and more experience, I hope, will cure me——Your servant, Sir—Indeed he is a fine old Grecian! [*Exit* Taylor.

Esop. Poor fellow I pity him.

Enter MERCURY.

Mer. What can be the meaning, Esop, that there are no more mortals coming over? I perceive there is a great bustle on the other side the Styx, and Charon has brought his boat over without passengers.

Esop. Here he is to answer for himself.

Enter CHARON, *laughing.*

Char. Oh! oh! oh!

Mer. What diverts you so, Charon?

Char. Why there's the devil to do among the mortals yonder; they are altogether by the ears.

Esop. What's the matter?

Char. There are some ladies who have been disputing so long and so loud, about taking place and precedency, that they have set their relations a tilting at one another, to support their vanity; the standers-by are some of them so frighted, and some of them so diverted at the quarrel, that they have not time to think of their misfortunes; so I e'en left them to settle their prerogatives by themselves, and be friends at their leisure.

Mer. What is to be done, Esop.

Esop. Discharge these we have, and finish the business of the day.

Enter DRUNKEN MAN *and* Mrs RIOT.

Drunken Man. I never went to pick up a whore in my life, but the first woman I laid hold of was my dear virtuous wife, and here she is——

Esop. Is that lady your wife?

Drunken Man. Yes, Sir; and yours, if you please to accept of her—

Esop. Tho' she has formerly given too much into fashionable follies, she now repents, and will be more prudent for the future.

Drunken Man, Lookee, Mr Esop, all your preaching

and

and morality signifies nothing at all—but since your wisdom seems bent upon our reformation, I'll tell you the only way, old boy, to bring it about. Let me have enough of your water to settle my head; and throw madam into the river.

Esop. 'Tis in vain to reason with such beings; therefor, Mercury, summon the mortals from the grove, and we'll dismiss them to earth, as happy as Lethe can make 'em——

S O N G.

By Mercury.

I.

Come, mortals, come ; come follow me.
Come follow, follow, follow me,
To mirth, and joy, and jollity :
Hark, hark, the call ; come, come and drink,
And leave your cares by Lethe's brink.

CHORUS.

Away then come, come, come away,
And life shall hence be holiday ;
Nor jealous fears, nor strife, nor pain,
Shall vex the jovial heart again.

II.

To Lethe's brink then follow all,
Then follow, follow, follow all,
'Tis pleasure courts, obey the call ;
And mirth, and jollity, and joy,
Shall every future hour employ,

CHORUS.

Away then come ; come come away
And life shall hence be holiday :
Nor jealous fears, nor strife, nor pain,
Shall vex the jovial heart again.

[During the song, the characters enter from the grove.]

Esop.

Esop. Now, mortals, attend; I have perceived from your examinations, that you have mistaken the effect of your distempers for the cause—you would willingly be relieved from many things which interfere with your passions and affections; while your vices, from which all your cares and misfortunes arise, are totally forgotten and neglected.—Then follow me, and drink to the forgetfulness of vice——

'Tis vice alone disturbs the human breast;
Cure dies with guilt; be virtuous, and be blest.

FINIS.

THE
LYING VALET.

DRAMATIS PERSONÆ.

Sharp, [the Lying Valet] Mr Garrick.
Gayless, Mr Blakes.
Justice Guttle, Mr Taswell.
Beau Trippet, Mr Neal.

Dick, Mr Yates.

Melissa, Miss Bennet.
Kitty Pry, Mrs Clive.
Mrs Gadabout, Mrs Cross.
Mrs Trippet, Mrs Ridout.

ACT I. SCENE I.

Gayless's Lodgings.

Enter GAYLESS *and* SHARP.

Sharp.

HOW, Sir, shall you be married to-morrow? Eh, I'm afraid you joke with your poor humble servant.

Gayl. I tell thee, Sharp, last night Melissa consented, and fixed to-morrow for the happy day.

Sharp. 'Tis well she did, Sir, or it might have been a dreadful one for us in our present condition: all your money spent; your moveables sold; your honour almost ruined, and your humble servant almost starved; we could not possibly have stood it two days longer——But if this young lady will marry you, and relieve us, o' my conscience I'll turn friend to the sex, rail no more at matrimony, but curse the whores, and think of a wife myself.

Gayl. And yet, Sharp, when I think how I have imposed upon her, I am almost resolved to throw myself at her feet, tell the real situation of my affairs, ask her pardon, and implore her pity.

Sharp. After marriage with all my heart, Sir; but don't let your conscience and honour so far get the better of your poverty and good sense, as to rely on so great uncertainties as a fine lady's mercy and good-nature.

Gayl..

Gayl. I know her generous temper, and am almost persuaded to rely upon it: what, because I am poor, shall I abandon my honour?

Sharp. Yes, you must, Sir, or abandon me: so, pray, discharge one of us; for eat I must, and speedily too: and you know very well that that honour of yours will neither introduce you to a great man's table, nor get me credit for a single beef-steak.

Gayl. What can I do?

Sharp. Nothing, while honour sticks in your throat: do gulp, master, and down with it.

Gayl. Prithee leave me to my thoughts.

Sharp. Leave you! no, not in such bad company, I'll assure you: why you must certainly be a very great philosopher, Sir, to moralize and declaim so charmingly, as you do, about honour and conscience, when your doors are beset with bailiffs, and not one single guinea in your pocket to bribe the villains.

Gayl. Don't be witty, and give your advice, sirrah!

Sharp. Do you be wise, and take it, Sir. But to be serious, you certainly have spent your fortune, and out-liv'd your credit, as your pockets and my belly can testify; your father has disown'd you; all your friends forsook you, except myself, who am starving with you. Now, Sir, if you marry this young lady, who as yet, thank heaven, knows nothing of your misfortunes, and by that means procure a better fortune than that you squander'd away, make a good husband, and turn œconomist; you still may be happy, may still be Sir William's heir, and the lady too no loser by the bargain: there's reason and argument, Sir.

Gayl. 'Twas with that prospect I first made love to her; and though my fortune has been ill spent, I have, at least, purchased discretion with it.

Sharp. Pray then convince me of that, Sir, and make no more objections to the marriage. You see I am reduced to my waistcoat already; and when necessity has undress'd me from top to toe, she must begin with you; and then we shall be forced to keep house and die by inches. Look you, Sir, if you won't resolve to take my advice, while you have one coat to your back, I must e'en take to my heels while I have strength to run, and something to cover me: so, Sir, wishing you much comfort and consolation with

your

your bare conscience, I am your most obedient and half-starv'd friend and servant. [*Going.*

Gayl. Hold, Sharp, you won't leave me.

Sharp. I must eat, Sir; by my honour and appetite I must!

Gayl. Well then, I am resolv'd to favour the cheat; and as I shall quite change my former course of life, happy may be the consequences: at least of this I am sure——

Sharp. That you can't be worse than you are at present.

Gayl. (A *knocking without.*)——Who's there?

Sharp. Some of your former good friends, who favour-ed you with money at fifty per cent, and helped you to spend it; and are now become daily memento's to you of the folly of trusting rogues, following whores, and laugh-ing at my advice.

Gayl. Cease your impertinence! to the door! if they are duns, tell 'em my marriage is now certainly fix'd, and persuade 'em still to forbear a few days longer, and keep my circumstances a secret for their sakes as well as my own.

Sharp. O never fear it, Sir; they still have so much friendship for you, not to desire your ruin to their own disadvantage.

- *Gayl.* And do you hear, Sharp, if it shou'd be any body from Melissa, say I am not at home, lest the bad appear-ance we make here should make 'em suspect something to our disadvantage.

Sharp. I'll obey you, Sir;——but I am afraid they will easily discover the consumptive situation of our affairs by my chop-fallen countenance. [*Exit* Sharp.

Gayl. These very rascals, who are continually dunning and persecuting me, were the very persons who led me to my ruin, partook of my prosperity, and profess'd the great-est friendship.

Sharp. (*without.*) Upon my word, Mrs Kitty, my ma-ster's not at home.

Kit. (*without.*) Lockee, Sharp, I must and will see him!

Gayl. Ha, what do I hear? Melissa's maid! what has brought her here? my poverty has made her my enemy too——She is certainly come with no good intent——No friendship there, without fees——She's coming up stairs.——What must I do?—I'll get into this closet and listen.
[*Exit* Gayless.

Enter

Kit. I must know where he is, and will know too, Mr Impertinence!

Sharp. Not of me you won't. [*Aside.*] He's not within, I tell you, Mrs Kitty; I don't know myself: do you think I can conjure?

Kit. But I know you will lie abominably; therefore don't trifle with me. I come from my mistress, Melissa; you know, I suppose, what's to be done to-morrow morning?

Sharp. Ay, and to-morrow night too, girl!

Kit. Not if I can help it. *Aside.*]—But come, where is your master? for see him I must.

Sharp. Pray, Mrs Kitty, what's your opinion of this match between my master and your mistress?

Kit. Why I have no opinion of it at all; and yet most of our wants will be reliev'd by it too : for instance now, your master will get a fortune, that's what I'm afraid he wants ; my mistress will get a husband, that's what she has wanted for some time : you will have the pleasure of my conversation, and I an opportunity of breaking your head for your impertinence.

Sharp. Madam, I'm your most humble servant! But I'll tell you what, Mrs Kitty, I am positively against the match ; for, was I a man of my master's fortune——

Kit. You'd marry, if you cou'd, and mend it. Ha, ha, ha! Pray, Sharp, where does your master's estate lie?

Guyl. Oh the devil! what a question was there!

[*Aside.*

Sharp. Lie, lie; why it lies——faith, I can't name any particular place, it lies in so many : his effects are divided, some here, some there; his steward hardly knows himself.

Kit. Scatter'd, scatter'd, I suppose. But harkee, Sharp, what's become of your furniture ? You seem to be a little bare here at present.

Guyl. What, has she found out that too? [*Aside.*

Sharp. Why, you must know, as soon as the wedding was fixed, my master order'd me to remove goods into a friend's house, to make room for a ball which he designs to give here the day after the marriage.

Kit. The luckiest thing in the world! for my mistress designs to have a ball and entertainment here to-night

before

before the marriage; and that's my business with your master.

Sharp. The devil it is! [*Aside.*

Kit. She'll not have it public, she designs to invite only eight or ten couple of friends.

Sharp. No more?

Kitty. No more: and she ordered me to desire your master not to make a great entertainment.

Sharp. Oh, never fear——

Kit. Ten or a dozen little nice things, with some fruit, I believe, will be enough in all conscience.

Sharp. Oh, curse your conscience! [*Aside.*

Kit. And what do you think I have done of my own head?

Sharp. What?

Kit. I have invited all my lord Stately's servants to come and see you, and have a dance in the kitchen; won't your master be surpriz'd?

Sharp. Much so indeed!

Kit. Well, be quick and find out your master, and make what haste you can with your preparations: you have no time to lose.——Prithee, Sharp, what's the matter with you? I have not seen you for some time, and you seem to look a little thin.

Sharp. Oh my unfortunate face! [*Aside.*] I'm in pure good health, thank you, Mrs Kitty; and I'll assure you, I have a very good stomach, never better in my life, and I am as full of vigour, hussy! [*Offers to kiss her.*

Kit. What, with that face! well, bye, bye, [*going*]—— oh, Sharp, what ill-looking fellows are those, were standing about your door when I came in? They want your master too, I suppose.

Sharp. Hum! Yes, they are waiting for him.——They are some of his tenants out of the country that want to pay him some money.

Kit. Tenants! what, do you let his tenants stand in the street?

Sharp. They chuse it; as they seldom come to town they are willing to see as much of it as they can, when they do; they are raw, ignorant, honest people.

Kit. Well, I must run home, farewel!——But do you hear? Get something substantial for us in the kitchen—— a ham, a turkey, or what you will——We'll be very merry;

and

and be sure to remove the tables and chairs away there too, that we may have room to dance; I can't bear to be confined in my French dances; tal, tal, tal, [*dancing*.] Well, adieu! Without any compliment, I shall die if I don't see you soon.   [*Exit* Kitty.

Sharp. And without any compliment, I pray heaven you may!

Enter GAYLESS.

[*They look for some time sorrowful at each other.*]
Gayl. Oh, Sharp!
Sharp. Oh, master!
Gayl. We are certainly undone!
Sharp. That's no news to me.
Gayl. Eight or ten couple of dancers——ten or a dozen little nice dishes, with some fruit—my lord Stately's servant's, ham and turkey!
Sharp. Say no more; the very sound creates an appetite: and I am sure of late I have had no occasion for whetters and provocatives.
Gayl. Curs'd misfortune! What can we do?
Sharp. Hang ourselves; I see no other remedy; except you have a receipt to give a ball and a supper without meat or music.
Gayl. Melissa has certainly heard of my bad circumstances, and has invented this scheme to distress me, and break off the match.
Sharp. I don't believe it, Sir: begging your pardon.
Gayl. No, why did her maid then make so strick an enquiry into my fortune and affairs?
Sharp. For two very substantial reasons; the first to satisfy a curiosity, natural to her as a woman; the second, to have the pleasure of my conversation, very natural to her as a woman of taste and understanding.
Gayl. Prithee be more serious: is not our All at stake?
Sharp. Yes, Sir: and yet that All of ours is of so little consequence, that a man, with a very small share of philosophy may part from it without much pain or uneasiness. However, Sir, I'll convince you in half an hour, that Mrs Melissa knows nothing of your circumstances, and I'll tell you what too, Sir, she shan't be here to-night, and yet you shall marry her to-morrow morning.
Gayl. How, how, dear Sharp?

Sharp.

Sharp. 'Tis here, here, Sir! warm, warm, and delay will cool it; therefore I'll away to her, and do you be a merry as love and poverty will permit you.

Would you succeed, a faithful friend depute,
Whose head can plan, and front can execute.

I am the man, and I hope you neither dispute my friendship or qualification.

Gayl. Indeed, I don't; prithee be gone.

Sharp, I fly.   [*Exeunt.*

SCENE, *Melissa's Lodgings.*

Enter MELISSA *and* KITTY.

Mel. You surprise me, Kitty; the master not at home! the man in confusion! no furniture in the house! and ill-looking fellows about the doors! 'tis all a riddle.

Kit. But very easy to be explain'd.

Mel. Prithee explain it then, nor keep me longer in suspence.

Kit. The affair is this, madam; Mr Gayless is over head and ears in debt; you are over head and ears in love; you'll marry him to-morrow; the next day, your whole fortune goes to his creditors, and you and your children are to live comfortable upon the remainder.

Mel. I cannot think him base.

Kit. But I know they are all base——You are very young, and very ignorant of the sex; I am young too, but have more experience: you never was in love before; I have been in love with an hundred, and try'd 'em all; and know 'em to be a parcel of barbarous, perjur'd, deluding, bewitching devils.

Mel. The low wretches you have had to do with, may answer the character you give 'em; but Mr Gayless——.

Kit. Is a man, madam.

Mel. I hope so, Kitty, or I would have nothing to do with him.

Kit. With all my heart——I have given you my sentiments upon the occasion, and shall leave you to your own inclinations.

Mel. Oh, madam, I am much obliged to you for your
                                             great

great coneescension, ha, ha, ha! however, I have so great
a regard for your opinion, that had I certain proofs of his
villainy——

   Kit. Of his poverty you may have a hundred, I am sure
I have had none to the contrary.

   Mel. Oh, there the shoe pinches.   [*Aside.*

   Kit. Nay, so far from giving me the usual perquisites of
my place, he has not so much as kept me in temper with
little endearing civilities; and one might reasonably expect
when a man is deficient in one way, that he shou'd make
it up in another.   [*Knocking without.*

   Mel. See who's at the door. [*Exit* Kitty.]——I must
be cautious how I hearken too much to this girl: her bad
opinion of Mr Gayless seems to arise from his disregard of
her.——

Enter SHARP *and* KITTY.

   Kit. So, Sharp, have you found your master? will things
be ready for the ball and entertainment?

   Sharp. To your wishes, madam. I have just now bespoke the music and supper, and wait now for your ladyship's farther commands.

   Mel. My compliments to your master, and let him know
I and my company will be with him by six; we design to
drink tea, and play at cards, before we dance.

   Kit. So shall I and my company, Mr Sharp.   [*Aside.*

   Sharp. Mighty well, madam!

   Mel. Prithee, Sharp, what makes you come without your
coat? 'Tis too cool to go so airy, sure.

   Kit. Mr Sharp, madam, is of a very hot constitution, ha,
ha, ha!

   Sharp. If it had been ever so cool I have had enough, to
warm me since I came from home, I'm sure, but no matter
for that.   [*Sighing.*

   Mel. What d'ye mean?

   Sharp. Pray don't ask me, madam; I beseech you don't:
let us change the subject.

   Kit. Insist upon knowing it, madam——My curiosity
must be satisfied, or, I shall burst.   [*Aside.*

   Mel. I do insist upon knowing—On pain of my displeasure, tell me!

   Sharp. If my master should know——I must not tell
you, madam, indeed.

Mel.

Mel. I promise you, upon my honour, I never shall.

Sharp. But can your ladyship insure secrecy from that quarter?

Kit. Yes, Mr Jackanapes, for any thing you can say.

Mel. I engage for her.

Sharp. Why then, in short, madam, I cannot tell you.

Mel. Don't trifle with me.

Sharp. Then since you will have it, madam,—I lost my coat in defence of your reputation.

Mel. In defence of my reputation!

Sharp. I will assure you, madam, I've suffer'd very much in defence of it; which is more than I would have done for my own.

Mel. Prithee explain.

Sharp. In short, madam, you was seen about a month a-go, to make a visit to my master alone.

Mel. Alone! my servant was with me.

Sharp. What, Mrs Kitty? so much the worse; for she was looked upon as my property; and I was brought in guilty, as well as you and my master.

Kit. What, your property, Jackanapes?

Mel. What is all this?

Sharp. Why, madam, as I came out but now, to make preparation for you and your company to-night; Mrs Pryabout, the attorney's wife at next door, calls to me; harkee fellow! says she, do you and your modest master know that my husband shall indite your house, at the next parish meeting, for a nusance?

Mel. A nusance!

Sharp. I said so——A nusance! I believe none in the neighbourhood live with more decency and regularity than I and my master, as is really the case——Decency and re-gularity, cries she, with a sneer;——why, sirrah, does not my window look into your master's bed-chamber? and did not he bring in a certain lady, such a day? describing you, madam.   And did not I see——

Mel. See! O scandalous! What?

Sharp. Modesty requires my silence.

Mel. Did not you contradict her?

Sharp. Contradict her! Why, I told her I was sure she ly'd: for zounds! said I, for I could not help swearing, I am so well convinc'd of the lady's and my master's prudence;

dence, that I am sure, had they a mind to amuse themselves, they would certainly have drawn the window-curtains.

Mel. What, did you say nothing else? did you not convince her of her error and impertinence? —

Sharp. She swore to such things, that I could do nothing but swear and call names; upon which, out bolts her husband upon me, with a fine taper crab in his hand, and fell upon me with such violence, that being half delirious, I made a full confession.

Mel. A full confession! what did you confess?

Sharp. That my master lov'd fornication; that you had no aversion to it; that Mrs Kitty was a bawd, and your humble servant a pimp.

Kit. A bawd! a bawd! do I look like a bawd, madam?

Sharp. And so, madam, in the scuffle, my coat was torn to pieces as well as your reputation.

Mel. And so you join'd to make me infamous.

Sharp. For Heaven's sake, madam, what could I do? his proofs fell so thick upon me, as witness my head [*shewing his head plaister'd.*] that I would have given up all the maidenheads in the kingdom, rather than have my brains beat to a jelly.

Mel. Very well!—but I'll be reveng'd—And did not you tell your master of this?

Sharp. Tell him! no madam. Had I told him, his love is so violent for you, that he would certainly have murdered half the attorney's in town by this time.

Mel. Very well!—But I'm resolv'd not to go to your master's to night.

Sharp. Heaven's and my impudence be praised. [*aside.*

Kit. Why not, Madam? if you are not guilty, face your accusers.

Sharp. Oh the devil! ruin'd again! [*Aside.*] To be sure, face 'em by all means, madam,———They can't but be abusive, and break the windows a little:———Besides, madam, I have thought of a way to make this affair quite diverting to you.———I have a fine blunderbuss charg'd with half a hundred slugs, and my master has a delicate large Swiss broad sword; and between us madam, we shall so pepper and slice 'em, that you will die with laughing.

Mel. What at murder?

Kit.

Kit. Don't fear, madam, there will be no murder, if Sharp's concern'd.

Sharp. Murder, madam! 'Tis self-defence; besides, in these sorts of skirmishes there are never more than two or three killed; for, supposing they bring the whole body of militia upon us, down but with a brace of them, and a-way fly the rest of the covey,

Mel. Persude me never so much, I won't go; that's my resolution.

Kit. Why then, I'll tell you what, madam since you are resolved not to go to the supper, suppose the supper was to come to you; 'tis great pity such great preparations as Mr Sharp has made should be thrown away.

Sharp. So it is, as you say, Mrs Kitty. But I can immediately run back and unbespeak what I have order'd; 'tis soon done.

Mel. But then what excuse can I send to your master; he'll be very uneasy at my not coming.

Sharp. O terribly so!——But I have it—I'l' tell him you are very much out of order—that you were suddenly taken with the vapours or qualms; or what you please, madam.

Mel. I'll leave it to you, Sharp, to make my apology; and there's half a guinea for you to help your invention.

Sharp. Half a guinea!——'Tis so long since I had any. thing to do with money, that I scarcely know the current coin of my own country. Oh, Sharp, what talents hast thou! to secure thy master; deceive his mistress, out-lie her chambermaid; and yet be paid for thy honesty! But my joy will discover me [*Aside.*] Madam, you have eternally fix'd Timothy Sharp your most obedient humble servant——Oh the delights of impudence and a good understanding! [*Exit.* Sharp.

Kit. Ha, ha! ha! was there ever such a lying varlet! with his slugs and his broad swords; his attornies, and broken heads and nonsense! Well, madam, are you satisfied now? Do you want more proofs?

Mel. Of your modesty I do; but I find, you are resolved to give me none.

Kit. Madam?

Mel. I see thro' your little mean artifice; you are endeavouring to lessen Mr Gayless in my opinion, because

cause he has not paid you for services he had no occasion for.

Kit. Pay me, madam, I am sure I have very little occasion to be angry with Mr Gayless for not paying me, when I believe, 'tis his general practice.

Mel. 'Tis false! he's a gentleman and a man of honour, and you are——

Kit. Not in love, I thank heaven!   [*Curtseying.*
Mel. You are a fool.
Kit. I have been in love; but I am much wiser now.
Mel. Hold your tongue, impertinence!
Kit. That's the severest thing she has said yet.   [*Aside.*
Mel. Leave me.
Kit. Oh this love! this love is the devil!   [*Exit* Kitty.

Mel. We discover our weaknesses to our servants, make them our confidants, put 'em on an equality with us, and so they become our advisers——Sharp's behaviour tho' I seem'd to disregard it, makes me tremble with apprehensions; and tho' I have pretended to be angry with Kitty for her advice, I think it of too much consequence to be neglected.

Enter KITTY.

Kit. May I speak, Madam?
Mel. Don't be a fool, what do you want?
Kit. There is a servant just came out of the country, says, he belongs to Sir William Gayless, and has got a letter from his master upon very urgent business.

Mel. Sir William Gayless; what can this mean? where is the man.

Kit. In the little parlour, madam.
Mel. I'll go to him——My heart flutters strangely,
                    [*Exit* Melissa.

Kit. Oh woman, woman, foolish woman! she'll certainly have this Gayless; nay, were she as well convinc'd of his poverty as I am, she'd have him——A strong dose of love is worse than one of ratifia; when once it get's into our heads, it trips up our heels, and then good night to discretion. Here she is going to throw away fifteen thousand pounds? upon what? faith, little better than nothing—— He's a man, and that's all—and heaven knows mere man is but small consolation.

                                      Be

Be this advice pursu'd by each fond maid,
Ne'er slight the substance for a empty sdade ;
Rich weighty sparks alone should please and charm ye ;
For should spouse cool, his gold will always warm ye.

ACT. II.

Enter GAYLESS *and* SHARP.

GAYLESS.

PRITHEE be serious, Sharp. Hast thou really succeeded.

Sharp. To our wishes, Sir. In short I have managed the business with such skill and dexterity, that neither your circumstances nor my veracity are suspected.

Gayl. But how hast thou excused me from the ball and entertainment ?

Sharp. Beyond expectation, Sir.—But in that particular I was obliged to have recourse to truth, and declare the real situation of your affairs. I told her we had so long disused ourselves to dressing either dinners or suppers, that I was afraid we should be but aukward in our preparations. In short, Sir,——at that instant a cursed gnawing seized my stomach, that I could not help telling her, that both you and myself seldom make a good meal now-a-days once a quarter of a year.

Gayl. Hell and confusion, have you betray'd me villain ! did you not tell me this moment, she did not in the least suspect my circumstances.

Sharp. No more she did, Sir, till I told her.

Gayl. Very well ; and was this your skill and dexterity ?

Sharp. I was going to tell you ; but you won't hear reason ; my melancholy face and piteous narration had such an effect upon her generous bowels, that she freely forgives all that's past,

Gayl. Does she, Sharp ?

Sharp. Yes ; and desires never to see your face again ; and, as a farther consideration of so doing, she has sent you half a guinea. [*Shews the money.*

Gayl. What do you mean ?

Sharp. To spend, spend it, Sir ; and regale.

Gayl.

Gayl. Villian, you have undone me!

Sharp. What, by bringing you money, when you are not worth a farthing in the whole world? Well, well, then to make you happy again, I'll keep it myself; and wish somebody would take it in their head to load me with such misfortunes.　　　　　　　　[*Puts up the money.*

Gayl. Do you laugh at me rascal?

Sharp. Who deserves more to be laughed at? Ha, ha, ha. Never for the future, Sir, dispute the success of my negotiations, when even you, who know me so well can't help swallowing my hook. Why, Sir, I could have play'd you backwards and forwards at the end of my line, till I had put your senses into such a farmentation, that you should not have known in an hour's time whether you was a fish or a man.

Gayl. Why, what is all this you have been telling me?

Sharp. A down-right lie from beginning to end.

Gayl. And have you really excused me to her?

Sharp. No Sir; but I have got this half guinea to make her excuses to you; and, instead of a confederacy between you and me to deceive her, she thinks she has brought me over to put the deceit upon you.

Gayl. Thou excellent fellow!

Sharp. Don't lose time but slip out of the house immediately; the back-way, I believe, will be the safest for you, and to her as fast as you can; pretend vast surprise and concern that her indisposition has debarr'd you the pleasure of her company here to-night; you need know no more: away!

Gayl. But what shall we do, Sharp? here's her maid again.

Sharp. The devil she is——I wish I could poison her; for I'm sure, while she lives I can never prosper.

Enter KITTY.

Kit. Your door was open, so I did not stand upon ceremony.

Gayl. I am sorry to hear your mistress is taken so suddenly.

Kit. Vapours, vapours only, Sir; a few matrimonial omens, that's all: but I suppose Mr Sharp has made her excuses.

Gayl. And tells me I can't have the pleasure of her company

pany

pany to night. I had made a small preparation: but 'tis no matter; Sharp shall go to the rest of the company, and let them know it is put off.

Kit. Not for the world, Sir; my mistress was sensible you must have provided for her, and the rest of the company: so she is resolv'd, tho' she can't, the other ladies and gentlemen shall partake of your entertainment: she's very good natur'd.

Sharp. I had better run, and let 'em know 'tis deferr'd.
[*Going.*

Kit. [*Stopping him.*] I have been with 'em already, and told 'em my mistress insists upon their coming, and they have all promised to be here: so pray, don't be under any apprehensions, that your preparations will be thrown away.

Gayl. But as I can't have her company, Mrs Kitty, 'twill be a greater pleasure to me, and a greater compliment to her, to defer our mirth; besides I can't enjoy any thing at present, and she not partake of it.

Kit. Oh, no to be sure; but what can I do? My mistress will have it so: and Mrs Gad-about, and the rest of the company, will be here in a few minutes; there are two or three coachfuls of 'em.

Sharp. Then my master must be ruin'd in spite of my parts.

Gayl. [*Aside to* Sharp.] 'Tis all over, Sharp.

Sharp. I know it, Sir.

Gayl. I shall go distracted; what shall I do.

Sharp. Why, Sir, as our rooms are a little out of furniture at present, take 'em into the captain's that lodges here, and set 'em down to cards; if he should come in the mean time, I'll excuse you to him.

Kit. I have disconcerted their affairs, I find; I'll have some sport with 'em.—Pray, Mr Gayless, don't order too many things, they only make you a friendly visit; the more ceremony, you know, the less welcome. Pray, Sir, let me intreat you not to be profuse. If I can be of service, pray, command me: my mistress has sent me on purpose; while Mr Sharp is doing the business without doors, I may be employed within; if you'll lend me the keys of your side-board, [*to* Sharp.] I'll dispose of your plate to the best advantage.
[*Knocking.*
Sharp.

Sharp. Thank you, Mrs Kitty; but it is dispos'd of already.   [*Knocking at the door.*

Kit. Bless me the company's come! I'll go to the door and conduct 'em into your presence.   -   [*Exit* Kitty.

Sharp. If you'd conduct them into a horse-pond, and wait of 'em there yourself; we should be more oblig'd to you.

Gayl. I can never support this!

Sharp. Rouse your spirits and put on an air of gaiety, and I don't dispair of bringing you off yet.

Gayl. Your words have done it effectually.

Enter Mrs GAD-ABOUT, *her daughter and niece,* Mr GUT-
   - TLE, Mr TRIPPET, *and* Mrs TRIPPET.

Gad. Ah my dear Mr Gayless!   [*Kisses him.*
Gayl. My dear widow!   [*Kisses her.*
Gad. We are come to give you joy, Mr Gayless.
Sharp. You never was more mistaken in your life.
                                                  [*Aside.*

Gad. I have brought some company here, I believe, is not well known to you, and I protest I have been all about the town to get the little I have—Prissy, my dear——Mr Gayless, my daughter.

Gayl. And as handsome as her mother; you must have a husband shortly, my dear.

Pris. I'll assure you I don't dispair, Sir.

Gad. My neice too.

Gayl. I know by her eyes she belongs to you, widow.

Gad. Mr Guttle, Sir, Mr Gayless; Mrs Gayless, Justice Guttle.

Sharp. O destruction! one of the quorum.

Gut. Hem. tho' I had not the honour of any personal knowledge of you; yet at the instigation of Mrs Gad-about, I have, without any previous acquaintance with you, throw'd aside all ceremony to let you know that I joy to hear the solemnization of your nuptials is so near at hand.

Gayl. Sir, tho' I cannot answer you with the same elocution, however, Sir, I thank you with the same sincerity.

Gad. Mr and Mrs Trippit, Sir, the properest lady in the world for your purpose, for she'll dance for four and twenty hours together.

Trip. My dear Charles, I am very angry with you, faith: so near marriage, and not let me know, 'twas barbarous:
                                                           you

you thought, I suppose, I should rally you upon it; but dear Mrs Trippet, here has long ago eradicated all my antimatrimonial principles.

Mrs Trip. I eradicate! fye, Mr Trippet, don't be so obscene.

Kit. Pray, ladies, walk into the next room ; Mr Sharp can't lay his cloth till you are set down to cards.

Gad. One thing I had quite forgot; Mr Gayless, my nephew, who you never saw, will be in town from France presently, so I left word to send him here immediately, to make one.

Gayl. You do me honour, madam.

Sharp. Do the ladies chuse cards or the supper first?

Gayl. Supper! what does the fellow mean?

Gut. Oh, the supper by all means, for I have eat nothing to signify since dinner.

Sharp. Nor I, since Monday was a fortnight. *[Aside.*

Gayl. Pray, ladies, walk into the next room; Sharp, get things ready for supper, and call the music.

Sharp. Well said, master.

Gad. Without ceremony, ladies. *Exeunt ladies.*

Kit. I'll to my mistress, and let her know every thing is ready for her appearance. *[Exit* Kitty.

GUTTLE *and* SHARP.

Gut. Pray Mr what's your name, don't be long with supper; but harkee, what can I do in the mean time? Suppose you get me a pipe and some good wine, I'll try to divert myself that way till supper's ready.

Sharp. Or suppose, Sir, you was to take a nap till then, there's a very easy couch in that closet.

Gut. The best thing in the world, I'll take your advice; but be sure and wake me when the supper is ready.

[Exit Guttle.

Sharp. Pray heaven, you may not wake till then—What a fine situation my master is in at present : I have promised him my assistance, but his affairs are in so desperate a way that I am afraid it is out of my skill to recover 'em. Well, fools have fortune, says an old proverb, and a very true one it is, for my master and I are two of the most unfortunate mortals in the creation.

Enter

Enter GAYLESS.

Gayl. Well, Sharp, I have set them down to cards, and now what have you to propose?

Sharp. I have one scheme left, which in all probability may succeed. The good citizen, overloaded with his last meal, is taking a nap in that closet, in order to get him an appetite for yours. Suppose, Sir, we should make him treat us.

Gayl. I don't understand you.

Sharp. I'll pick his pocket, and provide us a supper with the booty.

Gayl. Monstrous! for, without considering the villainy of it, the danger of waking him, makes it impracticable.

Sharp. If he wakes, I'll smother him, and lay his death to indigestion—a very common death, among the justices.

Gayl. Prithee be serious, we have no time to lose; can you invent nothing to drive 'em out of the house?

Sharp. I can fire it.

Gayl. Shame and confusion, so perplex me, I cannot give myself a moment's thought.

Sharp. I have it; did not Mrs Gad-about say her nephew would be here?

Gayl. She did.

Sharp. Say no more, but in to your company; if I don't send 'em out of the house for the night, I'll at least frighten their stomachs away: and if this stratagem fails, I'll relinquish politics, and think my understanding no better than my neighbours.

Gayl. How shall I reward thee, Sharp?

Sharp. By your silence and obedience; away to your company, Sir. [*Exit* Gayless.] Now, dear madam Fortune, for once open your eyes and behold a poor unfortunate man of parts addressing you; now is your time to convince your foes, you are not that blind whimsical whore they take you for; but let 'em see, by your assisting me, that men of sense, as well as fools, are sometimes intitled to your favour and protection.—So much for prayer; now for a great noise and a lye. [*Goes aside and cries out.*] Help! help, master; help, gentlemen, ladies; murder, fire, brimstone; help, help, help!

Enter

Enter Mr GAYLESS *and the ladies, with cards in their hands, and* SHARP *enters running, and meets them.*

Gayl. What's the matter?

Sharp. Matter, Sir, if you don't run this minute with that gentleman, this lady's nephew will be murder'd; I am sure, 'twas he, he was set upon the corner of the street, by four; he has kill'd two, and if you don't make haste, he'll be either murdered or took to prison.

Gad. For heaven's sake, gentlemen, run to his assistance. How I tremble for Melissa! this frolic of her's may be fatal. *[Aside.*

Gayl. Draw, Sir, and follow me.
[Exit Gayless *and* Gad-about.

Trip. Not I; I don't care to run myself into needless quarrels; I have suffered too much formerly by flying into passions; besides, I have pawn'd my honour to Mrs Trippet, never to draw my sword again; and in her present condition, to break my word might have fatal consequences.

Sharp. Pray, Sir, don't excuse yourself, the young gentleman may be murdered by this time.

Trip. Then my assistance will be of no servise to him; however— I'll go to oblige you, and look on at a distance.

Mrs Trip. I shall certainly faint, Mr Trippet, if you draw.

Enter GUTTLE, *disorder'd as from sleep.*

Gut. What a noise and confusion is this?

Sharp. Sir, there's a man murder'd in the street.

Gut. Is that all.—zounds, I was afraid you had throw'd the supper down—a plague of your noise.—I shan't recover my stomach this half hour.

Enter GAYLESS *and* GAD-ABOUT, *with* MELISSA *in boy's cloaths dress'd in the* FRENCH *manner.*

Gad. Well, but my dear *Jemmy*, you are not hurt sure?

Mel. A little with riding post only.

Gad. Mr Sharp alarm'd us all with an accident of your being set upon by four men; and that you had kill'd two, and was attacking the other, when he came away, and when we met you at the door, we were running to your rescue.

Mel. I had a small encounter with half a dozen villa'n;

VOL. I. C but

but finding me resolute, they were wise enough to take their heels; I believe I scratch'd some of 'em.

[Laying her hand to her sword.

Sharp. His vanity has sav'd my credit. I have a thought come into my head may prove to our advantage, provided monsieur's ignorance bears any proportion to his impudence. *[Aside.*

Gad. Now my fright's over, let me introduce you, my dear, to Mr Gayless; Sir, this is my nephew.

Gayl. [*Saluting her.*] Sir, I shall be proud of your friendship.

Mel. I don't doubt but we shall be better acquainted in a little time.

Gut. Pray, Sir, what news in France?

Mel. Faith, Sir, very little that I know of in the political way; I had no time to spend among the politicians. I was——

Gayl. Among the ladies, I suppose.

Mel. Too much indeed. Faith, I have not philosophy enough to resist their solicitations; you take me.

[To Gayless aside.

Gayl. Yes, to be a most incorrigible fop; s'death, this puppy's impertinence is an addition, to my misery.

[Aside to Sharp.

Mel. Poor Gayless! to what shifts is he reduced? I cannot bear to see him much longer in this condition, I shall discover myself. *[Aside to* Gad-about.

Gad. Not before the end of the play; besides, the more his pain now, the greater his pleasure when relieved from it.

Trip. Shall we return to our cards? I have a *sans prendre* here, and must insist you to play it out.

Lad. With all my heart.

Mel. Allons donc.

[*As the company goes out,* Sharp *pulls* Melissa *by the sleeve.*]

Sharp. Sir, Sir, shall I beg leave to speak with you? Pray did you find a bank note in your way hither?

Mel. What, between here and Dover do you mean?

Sharp. No, Sir, within twenty or thirty yards of this house.

Mel. You are drunk, fellow.

Sharp. I am undone, Sir, but not drunk, I'll assure you.

Mel. What is all this?

Sharp.

Sharp. I'll tell you, Sir: a little while ago my master
sent me out to change a note of twenty pounds; but I unfortunately hearing a noise in the street of damn-me, Sir,
and clashing of swords, and rascal, and murder; I runs up
to the place, and saw four men upon one; and having
heard you was a mettlesome young gentleman, I immediately concluded it must be you; so run back to call my
master, and when I went to look for the note to change it,
I found it gone, either stole or lost; and if I don't get the
money immediately, I shall certainly be turned out of my
place, and lose my character——

Mel. I shall laugh in his face, [*Aside.*] Oh, I'll speak
to your master about it, and he will forgive you at my intercession.

Sharp. Ah, Sir! you don't know my master.

Mel. I'm very little acquainted with him; but I have
heard he's a very good-natur'd man.

Sharp. I have heard so too, but I have felt it otherwise;
he has so much good-nature, that, if I could compound
for one broken-head a day, I should think myself very
well off.

Mel. Are you serious, friend?

Sharp. Look'e Sir, I take you for a man of honour;
there is something in your face that is generous, open,
and masculine; you don't look like a foppish, effeminate
tell-tale; so I'll venture to trust you.——See here, Sir
[*shews his head.*] these are the effects of my master's good-
nature.

Mel. Matchless impudence! [*Aside.*] Why do you live
with him then after such usage?

Sharp. He's worth a great deal of money, and when
he's drunk, which is commonly once a day, he's very free,
and will give me any thing; but I design to leave him when
he's married for all that.

Mel. Is he going to be married then?

Sharp. To-morrow, Sir; and between you and I, he'll
meet with his match, both for humour and something
else too.

Mel. What, she drinks too?

Sharp. Damnably, Sir; but mum—You must know this
entertainment was design'd for madam to-night; but she
got so very gay after dinner, that she could not walk out
of her own house; so her maid, who was half gone too,

C 2

came

came here with an excuse, that Mrs Melissa had got the vapours; and so she had indeed violently; here, here, Sir.

[Pointing to his head.

Mel. This is scarcely to be borne. [*Aside.*] Melissa! I have heard of her; they say she's very whimsical.

Sharp. A very woman, and please your honour; and between you and I, none of the mildest of her sex—But to return, Sir, to the twenty pounds.

Mel. I am surprised, you, who have got so much money in his service, should be at a loss for twenty pounds, to save your bones at this juncture.

Sharp. I have put all my money out at interest; I never keep above five pounds by me; and if your honour would lend me the other fifteen and take my note for it.

[Knocking.

Mel. Somebody at the door.
Sharp. I can give very good security.   *[Knocking.*
Mel. Don't let the people wait Mr—
Sharp. Ten pounds will do.   *[Knocking.*
Mel. Allez vous en.
Sharp. Five, Sir.   *[Knocking.*
Mel. Je ne puis pas.
Sharp. Je ne puis pas.—I find we shan't understand one another, I do but lose time; and if I had any thought, I might have known these young fops return from their travels generally with as little money as improvement.

[Exit Sharp.

Mel. Ha, ha, ha, what lies does this fellow invent, and what rogueries does he commit for his master's service? There never sure was a more faithful servant to his master, or a greater rogue to the rest of mankind. But here he comes again, the plot thickens, I'll in and observe Gayless.

[Exit Melissa.

Enter SHARP *before several persons with dishes in their hands, and a cook drunk.*

Sharp. Fortune, I thank thee, the most lucky accident! [*Aside.*] This way, Gentlemen, this way.

Cook. I am afraid I have mistook the house. Is this Mr Treatwell's?

Sharp. The same, the same: what, don't you know me?

Cook. Know you!——Are you sure there was a supper bespoke here?

Sharp.

Sharp. Yes: upon my honour, Mr Cook, the company is in the next room, and must have gone without, had not you brought it. I'll draw a table. I see you have brought a cloth with you; but you need not have done that, for we have a pretty good stock of linen—at the pawnbrokers.

[Aside.—

[Exit, and returns immediately, drawing a table.] Come, come, my boys, be quick, the company began to be very uneasy; but I knew my old friend, Lick-spit here would not fail us.

Cook. Lick-spit! I am no friend of yours; so I desire less familiarity; lick-spit too!

Enter GAYLESS, *and stares.*

Gayl. What is all this?

Sharp. Sir, if the sight of the supper is offensive, I can easily have it removed.   *[Aside to Gayless..*

Gayl. Prithee explain thyself, Sharp.

Sharp. Some of our neighbours, I suppose have bespoke this supper; but the cook has drank away his memory, forgot the house, and brought it here; however, Sir, if you dislike it, I'll tell him of his mistake, and send him about his business.

Gayl. Hold, hold, necessity obliges me against my inclination to favour the cheat, and feast at my neighbour's expence.

Cook. Hark you, friend, is that your master?

Sharp. Ay, and the best master in the world.

Cook. I'll speak to him then——Sir, I have according to your commands, dress'd as genteel a supper as my art and your price would admit of.

Sharp. Good again, Sir, 'tis paid for. *[Aside to Gayless.*

Gayl. I don't in the least question your abilities, Mr Cook, and I am obliged to you for your care.

Cook. Sir, you are a gentleman;——and if you would look over the bill and approve it *(pulls out a bill)* you will over and above return the obligation.

Sharp. Oh the devil!

Gayl. *(looking on a bill.)* Very well, I'll send my man to pay you to-morrow.

Cook. I'll spare him that trouble, and take it with me, Sir—I never work but for ready money.

Gayl. Hah?

Sharp. Then you won't have our custom. [*Aside.*] My master is busy now, friend; do you think he won't pay you?

Cook. No matter what I think; either my meat or my money.

Sharp. 'Twill be very ill-convenient for him to pay you to-night.

Cook. Then I'm afraid it will be ill-convenient to pay me to-morrow; so d'ye hear——

Enter MELISSA.

Gayl. Prithee be advis'd, s'death I shall be discover'd.
                           [*Takes the cook aside.*

Mel. (*to* Sharp.) What's the matter?

Sharp. The cook has not quite answer'd my master's expectations about the supper, Sir, and he's a little angry at him, that's all.

Mel. Come, come, Mr Gayless, don't be uneasy, a batchelor cannot be supposed to have things in the utmost regularity; we don't expect it.

Cook. But I do expect, and will have it.

Mel. What does that drunken fool say?

Cook. That I will have my money, and I won't stay till to-morrow—and, and——

Sharp. (*runs and stops his mouth.*) Hold, hold, what are you doing? Are you mad?

Mel. What do you stop the man's breath for?

Sharp. Sir, he was going to call you names.——Don't be abusive, Cook; the gentleman is a man of honour, and said nothing to you; pray be pacify'd, you are in liquor.

Cook. I shall have my——

Sharp. (*holding still.*) Why, I tell you, fool, you mistake the gentleman, he is a friend of my master's, and has not said a word to you.——Pray, good Sir, go into the next room; the fellow's drunk, and takes you for another. —You'll repent this when you are sober, friend—Pray, Sir, don't stay to hear his impertinence.

Gayl. Pray, Sir, walk in—he's below your anger.

Mel. Damn the rascal! what does he mean by affronting me!—Let the scoundrel go, I'll polish his brutality, I warrant you; here's the best reformers of manners in the univese. [*Draws his sword.*]. Let him go, I say.

Sharp. So, so you have done finely, now—Get away as
                                        fast

fast as you can; he's the most courageous mettlesome young man in all England—Why, if his passion was up, he could eat you.—Make your escape, you fool!

Cook. I won't .——Eat me! He'll find me damn'd hard of digestion tho'

Sharp. Prithee come here; let me speak with you.
[*They walk aside.*

Enter KITTY.

Kit. Gad's me, is the supper on table already?——Sir pray defer it for a few moments; my mistress is better, and will be here immediately.

Gayl. Will she indeed! Bless me—I did not expect—but however Sharp?

Kit. What success, Madam?   [*Aside to* Melissa.

Mel. As we could wish, girl—but he is in such pain and perplexity, I can't hold it out much longer.

Kit. Ay, that not holding out, is the ruin of half our sex.

Sharp. I have pacify'd the cook, and if you can but borrow twenty pieces of that young prig, all may go well yet; you may succeed though I could not: remember what I told you——about it straight, Sir,——

Gayl. Sir, Sir, (*to* Melissa) I beg to speak a word with you; my servant, Sir, tells me he has had the misfortune, Sir, to lose a note of mine, of twenty pounds, which I sent him to receive,—and the bankers shops being shut up, and having very little cash by me, I should be much obliged to you if you would favour me with twenty pieces till to-morrow.

Mel. Oh Sir, with all my heart, (*Taking out her purse.*) and as I have a small favour to beg of you, Sir, the obligation will be mutual.

Gayl. How may I oblige you, Sir?

Mel. You are to be marry'd, I hear, to Melissa.

Gayl. To morrow, Sir.

Mel. Then you'll oblige me, Sir, by never seeing her again.

Gayl. Do you call this a small favour, Sir.

Mel. A mere trifle, Sir——breaking of contracts, suing for divorces, committing adultery, and such like, are all reckon'd trifles now-a-days; and smart young fellows, like you and myself, Gayless, should be never out of fashion.

C 4

Gayl.

Gayl. But pray, Sir, how are you concern'd in this affair!

Mel. Oh Sir, you must know I have a very great regard for Melissa, and indeed, she for me ; and by the by, I have a most despicable opinion of you ; for, *entre nous*, I take you, Charles to be a very great scoundrel.

Gayl. Sir!

Mel. Nay, don't look fierce, Sir ! and give yourself airs ————Damme, Sir, I shall be thro' your body else in the snapping of a finger.

Gayl. I'll be as quick as you, villain !

[*Draws and makes at* Melissa.

Kit. Hold, hold, murder ! you'll kill my mistress—the young gentleman I mean.

Gayl. Ah ! her mistress !   [*Drops his sword.*

Sharp. How ! Melissa ! nay, then drive away care—All's over now.

Enter all the COMPANY *laughing.*

Gad. What, Mr Gayless, engaging with Melissa before your time. Ha, ha, ha!

Kit. Your humble servant, good Mr Politician (*to Sharp.*) This is gentlemen, and ladies, the most celebrated and ingenious Timothy Sharp, Schemer-general and conductor-esquire to the most renowned and fortunate adventurer Charles Gayless, knight of the woeful countenance; Ha, ha, ha!————Oh that dismal face, and more dismal head of yours. [*Strikes* Sharp *upon the head.*

Sharp. 'Tis cruel in you to disturb a man in his last agonies.

Mel. Now, Mr Gayless !—what, not a word ! you are sensible I can be no stranger to your misfortunes, and I might reasonably expect an excuse for your ill treatment of me.

Gayl. No, madam, silence is my only refuge ; for to endeavour to vindicate my crimes would show a greater want of virtue than even the commission of them.

Mel. Oh, Gayless ! 'twas poor to impose upon a woman and one that lov'd you too.

Gayl. Oh most unpardonable: but my necessities————

Sharp. And mine, madam were not to be match'd, I'm sure, o' th's side starving.

Mel. His tears have softened me at once————Your necessities Mr Gayless, with such real contrition are too

powerful

powerful motives not to affect the breast already prejudic'd in your favour——You have suffer'd too much already for your extravagance; and as I take a part of your sufferings, 'tis easing myself to relieve you; know therefore, all that's past I freely forgive.

Gayl. You cannot mean it sure; I am lost in wonder.

Mel. Prepare yourself for more wonder—You have another friend in masquerade here; Mr Cook pray throw aside your drunkenness, and make your sober appearance——Don't you know that face, Sir?

Cook. Ay, master, what have you forgot your friend Dick, as you used to call me?

Gayl. More wonder indeed! don't you live with my father?

Mel. Just after your hopeful servant there had left me, comes this man from Sir William with a letter to me; upon which (being by that wholly convinced of your necessitous condition) I invented by the help of Kitty and Mrs Gadabout, this little plot, in which your friend Dick there has acted miracles, resolving to teaze you a little, that you might have a greater relish for a happy turn in your affairs. Now, Sir, read that letter, and compleat your joy.

Gayl. [*reads.*] Madam, I am father to that unfortunate
' young man whom I hear by a friend of mine (that by my
' desire has been a continual spy upon him) is making his
' addresses to you; if he is so happy as to make himself a-
' greeable to you (whose character I am charm'd with) I
' shall own him with joy for my son, and forget his
' former follies.
 ' I am, madam,
  ' Your most humble servant,
   ' William Gayless,
' P. S. I will be soon in town myself to congratulate his
' reformation and marriage.
Oh, Melissa, this is too much; thus let me shew my thanks and gratitude, [*kneeling she raises him.*] for here 'tis only due.

Sharp. A reprieve! a reprieve! a reprieve!

Kit. I have been, Sir, a most bitter enemy to you; but, since you are likely to be a little more conversant with cash than you have been, I am now, with the greatest sincerity,

C 5

your

your most obedient friend and humble servant.   And I
hope, Sir, all enmity will be forgotten.

Gayl. Oh, Mrs Pry, I have been too much indulged
with forgiveness myself not to forgive lesser offences in
other people.

Sharp. Well then, Madam, since my master has vouch-
saf'd pardon to your handmaid Kitty, I hope you'll not
deny it to his footman Timothy.

Mel. Pardon ! for what ?

Sharp. Only for telling you about ten thousand lies,
madam ; and, among the rest, insinuating, that your ladyship would——

Mel. I understand you ; and can forgive any thing
Sharp, that was design'd for the service of your master ;
and if Pry and you will follow our example, I'll give her
a small fortune as a reward for both your fidelities.

Sharp. I fancy madam, 'twould be better to halve the
small fortune between us, and keep us both single ; for
as we shall live in the same house in all probability we
may taste the comforts of matrimony, and not be troubled
with its inconveniences.   What say you, Kitty.

Kit. Do you hear, Sharp ? before you talk of the comforts of matrimony, taste the comforts of a good dinner,
and recover your flesh a little ; do, puppy.

Sharp. The devil backs her, that's certain ; and I am no
match for her at any weapon.

Mel. And now, Mr Gayless, to shew I have not provided for you by halves, let the music prepare themselves ;
and with the approbation of the company, we'll have a
dance.

All. By all means a dance.

Gut. By all means a dance——after supper tho'——

Sharp. Oh, pray Sir, have supper first, or I'm sure, I
shan't live till the dance is finish'd.

Gayl. Behold, Melissa, as sincere a convert as ever truth
and beauty made. The wild impetuous sallies of my youth
are now blown over, and a most pleasing calm of perfect
happiness succeeds.

> *Thus Ætna's flames the verdant earth consume ;*
> *But milder heat makes drooping nature bloom.*
> *So virtuous love, afford us springing joy.*
> *Whilst vicious passions, as they burn, destroy.*

F I N I S.

MISS in her TEENS.

DRAMATIS PERSONÆ.

Sir Simon Loveit, Mr Tas-
  well.
Captain Loveit, Mr Havard.
Fribble, Mr Garrick.
Flash, Mr Woodward.
Puff, Mr Yates.

Jasper, Mr Blakes.

Miss Biddy, Mrs Green.
Aunt, Mrs Cross.
Tag, Mrs Clive.

ACT I.   SCENE I.

SCENE, a Street.

Enter Captain LOVEIT *and* PUFF.

Captain.

THIS is the place we were directed to; and now,
Puff, if I can get no intelligence of her, what will become of me ?

Puff. And me too, Sir.——You must consider I am a
married man, and can't bear fatigue as I have done.——
But pray, Sir, why did you leave the army so abruptly,
and not give me time to fill my knapsack with common
necessaries ? half a dozen shirts, and your regimentals are
my whole cargo.

Cap. I was wild to get away, and as soon as I obtained
my leave of absence, I thought every moment an age till
I return'd to the place where I first saw this young, charm-
ing, innocent, betwitching creature.——

Puff, With fifteen thousand pounds for her fortune——
Strong motives, I must confess.——And now, Sir, as you
are pleased to say you must depend upon my care and abilities in this affair, I think I have a just right to be acquainted with the particulars of your passion, that I may be the
better enabled to serve you.

Capt. You shall have 'em—When I left the university,
which is now seven months since, my father, who loves

C 6

his

his money better than his son, and would not settle a far-thing upon me——

Puff. Mine did so by me——

Capt. Purchas'd me a pair of colours at my own request; but before I join'd the regiment, which was going abroad, I took a ramble into the country with a fellow-collegian, to see a relation of his who liv'd in *Berkshire.*——

Puff.——A party of pleasure, I suppose.

Capt. During a short stay there, I came acquainted with this young creature: she was just come from the boarding-school, and tho' she had all the simplicity of her age and the country, yet it was mix'd with such sensible vivacity, that I took fire at once.——

Puff. I was tinder myself at your age. But pray, Sir, did you take fire before you knew her fortune.

Capt. Before, upon my honour.

Puff. Folly and constitution—But on, Sir.

Capt. I was introduced to the family by the name of *Rhodophil,* (for so my companion and I had settled it;) at the end of three weeks I was obliged to attend the call of honour in *Flanders.*

Puff. Your parting, to be sure, was heart-breaking.

Capt. I feel it at this instant.—We vow'd eternal con-stancy, and I promis'd to take the first opportunity of re-turning to her: I did so, but we found the house was shut up, and all the information you know, that we could get from the neighbouring cottage was, that miss and her aunt remov'd to town, and liv'd somewhere near this part of it.

Puff. And now we are got to the place of action, pro-pose your plan of operation.

Capt. My father lives but in the next street, so I must decamp immediately for fear of discoveries; you are not known to be my servant, so make what enquiries you can in the neighbourhood, and I shall wait at the inn for your intelligence.

Puff. I'll patrol hereabouts, and examine all that pass; but I've forgot the word, Sir—Miss *Biddy*—

Capt. Bellair.——

Puff. A young lady of wit, beauty, and fifteen thousand pounds fortune——but Sir——

Capt. What do you say, Puff?

Puff. If your honour pleases to consider that I had a wife in town whom I left somewhat abruptly half a year

ago,

ago, you'll think it, I believe, but decent to make some enquiry after her first; to be sure it would be some small consolation to me to know whether the poor woman is living, or has made away with herself, or——

Capt. Pry'thee don't distract me; a moment's delay is of the utmost consequence; I must insit upon an immediate compliance with my commands.   [*Exit* Captain.

Puff. The devil's in these fiery young fellows! they think of no body's wants but their own. He does not consider that I am flesh and blood as well as himself. However I may kill two birds at once; for I shan't be surprized if I meet my lady walking in the streets——But who have we here? Sure I should know that face.

Enter JASPER *from a house.*

Who's that? my old acquaintance, Jasper?

Jas. What, Puff! are you here?

Puff. My dear friend! [*Kisses him.*] Well, and now, Jasper, still easy and happy! *Toujours le meme!*——What intrigues now? what girls have you ruin'd, and what cuckolds made, since you and I used to beat up together, Eh

Jas. Faith, business has been very brisk during the war; men are scarce, you know; not that I can say I ever wanted amusement in the worst of times—But harkee, Puff——

Puff. Not a word aloud, I am *incognito.*

Jas. Why faith, I should not have known you, if you had not spoke first; you seem to be a little *dishabille* too, as well as *incognito.* Whom do you honour with your service now? are you from the wars?

Puff. Piping hot, I assure you: fire and smoke will tarnish; a man that will go into such service as I have been in, will find his cloaths the worse for wear, take my word for it; but how is it with you, friend Jasper? what, you still serve, I see? You live at that house, I suppose?

Jas. I don't absolutely live, but I am most of my time there; I have been these two months enter'd into the service of an old gentleman, who hired a reputable servant, and dressed him as you see, because he has taken it into his head to fall in love.

Puff. False appetite, and second childhood! but pry'thee, what's the object of his passion?

Jas.

Jas. No less than a virgin of sixteen.

Puff. Oh, the toothless old dotard!

Jas. And he mumbles and plays with her till his mouth waters: then chuckles till he cries, and calls it his *Bid*, and his *Bidsy*, and is so foolishly fond——

Puff. Bidsy! what's that?

Jas. ——Her name is Biddy.

Puff. Biddy! what Miss Biddy Bellair!

Jas. The same——

Puff. I have no luck to be sure. [*Aside.*]——Oh! I have heard of her; she's of a pretty good family, and has some fortune, I know. But are things settled? Is the marriage fix'd?

Jas. Not absolutely; the girl I believe detests him; but her aunt, a very good prudent old lady, has given her consent, if he can gain her nieces; how it will end I can't tell. —but I am hot upon't myself.

Puff. ——The devil! not marriage, I hope.

Jas. That is not yet determined.

Puff. Who is the lady, pray?

Jas. A maid in the same family, a woman of honour, I assure you; she has one husband already, a scoundrel sort of a fellow that has run away from her, and listed for a soldier; so towards the end of the campaign she hopes to have a certificate that he's knock'd o' th' head; if not, I suppose we shall settle matters another way.

Puff. Well speed the plough——But harkye, consummate without the certificate if you can—keep your neck out of the collar—do—I have wore it these two years, and damnably gall'd I am.——

Jas. I'll take your advice; but I must run away to my master, who will be impatient for an answer to his message which I have just delivered to the young lady: so, dear Mr Puff, I am your most obedient humble servant.

Puff. And I must to our agent's for my arrears: if you have an hour to spare, you'll hear of me at George's or the Tilt-Yard——*Au Revoir*, as we say abroad. [*Exit* Jasper.] Thus we are as civil and as false as our betters; Jasper and I were always the *Beau Monde* exactly; we ever hated one another heartily, yet always kiss and shake hands—But now to my master with a head full of news, and a heart full of joy.   [*Going, starts.*

Angels, and ministers of grace defend me!

It:

It can't be ! by heavens, it is, that fretful porcupine, my wife ! I can't stand it; what shall I do, I'll try to avoid her.

Enter TAG.

Tag. It must be he ! I'll swear to the rogue at a mile's distance ; he either has not seen me, or won't know me; if I can keep my temper, I'll try him farther.

Puff. I sweat—I tremble—She comes upon me !

Tag. Pray, good Sir, if I may be so bold——

Puff. I have nothing for you, good woman, don't trouble me.

Tag. If your honour pleases to look this way.——

Puff. The kingdom is over-run with beggars ; I suppose the last I gave to has sent this ; but I have no more loose silver about me ; so pr'ythee, woman, don't disturb me.

Tag. I can hold no longer ; oh, you villain, you ! where have you been, scoundrel ? do you know me now, varlet ?

[*Seizes him.*

Puff. Here, watch, watch, zounds I shall have my pocket pick'd.

Tag. Own me this minute, hang-dog, and confess every thing, or by the rage of an injured woman, I'll raise the neighbouroood, throttle you, and send you to *Newgate.*

Puff. Amazement! what, my own dear Tag! Come to my arms, and let me press you to my heart, that pants for thee, and only thee, my true and lawful wife.—Now my stars have over-paid me for the fatigue and dangers of the field ; I have wandered about like Achilles in search of faithful Penelope, and the Gods have brought me to this happy spot. [*Embraces her.*

Tag. The fellow's crack'd for certain ! Leave your bombastic stuff, and tell me, rascal, why you left me, and where you have been these six months, heh ?

Puff. We'll reserve my adventures for our happy winter evenings——I shall only tell you now, that my heart beats so strong in my country's cause, and being instigated either by honour or the devil, (I can't tell which) I set out for *Flanders,* to gather laurels, and lay 'em at thy feet.

Tag. You left me to starve, villain, and beg my bread, you did so.

Puff. I left you too hastily I must confess, and often has my conscience stung me for it.—I am got into an officer's service, have been in several actions, gain'd some credit

by

by my behaviour, and am now return'd with my master to indulge the genteeler passions.

Tag. Don't think to sob me off with this nonsensical talk; what have you brought me home besides?

Puff. Honour and immoderate love.

Tag. I could tear your eyes out.

Puff. Temperance or I walk off.

Tag. Temperance, traitor, temperance! what can you say for yourself; leave me to the wide world——

Puff. Well I have been in the wide world too, han't I? what would the woman have?

Tag. Reduce me to the necessity of going to service.

[*Cries.*

Puff. Why, I'm in service too, your lord and master an't I you saucy jade, you? Come, where dost thou live, hereabouts? hast got good vails? dost go-to market? Come, give me a kiss, darling, and tell me where I shall pay my duty to thee.

Tag. Why there I live at that honse.

[*Pointing at the house* Jasper *came out of.*

Puff. What, there? that house?

Tag. Yes, there that house.

Puff. Huzza! we're made for ever, you slut you! huzza! every thing conspires this day to make me happy—Prepare for an inundation of joy! my master is in love with your Miss Biddy over head and ears, and she with him: I know she is courted by some old fumbler, and her aunt is not against the match; but now we are come, the town will be reliev'd, and the governor brought over; in plain *English,* our fortune is made; my master must marry the lady, and the old gentleman may go to the devil.

Tag. Heyday! what's all this?

Puff. Say no more, the dice are thrown, doubtless for us; away to your young mistress, while I run to my master, tell her Rhodophil! Rhodophil! will be with her immediately; then if her blood does not mount to her face like quick-silver in a weather-glass, and point to extreme hot, believe the whole a lye, and your husband no politician.

Tag. This is news indeed! I have had the place but a little while, and have not quite got into the secrets of the family; but part of your story is true, and if you bring

your master, and miss is willing, I warrant we'll be too
hard for the old folks.

Puff. I'll about it streight!—but hold, Tag, I had forgot——Pray how does Mr Jasper do?

Tag. Mr Jasper! what do you mean? I—I—I

Puff. What out of countenance, child? Oh fy! Speak
plain, my dear——And the certificate, when comes that
heh, love?

Tag. He has sold himself, and turn'd conjurer, or he
could never have known it.   [*Aside.*

Puff. Are not you a jade? Are not you a Jezebel——
Arn't you a——

Tag. O ho, temperance? or I walk off——

Puff. I know I'm not finished yet, and so am easy; but
more thanks to my fortune than your virtue, madam.

Aunt. [*within.*] Tag, Tag, where are you Tag?

Tag. Coming, madam.——My old lady calls; away to
your master, and I'll prepare his reception within.

Puff. Shall I bring the certificate with me?   [*Exit.*

Tag. Go, you graceless rogue, you richly deserve it.

[*Exit.*

S C E N E, changes to a Chamber.

Enter AUNT *and* TAG.

Aunt. Who was that man you were talking too, Tag?

Tag. A cousin of mine, madam, that brought me news
from my aunt in the country.

Aunt. Where's my niece? why are not you with her?

Tag. She bid me leave her alone——She's melancholy,
madam; I don't know what's come to her of late——

Aunt. The thoughtfulness that is natural upon the approach of matrimony, generally occasions a decent concern.

Tag. And do you think, madam, a husband of three-
score and five——

Aunt. Hold, Tag, he protests to me, he is but fifty and
five.

Tag. He is a rogue, madam, and an old rogue, which is
the worst of rogues.——

Aunt. Alas! youth or age, 'tis all one to her; she is all
simplicity without experience; but she's so innocent she
won't know the difference——

Tag.

Tag. Innocent! ne'er trust to that, madam; I was innocent myself once, but *live and learn* is an old saying, and a true one; I believe, madam, nobody is more innocent than yourself, and a good maid you are to be sure; but tho' you really don't know the difference, yet you can fancy it, I warrant you.

Aunt. I should prefer a large jointure to a small one, and that's all: but it's impossible that Biddy should have desires, she's but newly come out of the country, and just turn'd of sixteen.

Tag. That's a ticklish age, madam! I have observ'd she does not eat, nor she does not sleep: she sighs, and she cries, she loves moon-light; these I take it are very strong symptoms.

Aunt. They are very unaccountable, I must confess; but you talk from a deprav'd mind, Tag: her's is simple, and untainted.

Tag. She'll make him a cuckold tho' for all that, if you force her to marry him.

Aunt. You shock me Tag, with your coarse expressions, I tell you, her chastity will be her guard, let her husband be what he will.

Tag. Chastity? never trust to that, madam; get her a husband that's fit for her, and I'll be bound for her virtue; but with such a one as Sir Simeon, I'm a rogue if I'd answer for my own.

Aunt. Well, Tag, the child shall never have reason to repent of my severity; I was going before to my lawyer's to speak about the articles of marriage, I will now put a stop to 'em for some time, till we can make further discoveries.

Tag. Heaven will bliss you for your goodness; look where the poor bird comes, quite mop'd and melancholy; I'll set my pump to work, and draw something from her before you return, I warrant you. [*Exit* Aunt.] There goes a miracle; she has neither pride, envy, or ill nature, and yet is near sixty and a virgin.

Enter Biddy.

Bid. How unfortunate a poor girl am I? dare not tell my secrets to any body, and if I don't I'm undone—Heigh-ho! [*sighs.*] Pray Tag, is my aunt gone to her lawyer about me? Heigho!

Tag.

Tag. What's that sigh for my dear young mistress?

Bid. I did not sigh, not I——[*sighs*]

Tag. Nay never gulp 'em down, they are the worst hings you can swallow. There's something in that little ieart of yours, that swells it and puffs it, and will burst it at ast if you don't give it vent.

Bid. What would you have me tell you? [*sighs*]

Tag. Come, come, you are afraid I'll betray you, but you had as good speak, I may do you some service you little think of.

Bid. It is not in your power Tag, to give me what I want. [*sighs*]

Tag. Not directly, perhaps; but I may be the means of helping you to it; as for example—If you should not like to marry the old man your aunt designs for you, one may find a way to break——

Bid. His neck, Tag?

Tag. Or the match either; will do, child.

Bid. I don't care which indeed, so I was clear of him.—I don't think I'm fit to be marry'd,

Tag. To him you mean——You have no objection to marriage, but the man, and I applaud you for it; but come courage, miss, never keep it in, out with it all——

Bid. If you'll ask me any questions, I'll answer 'em, but I can't tell you any thing of myself, I shall blush if I do.

Tag. Well then—In the first place pray tell me, Miss Biddy Bellair, if you don't like somebedy better than old Simeon Loveit?

Bid. Heigho!

Tag. What's heigho, miss?

Bid. When I say heigho! it means yes.

Tag. Very well; and this somebody is a young handsome fellow?

Bid. Heigho!

Tag. And if you were once his, you'd be as merry as the best of us.

Bid. Heigho!

Tag. So far so good; and since I have got you to wet your feet, souse over head at once, and the pain will be over.

Bid. There then.—(*A long sigh.*) now help me out Tag, as fast as you can.

Tag

Tag. When did you hear from your gallant?

Bid. Never since he went to the army.

Tag. How so?

Bid. I was afraid the letters would fall into my aunt's hands, so I would not let him write to me : but I had better reason then.

Tag. Pray let us hear that too.

Bid. Why, I thought if I should write to him and promise him to love nobody else, and should afterwards change my mind, he might think I was inconstant, and call me a coquette.

Tag. What a simple innocent it is! [*aside*] And have you chang'd your mind, miss?

Bid. No indeed, Tag, I love him the best of any of 'em.

Tag. Of any of 'em! why have you any more?

Bid. Pray don't ask me.

Tag. Nay, miss, if you only trust me by halves you can't expect——

Bid. I will trust you with every thing—When I parted with him, I grew melancholy; so in order to divert me, I have let two others court me till he returns again.

Tag. Is that all, my dear? mighty simple indeed.

[*Aside.*

Bid. One of 'em is a fine blustering man, and is called captain Flash; he's always talking of fighting and wars; he thinks he's sure of me, but I shall baulk him; we shall see him this afternoon, for he press'd strongly to come and I have given him leave, while my aunt's taking her afternoon's nap.

Tag. And who is the other pray?

Bid. Quite another sort of a man; he speaks like a lady for all the world, and never swears as Mr Flash does, but wears nice white gloves, and tells me what ribbons become my complexion, where to stick my patches, who is the best milliner, where they sell the best tea, and which is the best wash for the face, and the best paste for the hands; he is always playing with my fan, and shewing his teeth, and whenever I speak he pats me——so——and cries *The devil take me, Miss Biddy, but you'll be my perdition.*—Ha, ha, ha!

Tag. Oh the pretty creature! and what do you call him, pray?

Bid. His name is Fribble; you shall see him too, for by

mistake

mistake I appointed 'em at the same time; but you must help me out with them.

Tag. And suppose your favourite should come too——

Bid. I should not care what become of the others.

Tag. What's his name?

Bid. It begins with R—h—o—

Tag. I'll be hang'd if it is not Rhodophil.

Bid. I am frighten'd at you! you are a witch, Tag!

Tag. I am so, and can I tell your fortune too. Look me in the face. The gentleman you love most in the world will be at our house this afternoon; he arriv'd from the army this morning and dies till he sees you.

Bid. Is he come, Tag? don't joke with me——

Tag. Not to keep you longer in suspence, you must know the servant of your Strephon, by some unaccountable fate or other, is my lord and master; he has just been with me, told me of his master's arrival and impatience——

Bid. O my dear, dear, Tag, you have put me out of my wits—I am all over in a flutter.—I shall leap out of my skin—I don't know what to do with myself—Is he come, Tag?—I am ready to faint—I'd give the world I had put on my pink and silver robings to-day.

Tag. I assure you, miss, you look charmingly!

Bid. Do I indeed tho'? I'll put a little patch under my left eye, and powder my hair immediately.

Tag. We'll go to dinner first, and then I'll assist you.

Bid. Dinner! I can't eat a morsel—I don't know what's the matter with me—my ears tingle, my heart beats, my face blushes, and I tremble every joint of me—I must run in and look at myself in the glass this moment.

Tag. Yes, she has it, and deeply too; this is no hypocrisy——

> Not art, but nature now performs her part,
> And every word's the language of the heart.

ACT.

ACT. II　　SCENE. I.

SCENE Continues.

Enter Captain LOVEIT, BIDDY, TAG, *and* PUFF

CAPTAIN.

TO find you still constant, and to arrive at such a critical juncture, is the height of fortune and happiness.

Bid. Nothing shall force me from you; and if I am secure of your affections——

Puff. I'll be bound for him, madam, and give you any security you can ask.

Tag. Every thing goes on to our wish, Sir, I just now had a second conference with my old lady, and she was so convinced by my arguments, that she returned instantly to the lawyer to forbid the drawing out of any writings at all, and she is determined never to thwart Miss's inclinations, and left it to us to give the old gentleman his discharge at the next visit.

Capt. Shall I undertake the old dragon?

Tag. If we have occasion for help, we shall call for you.

Bid. I expect him every moment, therefore I'll tell you what, Rhodophil; you and your man shall be lock'd up in my bed-chamber till we have settled matters with the old gentleman.

Capt. Do what you please with me.

Bid. You must not be impatient tho'.

Capt. I can undergo any thing with such a reward in view : one kiss and I'll be quite resign'd——and now shew me the way.　　　　　　　　　　　[*Exeunt.*

Tag. Come sirrah, when I have got you under lock and key, I shall bring you to reason.

Puff. Are your wedding cloaths ready, my dove? the certificate's come.

Tag. Go follow your captain, sirrah—march—you may thank heav'n I had patience to stay so long.

　　　　　　　　　　　　[*Exeunt* Tag *and* Puff.
　　　　　　　　　　　　　　　　Enter

Enter BIDDY.

Bid. I was very much alarm'd for fear my two gallants should come in upon us unawares; we should have had sad work if they had; I find I love Rhodophil vastly, for tho' my other sparks flatter me more, I can't abide thoughts of 'em now——I have business upon my hands enough to turn my little head; but egad my heart's good, and a fig for dangers——let me see, what shall I do with my two gallants? I must, at least part with 'em decently; suppose I set 'em togther by the ears?——The luckiest thought in the world! For if they won't quarrel (as I believe they (won't I can break with 'em for cowards, and very justly dismiss 'em my service; if they will fight, and one of 'em should be kill'd, the other will certainly be hang'd, or run away; and so I shall very handsomely get rid of both ——I am glad I have settled it so purely.

Enter TAG.

Well, Tag, are they safe!

Tag. I think so, the door's double-locked, and I have the key in my pocket.

Bid. That's pure; but have you given them any thing to divert 'em.

Tag. I have given the captain one of our old gloves to mumble; but my Strephon is diverting himself with the more substantial comforts of a cold venison pasty.

Bid. What shall we do with the next that comes?

Tag. If Mr Fribble comes first; I'll clap him up in my lady's store-room; I suppose he is a great maker of marmalads himself, and will have an opportunity of making some critical remarks upon our pasty and sweat-meats.

Bid. When one of 'em comes, do you go and watch for the other, and as soon as you see him, run in to us and pretend it is my aunt, and so we shall have an excuse to lock him up till we want him.

Tag. You may depend upon me, here's one of them—

Enter FRIBBLE.

Bid. Mr Fribble your servant.

Frib. Miss Biddy your slave—I hope I have not come upon you abruptly; I should have waited upon you sooner-

er,

er, but an accident happen'd that discompos'd me so, that I was obliged to go home again to take drops.   –

Bid. Indeed you don't look well, Sir.—Go, Tag, and do as I bid you.

Tag. I will, madam.   [*Exit.*

Tag. I have set my maid to watch my aunt, that we may'n't be surpriz'd by her.

Frib. Your prudence is equal to your beauty, miss, and I hope your permitting me to kiss your hands will be no impeachment to your understanding.

Bid. I hate the sight of him. [*Aside.*] I was afraid I should not have had the pleasure of seeing you ; pray let me know what accident you met with, and what's the matter with your hand?

Frib. Well, I vow, Miss Biddy you're a good *Creter,* ————I'll endeavour to muster up what little spirits I have, and tell you the whole affair——Hem !—But first you must ive me leave to make you a present of a small pot of my lip-salve ; my servant made it this morning—the ingredients are innocent, I assure you ; nothing but the best virgin-wax, conserve of roses, and lilly of the valley water,

Bid. I thank you sir ; but my lips are generally red, and when they a'nt I bite 'em.

Frib. I bite my own, sometimes, to pout 'em a little, but this will give shem a softness, colour, and an a agreeable *moister.*————Thus let me make a humble offering at that shrine, where I have already sacrific'd my heart.

[*Kneels and gives the pot.*

Bid. Upon my word that's very prettily express'd ; you are positively the best company in the world——I wish he was out of the house.   [*Aside.*

Frib. But to return to my accident, and the reason why my hand is in this condition—I beg you'll excuse the appearance of it, and be satisfied that nothing but mere necessity could have forc'd me to appear thus muffled before you.

Bid. I am very willing to excuse any misfortunes that happens to you, Sir.   [*Curtsies.*

Frib. You are vastly good, indeed,——thus it was—— Hem !——You must know, Miss, there is not an animal in the creation I have so great an aversion to, as those hackney-coach fellows——As I was coming out of my

lodgings,

lodgings,——Says one of 'em to me, *Would your honour have a coach?*——No, man, said I, not now (with all the civility imaginable)——*I'll carry you and your Doll too?* (said he) *miss Margery, for the same price.*—Upon which the masculine beasts about us fell a laughing; then I turn'd round in a great passion, curse me, (says I) fellow, but I'll trounce thee.——And as I was holding out my hand in a threatening *poster*—thus—he makes a cut at me with his whip, and striking me over the nail of my little finger, it gave me such exquisite *torter* that I fainted away; and while I was in this condition, the mob pick'd my pocket of my purse, my scissars, my *mocco* smelling-bottle, and my huswife?

Bid. I shall laugh in his face. [*Aside.*] I am afraid you are in great pain; pray sit down, Mr Fribble, but I hope your hand is in no danger.   [*They sit.*

Frib. Not in the least, maam; pray don't be apprehensive—A milk-poultice, and a gentle sweat to-night, with a little manna in the morning, I am confident, will relieve me entirely.

Bid. But pray, Mr Fribble, do you make use of a huswife?

Frib. I can't do without it, maam; there is a club of us, all young bachelors, the sweetest society in the world; and we meet three times a week at each others lodgings, where we drink tea, hear the chat of the day, invent fashions for the ladies, make models of 'em, and cut out patterns in paper. We were the first inventors of knotting, and this fringe is the original produce and joint labour of our little community.

Bid. And who are your pretty set, pray?

Frib. There's *Phil Whiffle, Jacky Wagtail,* my lord *Trip, Billy Dimple,* Sir *Dilbery Diddle,* and your humble——

Bid. What a sweet collection of happy creatures!

Frib. Indeed and so we are, miss——But a prodigious *fracas* disconcerted us some time ago at Billy Dimple's—three drunken naughty women of the town burst into our club-room, curst us all, threw down the china, broke six looking-glasses, scalded us with the slop-bason, and *scrat* poor Phil Whiffle's cheek in such a manner that he has kept his bed these three weeks.

Bid. Indeed, Mr Fribble, I think all our sex have great reason to be angry; for if you are so happy now you are bachelors, the ladies may wish and sigh to very little purpose.

Frib. You are mistaken, I assure you; I am prodigiously rallied about my passion for you, I can tell you that, and am look'd upon as lost to our society already; he, he, he!

Bid. Pray, Mr Fribble, now you have gone so far, don't think me impudent if I long to know how you intended to use the lady who shall be honour'd with your affections?

Frib. Not as most other wives are used, I assure you; all the domestic business will be taken off her hands; I shall make the tea, comb the dogs, and dress the children myself; so that tho' I'm a commoner, Mrs Fribble will lead the life of a woman of quality! for she will have nothing to do, but lie in bed, play at cards, and scold the servants.

Bid. What a happy creature she must be!

Frib. Do you really think so? then pray let me have a little *serous* talk with you.——Though my passion is not of a long standing, I hope the sincerity of my intentions——

Bid. Ha, ha, ha!

Frib. Go thou wild thing. [*Puts her.*] The devil take me but there is no talking to you.—How can you use me in this barbarous manner! if I had the constitution of an alderman it would sink under my sufferings.—*Hooman nater* can't support it.——

Bid. Why, what would you do with me, Mr Fribble?

Frib. Well, I vow I'll beat you if you talk so——Don't look at me in that manner—Flesh and blood can't bear it —I could—but I won't grow indecent——

Bid. But pray, Sir, where are the verses you were to write upon me? I find if a young lady depends too much upon such fine gentlemen as you, she'll certainly be disappointed.

Frib. I vow, the flutter I was put into this afternoon has quite turn'd my senses—here they are tho'—and I believe you'll like 'em.——

Bid. There can be no doubt of it.   [*Curtseys.*

Frib. I protest, miss, I don't like that curtsy—Look at me, and always rise in this manner. [*Shews her.*] But, my dear *creteer*, who put on your cap to-day? They have

ade

made a fright of you, and it is as yellow as old lady *Crow-foot's* neck.——When we are settled, I'll dress your heads myself.

Bid. Pray read the verses to me, Mr Fribble.

Frib. I obey—Hem !—William Fribble, Esq; to miss Biddy Bellair—greeting.

No ice so hard, so cold as I,
'Till warm'd and soften'd by your eye :
And now my heart dissolves away
In dreams by night, in sighs by day ;
No brutal passions fire my breast,
Which loaths the object when possess'd ;
But one of harmless, gentle kind,
Whose joys are center'd——in the mind ;
Then take with me Love's better part,
His downy wing, but not his dart.

How do you like 'em ?

Bid. Ha, ha, ha ! I swear they are very pretty—but I don't quite understand 'em.

Frib. These light pieces are never so well understood in reading as singing; I have set 'em myself, and will endeavour to give 'em you *La—lā—*I have an abominable cold, and can't sing a note: however the tune's nothing, the manner's all.

No ice so hard, &c.   [*Sings.*]

Enter TAG, *running.*

Tag. Your aunt, your aunt, your aunt, madam !

Frib. What's the matter ?

Bid. Hide, hide Mr Fribble, Tag, or we are ruin'd.

Frib. Oh ! for heaven's sake, put me any where, so I don't dirty my cloths.

Bid. Put him into the store-room Tag, this moment.

Frib. Is it a damp place, Mrs Tag? The floor is boarded, I hope ?

Tag. Indeed it is not, Sir.

Frib. What shall I do? I shall certainly catch my death ! where's my cambric handkerchief, and my salts ? I shall certainly have my hysterics !   [*Runs out.*

Bid. In, in, in——So now let the other come as soon

as he will; I do not care if I had twenty of 'em, so they would but come one-after another.

Enter TAG.

Was my aunt coming?

Tag. No, 'twas Mr Flash, I suppose, by the length of his stride, and the cock of his hat. He'll be here this minute—What shall we do with him?

Bid. I'll manage him, I warrant you, and try his courage; be sure you are ready to second me—we shall have pure sport.

Tag. Hush! here he comes.

Enter FLASH, *singing.*

Flash. Well, my blossom, here am I! what hopes for a poor dog, eh? how! the maid here! then I've lost the town, dammee! not a shilling to bribe the governor; she'll spring a mine, and I shall be blown to the devil.

Bid. Don't be asham'd, Mr Flash; I have told Tag the whole affair, and she's my friend I can assure you.

Flash. Is she? then she won't be mine, I am certain. [*Aside.*] Well, Mrs Tag, you know, I suppose, what's to be done: this young lady and I have contracted ourselves; and so, if you please to stand bride-maid, why, we'll fix the wedding-day directly.

Tag. The wedding-day, Sir?

Flash. The wedding-day, Sir? Ay, Sir, the wedding-day, Sir; what have you to say to that, Sir?

Bid. My dear Captain Flash, don't make such a noise you'll wake my aunt.

Flash. And suppose I did, Child, what then?

Bid. She'd be frighten'd out of her wits.

Flash. At me, Miss! frighten'd at me? *Tout au contraire*, I assure you; you mistake the thing, child; I have some reason to believe, I am not quite so shocking.

[*Affectedly.*

Tag. Indeed, Sir, you flatter yourself—But pray, Sir, what are your pretensions?

Flash. The lady's promises, my own passion, and the best mounted blade in the three kingdoms. If any man can produce a better title, let him take her; if not, the d—l mince me if I give up an atom of her.

Bid. He's in a fine passion, if he would but hold it.

Tag.

Tag. Pray, Sir, hear reason a little.

Flash. I never do, Madam; it is not my method of proceeding; here is my logic! [*Draws his sword.*] Sa, sa, ——my best argument is cart over arm, madam, ha, ha, [*lunges.*] and if he answers that, madam, through my small guts, my breath, blood, and mistress, are all at his service—Nothing more, madam.

Bid. This 'll do, this 'll do.

Tag. But Sir, Sir, Sir?

Flash. But madam, madam, madam: I profess blood, madam, I was bred up to it from a child; I study the book of fate, and the camp is my university; I have attended the lectures of Prince Charles upon the Rhine, and Bathiani upon the Po, and have extracted knowledge from the mouth of a cannon; I'm not to be frighten'd with squibs, madam, no, no.

Bid. Pray, dear Sir, don't mind her, but let me prevail with you to go away this time—Your passion is very fine to be sure, and when my aunt and Tag are out of the way, I'll let you know when I'd have you come again.

Flash. When you'd have me come again, child? And suppose I never would come again, what do you think of that now, ha? You pretend to be afraid of your aunt; your aunt knows what's what, too well to refuse a good match when 'tis offer'd—Lookee, miss, I'm a man of honour, glory is my aim, I have told you the road I am in, and do you see here, child, [*Shewing his sword.*] no tricks upon travellers.

Bid. But pray, Sir, hear me.

Flash. No, no, no, I know the world, madam: I am as well known at *Covent-Garden* as the dail, madam: I'll break a lamp, bully a constable, bam a justice, or bilk a box-keeper, with any man in the liberties of *Westminster;* what do you think of me now, madam?

Bid. But pray, Sir, hear me.

Flash. Come, come, come, few words are best, somebody's happier than somebody, and I'm a poor silly fellow; ha, ha,——That's all—Look you, child, to be short, (for I'm a man of reflection) I have but a *bagatelle* to say to you: I am in love with you up to hell and desperation; may the sky crush me if I am not——But since there is another more fortunate than I, adieu, Biddy! prosperity to the happy rival, patience to poor Flash; but the first

time

time we meet,—gunpowder be my perdition, but I'll have the honour of cutting a throat with him.   [*Going*.

Bid. [*Stopping him.*] You may meet with him now, if you please.

Flash. Now, may I!—Where is he, I'll sacrifice the villain.   [*Aloud*.

Tag. Hush! he's but in the next room.

Flash. Is he! Ram me [*Low.*] into a mortar piece, but I'll have vengeance; my blood boils to be at him—Don't be frighten'd, miss?

Bid. No Sir, I never was better pleas'd, I assure you.

Flash. I shall soon do his business.

Bid. As soon as you please, take your own time.

Tag. I'll fetch the gentlemen to you immediately.
          [*Going*.

Flash. (*Stopping her.*) Stay, stay, a little; what a passion I am in!—are you sure he is in the next room?—I shall certainly tear him to pieces——I would fain murder him like a gentleman too——Besides, this family shan't be brought into trouble upon my account.——I have it—I'll wait for him in the street, and mix his blood with the puddle of the next kennel.   [*Going*.

Bid. (*Stopping him.*) No, pray, Mr Flash, let me see the battle, I shall be glad to see you fight for me, you shan't go, indeed.   [*Holding him.*

Tag. (*Holding him.*) Oh, pray let me see you fight; there were two gentlemen fit yesterday, and my mistress was never so diverted in her life—I'll fetch him out. [*Exit.*

Bid. Do, stick him, stick him, captain Flash; I shall love you the better for it.

Flash. D—n your love, I wish I was out of the house.
          [*Aside*.

Bid. Here he is—Now speak some of your hard words, and run him through——

Flash. Don't be in fits now——[*Aside* to Biddy.

Bid. Never fear me.

Enter TAG and FRIBBLE.

Tag. (*To* Fribble.) Take it on my word, Sir, he is a bully and nothing else.

Frib. (*Frighten'd.*) I know you are my good friend, but perhaps you don't know his disposition.

Tag. I am confident he is a coward.

Frib.

Frib. Is he? Nay then, I'm his man.

Flash. I like his looks, but I'll not venture too far at first.

Tag. Speak to him, Sir.

Frib. I will—I understand, Sir,—hem—that you—by Mrs Tag here,—Sir,—who has inform'd me—hem—that you have sent her, to inform me—Sir—that you would be glad to speak with me—Demmee———   [*Turns off.*

Flash. I can speak to you Sir,——or to any body Sir—or I can let it alone and hold my tongue,—if I see occasion, Sir, damme e———   *Turns off.*

Bid. Well said, Mr Flash, be in a passion.

Tag. (*To* Fribble.) Don't mind his looks, he changes colour already; to him, to him.   - *Pushes him.*

Frib. Don't hurry me, Mrs Tag, for heaven's sake, I shall be out of breath before I begin, if you do,—Sir,—(*To* Flash.) If you can't speak to a gentleman in another manner, Sir,——why then I'll venture to say you had better hold your tongue——Oons.

Flash. Sir, you and I are of different opinions.

Frib. You and your opinion may go to the devil—Take that.   [*Turns off to Tag.*

Tag. Well said, Sir, the day's your own.

Bid. What's the matter, Mr Flash? is all your fury gone? do you give me up?

Frib. I have done his business.   [*Struts about.*

Flash. Give you up, madam! No, madam; when I am determined in my resolutions, I am always calm; 'tis our way, madam; and now I shall proceed to business.—Sir, I beg to say a word to you in private.

Frib. Keep your distance, fellow, and I'll answer you. —That lady has confess'd a passion for me, and as she has deliver'd up her heart into my keeping, nothing but my 'arts blood will purchase it.   Damnation!

Tag. Bravo! Bravo!

Flash. If those are the conditions, I'll give you earnest for it directly. (*Draws.*) Now, villain, renounce all right and title this minute, or the torrent of my rage will overflow my reason, and I shall annihilate the nothingness of your soul and body in an instant.

Frib. I wish there was a constable at hand to take us both up; we shall certainly do one another a prejudice.

Tag. No, you won't indeed, Sir; pray bear up to him;
D 4

it

if you wou'd but draw your sword, and be in a passion, he would run away directly.

Frib. Will he? *(Draws his sword.)* Then I can no longer contain myself.—Hell and the furies! Come on, thou savage brute.

Tag. Go, on Sir.

Here they stand in fighting postures, while Biddy *and* Tag *push 'em forward.*

Flash. Come on.

Bid. Go on.

Frib. Come on, rascal.

Tag. Go on, Sir.

Enter Captain Loveit *and* Puff.

Capt. What's the matter, my dear?

Bid. If you won't fight, here's one that will. Oh, Rhodophil, these two sparks are your rivals, and have pester'd me these two months with their addresses; they forc'd themselves into the house, and have been quarrelling about me, and disturbing the family; they won't fight, pray kick them out of the house.

Capt. What's the matter, gentlemen?

[*They both keep their fencing posture.*

Flash. Don't part us, Sir.

Frib. No, pray, Sir, don't part us, we shall do you a mischief.

Capt. Puff, look to the other gentleman, and call a surgeon?

Bid. and Tag. Ha, ha, ha!

Puff. Bless me! how can you stand under your wounds, Sir?

Frib. Am I hurt, Sir?

Puff. Hurt, Sir! why you have——let me see——pray stand in the light——one, two, three, thro' the heart; and let me see——hum——eight thro' the small guts! come, Sir, make it up the round dozen, and then we'll part you.

All. Ha, ha, ha!

Capt. Come here, Puff　　[*Whispers and looks at* Flash.

Puff. 'Tis the very same, Sir.

Capt. (*To* Flash.) Pray, Sir, have I not had the pleasure of seeing you abroad?

Flash. I have serv'd abroad.

Capt.

Capt. Had not you the misfortune Sir, to be missing at the last engagement in Flanders?

Flash. I was found amongst the dead in the field of battle.

Puff. He was the first that fell, Sir; the wind of a cannon-ball struck him flat upon his face; he had just strength enough to creep into a ditch, and there he was found after the battle in a most deplorable condition.

Capt. Pray, Sir, what advancement did you get by the service of that day?

Flash. My wounds render'd me unfit for service, and I sold out.

Puff. Stole out, you mean.—We hunted him by scent, to the water-side, thence he took shipping for England, and, taking the advantage of my master's absence, has attack'd the citadel, which we are luckily come to relieve, and drive his honour into the ditch again.

All. Ha, ha, ha!

Frib. He, he, he!

Capt. And now, Sir, how have you dar'd to shew your face again in open day, or wear even the outside of a profession you have so much scandaliz'd by your behaviour? I honour the name of a soldier, and as a party concerned am bound not to see it disgrac'd. As you have forfeited your title to honour, deliver up your sword this instant.

Flash. Nay, good captain——

Capt. No words, Sir.   [*Takes his sword.*

Frib. He's a sad scoundrel; I wish I had kick'd him.

Capt. The next thing I command——leave this house, change the colour of your cloths and fierceness of your looks, appear from top to toe the wretch thou art; if e'er I meet thee in the military dress again, or if thou put on looks that belye the native baseness of thy heart, be it where it will, this shall be the reward of thy impudence and disobedience.   [*Kicks him, he runs off.*

Bid. Oh, my dear Rhodophil!

Frib. What an infamous rascal it is! I thank you, Sir, for this favour, but I must after and cane him.

            [*Going. is stopt by the* Captain.

Capt. One word with you too, Sir.

Frib. With me, Sir?

Capt. You need not tremble, I shan't use you roughly.

Frib. I am certain of that, Sir; but I am sadly troubled with weak nerves.

Capt. Thou art of a species too despicable for correction; therefore be gone, and if I see you here again, your insignificancy shan't protect you.

Frib. I am oblig'd to you for your kindness; well, if ever I have any thing to do with intrigues again!—[*Exit.*

All. Ha, ha, ha!

Puff. Shall I ease you of your trophy, Sir?

Capt. Take it, Puff, as some small recompence for thy fidelity, thou canst better use it than its owner.

Puff. I wish your honour had a patent to take such trifles from every pretty gentlemen that could spare 'em; I would set up the largest cutler's shop in the kingdom.

Capt. Well said, Puff.

Bid. But pray, Mr Fox, how did you get out of your hole? I thought you was lock'd in?

Capt. I shot the bolt back when I heard a noise; and thinking you were in danger I broke my confinement without any other consideration than your safety.

[*Kisses her hand.*

Sir Simon. (*Without.*) Biddy, Biddy, why Tag, Tag.

Bid. There's the old gentleman; run in, run in.

[*Exeunt.* Captain *and* Puff. Tag *opens the door.*

Enter Sir Simon *and* Jasper.

Sir *Sim.* Where have you been, Biddy? Jasper and I have knock'd and call'd as loud and as long as we were able; what were you doing, child?

Bid. I was reading part of a play to Tag, and we came as soon as we heard you.

Sir *Sim.* What play, Moppet?

Bid. The *Old Batchelor*; and we were just got to old *Nykyn* as you knock'd at the door.

Sir *Sim.* I must have you burn your plays and romances now you are mine; they corrupt your innocence; and what can you learn from 'em?

Bid. What, you can't teach me, I'm sure.

Sir *Sim.* Fy, fy, child; I never heard you talk at this rate before; I'm afraid, Tag, you put these things into her head.

Tag. I Sir? I vow, Sir Simon, she knows more than you can conceive; she surprises me, I assure you, though

I have

I. have been married these two years, and liv'd with batchelors most part of my life.

Sir *Sim.* Do you hear, Jasper? I'm all over in a sweat.
—Pray, miss, have not you had company this afternoon?
I saw a young fop go out of the house as I was coming hither.

Bid. You might have seen two, Sir Simon, if your eyes had been good.

Sir *Sim.* Do you hear, Jasper?—Sure the child is possess'd—Pray, miss, what do they want here?

Bid. Me, Sir; they wanted me.

Sir *Simon.* What did they want with you, I say?

Bid. Why, what do you want with me?

Sir *Sim.* Do you hear, Jasper?—I am thunder-struck!
I can't believe my own ears! Tell me the reason, I say,
why——

Tag. I'll tell you the reason why, if you please, Sir Simon. Miss, you know, is a very silly young girl, and having found out (Heaven knows how!) that there is some little difference between sixty-five and twenty-five, she's ridiculous enough to choose the latter; when if she'd take my advice——

Sir *Sim.* You are right, Tag, she wou'd take me? Eh?

Tag. Yes, Sir, as the only way to have both; for if she marries you, the other will follow of course.

Sir *Sim.* Do you hear, Jasper?

Bid. 'Tis very true, Sir Simon; from knowing no better, I have set my heart upon a young man, and a young one I'll have; there have been three here this afternoon.

Sir *Sim.* Three, Jasper?

Bid. And they have been quarrelling about me, and one has beat the other two. Now, Sir Simon, if you'll take up the conqueror and kick him, as he has kick'd the others, you shall have me for your reward, and my fifteen thousand pounds into the bargain. What says my hero?
Eh?

[*Slaps him on the back.*

Sir *Sim.* The world's at an end——What's to be done,
Jasper?

Jas. Pack up and be gone; don't fight the match, sir.

Sir *Sim.* Flesh and blood can't bear it——I'm all over agitation—Hugh, hugh!—am I cheated by a baby, a doll?

Where's your aunt, you young cockatrice?—I'll let her know—she's a base woman, and you are——

Bid. You are in a fine humour to shew your valour. Tag, fetch the captain this minute, while sir Simon is warm, and let him know, he is waiting here to cut his throat [*Exit* Tag.] I lock'd him up in my bed-chamber till you came.

Sir Sim. Here's an imp of darkness! what would I give that my son Bob was here to thrash her spark, while I—ravish'd the rest of the family.

Jas. I believe we had best retire, Sir.

Sir Sim. No, no, I must see her bully first; and, do you hear, Jasper, if I put him in a passion do you knock him down.

Jas. Pray, keep your temper, sir.

Enter CAPTAIN, TAG, *and* PUFF.

Capt. [*Approaching angrily.*] What's the meaning, sir?——Ounds! it is my father, Puff; what shall I do?

[*Aside.*

Puff. [*Drawing him by the coat.*] Kennel again, sir.

Sir Sim. I am enchanted!

[*Starting.*

Capt. There is no retreat, I must stand it!

Bid. What's all this?

Sir Sim. Your humble servant, captain Fire-Ball.—You are welcome from the wars, noble captain. I did not think of being knock'd o' th' head, or cut up alive by so fine a gentleman.

Capt. I am under such confusion, sir, that I have no power to convince you of my innocence.

Sir Sim. Innocence! pretty lamb! and so, sir, you have left the regiment, and the honourable employment of fighting for your country, to come home and cut your father's throat; why, you'll be a great man in time, *Bob!*

Bid. His father, Tag!

Sir Sim. Come, come, 'tis soon done—one stroke does it—or if you have any qualms, let your 'squire there perform the operation.

Puff. Pray, sir, don't throw such temptations in my way.

Capt.

Capt. Hold your impudent tongue!.

Sir *Sim.* Why don't you speak, Mr Modesty; what excuse have you for leaving the army, I say?

Capt. My affection to this lady.

Sir *Sim.* Your affection, puppy!

Capt. Our love, sir, has been long and mutual; what accidents have happen'd since my going abroad, and her leaving the country, and how I have most unaccountably met you here, I am a stranger to; but whatever appearances may be, I still am, and ever was, your dutiful son.

Bid. He talks like an angel, Tag!

Sir *Sim.* Dutiful, sirrah! have not you rivall'd your father?.

Capt. No, sir, you have rivall'd me; my claim must be prior to yours.

Bid. Indeed, sir Simon, he can shew the best title to me.

Jus. Sir, sir, the young gentleman speaks well, and as the fortune will not go out of the family, I would advise you to drop your resentment, be reconcil'd to your son, and relinquish the lady.

Sir *Sim.* Ay, ay, with all my heart——Look ye, son, I give you the girl, she's too much for me, I confess;—and take my word, Bob, you'll catch a tartar..

Bid. I assure you, sir Simon, I'm not the person you take me for; if I have us'd you any ways ill, 'twas for your son's sake, who had my promise and inclinations before you; and tho' I believe I should have made you a most uncomfortable wife, I'll be the best daughter to you in the world; and if you stand in need of a lady, my aunt is disengag'd, and is the best nurse——

Sir *Sim.* No, no, I thank you, child; you have so turn'd my stomach to marriage, I have no appetite left——But where is this aunt? won't she stop your proceedings, think you?

Tag. She's now at her lawyer's, sir, and if you please to go with the young couple, and give your approbation, I'll answer for my old lady's consent.

Bid. The Captain, and I, sir——

Sir *Sim.* Come, come, Bob, you are but an ensign, don't impose on the girl neither.

Capt. I had the good fortune, sir, to please my royal general

neral

neral by my behaviour in a small action with the enemy, and he gave me a company.

Sir Sim. Bob, I wish you joy! this is news indeed! and when we celebrate your wedding, son, I'll drink a half pint bumper myself to your benefactor.

Capt. And he deserves it, sir; such a general, by his example and justice, animates us to deeds of glory, and insures us conquest.

Sir Sim. Right, my boy,——come along then. [*Going.*

Puff. Halt a little, gentlemen and ladies, if you please: every body here seems well satisfied but myself.

Capt. What's the matter with Puff?

Puff. Sir, as I would make myself worthy of such a master, and the name of a soldier, I cannot put up the least injury to my honour.

Sir Sim. Heyday! what flourishes are these?

Puff. Here is the man; come forth, caitiff. (*To* Jasper.) He hath confess'd this day, that in my absence, he hath taken freedoms with my lawful wife, and had dishonourable intentions against my bed; for which I demand satisfaction.——

Sir Sim. (*Striking him.*) What stuff is here, the fellow's brain's turn'd.

Puff. And crack'd too, sir; but you are my master's father, and I submit.

Capt. Come, come, I'll settle your punctilios, and will take care of you and Tag hereafter, provided you drop all animosities, and shake hands this moment.

Puff. My revenge gives way to my interest, and I once again, Jasper, take thee to my bosom.

Jas. I'm your friend again, Puff——but harkye——I fear you not; and if you'll lay aside your steel there, as far as a broken head or a black eye, I'm at your service upon demand.

Tag. You are very good at crowing indeed, Mr Jasper; but let me tell you, the fool that is rogue enough to brag of a woman's favours must be a dunghill every way—As for you my dear husband, shew your manhood in a proper place, and you need not heed these sheep-biters.

Sir Sim. The Abigail is pleasant I confess, he, he!

Bid. I'm afraid the town will be ill-natured enough to think I have been a little coquetish in my behaviour; but,

I hope

I hope, as I have been constant to the Captain, I shall be excus'd diverting myself with pretenders.

> Ladies, to fops and braggarts ne'er be kind,
> No charms can warm 'em, and no virtues bind;
> Each lover's merit by his conduct prove,
> Who fails in honour, will be false in love.　*[Exeunt.*

FINIS.

ROMEO and JULIET.

DRAMATIS PERSONÆ.

Romeo, Mr Garrick.
Escalus, Mr Bransby.
Paris, Mr Scrase.
Mountague, Mr Burton.
Capulet, Mr Berry.
Mercutio, Mr Woodward.
Benvolio, Mr Mozeen.
Tibalt, Mr Blakes.
Old Capulet, Mr Johnson.
Friar Lawrence, Mr Havard.

Friar John, Mr Jefferson.
Balthasar, Mr Ackman.
Gregory, Mr W. Vaughan.
Sampson, Mr Clough.
Abram, Mr Mare.

Juliet, Mrs Cibber.
Lady Capulet, Mrs Bennet.
Nurse, Mis Maklin.

Citizens of Verona, *several men and women relations to Ca-*
pulet, maskers, guards, and other attendants.

The SCENE, *in the beginning of the fifth Act is in Man-*
tua; during all the rest of the Play, in and near Verona.

ACT I.   SCENE I.

The street in VERONA.

Enter Sampson *and* Gregory.

Sampson.

GREGORY, I strike quickly, being moved.
 Greg. But thou art not quickly mov'd to strike.
Sam. A dog of the house of *Mountague* moves me.
Greg. Draw thy tool then, for here come of that house.

Enter Abram *and* Balthasar.

Sam. My naked weapon is out; quarrel, I will back
thee, but——Let us take the law of our sides: let them
begin.
 Greg. I will frown as I pass by, and let them take it as
they list.

Sam.

Sam. Nay as they dare.   I will bite my thumb at them, which is a disgrace to them, if they bear it.

Abra. Do you bite your thumb at us, Sir?

Sam. I do bite my thumb, Sir.

Abra. Do you bite your thumb at us, Sir.

Sam. Is the law on our side, if I say ay?

Greg. No.

Sam. No, Sir, I do not bite my thumb at you, Sir: but I bite my thumb, Sir.

Greg. Do you quarrel, Sir?

Abra. Quarrel, Sir? no, Sir.

Sam. If you do, Sir, I am for you: I serve as good a man as you.

Abra. No better, Sir.

Sam. Well, Sir.

Enter BENVOLIO.

Greg. Say better: here comes one of my master's kins-men.

Sam. Yes, better, Sir.

Abra. You lye.

Sam. Draw, if you be men.   Gregory, remember thy swashing blow.   [*They fight.*

Ben. Part, fools, put up your swords, you know not what you do.

Enter TIBALT.

Tib. What art thou drawn among these heartless hinds? Turn thee, Benvolio, look upon thy death.

Ben. I do but keep the peace; put up thy sword, Or manage it to part these men with me.

Tib. What drawn, and talk of peace? I hate the word As I hate hell, all Mountagues and thee:
Have at thee, coward.

Enter three or four Citizens with clubs.

Offi. Clubs, bills, and partizans! strike, beat them down. Down with the Capulets, down with the Mountagues.

Enter Old CAPULET *in his Gown.*

Cap. What noise is this? give me my sword, My sword, I say: old Mountague is come, And flourishes his blade in spite of me.

Enter

Enter Old MOUNTAGUE.

Moun. Thou villain, Capulet——Hold me not, let me go.

Enter PRINCE *with Attendants.*

Prin. Rebellious subjects, enemies to peace,
Profaners of your neighbour-stained steel——
Will they not hear? what ho! you men! you beasts,
That quench the fire of your pernicious rage,
With purple fountains issuing from your veins;
On pain of torture, from those bloody hands
Throw your mis-temper'd weapons to the ground,
And hear the sentence of your moved prince.
Three civil broils, bred of an airy word,
By thee, old Capulet, and Mountague,
Have thrice disturb'd the quiet of our streets;
And made Verona's ancient citizens
Cast by their great beseeming ornaments,
To wield old partizans in hands as old;
If ever you affright your streets again,
Your lives shall pay the forfeit of the peace.
For this time all the rest depart away.
You, Capulet, shall go along with me;
And Mountague, come you this afternoon
To know our father's pleasure in this case.
Once more on pain of death, all men depart.

               [*Exeunt* Prince *and* Capulet, *etc.*

SCENE II.

Manent MOUNTAGUE *and* BENVOLIO.

Moun. WHO set this ancient quarrel now abroach?
       Speak, nephew, were you by when it began?
Ben. Here were the servants of your adversary,
And yours, close fighting, ere I did approach;
I drew to part them: in the instant came
The fiery Tibalt, with his sword prepar'd,
Which as he breath'd defiance to my ears,
He swung about his head, and cut the winds:
While we were interchanging thrusts and blows,

                                  Came

Came more and more, and fought on part and part,
'Till the prince came.

Moun. O where is Romeo? Saw you him to-day?
Right glad am I, he was not at this fray.

Ben. My lord, an hour before the worshipp'd sun
Peer'd through the golden window of the East,
A troubled mind drew me to walk abroad;
Where underneath the grove of sycamoor,
That westward rooteth from the city side,
So early walking did I see your son.
Tow'rds him I made, but he was 'ware of me,
And stole into the covert of a wood.
I, measuring his affections by my own,
(That most are busied when there most alone,)
Pursu'd my honour: nor pursuing him,
And gladly shun'd, who gladly fled from me.

Moun. Many a morning hath he there been seen
With tears augmenting the fresh morning dew;
But all so soon as the all chearing sun
Should, in the farthest east, begin to draw
The shady curtains from Aurora's bed;
Away from light steals home my heavy son,
And private in his chamber pens himself;
Shuts up his windows, locks fair day-light out,
And makes himself an artificial night.
Black and portentous must this humour prove.
Unless good counsel may the cause remove.

Ben. My noble uncle, do you know the cause?
Moun. I neither know it, nor can learn it of him.
Ben. Have you importun'd him by any means?
Moun. Both by himself and many other friends;
But he his own affections' counsellor,
Is to himself, I will not say, how true:
But to himself so secret and so close,
So far from sounding and discovery,
As is the bud, but with an envious worm,
Ere he can spread his sweet leaves to the air,
Or dedicate his beauty to the sun.

Ben. So please you, Sir, Mercutio and myself
Are most near to him; be it that our years,
Statures, births, fortunes, studies, inclinations,
Measure the rule of his, I know not; but
Friendship still loves to sort him with his like.

We

We will attempt upon his privacy,
And could we learn from whence his sorrows grow,
We would as willingly give cure, as knowledge.
Moun. 'Twill bind us to you: good Benvolio, go.
Ben. We'll know his grievance, or be hard denied.

           [Exeunt severally.

SCENE III.

Before CAPULET's *House.*

Enter CAPULET, PARIS, *and a Servant.*

Cap. AND Mountague is bound as well as I,
   In penalty alike; and 'tis not hard
For men so old as we to keep the peace.
 Par. Of honourable reck'ning are you both,
And pity 'tis you liv'd at odds so long:
But now, my lord, What say you to my suit?
 Cap. But saying o'er what I have said before,
My child is yet a stranger in the world,
She hath not seen the change of eighteen years;
Let two more summers wither in their pride,
Ere we may think her ripe to be a wife.
 Par. Younger than she are happy mothers made.
 Cap. And too soon marr'd are those so early made:
The earth hath swallow'd all my hopes with her.
But woo her, gentle Paris, get her heart;
If she agree, within her scope of choice
Lies my consent; so woo her, gentle Paris.
This night I hold an old accustom'd feast,
Whereto I have invited many a friend,
Such as I love, and you among the rest;
Once more most welcome!
Come go with me. Go, sirrah, trudge about.

           [To a Servant.

Through fair Verona; find those persons out,
Whose names are written there, and to them say,
My house and welcome on their pleasures stay. *[Exeunt.*

SCENE

SCENE IV.

Wood near VERONA.

Enter BENVOLIO and MERCUTIO.

Mer. SEE where he steals—Told I you not, Benvolio,
That we should find this melancholy Cupid
Lock'd in some gloomy covert, under key
Of cautionary silence; with his arms
Threaded, like these cross boughs, in sorrow's knot.

Enter ROMEO.

Ben. Good-morrow, cousin.
Rom. Is the day so young?
Ben. But new struck nine.
Rom. Ah, me! sad hours seem long,
Mer. Pry'thee, what sadness lengthens Romeo's hours?
Rom. Not having that, which having makes them short,
Ben. In love, me seems!
Alas, that love so gentle to the view,
Should be so tyrannous and rough in proof!
Rom. Where shall we dine!—O me—Cousin Benvolio,
What was the fray this morning with the Capulets?
Yet, tell me not, for I have heard it all.
Here's much to do with hate, but more with love:
Love, heavy lightness! serious vanity!
Mis-shapen chaos of well seeming forms!
This love feel I; but such my froward fate,
That there I love where most I ought to hate.
Dost thou not laugh, my friend!—Oh Juliet! Juliet!
Ben. No, coz, I rather weep.
Rom. Good heart, at what?——
Ben. At thy good heart's oppression,
Mer. Tell me in sadness, who she is you love?
Rom. In sadness then, I love a woman.
Mer. I aim'd so near, when I suppos'd you lov'd.
Rom. A right good marksman! and she's fair I love:
But knows not of my love, 'twas through my eyes
The shaft empierc'd my heart, change gave the wound,
Which time can never heal: no star befriends me,
To each sad night succeeds a dismal morrow.

And

And still 'tis hopeless love, and endless sorrow.

   Mer. Be rul'd by me, forget to think of her.

   Rom. O teach me how I should forget to think!

   Mer. By giving liberty into thine eyes:
Take thou some new infection to thy heart,
And the rank poison of the old will die.
Examine other beauties.

   Rom. He that is strucken blind cannot forget
The precious treasure of his eye-sight lost.
Shew me a mistress that is passing fair;
What doth her beauty serve but as a note,
Remembring me, who past that passing fair;
Farewel, thou can'st not teach me to forget.

   Mer. I warrant thee.   If thou'lt but stay to hear,
To-night there is an ancient splended feast
Kept by old Capulet, our enemy,
Where all the beauties of Verona meet.

   Rom. At Capulet's my friend ;
Go there, and with an unattainted eye,
Compare her face with some that I shall show,
And I will make thee think thy swain a crow.

   Rom. When the devout religion of mine eye
Maintains such falsehoods, then turn tears to fires;
And burn the heretics.   All-seeing Phœbus
Ne'er saw her match, fince first his course began.

   Mer. Tut, tut, you saw her fair, none else being by,
Herself pois'd with herself; but let be weigh'd
Your lady-love against some other fair,
And she will shew scant well.

   Rom. I will along, Mercutio.

   Mer. 'Tis well.   Look to behold at this high feast,
Earth-treading stars, that might dim heaven's lights,
Hear all, all see, try all ; and like her most,
That most shall merit thee.

   Rom. My mind is chang'd——
I will not go to-night.

   Mer. Why, may one ask ?

   Rom. I dream'd a dream last night.

   Mer. Ha ! ha ! a dream !
O then I see queen Mab hath been with you.
She is the fancy's mid-wife, and she comes
In shape no bigger than an agat-stone
On the fore-finger of an Alderman,

Drawn

Drawn with the team of little atomies,
Athwart mens as they lie asleep:
Her waggon-spokes made of long spinners legs;
The cover, of the wings of grashoppers;
The traces, of the smallest spider's web;
The collars, of the moon-shine's wat'ry beams;
Her whip, of cricket's bone; the lash, of film:
Her waggoner a small grey-coated gnat,
Not half so big as a round little worm,
Prick'd from the lazy finger of a maid.
Her chariot is an empty hazel nut,
Made by the joiner squirrel, or old grub,
Time out of mind the fairies coach-makers:
And in this state she gallops night by night,
Through lovers brains, and then they dream of love;
On courtiers knees, that dream on curt'sies straight:
O'er lawyer's fingers, who straight dream on fees;
O'er ladies lips, who straight on kisses dream.
Sometimes she gallops o'er a lawyer's nose,
And then dreams he of smelling out a suit:
And sometimes comes she with a tith's-pig's tail,
Tickling the parson as he lies asleep;
Then dreams he of another benefice,
Sometimes she driveth o'er a soldier's neck,
And then dreams he of cutting foreign throats,
Of breaches, ambuscadoes, Spanish blades,
Of healths five fathom deep; and then anon
Drums in his ears, at which he starts and wakes,
And being thus frighted, swears a prayer or two,
And sleeps again. This is that Mab——
   Rom. Peace, peace,
Thou talk'st of nothing.
   Mer. True, I talk of dreams;
Which are the children of an idle brain,
Begot of nothing, but vain phantasy,
Which is as thin of substance as the air,
And more unconstant than the wind.
   Ben. This wind you talk of, blows us from ourselves,
And we shall come too late.
   Rom. I fear too early: for my mind misgives
Some consequence, yet hanging in the stars,
From this night's revels—lead, gallant friends;
Let come what may, once more I will behold

My Juliet's eyes, drink deeper of affliction:
I'll watch the time; and, mask'd from observation,
Make known my sufferings, but conceal my name:
Tho' hate and discord 'twixt our sires increase,
Let in our hearts dwell love and endless peace.

[*Exeunt* Mercutio *and* Benvolio.

SCENE. V.

CAPULET's *House.*

Enter Lady CAPULET *and* NURSE.

L. *Cap.* NURSE, where's my daughter? call her forth
to me.

Nurse. Now (by my maidenhead at twelve years old
I bade her come; what lamb, what lady-bird, God forbid
———where's this girl? what *Juliet?*

Enter JULIET.

Jul. How now? who calls?

Nurse. Your mother.

Jul. Madam, I am here, what is your will?

La. *Cap.* This is the matter———Nurse give leave a
while, we must talk in secret: Nurse, come back again,
I have remember'd me, thou shal't hear mycounsel: thou
know'st my daughter's of a pretty age.

Nurse. Faith I can tell her age unto an hour.

La *Cap.* She's not eighteen.

Nurse. I'll lay eighteen of my teeth, and yet to my teeth
be it spoken, I have but eight, she's not eighteen; how
long is it now to Lammas-tide?

La. *Cap.* A fortnight and odd days.

Nurse. Even or odd, of all the days in the year come,
Lammas-eve at night shall she be eighteen. Susan and she
(God rest all Christian souls) were of an age. Well, Susan
is with God; she was too good for me. But as I said
on, Lammas-eve at night shall she be eighteen, that shall
she, marry, marry, I remember it well. 'Tis since the
earthquake now fifteen years, and she was wean'd, I never shall forget it, of all the days in the year upon that
day; for I had then laid wormwood to my breast, sitting
in the sun, under the dove-house wall; my lord and you

were

were then at Mantua——nay, I do bear a brain.   But as
I said, when it did taste the wormwood on the nipple of
the breast, and felt it bitter, pretty fool, to see it teachy
and fall out with the breast.   Shake, quoth the dove-
house——'twas no need I trow to bid me trudge; and
since that time it is fifteen years, for then she could stand
alone, nay, by th' rood she could have run, and wad-
dled all about; for even the day before she broke her brow ;
and then my husband (God be with his soul, a' was a
merry man,) took up the child ; yea, quoth he, dost
thou fall upon thy face ? thou wilt fall backward when
thou hast more wit : wilt thou not, Jule ? and by my holy
dam, the pretty wretch left crying, and said, ay ; to see
now how a jest shall come about I warrant, and I should
live a thousand years I should not forget it ; wilt thou
not, Jule, quoth he ? and pretty fool, it stinted, and said,
ay.

 Jul. And stint thee too, I pray thee, peace.
 Nurse. Peace, I have done; God mark thee to his grace.
Thou wast the prettiest babe that ere I nurst.
An' I might live to see thee married once,
I have my wish.
 La. *Cap.* And that same marriage is the very theme,
I came to talk of.   Tell, me, daughter Juliet,
How stands your disposition to be married ?
 Jul. It is an honour that I dreamt not of.
 Nurse. An honour ? Were not I thine only nurse,
I'd say thou hadst suck'd wisdom from thy teat.
 La. *Cap.* Well, think of marriage now ; younger than you
Here in Verona, ladies of esteem,
Are made already mothers, by my 'count,
I was your mother much upon these years
That you are now a maid.   Thus then in brief,
The valiant Paris seeks you for his love.
 Nurse. A man, young lady : lady such a man
As all the world——Why, he's a man of wax.
 La. *Cap.* Verona's summer hath not such a flower.
 Nurse. Nay, he's a flower in faith, a very flower.
 La. *Cap.* Speak briefly, can you like of Paris' love.
 Jul. I'll look to like, if looking liking move;
But no more deep will I indart my eye,
Than your consent gives strength to make it fly.
 VOL. I.   E   *Enter.*

Enter GREGORY.

Greg. Madam, new guests are come, and brave one's
all in masks. You are call'd; my young lady ask'd for
the nurse curs'd in the pantry; supper almost ready to be
serv'd up, and every thing in extremity. I must hence
and wait.

La. *Cap.* We follow thee.   [*Exeunt.*

SCENE. VI.

A Hall in CAPULET's *House.*

The CAPULET's, LADIES, GUESTS, *and* MASKERS, *are discover'd.*

Cap. WELCOME, gentlemen. Ladies, that have your
     feet
Uuplagu'd with corns, we'll have about with you.
Who'll now deny to dance ? She thatmakes dainty,
I'll swear hath corns.   Am I come near you now ?
Welcome all gentlemen ; I've seen the day
That I have worn a viser, and could tell,
A whispering-tale in a fair lady's ear,
Such as would please; 'tis gone; 'tis gone ; 'tis gone !
                        [*Music plays and they dance.*
More light ye knaves, and turn the table up ;
And quench the fire, the room is grown too hot.
Ah, sirrah, this unlook'd-for sport comes well.
Nay, sit, nay, sit good cousin Capulet,
For you and I are past our dancing days :
How long is't now since last yourself and I
Were in a mask ?

   2 Cap. By'r lady thirty years.

   Cap. What, man ! 'tis not so much, 'tis not so much !
'Tis since the nuptial of Lucentio,
Come Pentecost as quickly as it will,
Some five and twenty years and then we mask'd.

   2 Cap. 'Tis more, 'tis more ; his son is elder Sir,
His son is thirty.

   Cap. Will you tell me that ?
His son was but a ward two years ago.

                                        Rom.

Rom. Cousin Benvolio, do you mark that lady which
Doth enrich the hand of yonder gentleman?
Ben. I do.
Rom. Oh, she doth teach the torches to burn bright!
Her beauty hangs upon the cheek of night,
Like a rich jewel in an Ethiops' ear:
The measure done, I'll watch her to her place,
And touching hers, make happy my rude hand.
Be still, be still, my fluttering heart.
Tib. This, by his voice, should be a Montague,
Fetch me my rapier, boy; what, dares the slave
Come hither cover'd with an antic face,
To steer and scorn at our solemnity.
Now by the stock and honour of my race,
To strike him dead I hold it not a sin.
Cap. Why, how now, kinsman wherefore storm you
    thus?
Tib. Uncle, this is a Montague, or foe:
A villain that has hither come in spite,
To scorn and flout at our solemnity.
Capt. Young Romeo, is't?
Tib. That villian Romeo.
Cap. Content thee, gentle coz, let him alone,
He bears him like a courtly gentleman;
And, to say truth, Verona brags of him,
To be a virtuous and well govern'd youth.
I would not for the wealth of all this town,
Here in my house do him disparagement;
Therefore be patient take no note of him. .
Tib. It fits when such a villain is a guest.
I'll not endure him.
Cap. He shall be endur'd.
Be quiet cousin, or I'll make you quiet——
Tib. Patience perforce with wilful choler meeting,
Makes my flesh tremble in their difference.
I will withdraw; but this intrusion shall,
Now seeming sweet covert to bitter gall.   [*Dance here.*
Rom. If I profane with my unworthy hand   [*To* Juliet.
This holy shrine, the gentle fine is this.   [*Kiss.*
Jul. Good pilgrim, you do wrong your hands too much.
For palm to palm is holy palmer's kiss.
Rom. Have not saints lips, and holy palmers too?
Jul. Ay, pilgrim, lips that they must use in prayer.
                    E 2   *Rom.*

Rom. Thus then, dear saint, let lips put up their prayers.
                                        [*Kiss.*

Nurse. Madam, your mother craves a word with you.
Ben. What is her mother?   [*To her Nurse.*
Nurse. Marry batchelor,
Her mother is the lady of the house,
And a good lady and a wise and virtuous,
I nurs'd her daughter that you talk withal;
I tell you, he that can lay hold on her
Shall have the chink.
Ben. Is she a Capulet?
Romeo, let's be gone, the sport is over.
Rom. Ay so I fear the more is my mishap.   [*Exeunt.*
Cap. Nay, gentlemen, prepare not to be gone,
We have a trifling foolish banquet towards.
Is it e'en so? why then, I thank you all.
I thank you honest gentlemen, good night;
More torches here—come on then, lets to supper. [*Exeunt.*
Jul. Come hither nurse.   What is yon gentleman?
Nurse. The son and heir of old Tiberio.
Jul. What's he that is now going out of door?
Nurse. That as I think, is young Mercutio.
Jul. What's he that fellows here, that would not dance.
Nurse. I know not.
Jul. Go ask his name.   If he be married,
My grave is like to be my wedding-bed.
Nurse. His name is Romeo, and a Montague,
The only son of your great enemy.
Jul. My only love sprung from my only hate!
Too early seen, unknown; and known too late.
Nurse. What's this? what's this!
Jul. A rhyme I learn't e'en now
Of one I talk'd withal.   [*One calls within* Juliet.
Nurse. Anon, anon——
Come, let's away, the strangers are all gone.   [*Exeunt.*

ACT.

ACT. II.   SCENE. I.

The *STREET.*

Enter ROMEO *alone.*

ROMEO.

CAN I go forward when my heart is here ;
Turn back, dull earth, and find thy center out. [*Exit.*

Enter BENVOLIO *with* MERCUTIO.

Ben. Romeo, my cousin Romeo.
Mer. He is wise,
And on my life has stol'n him home to bed.
Ben. He ran this way, and leap'd this orchard wall,
Call, good Mercutio.
Mer. Nay, I'll conjure too.
Why, why, Romeo ! humours ! madam, passion ! lover !
Appear thou in the likeness of a sigh.
Speak but one rhyme and I am satisfy'd.
Cry but *Ab me !* couple but *love* and *dove,*
Speak to my gossip Venus one fair word,
One nick-name to her pur-blind son and heir ;
I conjure thee by thy mistres' bright eyes,
By her fine foot, straight leg, and quivering thigh,
And the demeasns that there adjacent lie,
That in thy likeness thou appear to us.
Ben. And if he hear thee, thou wilt anger him.
To raise a spirit in his mistres' circle,
'Till she had laid it.   My invocation is
Honest and fair, in his mistres' name,
I conjure only but to raise him up.
Ben. Come, he hath hid himself among these trees,
To be consorted with the hum'rous night.
Mer. Romeo, good night, I'll to my truckle bed,
This field-bed is too cold for me to sleep ;
Come, shall we go ?
Ben. Go then, for 'tis in vain
To seek him here that means not to be found. [*Exeunt.*

E 3

ACT.

S C E N E. II.

A Garden.

Enter ROMEO.

Rom. HE jests at scars that never felt a wound———
But soft, what light thro' yonder window
breaks ?
It is the east, and Juliet is the sun !

> [Juliet *appears above at a window.*

Arise, fair sun, and kill the envious moon,
Who is already sick and pale with grief,
That thou, her maid, art far more fair than she.
She speaks, yet she says nothing ; what of that ?
Her eye discourses, I will answer it ;
I am too bold———Oh were those eyes in heav'n,
They'd through the airy region stream so bright,
That birds would sing and think it were the morn ;
See how she leans her cheek upon her hand,
O that I were a glove upon that hand,
That I might touch that cheek.

Jul. Ah me !

Rom. She speaks, she speaks !
Oh speak again bright angel for thou art
As glorious to this sight, being o'er my head,
As is a winged messenger from heav'n,
To the upturn'd wond'ring eyes of mortals
When he bestrides the lazy-passing clouds,
And sails upon the bosom of the air.

Jul. O Romeo, Romeo—wherefore art thou Romeo ?
Deny thy father, and refuse thy name ;
Or if thou wilt not, be but sworn my love,
And I'll no longer be a Capulet.

Rom. Shall I hear more, or shall I speak at this ? [*Aside.*

Jul. 'Tis but thy name that is my enemy ;
What's in a name ? that which we call a rose,
By any other name would smell as sweet.
So Romeo would, were he not Romeo call'd,
Retain that dear perfection which he owes,
Without that title ; Romeo, quit thy name,
And for that name, which is no part of thee,

Take

Take all myself.

Rom. I take thee at thy word;
Call me but love, I will forswear thy name,
And never more be Romeo.
What man art thou that thus bescreen'd in night
So stumblest on my counsel.
I know not how to tell thee who I am:
My name, dear saint, is hateful to myself,
Because it is an enemy to thee.

Jul. My ears have not yet drunk a hundred words
Of that tongue's uttering, yet I know the sound.
Art thou not Romeo, and a Montague?

Rom. Neither, fair saint, if either thee displease.

Jul. How cam'st thou hither, tell me, and for what?
The orchard walls are high, and hard to climb,
And the place death, considering who thou art,
If any of my kinsmen find thee here.

Rom. With love's light wings did I oe'r-perch these walls,
For stony limits cannot hold love out,
And what love can do, that dares love attempt;
Therefore thy kinsmen are no stop to me.

Jul. If they do see thee, they will murder thee.

Rom. Alack there lies more peril in thine eye,
Than twenty of their swords; look thou but sweet,
And I am proof against their enmity.

Jul. I would not for the world they saw thee here,
By whose direction found'st thou out this place?

Rom. By love that first did prompt me to enquire,
He lent me counsel and I lent him eyes;
I am no pilot, yet wert thou as far
As that vast shore, wash'd with the farthest sea,
I would adventure for such a merchandize,

Jul. Thou knowst the mask of night is on my face,
Else would a maiden blush bepaint my cheek
For that which thou hast heard me speak to-night,
Fain would I dwell on form, fain fain, deny
What I have spoke—but farewell compliment;
Dost thou love me? I know thou wilt say, ay,
And I will take thy word——yet if thou swear'st,
Thou may'st prove false; at lover's perjuries
They say *Jove* laughs. Oh gentle *Romeo!*
If thou dost love, pronounce it faithfully;
Or if thou think I am too quickly won,

E 4

I'll frown and be perverse and say thee nay,
So thou wilt woo; but else not for the world.
In truth, fair Montague, I am too fond;
And therefore thou may'st think my 'haviour light;
But trust me, gentlemen, I'll prove more true,
Than those that have more cunning to be strange.
I should have been more strange, I must confess,
But thou over-heard'st, ere I was 'ware,
My true love's passion: therefore pardon me,
And not impute this yielding to light love,
Which the dark night hath so discover'd.

   Rom. Lady by yonder blessed moon I vow——

   Jul. O swear not by moon, th' inconstant moon,
That monthly changes in her circled orb;
Lest that thy love prove likewise variable.

   Rom. What shall I swear by?

   Jul. Do not swear at all;
Or if thou wilt, swear by thy gracious self,
Which is the god of my idolatry,
And I'll believe thee.

   Rom. If my true heart's love——

   Jul. Well, do not swear—although I joy in thee,
I have no joy of this contract to-night:
It is too rash, too unadvis'd, too sudden,
Too like the lightning which doth cease to be
Ere one can say, it lightens—sweet, good night,
This bud of love by summer's ripening breath
May prove a beauteous flower when next we meet:
Good night, good night—as sweet repose and rest
Come to thy heart, as that within my breast.

   Rom. O wilt thou leave me so unsatisfied?

   Jul. What satisfaction canst thou have to-night?

   Rom. Th' exchange of thy love's faithful vow for mine.

   Jul. I gave thee mine before thou didst request it,
And yet I would it were to give again.

   Rom. Would'st thou withdraw it? for what purpose,
     love?

   Jul. But to be frank, to give it thee again.
My bounty is as boundless as the sea,
My love as deep; the more I give to thee,
The more I have, for both are infinite.
I hear some noise within; dear love, adieu.

                [*Nurse calls within.*
                    Anon,

Anon, good Nurse—Sweet Montague, be true;
Stay but a little I will come again.   [*Exit.*
   Rom. O blessed, blessed night.   I am afraid:
Being in night, all this is but a dream !
Too flattering-sweet to be substantial.

Re-enter JULIET *above.*

   Jul. Three words, dear Romeo, and good night indeed ;
If that thy bent of love be honourable,
Thy purpose, marriage, send me word to-morrow
By one that I'll procure to come to thee,
Where, and what time thou wilt perform the rite ;
And all my fortunes at thy foot I'll lay,
And follow thee, my love throughout the world.
                     [*Within* Madam.
I come anon,—but if thou mean'st not well,
I do beseech thee—[*Within* Madam.] By and by I come—
To cease thy suit, and leave me to my grief.
To morrow I will send.
   Rom. So thrive my soul.
   Jul. A thousand times good night.
   Rom. A thousand times the worse to want thy light.

Enter JULIET *again.*

   Jul. Hist ! Romeo, hist ! O for a falk'ner's voice,
To lure this tassel gentle back again——
Bondage is hoarse and may not speak aloud,——
Else would I tear the cave where Echo lies,
And make her angry tongue more hoarse than mine
With repetition of my Romeo.
   Rom. It is my love that calls upon my name.
How silver-sweet sound lover's tongues by night,
Like softest music to attending ears.
   Jul. Romeo !
   Rom. My sweet !
   Jul. At what o'clock to-morrow
Shall I send to thee ?
   Rom. By the hour of nine.
   Jul. I will not fail, 'tis twenty years till then ——
I have forgot why did I call thee back.
   Rom. Let me stand here till thou remember it.
   Jul. I shall forget to have thee still stand there,
Remembering how I love thy company.
E 5

Rom.

Rom. And I'll stay here to have thee still forget,
Forgetting any other home but this.

Jul. 'Tis almost morning.   I would have thee gone,
And yet no further than a wanton's bird,
That lets it hop a little from her hand,
And with a silk thread plucks it back again,
So living-jealous of his liberty.

Rom. I would I were thy bird.

Jul. Sweet, so would I,
Yet I should kill thee with much cherishing.
Good night, good night.   Parting is such sweet sorrow,
That I shall say good-night 'till it be morrow. .   [*Exit.*

Rom. Sleep dwell upon thine eyes, peace in thy breast;
Would I were sleep and peace, so sweet to rest!
Here will I to my ghostly father's cell,
His help to crave and my dear hap to tell.   [*Exit.*

S C E N E. III.

A Monastery.

Enter Friar Lawrence *with a basket.*

Fri. THE grey-ey'd morn smiles on the frowning night,
    Check'ring the eastern clouds with streaks of light,
Now ere the sun advance his burning eye,
The day to chear, and night's dank dew to dry,
I must fill up this osier cage of ours
With baleful weeds, and precious juiced flowers.
O mickle is the powerful grace that lies
In plants, herbs, stones, and their true qualities !
For nought so vile, that on the earth doth live,
But to the earth some special good doth give ;
Nor ought so good, but strain'd from that fair use,
Revolts to vice, and stumbles on abuse.
Virtue itself turns vice, being misapplied,
And vice sometimes by actions dignified.
Within the infant rind of this small flower
Poison hath residence, and med'cine power ;
For this being smelt, with that sense cheers each part ;
Being tasted, slays all senses with the heart.
Two such opposed foes encamp them still
In man, as well as herbs ; Grace, and rude Will ;

And

And where the worser is predominant,
Full soon the canker death eats up that plant.

Enter ROMEO.

Rom. Good-morrow, father.
Fri. Benedicite,
What early tongue so sweet saluteth me?
Young son, it argues a distemper'd head?
So soon to bid good-morrow to thy pillow;
Care keeps his watch on every old man's eye;
And where care lodgeth, sleep will never bide;
But where with unstuft brain unbruised youth
Doth couch his limbs, there golden sleep resides;
Therefore thy earliness assureth me
Thou art up-rous'd by some distemp'rature;
What is the matter, son?
Rom. I tell thee, ere thou ask it me again;
I have been feasting with mine enemy,
Where to the heart's core one hath wounded me,
That's by me wounded; both our remedies
Within thy help and holy physic lie.
Fri. Be plain, good son, and homely in thy drift.
Rom. Then plainly know, my heart's dear love is set
On Juliet, Capulet's fair daughter;
As mine on her's, so hers is set on mine:
When, and where, and how
We met, we woo'd, and made exchange of vows,
I'll tell thee as we pass; but this I beg
That thou consent to marry us to-day.
Fri. Holy saint Francis, what a change is this!
But tell me, son, and call thy reason home,
Is not this love the offspring of thy folly,
Bred from thy wantonness and thoughtless brain?
Be heedful, and see you stop by times,
Lest that thy rash ungovernable passions,
O'er-leaping duty, and each dew regard,
Hurry thee one, thro' short-liv'd, dear-bought pleasures,
To cureless woes, and lasting penitence.
Rom. I pray thee, chide me not, she whom I love,
Doth give me grace for grace, and love for love;
Do thou with heav'n smile upon our union;
Do not withhold thy benediction from us,
But make two hearts, by holy marriage, one.

Fri. Well, come, my pupil, go along with me,
In one respect I'll give thee my assistance;
For this alliance may so happy prove,
To turn your household rancour to pure love.

Rom. O let us hence, Love stands on sudden haste.

Fri. Wisely and slow; they stumble that run fast.

[*Exeunt.*

S C E N E IV.

The STREET.

Enter BENVOLIO *and* MERCUTIO.

Mer. WHERE the devil should this Romeo be? came
he not home to night?

Ben. Not to his father's; I spoke with his man.

Mer. Why that same pale hard-hearted wench, that Rosaline, torments him so, that he will sure run mad.

Ben. Tibalt, the kinsman of old Capulet, hath sent a letter to his father's house.

Mer. A challenge, on my life.

Ben. Romeo will answer it.

Mer. Alas, poor Romeo, he is already dead! stabb'd
with a white wench's black eye, run through the ear with
a love-song, the very pin of his heart cleft with the blind
bow-boy's but-shaft; and is he a man to encounter Tibalt?

Ben. Why, what is Tibalt?

Mer. O, he's the courageous captain of compliments;
he fights as you sing prick-song, keeps time, distance, and
proportion: rests his minum one, two, and the third in
your bosom; the very butcher of a silk-button, a duellist,
a duellist; a gentleman of the very first house, of the first
and second cause; ah, the immortal passado, the punto reverso, the hay——

Ben. The what?

Mer. The pox of such antic, lisping, affected phantasies,
these new tuners of accents:—Jesu a very good blade—a
very tall man—a very good whore——Why is not this a
lamentable thing, grandsire, that we should be thus afflicted
with these strange flies, these fashion-mongers, these *pardonnez moy's?*

Ben. Here comes Romeo.

Mer.

Mer. Without his roe, like a dried herring. O flesh, flesh, how art thou fishified? Now is he for the numbers that Petrarch flowed in: Laura to his lady was but a kitchen-wench; marry, she had a better love to be-rhyme her; Dido, a dowdy; Cleopatra, a gipsy, Helen and Hero hildings and harlots; Thisbe, a gray eye or so, but not to the purpose.

Enter ROMEO.

Signior Romeo, *bonjour*, there's a French salutation for you.

Rom. Good-morrow to you both.

Mer. You gave us the counterfeit fairly last night.

Rom. What counterfeit did I give you?

Mer. The slip, Sir, the slip: can you not conceive?

Rom. Pardon, Mercutio, my business was great, and in such a case as mine, a man may strain curtsey.

Enter NURSE *and her* MAN.

Ben. A sail! a sail!

Mer. Two, two, a shirt and a smock.

Nurse. Peter.

Pet. Anon.

Nurse. My fan, Peter.

Mer. Do, good Peter, to hide her face.

Nurse. Good ye good-morrow, gentlemen.

Mer. Good ye good-den, fair gentlewoman.

Nurse. Gentlemen, can any of you tell me where I may find young Romeo?

Rom. I am the youngest of that name, for fault of a worse.

Nurse. You say well. If you be he, Sir, I desire some *confidence* with you.

Ben. She will *indite* him to supper presently.

Mer. A bawd, a bawd, a bawd: so ho.

Rom. What hast thou found?

Mer. No, hare, Sir, but a bawd. Romeo, will you come to your father's? we'll to dinner thither.

Rom. I will follow you.

Mer. Farewel, ancient lady.

Exeunt Mercutio *and* Benvolio.

Nurse. I pray you, Sir, what saucy merchant was this that was so full of his roguery?

Rom. A gentleman, Nurse, that loves to hear himself

talk

talk, and will speak more in a minute, than he will stand
to in a month.

Nurse. An' a speak any thing against me, I'll take him
down an' he were lustier than he is, and twenty such jacks:
and if I cannot, I'll find those that shall. Scurvy knave, I
am none of his flirty-girls; and thou must stand by too,
and suffer every knave to use me at his pleasure.

[*To her man.*

Pet. I saw no man use you at his pleasure: if I had,
my weapon should quickly have been out I warrant you.
I dare draw as soon as another man, if I see occasion in a
good quarrel, and the law on my side.

Nurse. Now, afore God, I am so vext, that every part a-
bout me quivers.——Scurvy knave! Pray you, Sir, a
word: and as I told you, my young lady bid me enquire
you out. What she bid me say, I will keep to myself:
but first let me tell ye, if ye should lead her into fool's paradise, as they say, it were a very gross kind of behaviour,
as they say; for the gentlewoman is young, and therefore
if you should deal double with her, truly it were an ill
thing to be offered to any gentlewoman.

Rm. Commend me to thy lady and mistress, I protest
unto thee——

Nurse. Good heart, and i'faith, I will tell her as much;
lord, lord, she will be a joyful woman.

Rom. What wilt thou tell her, Nurse? thou dost not
mark me.

Nurse. I will tell her, Sir, that you do protest; which,
as I take it is a gentleman-like offer.

Rom. Bid her advise some means to come to shrift this
afternoon.
And there shall she at friar Laurence' cell
Be shriev'd and married; here is for thy pains.

Nurse. No truly, Sir, not a penny.

Rom. Go to, I say, you shall.

Nurse. This afternoon, Sir? well, she shall be there.

Rom. And stay, good Nurse, behind the abbey-wall:
Within this hour my man shall be with thee,
And bring thee cords made like a tackled stair,
Which to the high top-gallant of my joy
Must be my convoy in the secret night.
Farewel, be trusty, and I'll quit thy pains.

Nurse. Well, Sir, my mistress is the sweetest lady; lord,
lord,

lord, when 'twas a little pratting thing——Oh, there is a nobleman in town, one Paris, that would fain lay knife abroad;.but she, good soul, had as lieve see a toad, a very toad, as see him: I anger her sometimes, and tell her that Paris is the properer man; but I'll warrant you, when I say so, she looks as pale as any clout in the universal world.

Rom. Commend me to thy lady——   [*Exit* Romeo.
Nurse. A thousand times. Peter?
Pet. Anon.
Nurse. Take my fan, and go before.   *Exeunt.*

S C E N E V.

CAPULET's *House.*

Enter JULIET.

Jul. THE clock struck nine when I did send the nurse :
In half an hour she promis'd to return.
Perchance she cannot meet him—That's not so——.
Oh, she is lame; love's heralds should be thoughts,
Which ten times faster glide than the sun-beams,
Driving back shadows over-low'ring hills.
Therefore do nimble pinion'd doves draw love,
And therefore hath the wind-swift Cupid wings.
Now is the sun upon the highmost hill
Of this day's journey, and from nine till twelve,——.
Is three long hours—and yet she is not come;
Had she affections and warm youthful blood,
She'd be as swift in motion as a ball,
My words would bandy her to my sweet love,
And his to me.

Enter NURSE.

O heav'n! she comes.   O honey nurse what news?
Hast thou met with him ? send thy man away.
Nurse. Peter, stay at the gate.   [*Exit* Peter.
Jul. Now, good sweet nurse——
Oh Lord, why look'st thou sad ?
Nurse. I am weary, let me rest a while
Ey, how my bones ake, what a jaunt have I had ?

Jul.

Jul. Nay, come, I pray thee speak——Good, good
    nurse, speak.
Is thy news good or bad? answer to that.
Say either, and I'll stay the circumstance;
Let me be satisfied, is't good or bad?

Nurse. Well, you have made a simple choice; you know
not how to choose a man; go thy ways, wench, serve God
—What, have you dined at home?

Jul. No, no,—but all this did I know before;
What says he of our marriage? what of that?

Nurse. Lord, how my head akes? what a head have I?
It beats as it would fall in twenty pieces;
My back o' th' other side—O my back, my back;
Beshrew your heart for sending me about,
To catch my death with jaunting up and down.

Jul. I' faith I'm sorry that thou art so ill;
Sweet, sweet, sweet nurse, tell me what says my love.

Nurse. Your love says like an honest gentleman,
And a courteous, and a kind, and a handsome,
And I warrant a virtuous—where is your mother?

Jul. Where is my mother? why, she is within,
Where should she be? how odly thou reply'd?
Your love says like an honest gentleman:
Where is your mother——

  Nurse. Oh, our lady dear,
Are you so hot? marry, come up! I trow.
Is this the poultice for my aking bones?
Hence-forward do your messages yourself.

Jul. Here's such a coil; come, what says Romeo?
Nurse. Have you got leave to go to shrift to-day?
Jul. I have.
Nurse. Then hie hence to friar Lawrence' cell,
There stays a husband to make you a wife.
Now comes the wanton blood up in your cheeks——
Hie you to church, I must another way,
To fetch a ladder by the which your love
Must climb a bird's nest soon, when it is dark.
I am the drudge and toil in your delight,
But you shall bear the burden soon at night.
Go, I'll to dinner, hie you to the cell.

Jul. Hie to high fortune: honest nurse, farewell.

                           Exeunt.

                           SCENE.

SCENE. VI.

The MONASTERY.

Enter Friar LAURENCE *and* ROMEO.

Fri. SO smile the heavens upon this holy act,
That after-hours of sorrow chide us not!
Rom. Amen, amen, but come what sorrow can,
It cannot countervail th' exchange of joy,
That one short minute gives me in her sight.
Do thou but close our hands with holy words,
Then love-devouring death do what he dare,
It is enough I may but call her mine.
Fri. These violent delights have violent ends,
And in their triumph die: like fire and powder:
Which as they meet consume. The sweetest honey
Is loathsome in its own deliciousness,
And in the taste confounds the appetite:
Therefore love mod'rately.
Enter JULIET.
Here comes the lady. O so light a foot
Will ne'er wear out the everlasting flint;
A lover may bestride the gossamour,
That idles in the wanton summer air,
And yet not fall, so light is vanity.
Jul. God-even to my ghostly confessor.
Fri. Romeo shall thank thee, daughter, for us both.
Rom. Ah Juliet, if the measure of thy joy
Be heapt like mine, and that thy skill be more
To blazon it: then sweeten with thy breath
This neighbour air, and let rich music's tongue
Unfold the imagin'd happiness, that both
Receive in either, by this dear encounter.
Jul. Conceit more rich in matter than in words,
Brags of his substance, not of ornament.
They are but beggars that can court their worth;
But my true love is grown to such access,
I cannot sum up one half of my wealth.
Fri. Come, come with me;
For, by your leaves you shall not stay alone,
Till holy church incorp'rate two in one. [*Exeunt.*
ACT.

A C T III.   SCENE I.

The STREET.

Enter MERCUTIO, BENVOLIO, *and Servants.*

BENVOLIO.

I PRAY thee good Mercutio, let's retire;
The day is hot, the Capulet's abroad;
And, if we meet, we shall not 'scape a brawl.

Mer. Thou art like one of these fellows, that when he enters the confines of a tavern, claps me his sword upon the table, and says, God send me no need of thee; and by the operation of a second cup, draws it on the drawer when indeed, there is no need.

Ben. Am I like such a fellow?

Mer. Come, come, thou art as hot a Jack in thy mood as any in Italy; an' there were two such, we should have none shortly, for one would kill the other. Thou! why thou wilt quarrel with a man that hath a hair more, or a hair less in his head than thou hast: thou wilt quarrel with a man for cracking nuts, having no other reason, but because thou hast hazel eyes; thou hast quarrel'd with a man for coughing in the street, because he hath wakened thy dog that hath lain asleep in the sun. Didst thou not fall out with a taylor for wearing his new doublet before Easter; with another, for tying his shoes with old ribbands! and yet thou wilt tutor me for quarrelling!

Ben. If I were so apt to quarrel as thou art, any man should buy the fee-simple of my life for an hour and a quarter.

Enter TIBALT, PETRUCHIO, *and others.*

Ben. By my head, here come the capulets.

Mer. By my heel, I care not.

Tib. Be near at hand, for I will speak to them: Gentlemen, good den, a word with one of you.

Mer. And but one word with one of us? couple it with something, make it a word and a blow.

Tib. You shall find me apt enough to that Sir, if you will give me occasion.

Mer. Could you not take some occasion without giving?

Tib.

Tib. Mercutio, thou cónsort'st with Romeo.

Mer. Consort? what dost thou make us minstrels! if thou make minstrels of us, look to hear nóthing but discords: here's my fiddle-stick, here's that shall make you dance, zounds! consort?   [*Laying his hand on his sword.*

Ben. We talk here in the public haunt of man : Either withdraw into some private place, Or reason coolly of your grievances, Or else depart; here all eyes gazes on us.

Mer. Men's eyes were made to look, and let them gaze, I will not budge for one man's pleasure, I.

Enter ROMEO.

Tib. Well, peace be with you, Sir, here comes my man.

Mer. But I'll be hang'd, Sir, if he wear your livery.

Tib. Romeo, the love I bear thee can afford No better term than this; thou art a villain.

Rom. Tibalt the reason that I have to love thee, Doth much excuse the appertaining rage To such a greeting: villain I am none, Therefore farewell, I see thou know'st me not.

Tib. Boy, this shall not excuse the injuries. That thou hast done me, therefore turn and draw.

Rom. I do protest I never injur'd thee, But love thee better than thou cans't devise; And so, good Capulet, (whose name I tender As dearly as my own) be satisfied.

Mer. O calm, dishonourable, vile submission! Ha! *la stoccata* carries it away—Tibalt—you rat-catcher.

Tib. What would thou have with me?

Mer. Good king of cats, nothing but one of your nine lives, that I mean to make bold withal: will you pluck your sword out of his pilchar by the ears? Make haste, lest mine be about your ears, ere it be out.

Tib. I am for you, Sir   ·   [*Drawing.*

Rom. Gentle Mercutio, put thy rapier up.

Mer. Come, Sir, your passado.   [Mer. *and* Tib. *fight.*

Rom. Draw, Benovolio—beat down their weapons—— Gentlemen—for shame forbear this outrage—— Hold Tibalt, good Mercutio——   [*Exit* Tibalt.

Mer. I am hurt—— A plague of both your houses! I am sped : Is he gone, and hath nothing?

                                                Ben.

Ben. What, art thou hurt?

Mer. Ay, ay, a scratch, a scratch, marry, 'tis enough:
Go, fetch a surgeon.

Rom. Courage, man, the hurt cannot be much.

Mer. No, 'tis not so deep as a well, nor so wide as
church door, but 'tis enough, 'twill serve: I am pepper'c
I warrant, for this world—a plague of both your houses
—What? a dog, a rat, a mouse, a cat, to scratch a man t
death; a braggart, a rogue, a villain, that fights by the
book of arithmetic? why the devil came you between us.
I was hurt under your arm.

Rom. I thought all for the best.

Mer. Help me into some house, Benvolio,
Or I shall faint; a plague o' both your houses!
They have made worms meat of me,
I have it, and soundly too: plague o' both your houses!

[*Exeunt* Mercutio *and* Benvolio

S C E N E II.

Rom. THIS gentleman, the prince's near ally,
My very friend, hath got his mortal hurt
In my behalf: my reputation's stain'd
With Tibalt's slander: O sweet Juliet!
Thy beauty hath made me effeminate,
And in thy temper softened valour's steel.

Enter BENVOLIO.

Ben. O Romeo, Romeo, brave Mercutio's dead,
That gallant spirit hath aspir'd the clouds,
Which too untimely here did scorn the earth.

Enter TIBALT.

Ben. Here comes the furious Tibalt back again.

Rom. Alive? in triumph? and Mercutio slain?
Away to heav'n, respective lenity,
And fire-ey'd fury be my conduct now!
Now, Tibalt, take the villain back again,
That late thou gav'st me: for Mercutio's soul
Is but a little way above our heads,
And thou or I must keep him company.

Tib. Thou wretched boy, that didst consort him here,
Shalt with him hence.

Rom.

Rom. This shall determine that.

                        [*They fight,* Tibalt *falls.*

Ben. Romeo, away, begone ;
The citizens are up, and Tibalt slain——
Stand not amaz'd; the prince will doom thee death,
If thou art taken ; hence, begone, away.
   Rom. O ! I am fortune's fool.   [*Exit* Romeo.

SCENE. III.

Enter PRINCE, MOUNTAGUE, CAPUTET, *citizens, etc.*

Prince. WHERE are the vile beginners of this fray ?
         Ben. O noble prince, I can discover all
The unlucky manage of this fatal quarrel ;
There lies the man slain by young Romeo,
That slew thy kinsman brave Mercutio.
   Cap. Unhappy sight ! alas, the blood is spill'd
Of my dear kinsman——Now as thou art a prince,
For blood of ours, shed blood of Mountague.
   Prin. Benvolio, who began this fray ?
   Ben. Tibalt, here slain ;
Romeo bespoke him fair, bid him bethink
How nice the quarrel was, and urg'd withal
Your high displeasure : all this uttered
With gentle breath, calm looks, knees humbly bow'd,
Could not make truce with the unruly spleen
Of Tibalt, deaf to peace ; but that he tilts
With piercing steel at bold Mercutio's breast ;
Who all as hot, turns deadly point to point,
And with a martial scorn with one hand beats
Cold death aside, and with the other sends
It back to Tibalt, whose dexterity
Retorts ; Romeo, he cries aloud,
Hold friends, friends part ! and swifter than his tongue,
His agile arm beats down their fatal points,
And twixt them rushes ; underneath whose arm,
An envious thrust from Tibalt hit the life
Of stout Mercutio, and then Tibalt fled ;
But by and by comes back to Romeo,
Who had but newly entertain'd revenge,
And to't they go like lightening : for ere I
Could draw to part them, was stout Tibalt slain ;

                            And

And, as he fell, did Romeo turn to fly;
This is the truth, or let Benvolio suffer.
    Cap. He is a kinsman to the Mountague,
Affection makes him false; he speaks not true;
I beg for justice; justice, gracious prince;
Romeo slew Tibalt, Romeo must not live.
    Prin. Romeo slew him, he slew Mercutio;
Who now the price of his dear blood doth owe?
    Mount: Romeo but took the forfeit life of Tibalt,
    Prin. And we for that offence do banish him.
I have an int'rest in your heady brawls,
My blood doth flow from brave Mercutio's wounds.
But I'll amerce you with so strong a fine,
That you shall all repent my loss in him,
I will be deaf to pleading and excuse,
Nor tears nor prayers shall purchase our repeal;
Therefore use none, let Romeo be gone,
Else when he is found, that hour is his last.
Bear hence this body, and attend our will:
Mercy but murders, pardoning those that kill.   [*Exeunt.*

S C E N E IV.

An Apartment in CAPULET's *House.*

Enter JULIET *alone.*

Jul. GALLOP apace, you fiery-footed steeds
        To Phœbus' mansion; such a waggoner,
As Phaeton, would whip you to the West,
And bring in cloudy night immediately.
Spread thy close curtain, love-performing night,
That the run-away's eyes may wink; and Romeo
Leap to these arms, untalkt of and unseen.
Come night, come Romeo! come thou day in night
For thou wilt lie upon the wings of night,
Whiter than snow upon the raven's back:
Give me my Romeo, Night, and when he dies,
Take him and cut him out in little stars,
And he will make the face of heav'n so fine,
That all the world will be in love with night,
And pay no worship to the garish sun:——
Oh, I have bought the mansion of a love,

                                            But

But not posess'd it; so tedious is the day,
As is the night before the festival,
To an impatient child that hath new robes,
And may not wear them.   Oh, here comes my nurse!

Enter NURSE.

And she brings news, and every tongue that speaks
But Romeo's name, speaks heav'nly eloquence ;
Now, nurse, what news ?
Why dost thou wring thy hands?
   Nurse. Ah, welladay he's dead, he's dead, he's dead!
We are undone, lady, we are undone——
   Jul. Can heav'n be so envious ?
   Nurse. Romeo can,
Though heav'n cannot.   Oh Romeo ! Romeo !
   Jul. What devil art thou that does torment me thus ?
This torture should be roar'd in dismal hell.
Hath Romeo slain himself? say thou but ay,
And that bare little word shall poison more
Than the earth-darting eye of cockatrice.
   Nurse. I saw the wound, I saw it with mine eyes,
Here on his manly breast.—A piteous coarse,
A bloody piteous coarse, pale, pale as ashes,
I swooned at the sight.
   Jul. Oh break my heart !——poor bankrupt, break at
      once !
To prison, eyes ! ne'er look on liberty ;
Vile earth to earth resign, and motion here,
And thou and Romeo press one heavy brier !
   Nurse. Oh Tibalt, Tibalt, the best friend I had ;
That ever I should leave to see thee dead !
   Jul. What storm is this that blows so contrary ?
Is Romeo slaughter'd? and is Tibalt dead ?
   Nurse. Tibalt is dead, and Romeo banished.
Romeo that kill'd him, he is banished.
   Jul. Oh heav'n ! did Romeo's hand shed Tibalt's blood ?
   Nurse. It did, it did, alas the day ! it did.
   Jul. Oh nature ! what hadst thou to do in hell,
When thou didst bower the spirit of a fiend
In mortal paradise of such sweet flesh? Oh that deceit
      should dwell
In such a gorgeous palace !
   Nurse. There is no trust,

No

No faith, no honesty in men ; all perjur'd;
Shame come to Romeo!

Jul. Blister'd be thy tongue,
For such a wish; he was not born to shame,
Upon his brow shame is asham'd to sit:
For 'tis a throne where honour may be crown'd,
Sole monarch of the universal earth.
Oh what a wretch was I to chide him so ?

Nurse. Will you speak well of him, that kill'd your
    cousin ?

Jul. Shall I speak ill of him that is my husband ?
Ah, poor my lord, what tongue shall smooth thy name,
When I thy three hours wife have mangled it ?
Back foolish tears, back to your native spring :
Your tributary drops belong to woe,
Which you, mistaking, offer up to joy.
My husband lives that Tibalt would have slain,
And Tibalt's dead that would have kill'd my husband;
All this is comfort; wherefore weep I then?
Some word there was worser than Tibalt's death
That murder'd me; I would forget it fain,
But oh it presses to my memory,
Like damned guilty deeds to sinners minds;
Tibalt *is dead, and* Romeo *banished*,
That *banished*, that one word *banished*,
Hath slain ten thousand Tibalt's : in that word
Is father, mother, Tibalt, Romeo, Juliet,
All slain, all dead !—Romeo *is banished!*
Where is my father, and my mother, nurse?

Nurse. Weeping and wailing over Tibalt's corpse:
Will you go to them ? I will bring you thither.   [flow

Jul. Wash they his wounds with tears ! my eyes shall
When theirs are dry, for Romeo's banishment.

Nurse. Hie to your chamber, I'll find Romeo
To comfort you.   I wot well where he is.
Hark ye, your Romeo will be here at night;
I'll to him, he is hid at Laurence's cell.

Jul. Oh find him, give this ring to my true lord,
And bid him come to take his last farewel.   [*Exeunt.*

SCENE

SCENE V.

The Monastery.

Enter Friar Lawrence *and* Romeo.

Fri. ROMEO, come forth; come forth, thou feaiful
          man,
Affliction is enamour'd of thy parts;
And thou art wedded to calamity:
  Rom. Father, what news? what is the prince's doom?
What sorrow craves acquaintance at my hand,
That I yet know not?
  Fri. Too Familiar
Is my dear son with such sour company,
I bring thee tidings of the prince's doom.
  Rom. What less than death can be the prince's doom?
  Fri. A gentler judgment vanish'd from his lips,
Not body's death, but body's banishment.
  Rom. Ha! banishment? be merciful, say death;
For exile hath more terror in his look,
Much more than death; do not say banishment;
'Tis death mis-term'd calling death banishment;
Thou cut'st my head off with a golden ax,
And smil'st upon the stroke that murders me.
  Fri. O deadly sin! O rude unthankfulness!
Thy fault our law calls death; but the kind prince,
Taking thy part, hath push'd aside the law,
And turn'd that black word death to banishment,
This is dear mercy, and thou seest it not.
  Rom. 'Tis torture, and not mercy: heav'n is here
Where Juliet lives.   There's more felicity
In carrion-flies, than Romeo: they may seize
On the white wonder of dear Juliet's hand,
And steal immortal blessings from her lips;
But Romeo may not, he is banished!
Oh father, hast thou no strong poison mixt,
Nor sharp-ground knife, no present means of death,
But banishment to torture me withal.
  Fri. Fond mad-man, hear me speak,
I'll give thee armour to bear of that word,
Adversity's sweet milk, philosophy,

To comfort thee tho' thou art banished.

Rom. Yet banished? hang up philosophy:
Unless philosophy can make a Juliet,
It helps not, it prevails not; talk no more——

Fri. Let me dispute with thee of thy estate.

Rom. Thou canst not speak of what thou dost not feel:
Wert thou as young as I, Juliet thy love,
An hour but married, Tibalt murdered:
Doting like me, and like me banished;
Then might'st thou speak, then mightst thou tear thy hair,
And fall upon the ground as I do now,
Taking the measure of an unmade grave.

> [*Throwing himself upon the ground.*

Fri. Arise, one knocks; good Romeo, hide thyself.

> [*Knock within.*

Rom. Not I; unless the breath of heart-sick groans,
Mist-like, infold me from the search of eyes.

Fri. Hark, how they knock—Romeo arise,
Who's there?
Thou wilt be taken—stay a while,—stand up;   [*Knocks.*
Run to my study—By and by—God's will;
What wilfulness is this!—I come, I come.   [*Knocks.*
Who knocks so hard? whence come you? what's your
    will?

Nurse. (*within.*) Let me come in, and you shall know
    my errand;
I come from lady Juliet.

Fri. Welcome then.

Enter NURSE.

Nurse. Oh holy Friar, oh tell me, holy Friar,
Where is my lady's lord? where's Romeo?

Fri. There, on the ground, with his own tears made
    drunk.

Nurse. O he is even in my mistres's case,
Just in her case: Oh Juliet, Juliet!

Rom. Speak'st thou of Juliet! how is it with her?
Since I have stain'd the childhood of our joy
With blood.——
Where is she? how does she? what says she?

Nurse. Oh, she says nothing, Sir, but weeps and weeps,
And now falls on her bed, and then starts up,
And Tibalt cries, and then on Romeo calls,

And

And then falls down again.

Rom. As if that name
Shot from the deadly level of a gun
Did murder her. Oh tell me, Friar, tell me,
In what vile part of this anatomy
Doth my name lodge? tell me, that I may sack
The hateful mansion.

Fri. Hold thy desperate hand:
Art thou a man? thy form cries out thou art;
Thy tears are womanish, thy wild acts note
Th' unreasonable fury of a beast.
Thou hast amazed me. By my holy order,
I thought thy disposition better-temper'd.
Hast thou not slain Tibalt? wilt thou slay thyself?
And slay thy lady too, that lives in thee?
What, rouze thee, man, thy Juliet is alive;
Go, get thee to thy love, as was decreed;
Ascend her chamber; hence, and comfort her:
But look thou stay not till the watch be set,
For then thou can'st not pass to Mantua,
Where thou shalt live, 'till we can find a time
To blaze your marriage, reconcile your friends,
Beg pardon of thy prince, and call thee back,
With twenty hundred thousand times more joy,
Than thou went'st forth in lamentation.
Go, before, nurse; commend me to thy lady,
And bid her hasten all her house to rest,
Romeo is coming.

Nurse. O Lord, I could have staid here all night long
To hear good counsel; oh what learning is!
My lord, I'll tell my lady you will come.

Rom. Do so, and bid my sweet prepare to chide.

Nurse. Here, Sir, a ring she bid me give you, Sir:
Hie you, make haste, for it grows very late.

Rom. How well my comfort is reviv'd by this!

Fri. Sojourn in Mantua; I'll find out your man,
And he will signify from time to time
Every good hap to you that chances here:
Give me thy hand, 'tis late, farewel, good night.

Rom. But that a joy, past joy, calls out on me,
It were a grief so soon to part with thee. [*Exeunt.*

SCENE VI.

CAPULET's *House.*

Enter CAPULET, Lady CAPULET, *and* PARIS.

Cap. THINGS have fall'n out, Sir, so unluckily
That we have had no time to move our daugh-
ter:
Look you, she lov'd her kinsman Tibalt dearly,
And so did I——Well, we were born to die——
'Tis very late, she'll not come down to-night.
　Par. These times of grief afford no time to woo;
Madam, good night; commend me to your daughter.
　Cap. Sir Paris, I will make a desperate tender
Of my child's love: I think she will be rul'd
In all respects by me; nay more, I doubt it not.
But, soft; what day? Well, Wednesday is too soon,
On Thursday (let it be:) you shall be marry'd.
We'll keep no great ado—a friend or two——
For, hark you, Tibalt being slain so late,
It may be thought we held him carelessly,
Being our kinsman, if we revel much:
Therefore we'll have some half a dozen friends,
And there's an end. But what say you to Thursday?
　Par. My lord, I would that Thursday were to-morrow.
　Cap. Well, get you gone—on Thursday be it then;
Go you to Juliet ere you go to bed: [*To Lady Capulet.*
Prepare her, wife, against the wedding-day.
Farewel, my lord——light to my chamber, hoa!
Good-night. [*Exeunt.*

SCENE. VII.

The Garden.

Enter ROMEO *and* JULIET *above at the window; a ladder
of Ropes set.*

Jul. WILT thou be gone? it is not yet near day;
It was the nightingale, and not the lark,
That pierc'd the fearful hollow of thine ear;

Nightly

Nightly she sings on yon pomegranate tree;
Believe me, love, it was the nightingale.

   Rom. It was the lark, the herald of the morn,
No nightingale.   Look, love, what envious streaks
Do lace the severing clouds in yonder East:
Night's candles are burnt out, and jocund day
Stands tip-toe on the misty mountain tops,
I must be gone and live, or stay and die.

   Jul. Yon light is not day-light, I know it well;
It is some meteor that the sun exhales,
To be this night a torch-bearer,
And light thee on thy way to Mantua;
Then stay a while thou shalt not go so soon,

   Rom. Let me be ta'en; let me be put to death,
I am content, if thou wilt have it so.
I'll say yon gray is not the morning eye,
'Tis but the pale reflex of Cynthia's brow,
I'll say 'tis not the lark whose notes do beat
The vaulty heav'ns so high above our heads:
Come death and welcome: Juliet wills it so.
What says my love, let's talk, it is not day.

   Jul. It is, it is, hie hence away, be gone;
It is the lark that sings so out of tune,
Straining harsh discords, and unpleasing sharps.
Oh now be gone, more light and light it grows.

   Rom. More light and light?—more dark and dark our
Farewel, my love; one kiss and I'll be gone.   [woes.
Enter NURSE.

  Nurse. Madam..
  Jul. Nurse.
  Nurse. Your lady mother's coming to your chamber:
The day is broke, be wary, look about.

   Jul. Art thou gone so? love! lord! ah, husband, friend!
I must hear from thee ev'ry hour in th' day,
For in love's hours there are many days.
O by this count I shall be much in years,
Ere I again behold my Romeo!

   Rom. Farewel: I, will admit no opportunity,
That may convey my greetings to thee, love.

   Jul. O think'st thou we shall ever meet again?

   Rom. I doubt it not, and all these woes shall serve
For sweet discourses, in our time to come.

F 3   *Jul.*

Jul. O heav'n! I have an ill-divining soul.
Methinks I see thee, now thou'rt parting from me,
As one dead in the bottom of a tomb!
Either my eye-sight fails, or thou look'st pale.
  Rom. And trust me, love, in mine eye so do you:
Dry sorrow drinks our blood.   Adieu!
My life, my love, my soul.   Adieu!

S C E N E VIII.

Juliet's Chamber.

Enter JULIET.

Jul. O FORTUNE, fortune, all men call thee fickle.
        If thou art fickle, what dost thou with him
That is renown'd for faith? be fickle, fortune:
For then I hope thou wilt not keep him long,
But send him back again.

Enter Lady CAPULET.

  La Cap. Ho, daughter, are you up?
  Jul. Who is't that calls? is it my lady mother?
What unaccustom'd cause procures her hither?
  La Cap. Why how now, Juliet?
  Jul. Madam, I am not well.
  La Cap. Evermore weeping for your cousin's death?
What, wilt thou wash him from his grave with tears?
  Jul. Let me weep for such a feeling loss.
  La Cap. I come to bring thee joyful tidings, girl.
  Jul. And joy comes well in such a needful time.
What are they, I beseech your ladyship?
  La Cap. Well, well, thou hast a careful father, child;
One who to put thee from thy heaviness,
Hath sorted out a sudden day of joy,
That thou expect'st not, nor I look'd not for,
  Jul. Madam, in happy time, what day is this?
  La Cap. Marry, my child, early next Thursday morn,
The gallant, young and noble gentleman,
The County Paris, at St Peter's church,
Shall happily make thee a joyful bride.
  Jul. I wonder at this haste, that I must wed
Ere he that must be husband comes to woo.

                                    I pray

I pray you tell my lord and father, madam,
I cannot marry yet.

La Cap. Here comes your father, tell him so yourself,
And see how he will take it at your hands.

Enter CAPULET *and* NURSE.

Cap. How now? a conduit, girl? what, still in tears;
Evermore showering? why how now, wife?
Have you deliver'd to her our decree?

La Cap. Ay, Sir; but she will none, she gives you
    thanks:
I would the fool were married to her grave.

Cap. Soft, take me with you, take me with you, wife,
How, will she none? doth she not give us thanks?
Is she not proud? doth she not count her blest,
(Unworthy as she is,) that we have wrought
So worthy gentleman to be her bridegroom?

Jul. Proud can I never be of what I hate,
But thankful even for hate that is meant love.

Cap. Thank me no thankings,
But settle your fine joints 'gainst Thursday next,
To go with Paris to St Peter's church:
Or I will drag thee on a hurdle hither.

La Cap. Fy, fy, what are you mad?

Jul. Good father, I beseech you on my knees,
Hear me with patience, but to speak a word.

Cap. Hang thee, young baggage, disobedient wretch,
I'll tell thee what, get thee to church o' Thursday,
Or never after look me in the face.
Speak not, reply not, do not answer me.
Wife, we scarce thought us blest,
That god had sent us but this only child,
But now I see this one is one too much,
And that we have a curse in having her:
Out on her, hilding.

Nurse. Heav'n bless her:
You are to blame, my lord, to rate her so.

Cap. And why, my lady wisdom? hold your tongue;
Good prudence, smatter with your gossips, go.

Nurse. I speak no treason.

La Cap. Peace, you mumbling fool;
Utter your gravity o'er a gossip's bowl,
For here we need it not.

F 4

Cap.

Cap. Good wife, it makes me mad; day, night, late,
At home, abroad; alone, in company, early,]
Waking or sleeping; still my care hath been
To have her match'd; having now provided
A gentleman of noble parentage,
Of fair demeans; youthful and nobly allied,
Proportion'd as one's thought would wish a man:
And then to have a wretched puling fool,
A whining mammet, in her fortune's tender,
To answer, I'll not wed, I cannot love,
I am too young, I pray you pardon me.
But if you will not wed, look to't, think on't,
I do not use to jest——Thursday is near.
If you be mine, I'll give you to my friends:
If you be not, hang, beg, starve, die i' th' streets;
For, by my soul, I'll ne'er acknowledge thee.   [*Exit.*

Jul. Is there no pity sitting in the clouds,
That sees into the bottom of my grief?
O sweet, my mother, cast me not away,
Delay this marriage for a month, a week;
Or if you do not, make the bridal bed,
In that dim monument where Tibalt lies.

La Cap. Talk not to me, for I'll not speak a word:
Do as thou wilt, for I have done with thee.   [*Exit.*

Jul. O heav'n! O nurse, how shall this be prevented?
Alack, alack, that heav'n should practise stratagems
Upon so soft a subject as myself.

Nurse. Rise, faith here it is:
Romeo is banish'd: all the world to nothing,
That he dares ne'er come back to challenge you
Or if he do, it needs must be by stealth;
Then since the case so stands, I think it best
You married with the count.

Jul. Speak'st thou from thy heart?

Nurse. And from my soul too,
Or else beshrew them both.

Jul. Amen, amen.

Nurse. What?

Jul. Well, thou hast comforted me marvellous much;
Go in, and tell my lady I am gone,
Having displeas'd my father, to Laurence cell,
To make confession, and to be absolv'd.

Nurse. Marry, I will, and this is wisely done.   [*Exit.*
Jul.

Jul. Ancient damnation! Oh most wicked fiend!
Is it more sin to wish me thus forsworn,
Or to dispraise my lord with that same tongue
Which she hath prais'd him with above compare,
So many thousand times? go counsellor,
Thou and my bosom henceforth shall be twain;
I'll to the friar to know his remedy;
If all else fail, myself have power to die.

ACT. IV. SCENE I.

The Monastery.

Enter Friar LAWRENCE *and* PARIS.

FRIAR.

ON Thursday, Sir! the time is very short.
  Par. My father Capulet will have it so,
And I am nothing slow to slack his haste.
  Fri. You say, you do not know the lady's mind:
Uneven is this coarse, I like it not.
  Par. Immoderately she weeps for Tibalt's death,
And therefore have I little talk'd of love,
For Venus smiles not in a house of tears.
Now, Sir, her father counts it dangerous
That she should give her sorrow so much sway;
And in his wisdom hastes our marriage,
To stop the inundation of her tears;
Now do you know the reason of this haste?
  Fri. I would I knew not why it should be flow'd:
Look, Sir, here comes the lady tow'rds my cell.

Enter JULIET.

  Par. Welcome my love, my lady and my wife.
  Jul. That may be, Sir, when I may be a wife.
  Par. That may be, must be, love, on Thursday next.
  Jul. What must be, shall be.
  Par. Come you to make confession to this father?
  Jul. To answer that were to confess to you:
Are you at leisure, holy father, now,
Or shall I come to you at evening mass?
  Fri. My leisure serves me, pensive daughter, now.

My lord, I must intreat the time alone,
  Par. Heav'n shield, I should disturb devotion:
Juliet, on Thursday early will I rouze you:
Till then adieu? and keep this holy kiss.   [*Exit* Paris.
  Jul. Go, shut the door; and when thou hast done so,
Come weep with me, past hope, past cure, past help,
  Fri. O Juliet, I already know thy grief.
  Jul. Tell me not, Friar, that thou know'st my grief,
Unless thou tell me how I may prevent it;
If in thy wisdom thou can'st give no help,
Do thou but call my resolution wise,
And with this steel I'll help it presently.
Heav'n join'd my heart and Romeo's; thou our hands,
And ere this hand, by thee to Romeo seal'd,
Shall be the label to another deed,
Or my true heart with treacherous revolt
Give to another, this shall slay them both:
Therefore out of thy long-experienc'd time,
Give me some present counsel, or behold
'Twixt my extremes and me this bloody dagger
Shall play the umpire;——
Speak now, be brief; for I desire to die,
If what thou speak'st speak not of remedy.
  Fri. Hold, daughter; I do espy a kind of hope,
Which craves as desperate an execution,
As that is desperate which we would prevent.
If rather than to marry County Paris
Thou hast the strength or will to slay thyself,
Then it is likely, thou wilt undertake
A thing like death to free thee from this marriage,
And if thou dar'st, I'll give thee remedy.
  Jul. O bid me leap, rather than marry Paris,
From off the battlements of yonder tower:
Or chain me to some steepy mountains top,
Where roaring bears and savage lions roam:
Or shut me nightly in a charnel-house,
O'er cover'd quite with dead-mens rattling bones,
With reeky shanks, and yellow chapless sculls,
Or bid me go into a new-made grave,
And hide me with a dead man in his shroud,
Things that to hear them nam'd, have made me tremble;
And I will do it without fear or doubt,
To live an unstain'd wife to my sweet love.

                                            Fri.

Fri. Hold then, go home, be merry, give consent
To marry Paris ; look thou lie alone.
(Let not thy nurse lie with thee in thy chamber.)
And when thou art alone, take thou this phial,
And this distilled liquor drink thou off ;
When presently through all thy veins shall run
A cold and drowsy humour, which shall seize
Each vital spirit ; for no pulse shall keep
His nat'ral progress, but surcease to beat.
No warmth, no breath shall testify thou liv'st ;
The roses in thy lips and cheeks shall fade
To paly ashes ; thy eyes' windows fall,
Like death, when he shuts up the day of life ;
And in this borrowed likeness of shrunk death
Thou shalt continue two and forty hours,
And then awake, as from a pleasant sleep.
Now when the bridegroom in the morning comes
To rouze thee from thy bed, there art thou dead :
Then, as the manner of our country is,
In thy best robes uncover'd on the bier,
Thou shalt be born to that same ancient vault,
Where all the kindred of the Capulets lie.
In the mean time, against thou shalt awake,
Shall Romeo by my letters know our drift,
And hither shall he come ; and he and I
Will watch thy waking, and that very night
Shall Romeo bear thee hence to Mantua ;
And this shall free thee from this present shame,
If no unconstant toy nor womanish fear
Abate thy valour in the acting it.

Jul. Give me, O give me, tell me not of fear.
[*Taking the phial.*

Fri. Hold, get you gone, be strong and prosperous
In this resolve ; I'll send a Friar with speed
To Mantua, with my letters to thy lord.

Jul. Love, give me strength, and strength shall help af‑
ford.
Farewel, dear father——

F 6.   SCENE.

SCENE. II.

CAPULET'S *House*.

Enter CAPULET, *Lady* CAPULET, *and* NURSE.

Cap. WHAT, is my daughter gone to Friar Lawrence?
  Nurse. Ay, forsooth.
 Cap. Well he may chance to do some good on her;
A peevish self-will'd harlotry it is.

Enter JULIET.

Nurse. See where she comes from shrift with merry look.
 Cap. How now my head-strong? where have you been
  gadding?
 Jul. Where I have learnt me to repent the sin
Of disobedient opposition:
To you and your behests; and am enjoin'd
By holy Lawrence, to fall prostrate here,
And beg your pardon; pardon I beseech you!
Hence forward I am ever-rul'd by you.
 Cap. Send for the County, go tell him of this,
I'll have this knot knit up to-morrow morning.
 Jul. Nurse, will you go with me into my closet,
To help me sort such needful ornaments
As you think fit to furnish me to-morrow.
 La. Cap. No, not 'till Thursday, there is time enough.
 Cap. Go, nurse, go with her; we'll to church to-morrow.
       [*Exeunt* Juliet *and* Nurse.
 La. Cap. We shall be short in our provision;
'Tis now near night.
 Cap. Tush, all things shall be well.
Go thou to Juliet, help to deck up her:
I'll not to bed; but walk myself to Paris,
T' appoint him 'gainst to-morrow. My heart's light,
Since this same wayward girl is so reclaim'd:
     [*Exeunt* Capulet *and* Lady Capulet.

SCENE. III.

Juliet's Chamber.

Enter Juliet and Nurse.

Jul. AY, those attires are best; but gentle Nurse,
I pray thee leave me to myself to night,
For I have need of many orisons
To move the heav'ns to smile upon my state,
Which thou well know'st is cross and full of sin.

Enter Lady Capulet.

La. Cap. What, are you busy? do you need my help?
Jul. No, madam, we have cull'd such necessaries
As are behoveful for our state to-morrow;
So please you, let me now be left alone,
And let the nurse this night set up with you;
For I am sure you have your hands full all,
In this so sudden business.
La. Cap. Then good night;
Get thee to bed and rest, for thou hast need.   [*Exeunt.*
Jul. Farewel—heav'n knows when we shall meet again!
I have a faint cold fear thrils through my veins,
That almost freezes up the heat of life.
I'll call them back again to comfort me.
Nurse—yet what should they do here?
My dismal scene I needs must act alone;
                                        [*Takes out the phial.*
Come, phial—What if this mixture do not work at all?
Shall I of force be married to the Count?
No, no, this shall forbid it; lie thou there——
                                        [*Pointing to a dagger.*
What if it be a poison, which the Friar
Subtly hath ministred, to have me dead,
Lest in this marriage he should be dishonour'd,
Because he married me before to Romeo?
I fear it is; and yet methinks it should not,
For he hath still been tried a holy man——
How, if when I am laid into the tomb,
I wake before the time that Romeo
Comes to redeem me? there's a fearful point!

Shall

Shall I not then be stifled in the vault,
To whose foul mouth no healthsome air breathes in?
And there be strangled ere my Romeo comes?
Or if I leave, is it not very like
The horrible conceit of death and night,
Together with the terror of the place,
(As in a vault, an ancient receptacle,
Where for these many hundred years, the bones
Of all my buried ancestors are pack'd;
Where bloody Tibalt, yet but green in earth,
Lies festring in his shroud; where, as they say,
At some hours in the night spirits resort——)
Alas, alas! is it not like, that I
So early waking, with what loathsome smells,
And shrieks like mandrakes torn out of the earth,
That living mortals hearing them, run mad——
Or if I wake, shall I not be distraught,
(Inviron'd with all these hideous fears),
And madly play with my forefather's joints,
And pluck the mangled Tibalt from his shroud?
And in this rage, with some great kinsman's bone
As with a club dash out my desp'rate brains?
O look! methinks I see my cousin's ghost
Seeking out Romeo——Stay, Tibalt, stay!
Romeo, I come! this do I drink to thee.   [Drinks.
                    [She throws herself on the bed.

SCENE IV.

A HALL.

Enter Lady CAPULET *and* NURSE.

L. *Cap.* HOLD take these keys, and fetch more spices,
             Nurse.
Nurse. They call for debts and quinces in the pastry.

Enter CAPULET *and* LADY, *meeting.*

Cap. Come, stir, stir, stir, the second cock hath crow'd,
The curphew bell hath rung, 'tis three o'clock:
Look to the bak'd meats, good Angelica.
Spare not for cost.
  Nurse. Go, go, you cot-quean go;

                                        Get

Get you to bed; faith you'll be sick to-morrow,
For this night's watching.   [*Exit.*

   Cap. No not a whit; what, I have watch'd ere now
All night for a less cause, and ne'er been sick.
                               [*Play music.*
The County will be here with music straight.
For so he said he would.—I hear him near,
Nurse,——wife.——what ho?..what Nurse, I say?

Enter NURSE.

Go waken Juliet, go and trim her up.
I'll go and chat with Paris; hie; make haste;
Make haste, I say.   [*Exit* Capulet.

S C E N E. V.

SCENE *draws, and discovers* JULIET *on a bed.*

Nurse. MISTRESS, what mistress! Juliet——Fast I
            warrant her.
Why, lamb—why, lady—Fy, you slug-a-bed——
Why, love, I say—Madam, sweet-heart—why, bride——
What, not a word! you take your pennyworths now;
Sleep for a week; for the next night, I warrant,
That you shall rest but little—God forgive me——
Marry and amen——How sound is she asleep!
I must needs wake her; madam, madam, madam,
Ay, let the County take you in your bed——
He'll fright you up, i'faith. Will it not be?
What drest, and in your cloaths—and down again!
I must needs wake you; lady, lady, lady,——
Alas, alas! help! help! my lady's dead,
O well a-dead, that ever I was born!
Ho! my lord, my lady!

Enter Lady CAPULET.

   La. Cap. What noise is here?
   Nurse. O lamentable day!
   La. Cap. What is the matter?
   Nurse. Look,—oh, heavy day!
   Cap. Oh me, my child, my only life!
Revive, look up, or I will die with thee!
Help, help! call help.

Enter CAPULET.

Cap. For shame, bring Juliet forth, her lord is come.
Nurse. She's dead, she's dead: alack the day!
Cap. Ha! let me see her——Out alas, she's cold,
Her blood is settled, and her joints are stiff
Life and these lips have long been separated;
Death lies on her like an untimely frost.
Upon the sweetest flower of the field.
Accursed time! unfortunate old man!!

Enter Friar LAWRENCE, *and* PARIS *with Musicians*.

Fri. Come, is the bride ready to go to church?
Cap. Ready to go, but never to return.
O son, the night before the wedding day.
Death has embrac'd thy wife; see there she lies,
Flower as she was, nip'd in the bud by him.
Oh Juliet, oh my child, my child!
Par. Have I thought long to see this morning's face,
And doth it give me such a sight as this?
La. *Cap.* Accurst, unhappy, wretched, hateful day.
Cap. Most miserable hour, that time e'er saw
In lasting labour of his pilgrimage.
But one, poor one, one poor and loving child,
But one thing to enjoy and solace in,
And cruel death hath catcht it from my sight.
Fri. Your daughter lives in death and happiness;
Heav'n and yourself had part in this fair maid,
Now heav'n hath all——dry up your fruitless tears;
Come, stick your rosemary on this fair corps;
And, as the custom of our country is,
Convey her where her ancestors lie tomb'd.
Cap. All things that were ordain'd to festival
Turn from their office to black funeral;
Our instruments to melancholy bells;
Our wedding chear to a sad burial feast;
Our solemn hymns to sullen dirges change;
And bridal flowers serve for a burial coarse,
And all things change them to the contrary.
Fri. Sir, go you in, and, Madam, go with him;
And go, Sir Paris, every one prepare,
To follow this fair coarse unto her grave.
The heav'ns do low'r upon you, for some ill:
Move them no more by crosssing their high will. [*Exeunt.*
ACT

ACT. V.   SCENE. I.

The inside of a Church.

Enter the funeral procession *of* JULIET, in which the following Dirge is sung.

CHORUS.

R ISE, rise ;
    Heart-breaking sighs,
The woe-fraught bosom swell ;
    For sighs alone,
    And dismal moan,
Should echo Juliet's knell.

AIR.

She's gone——the sweetest flow'r of May,
    That blooming blest our sight :
Those eyes which shone, like breaking day,
    Are set in endless night !

CHORUS.

Rise, rise ! etc.

AIR.

She's gone, she's gone, nor leaves behind
So fair a form, so pure a mind ;
How could'st thou, Death, at once destroy,
The Lover's hope, the Parent's joy ?

CHORUS.

Rise, rise ! etc.

AIR.

Thou spotless soul, look down below,
    Our unfeign'd sorrow see :
Oh give us strength to bear our woe,
    To bear the loss of thee !

CHORUS.

Rise, rise ! etc.

SCENE.

S C E N E. II.

MANTUA.

Enter ROMEO.

IF I may trust the flattery of sleep,
  My dreams presage some joyful news at hand;
My bosom's lord sits lightly on his throne,
And all this day an unaccustom'd spirit
Lift's me above the ground with chearful thoughts.
I dreamt, my lady came and found me dead,
And breath'd such life with kisses on my lips,
That I reviv'd and was an Emperor.
Ah me! how sweet is love itself possest,
When but love's shadows are so rich in joy?

Enter BALTHASAR.

News from Verona—How now, Belthasar?
Dost thou bring me letters from the Friar?
How doth my lady? is my father well?
How doth my Juliet? that I ask again,
For nothing can be ill if she be well?
  Bal. Then she is well, and nothing can be ill,
Her body sleeps in Capulet's monument,
And her immortal part with angels lives;
I saw her carried to her kindreds vault,
And presently took post to tell it you;
O, pardon me for bringing these ill news.
  Rom. Is it even so? then I defy you stars——
  Bal. My lord!
  Rom. Thou knowst my lodging, get me ink and paper,
And hire post horses.   I will hence to-night.
  Bal. Pardon me, Sir, I dare not leave you thus.
Your looks are pale and wild, and do import
Some misadventure.
  Rom. Go, thou art deceiv'd;
Leave me, and do the thing I bid thee do:
Hast thou no letters to me from the Friar?
  Bal. No, good my lord.
  Rom. No matter; get thee gone,

And

And hire those horses, I'll be with thee straight.
[*Exit* Balthasar.

Well, Juliet, I will lie with thee to night:——
Let's see for means—O mischief! thou art swift
To enter in the thought of desperate men!
I do remember an apothecary,
And hereabouts he dwells, who late I noted
In tatter'd weeds with overwhelming brows,
Culling of simples: meagre were his looks,
Sharp misery had worn him to the bones;
And in his needy shop a tortoise hung,
An alligator stufft, and other skins
Of ill-shap'd fishes; and about his shelves
A beggarly account of empty boxes;
Green earthen pots, bladders, and musty seeds,
Remnants of packthread, and old cakes of roses
Were thinly scatter'd, to make up a shew.
Noting his penury, to my self I said,
An' if a man did need a poison now,
Here lives a caitiff wretch would sell it him.
Oh this same thought did but forerun my need!
As I remember this should be the house.
Being holy-day the beggar's shop is shut.
What, ho! Apothecary!

Enter APOTHECARY.

Ap. Who calls aloud?

Rom. Come hither, man; I see that thou art poor;
Hold, there are forty ducats; let me have
A dram of poison, such soon speeding geer,
As will disperse itself through all the veins,
That the life-weary taker may soon die.

Ap. Such mortal drugs I have, but Mantua's law
Is death to any he that utters them.

Rom. Art thou so bare and full of wretchedness,
And fear'st to die? famine is in thy cheeks;
Need and oppression stare within thine eyes,
Contempt and beggary hang on thy back;
The world is not thy friend nor the world's law:
The world affords no law to make thee rich;
Then be not poor, but break it and take this.

Ap. My poverty, but not my will consents.　　[*Exit.*

Rom. I pay thy poverty, and not thy will.
[Apothecary *returns.*
Ap.

Ap. Put this in any liquid thing you will,
And drink it off, and if you had the strength
Of twenty men it would dispatch you straight.

Rom. There is thy gold, worse poison to men souls,
Doing more murder in this loathsome world,
Than these poor compounds that thou may'st not sell;
I sell thee poison, thou hast sold me none.
Farewel, buy food, and get thee into flesh.
Come cordial, and not poison, go with me
To Juliet's grave, for there I must use thee.　　*Exeunt.*

S C E N E. III.

The Monastery at VERONA.

Enter Friar JOHN *to* Friar LAWRENCE.

John. HOLY Franciscan Friar! brother! ho!
　　Law. This same should be the voice of
Friar John.
Welcome from Mantua: what says Romeo?
Or if his mind be writ, give me his letter.

John. Going to find a barefoot brother out,
One of our order to associate me,
Here in this city visiting the sick;
And finding him, the searchers of the town,
(Suspecting that we both were in a house
Where the infectious pestilence did reign)
Seal'd up the doors, and would not let us forth,
So that my speed to Mantua there was staid.

Law. Who bore my letter then to Romeo?

John. I could not send it; here it is again,
Nor get a messenger to bring it thee,
So fearful were they of infection.

Law. Unhappy fortune! by my brotherhood,
The letter was not nice, but full of charge,
Of dear import, and the neglecting it
May do much danger. Friar John, go hence,
Get me an iron crow, and bring it straight
Unto my cell.

John. Brother I'll go and bring it thee.　　[*Exit.*

Law. Now must I to the monument alone;
Within these three hours will fair Juliet wake;

　　　　　　　　　　　　　　　　　　　She

She will beshrew me much that Romeo
Hath had no notice of these accidents;
But I will write again to Mantua,
And keep her at my cell 'till Romeo come.
Poor living coarse clos'd in a dead man's tomb!   [*Exit.*

SCENE. IV.

A Church-yard; In it, a Monument belonging to the Ca-
pulets.

Enter Paris and his Page with a light.

Par. GIVE me thy torch, boy! hence, and stand aloof.
　　Yet put it out, for I would not be seen;
Under yon 'yew-tree lay thee all along,
Placing thy ear close to the hollow ground,
So shall no foot upon the church-yard tread,
(Being loose, unfirm, with digging up of graves)
But thou shalt hear it; whistle then to me,
As signal that thou heard'st something approach.
Give me those flow'rs.   Do as I bid thee; go.
　　Page. I am almost afraid to stand alone,
Here in the church-yard, yet I will adventure.   [*Exit.*
　　Par. Sweet flow'rs! with flow'rs thy bridal bed I strow;
　　　　　　　　　　　　　　[*Strewing flowers.*
Fair Juliet that with angels doth remain,
Accept this latest favour at my hand,
That living honour'd thee, and, being dead,
With fun'ral obsequies adorn thy tomb. [*The boy whistles.*
—The boy gives warning, something doth approach——
What cursed foot wanders this way to-night,
To cross my obsequies? and true love's rite?
What, with a torch? muffle me, night a while.
　　　　　　　　　　　　　[*Paris retires.*

SCENE. V.

Enter Romeo and Balthasar with a light.

Rom. GIVE me the wrenching iron.
　　　　Hold, take this letter, early in the morning
See thou deliver to my lord and father.

　　　　　　　　　　　　　Put

Put out the torch, and on thy life I charge thee,
Whate'er thou hear'st or seest, stand all aloof,
And do not interrupt me in my course.
Why I descend into this bed of death,
Is partly to behold my lady's face;
But chiefly to take thence from her dead finger,
A precious ring, a ring that I must use
In dear employment! therefore hence, be gone;
But if thou, jealous, dost return to pry
In what I further shall intend to do,
By heav'n, I will tear thee joint by joint,
And strew this hungry church-yard with thy limbs;
The time and my intents are savage, wild,
More fierce and more inexorable far
Than empty tigers, or the roaring sea.

    Bal. I will be gone, Sir, and not trouble you.

    Rom. So shalt thou win my favour. Take thou that,
Live and be prosp'rous, and farewell, good fellow.

    Bal. For all this same, I'll hide me near this place:
His looks I fear, and his intents I doubt.   [*Exit.*

    Rom. Thou detestable maw, thou womb of death,
Gorg'd with the dearest morsel of the earth;
Thus I inforce thy rotten jaws to open.
                [*Breaking open the monument.*
And in despite I'll cram thee with more food.

    Par. (*Shewing himself.*) Stop thy unhallow'd toil, vile
      Montague:
Can vengeance be pursu'd further than death?
Condemn'd villain, I do apprehend thee;
Obey and go with me, for thou must die.

    Rom. I must indeed, and therefore came I thither——
Good, gentle youth, tempt not a desp'rate man;
Fly hence and leave me;
By heav'n I love thee better than myself;
For I came hither arm'd against myself.

    Par. I do defy thy pity and thy counsel,
And apprehend thee for a felon here.

    Rom. Wilt thou provoke me? then have at thee boy.
                [*They fight* Paris *falls.*

    Page. Oh lord, they fight! I will go call the watch.

    Par. Oh, I am slain; if thou be merciful,
Open the tomb, lay me with Juliet.

    Rom. In faith, I will; let me peruse this face——
                          Mercutio's

Mercutio's kinsman ! noble County Paris !
Give me thy hand——
One writ with me in sour misfortune's book ;
I'll bury thee in a triumphant grave,
For here lies Juliet—Oh my love, my wife !
Death that hath suckt the honey of my breath,
Hath had no power yet upon thy beauty ;
Thou art not conquer'd, beauty's ensign yet
Is crimson in thy lips, and in thy cheeks,
And death's pale flag is not advanced there.
Oh Juliet, why art thou yet so fair—here, here
Will I set up my everlasting rest ;
And shake the yoke of inauspicious stars
From this world-weary flesh ;
Come bitter conduct, come unsav'ry guide,
Thou desp'rate pilot, now at once run on
The dashing rocks my sea-sick weary bark ;
No more—here's to my love !—eyes look your last ;
        [*Drinking the poison.*
Arms take your last embrace ; and lips do you
The doors of breath seal with a righteous kiss ;——
Soft—she breathes, and stirs !   [Juliet *wakes.*

Jul. Where am I ? defend me !

Rom. She speaks, she lives ! and we shall still be bless'd !
My kind propitious stars o'erpay me now
For all my sorrows past—rise, rise, my Juliet,
And from this cave of death, this house of horror,
Quick let me snatch thee to thy Romeo's arms,
There breathe a vital spirit in thy lips,
And call thee back to life and love.   [*Takes her hand.*

Jul. Bless me ! how cold it is ! who's there

Rom. Thy husband,
'Tis thy Romeo, Juliet ; rais'd from despair
To joy's unutt'rable ! quit, quit this place,
And let us fly together—— [*Brings her from the tomb.*

Jul. Why do you force me so ? I'll ne'er consent——
My strength may fail me, but my will's unmov'd,——
I'll not wed Paris—Romeo is my husband——

Rom. Her senses are unsettled—Heav'n restore 'em ?
Romeo is my husband ; I am that Romeo,
Nor all the opposing pow'rs of earth or man,
Shall break our bonds or tear thee from my heart.

Jul. I know ! that voice—Its magic sweetness wakes

            My

My tranced soul—I now remember well,
Each circumstance—Oh my lord, my husband——
                              [*Going to embrace him.*
Dost thou avoid me, Romeo? let me touch
Thy hand, and taste the cordial of thy lips——
You fright me—speak—O let me hear some voice
Besides my own in this drear vault of death,
Or I shall faint—support me—
    Rom. Oh I cannot,
I have no strength but want thy feeble aid;
Cruel poison!
    Jul. Poison! what means my lord? thy trembling
       Voice!
Pale lips! and swimming eyes! death's in thy face!
    Rom It is indeed—I struggle with him now ——
The transports that I felt to hear thee speak,
And see thy op'ning eyes, stopt for a moment
His impetuous course, and all my mind
Was happiness and thee; but now the poison
Rushes thro' my veins—I've not time to tell——
Fate brought me to this place—to take a last,
Last farewell of my love, and with thee die.
    Jul. Die! was the Friar false?
    Rom. I know not that——
I thought thee dead; distracted at the sight,
(Fatal speed) drank poison, kiss'd thy cold lips,
And found within thy arms a precious grave——
But in that moment—oh——
    Jul. And did I wake for this!
    Rom. My powers are blasted,
'Twixt death and life I'm torn—I'm distracted!
But death's strongest—and must I leave thee Juliet!
Oh cruel cursed fate! in sight of heav'n——
    Jul. Thou rav'st—lean on my breast——
    Rom. Father's have flinty hearts, no tears can melt 'em,
Nature pleads in vain—Children must be wretched——
    Jul. Oh my breaking heart——
    Rom. She is my wife—our hearts are twin'd together——
Capulet forbear—Paris loose your hold——
Pull not our heart-strings thus—they crack—they break——
Oh Juliet! Juliet!   [*Dies.*
    Jul. Stay, stay, for me, Romeo——
A moment stay: fate marries us in death,

                                                    And

And we are *one*—no pow'r shall part us.

                     [*Faints on* Romeo's *body.*

Enter Friar LAWRENCE *with Lantborn, Crow, and Spade.*

   Fri. St Francis be my speed ! how oft to-night,
Have my old feet stumbled at graves ? who's there ?
Alack, alack ! what blood is this which stains
The stony entrance of this sepulchre !
   Jul. Who's there ?
   Fri. Ah Juliet awake, and Romeo dead !
And Paris too—Oh what unkind hour
Is guilty of this lamentable chance !
   Jul. Here he is still, and I will hold him fast,
They shall not tear him from me——
   Fri. Patience lady——
   Jul. Who is that ? O thou cursed Friar ! patience !
Talk'st thou of patience to a wretch like me !
   Fri. O fatal error ! rise, thou fair distrest,
And fly this scene of death.
   Jul. Come thou not near me,
Or this dagger shall quit my Romeo's death !

                     [*Draws a dagger.*

   Fri. I wonder not thy griefs have made thee desp'rate.
What not noise without ? sweet Juliet let us fly——
A greater power than we can contradict,
Hath thwarted our intents—come, haste away,
I will dispose thee, most unhappy lady,
Among a sisterhood of holy nuns ;
Stay not to question—for the watch is coming,
Come, go, good Juliet——I dare not longer stay. [*Exit.*
   Jul. Go, get thee hence, I will not away——
What's here ! a phial——Romeo's timeless end.
O churl, drink all, and leave no friendly drop
To help me after—I will kiss thy lips,
Haply some poison yet doth hang on them—[*Kisses him.*

[WATCH *and* PAGE *within.*]

   Watch. Lead, boy, which way——
   Jul. Noise again !
Then I'll be brief——O happy dagger !
This is thy sheath, there rest and let me die. [*Kills herself.*
   Boy. This is the place——my liege.
VOL. I.   G   *Enter.*

Enter PRINCE, *etc.*

Prin. What misadventure is so early up,
That calls our person from its morning's rest?

Enter CAPULET.

Cap. What shall it be, that they so shriek abroad?
The people in the street cry Romeo,
Some Juliet; and some Paris; and all run
With open outcry tow'rds our monument.
 Prin. What fear is this which startles in your ears?
 Watch. Sovereign, here lies the County Paris slain,
And Romeo dead——Juliet thought dead before
Is warm and newly kill'd——
 Cap. Oh me, this sight of death is as a bell,
That warns my old age to a sepulchre.

Enter MOUNTAGUE.

Prin. Come, Mountague, for thou art early up,
To see thy son and heir now early fall'n——
 Mount. Alas, my liege, my wife is dead to-night,
Grief of my son's exile hath stopt her breath.
What further woe conspires against my age?
 Prin. Look there ——and see.
 Mount. Oh though untaught, what manners is in this,
To press before thy father to a grave!
 Prin. Seal up the mouth of outrage for a while
Till we can clear these ambiguities,
And know their spring and head—meantime forbear,
And let mischance be slave to patience;
Bring forth the parties of suspicion.
 Fri. I am the greatest.
 Prin. Then say at once what thou dost know of this.
 Fri. Let us retire from this dread scene of death,
And I'll unfold the whole; if ought in this
Miscarried by my fault, let my old life
Be sacrific'd some hour before its time
Unto the rigour of severest law.
 Prin. We still have known thee for a holy man;
Where be these enemies, Capulet! Mountague!
See what a scourge is laid upon your hate.
 Cap. Oh brother Mountague, give me thy hand,

This

This is my daughter's jointure ; for no more
Can I demand.
  Mount. But I can give thee more,
For I will raise her statue in pure gold,
That while Verona by that name is known,
There shall no figure at that rate be priz'd,
As that of true and faithful Juliet.
  Cap. As rich shall Romeo by his lady lie.
Poor sacrifices of our enmity !
  Prin. A gloomy piece this morning with it brings ;
Let Romeo's man and let the boy attend us :
We'll hence and scan these sad disasters ;
Well may you mourn, my lords, (now wise too late)
These tragic issues of your mutual hate ;
From private fueds, what dire misfortunes flow :
Whate'er the cause the sure effect is Woe.

FINIS.

Every MAN in his HUMOUR.

DRAMATIS PERSONÆ.

Kitely, a Merchant, Mr Garrick.

Captain Bobadil, Mr Woodward.

Kno'well, an old Gentleman, Mr Berry.

Ed. Kno'well, his Son, Mr Ross.

Brain-worm, the Father's Man, Mr Yates.

Mr Steven, a Country Gull, Mr Vernon.

Downright, a plain Squire, Mr Bransby.

Well-bred, his half-Brother, Mr Palmer.

Justice Clement, an old merry Magistrate, Mr Taswell.

Roger Formal, his Clerk, Mr Castollo.

Dame Kitely, Mrs Davies,

Mrs Bridget, Sister to Kitely, Miss Minors.

Mr Matthew, the Town Gull, Mr Vaughan.

Cash, Kitely's Man, Mr Blakes.

Cob, a Water-bearer, Mr Mozeen.

Tib, his Wife, Mrs Cross.

SCENE, LONDON.

ACT I. SCENE I.

SCENE, *A Court-yard before Kno'well's House.*

Enter KNO'WELL *and* BRAIN-WORM.

KNO'WELL.

A GOODLY day toward! and a fresh morning! *Brain-worm,*
Call up your young master: bid him rise, Sir.
Tell him I have some business to employ him.
   Brain. I will, Sir, presently.   *Kno.* But hear you, sirrah,
If he be at his book disturb him not,
   Bra. Well, Sir.   [*Exit.*
                                        Kno.

Kno. How happy yet, should I esteem myself,
Cou'd I (by any practice) wean the boy
From one vain course of study he affects.
He is a scholar, if a man may trust
The liberal voice of fame in her report,
Of good account, in both our *Universities;*
Either of which hath favoured him with graces:
But their indulgence must not spring in me
A fond opinion, that he cannot err.
Myself was once a student; and, indeed,
Fed with the self-same humour, he is now,
Dreaming on nought but idle *poetry,*
That fruitless, and unprofitable art, -
Good unto none, but least to the professors,
Which, then, I thought the mistress of all knowledge:
But since, time and the truth have wak'd my judgment,
And reason taught me better to distinguish
The vain from th' useful learnings.

Enter Master STEPHEN.

Cousin *Stephen!*
What news with you, 'that you are here so early ?
  Step. Nothing, but e'en come to see how you do, uncle.
  Kno. That's kindly done ; you are welcome, coz.
  Step. Ay, I know that, Sir; I would not ha' come else.
How doth my cousin *Edward,* uncle ?
  Kno. O, well, coz ; go in and see : I doubt he be scarce
stirring yet.
  Step. Uncle, afore I go in, can you tell me' an' he have
e'er a book of the sciences of hawking and hunting ? I
wou'd fain borrow it.
  Kno. Why, I hope you will not a hawking now; will
you ?
  Step. No wusse, but I'll practise against the next year,
uncle ; I have bought me a hawk, and a hood, and bells,
and all; I lack nothing but a book to keep it by.
  Kno. O, most ridiculous.
  Step. Nay, look you now, you are angry, uncle : why,
you know ; an' a man have not skill in the hawking and
hunting languages now-a-days, I'll not give a rush for him.
They are more studied than the *Greek,* or *Latin.* He is
for no gallant's company without 'em. And by gad's-lid I
scorn it; I, so I do, to be a consort for every *hum-drum;*

G 3

hang

hang 'em scroyls, there's nothing in 'em, i' the world.
What do you talk on it? because I dwell at *Hogsden*, I
shall keep company with none but the archers of *Finsbury?*
or the citizens that come a ducking to *Issington* ponds? A
fine jest i' faith; slid, a gentleman mun shew himself like a
gentleman. Uncle, I pray you be not angry, I know what
I have to do, I trow, I am no novice.

  Kno. You are a prodigal absurd coxcomb: go to.
Nay, never look at me, it's I that speak.
Take't as you will, Sir, I'll not flatter you.
Ha' you not yet found means enow, to waste
That, which your friends have ~~left you, but you must~~
Go cast away your money one a kite,
And know not how to keep it, when you've done?
O it's comely! this will make you a gentleman!
Well, cousin, well! I see you are e'en past hope
Of all reclaim. Ay, so, now you're told on it,
You look another way. *Step.* What would you ha' me do?

  Kno. What would I have you do? I'll tell you, kinsman;
Learn to be wise, and practise how to thrive,
That would I have thee do: and not to spend
Your coin on every bawble, that you fancy,
Or every foolish brain, that humours you.
I would not have you to invade each place,
Nor thrust yourself on a'l societies,
Till mens affections, or your own desert,
Should worthily invite you to your rank.
He that is so respectless in his courses,
Oft sells his reputation at cheap market.
Nor would I, you should melt away yourself
In flushing bravery, lest while you affect
To make a blaze of gentry to the world,
A little puff of scorn extiguish it,
And you be left, like an unsavoury snuff,
Whose property is only to offend.
I'd ha' you sober and contain yourself;
Not, that your sail be bigger than your boat:
But mod'rate your expences now (at first)
As you may keep the same proportion still,
Nor, stand so much on your gentility.
Which is an aery, and mere borrow'd thing,
From dead men's dust, and bones: and none of yours
Except you make, or hold it. Who comes here?

Enter

Enter a SERVANT.

Serv. Save you, gentleman.

Step. Nay, we do not stand much on our gentility, frie'd; yet, you are welcome; and I assure you, mine uncle here is a man of a thousands a-year, *Middlesex* land: he has but one son in all the world, I am his next heir (at the common law) master *Stephen*, as simple as I stand here; if my cousin die (as there's hope he will) I have a pretty living o' my own too, beside, hard by here.

Serv. In good time, Sir.

Step. In good time, Sir? Why? and in very good time, Sir. You do not flout, friend, do you?

Serv. Not I, Sir.

Step. Not you, Sir; you were not best, Sir; an' you should, here be them can perceive it, and that quickly too: go to. And they can give it again soundly too, an' need be.

Serv. Why, Sir, let this satisfy you: good faith, I had no such intent.

Step. Sir, an' I thought you had, I would talk with you, and that presently.

Serv. Good master *Stephen*, so you may, Sir, at your pleasure.

Step. And so I would, Sir, good my saucy companion! an' you were out o' my uncle's ground, I can tell you; tho' I do not stand upon my gentility neither in't.

Kno. Cousin! cousin! will this ne'er be left?

Step. Whorson base fellow? a mechanical serving man! By this cudgel, and 'twere not for shame, I would——

Kno. What wou'd you do, you peremptory gull? If you cannot be quiet, get you hence.
You see, the honest man demeans himself
Modestly t'wards you, giving no reply
To your unseason'd, quarrelling, rude fashion:
And still you huff it, with a kind of carriage,
As void of wit, as of humanity.
Go, get you in; 'fore heaven, I am asham'd
Thou hast a kinsman's interest in me.   [*Exit* Stephen.

Serv. I pray you, Sir, is this master *Kno'well's* house?

Kno. Yes, marry, is it, Sir.

Serv. I shou'd enquire for a gentleman here, one master *Edward Kno'well;* do you know any such, Sir, I pray you?

Kno.

Kno. I should forget myself else, sir.

Serv. Are you the gentleman? cry you mercy, sir: I was requir'd by a gentleman i' th' city, as I rode out at this end of the town, to deliver you this letter, sir.

Kno. To me, sir! [*To his most selected friend, master Edward Kno'well.*] What might the gentleman's name be, sir, that sent it?

Serv. One master *Well-bred*, sir.

Kno. Master *Well-bred!* A young gentleman? is he not?

Serv. The same, sir; master *Kitely* married his sister; the rich merchant i' the *Old Jewry*.

Kno. You say very true.   *Brain-worm!*

Enter BRAIN-WORM.

Brain. Sir.

Kno. Make this honest friend drink here: pray you go in.   [*Exeunt* Brain-worm *and servant.*
This letter is directed to my son:
Yet I am *Edward Kno'well* too, and may,
With the safe conscience of good manners, use
The fellow's error to my satisfaction.
Well, I will break it ope (old men are curious)
Be it for the stile's sake, and the phrase,
To see, if both do answer my son's praises,
Who is, almost, grown the idolater
Of this young *Well-bred:* what have we here? what's this?

[*The Letter.*]

Why, Ned, *I beseech thee, hast thou forsworn all thy friends i' th' Old Jewry? or dost thou think us all Jews that inhabit there? Leave thy vigilant father alone, to number over his green apricots, evening and morning, o' the north-west wall: an' I had been his son, I had sav'd him the labour long since; if, taking in all the young wenches that pass by, at the back-door, and coddling every kernel of the fruit for 'em would ha' served. But prithee, come over to me, quickly, this morning: I have such a present for thee (our Turkey company never sent the like to the Grand Signior.) One is a rhimer, Sir, o' your own batch, your own leven; but doth think himself poet-major o' the town; willing to be shewn, and worthy to be seen. The other—I*
will

will not venture bis description with you till you come, be-
cause I would ba' you make bitber with an appetite.   If
the worst of 'em be not worth your journey, draw your bill
of charges, as unconscionable as any Guild-Hall *verdict will*
give it you, and you shall be allowed your viaticum.
                              From the wind-mill..

From the *Burdello*, it might come as well;
The *spittle :* is this the man,
My son hath sung so, for the happiest wit,.
The choicest brain, the times hath sent us forth?
I know not what he may be, in the arts;
Nor what in schools: but surely, for his manners,.
I judge him a profane, and dissolute wretch:
Worse, by profession of such great good gifts,
Being the master of so loose a spirit:
Why, what unhallow'd ruffian would have writ;.
In such a scurrilous manner, to a friend?
Why should he think, I tell my apricots?
Or play the *Hisperian* dragon with my fruit,.
To watch it? Well, my son, I 'ad thought
You'd had more judgment, t' have made election
Of your companions, than t' have ta'en no trust
Such petulant, jeering gamesters, that can spare
No arguments, or subject from their jest.
But I perceive, *affection* makes a fool
Of any man, too much the father.   *Brain-worm.*
             Enter BRAIN-WORM.

   Brain. Sir:
   Kno. Is the fellow gone that brought this letter?
   Brain. Yes, Sir, a pretty while since.
   Kno. And where's your young master?
   Brain. In his chamber, sir.
   Kno. He spake not with the fellow, did he?
   Brain. No, sir, he saw him not.
   Kno. Take you this letter, seal it and deliver it my son;
But with no notice that I have open'd it on your life.
   Brain. O Lord, sir, that were a jest, indeed!
   Kno. I am resolv'd, I will not stop his journey;
Nor practise any violent means to stay
The unbridled course of youth in him: for that,
Restrain'd, grows more impatient; and, in kind,
Like to the eager, but the generous gray-hound,.
Who ne'er so little from the game withheld,.
             G 5.   Turn

Turns head, and leaps up at his holder's throat:
There is a way of winning, more by love,
And urging of the modesty, than fear:
Force works on servile natures, not the free,
He that's compell'd to goodness, may be good;
But, 'tis but for that fit: where others, drawn
By softness, and example, get a habit.
Then, if they stray, but warn 'em: and, the same
They shou'd for virtue do, they'll do for shame.

SCENE II,

Y. KNO'WELL's *Study.*

Enter Edw. KNO'WELL *and* BRAIN-WORM.

E Kno. Did he open it, say'st thou?

Brain. Yes, o' my word, sir, and read the contents.

E Kno. That's bad.   What countenance (pray thee) made he i' the reading of it? was he angry, or pleas'd?

Brain. Nay, sir, I saw him not read it, nor open it, assure your worship.

E Kno. No? how know'st thou then, that he did either?

Brain. Marry, sir, because he charg'd me on my life, to tell no body that he open'd it: which, unless he had done, he would never fear to have it reveal'd.

E Kno. That's true; well, I thank thee, *Brain-worm.*
Enter Master STEPHEN.

Step. O! *Brain-worm,* did'st thou not see a fellow here, in a what-sha'-call-him doublet? he brought mine uncle a letter e'en now.

Brain. Yes, master *Stephen;* what of him?

Step. O! I ha' such a mind to beat him—where is he? can'st thou tell?

Brain. Faith, he is not of that mind: he is gone, master *Stephen.*

Step. Gone! which way? when went he? how long since!

Brain. He is rid hence.   He took horse at the street door.

Step. And I stay'd i' the fields! Whorson, *Scanderbeg* rogue; O that I had but a horse to fetch him back again!

Brain.

Brain. Why, you may ha' my master's gelding, to save your longing, sir.

Step. But, I ha' no boots, that's the spite on't.

Brain. Why, a fine whisp of hay, roll'd hard, master Stephen.

Step. No, faith, it's no boot to follow him now; let him e'en go and hang. Pr'ythee, help to truss me a little. He does so vex me——

Brain. You'll be worse vex'd, when you are truss'd, master *Stephen.* But keep unbraced, and wa'k yourself till you be cold, your choler may founder you else.

Step. By my faith, and so I will, now thou teli'st me on't. How dost thou like my leg, *Brain-worm?*

Brain. A very good leg, mas'er *Stephen;* but the woollen stocking does not commend it so well.

Step. Fch, the stockings be good euough, now Summer is coming on, for the dust: I'll have a pair of silk against Winter, that I go to dwell i' the town. I think my leg would shew in a silk hose.

Brain. Believe me, master *Stephen,* rarely well.

Step. In sadness, I think it would; I have a reasonable good leg.

Brain. You have an excellent good leg, master *Stephen,* but I cannot stay to praise it longer now; I am very sorry for't.   [*Exit.*

Step. Another time will serve, *Brain-worm.* Gramercy, for this.

E Kno. Ha, ha, ha!

Step. 'Slid! I hope he laughs not at me, an he' do——

E Kno Here was a letter, indeed, to be intercepted by a man's father! He cannot bu' think most virtuously both of me and the sender, sure, that make the careful coster-monger of him in our *Familiar Epistles.* I wish I knew the end of it, which now is doubtful, and threatens—— What! my wise cousin! Nay, then I'll furnish our feast with one gull more tow'rd the mess. He writes to me of a brace, and here's one, that's three: O, for a fourth. Fortune! if ever thou'lt use thine eyes, I intreat thee——

Step. O, now I see who he laughs at. He laughs at somebody in a letter. By th's good light, an' he had laught at me——

E Kno. How now, cousin *Stephen,* melancholy?

G 6

Step.

Step. Yes, a little. I thought you had laught at me, cousin.

E Kno. Why, what an' I had, coz; what would you ha' done?

Step. By this light, I would ha' told mine uncle.

E Kno. Nay, if you would ha' told your uncle, I did laugh at you, coz.

Step. Did you indeed?

E Kno. Yes indeed?

Step. Why, then——

E Kno. What then?

Step. I am satisfied, it is sufficient.

E Kno. Why, be so, gentle coz. And I pray you, let me intreat a courtesy of you. I am sent for, this morning, by a friend i' the *Old Jewry*, to come to him: it's but crossing over the fields to *More-gate* : will you bear me company? I protest, it is not to draw you into bond, or any plot against the state, coz.

Step. Sir, that's all one, an' 'twere; you shall command me, twice so far as *More-gate*, to do you good in such a matter. Do you think I would leave you? I protest——

E Kno. No, no, you shall not protest, coz.

Step. By my fackins, but I will, by your leave; I'll protest more to my friend than I'll speak of at this time.

E Kno. You speak very well, coz.

Step. Nay, not so, neither, you shall pardon me: but I speak to serve my turn.

E Kno. Your turn, coz? do you know what you say? A gentleman of your sort, parts, carriage, and estimation, to talk o' your turn i' this company, and to me, alone, like a water-bearer at the conduit! fie. A wight, that (hitherto) his every step hath left the stamp of a great foot behind him, at every word the savour of a strong spirit! and he! this man! so graced, so gilded, or (as I may say) so *tinfoyl'd* by nature——Come, come, wrong not the quality of your desert, with looking downward, coz; but hold up your head, so; and let the *idea* of what you are, be portray'd i' your face, that men may read i' your physiognomy: *Here, within this place, is to be seen the true, rare, and accomplished monster, or miracle of nature,* which is all one. What think you of this, coz?

Step. Why, I do not think of it; and I will be more
proud,

proud, and melancholy, and gentleman-like, than I have been, I'll assure you.

E Kno. Why, that's resolute, master *Stephen!* Now, if I can but hold him up to his height, as it is happily begun, it will do well for a suburb-humour: we may hap have a match with the city, and play him for forty pound. Come coz.

Step. I'll follow you.

E Kno. Follow me? You must go before.

Step. Nay, an' I must, I will. Pray you, shew me, good cousin.   [*Exeunt.*

S C E N E. III.

The Street before COBB's *House.*

Enter Mr MATTHEW.

Mat. I think this be the house: what, hoa!

Enter COBB *from the House.*

Cob. Who's there.   O, master *Matthew!* gi' your worship good-morrow.

Mat. What! *Cob!* how dost thou, good *Cob?* dost thou inhabit here, *Cob?*

Cob. Ay, sir; I and my lineage, ha' kept a poor house there in our days.

Mat. Cob, canst thou shew me a gentleman, one captain *Bobadil,* where his lodging is?

Cob. O, my guest, sir? you mean?

Mat. Thy guest! alas! ha, ha.

Cob. Why do you laugh, sir? Do you not mean captain *Bobadil?*

Mat. Cob, 'pray thee, advise thyself well: do not wrong the gentleman and thyself too.   I dare be sworn he scorns thy house; he! he lodge in such a base, obscure place as thy house! Tut, I know his disposition so well, he would not lie in thy bed, if thou'ldst gi' it him.

Cob. I will not give him, though, sir.   Mass, I thought somewhat was in't we could not get him to bed, all night! well, sir, though he lie not o' my bed, he lies o' my bench: an't please you to go up, sir, you shall find him with two cushions under his head, and his cloke wrapped about him,

as

as though he had neither won nor lost; and yet (I warrant) he ne'er cast better in his life, than he has done, to-night.

Mat. Why? was he drunk?

Cob. Drunk, sir? You hear me not say so. Perhaps he swallowed a tavern-token. or some such device, Sir; I have nothing to do withal. I deal with water, and not with wine. Gi' me my bucket there, hoa. God b' w' you, sir, it's six o'clock: I should ha' carried two turns by this. What hoa? my stopple? come.

Mat. Lie in a water-bearer's house! a gentleman of his havings! well, I'll tell him my mind.

Cob. What *Tib*, shew this gentleman up to the captain.

[*Tib shews Mr Mat into the House.*

You wou'd ha, some now, wou'd take this Mr *Matthew* to be a gentleman at the least. His father is an honest man, a worshipful fishmonger, and so forth; and now does he creep, and wriggle into acquaintance with all the brave gallants about the town, such as my guest is: O, my guest is a fine man! he does swear the legiblest, of any man christened: by St *George*,——the foot of *Pharaoh*,——the body of me,——as I am a gentleman,——and a soldier; such dainty oaths! and withal, he does take this same filthy roguish *Tobacco*, the finest and cleanliest! it would do a man good to see the fume come forth out at's tonnels! Well, he owes me forty shillings (my wife lent him out of her purse by sixpence a time) besides his lodging; I would I had it. I shall ha' it, he says, the next *action*. *Helter, shelter*, hang sorrow, care'll kill a cat, up-tails all, and a louse for the hangman.

[*Exit.*

SCENE IV.

A Room in Cobb's *House.*

Bobadil *discover'd upon a Bench.* Tib *enters to him.*

Bob. Hostess, hostess.

Tib. What say you, sir?

Bob. A cup o' thy small-bear, sweet hostess.

Tib. Sir, there's a gentleman below, would speak with you.

Bob. A gentleman! 'ods so, I am not within.

Tib.

Tib. My husband told him you were, sir.

Bob. What a plague—what meant he?

Mat. [*within.*] Captain *Bobadil!*

Bob. Who's there? (take away the bason, good hostess) come up, sir.

Tib He would desire you to come up, Sir.   You come into a cleanly house here.

Enter Mr MATTHEW.

Mat. 'Save you, sir; 'save you, captain.

Bob. Gentle master *Mattbew!* is it you, sir? Please you sit down.

Mat. Thank you, good captain; you may see I am somewhat audacious.

Bob. Not so, sir.   I was requested to supper, last night, by a sort of gallants, where you were wish'd for, and drank to, I assure you.

Mat. Vouchsafe me by whom, good captain.

Bob. Marry, by young *Well-bred*, and others: why, hostess, a stool for this gentleman.

Mat. No haste, sir, 'tis very well.

Bob. Body of me! it was so late ere we parted last night, I can scarce open my eyes yet: I was but new risen, as you came: how passes the day abroad, sir? you can tell.

Mat. Faith some half-hour to seven: now, trust me, you have an exceeding fine lodging here, very neat, and private.

Bob. Ay, sir: sit down, I pray you, master *Mattbew*, (in any case) possess no gentleman of our acquaintance with notice of my lodging.

Mat. Who? I sir? no.

Bob. Not that I need to care who know it, for the cabbin is convenient, but in regard I would not be too popular and generally visited, as some are.

Mat. True, captain, I conceive you.

Bob. For, do you see, sir, by the heart of valour in me, except it be to some peculiar and choice spirits, to whom I am extraordinarily engaged, (as yourself, or so) I could not extend thus far.

Mat. O Lord, sir I resolve so.

[*Pulls out a paper and reads.*

Bob. I confess, I love a cleanly and quiet privacy, above all the tumult and roar of fortune.   What new piece ha' you there? Read it.

Mat

Mat. [reads.] *To thee purest object of my sense,*
The most refined essence heaven covers,
Send I these lines wherein I do commence
The happy state of turtle-billing lovers.

Bob. 'Tis good, proceed, proceed, Where's this?

Mat. This, sir, a toy o' mine own, in my nonage: the infancy of my muses: but, when will you come and see my study? Good faith, I can shew you some very good things, I have done of late——That boot becomes your leg, passing well, captain, methinks!

Bob. So, so, it's the fashion gentlemen now use.

Mat. Troth, captain, and now you speak o' the fashion, master *Well-bred's* elder brother, and I, are fall'n out exceedingly: this other day, I happen'd to enter into some discourse of a hanger, which I assure you, both for fashion and workmanship, was most peremptory beautiful, and gentleman-like! yet he condemn'd, and cry'd it down, for the most pied, and ridiculous that ever he saw.

Bob. 'Squire *Down-right*, the half brother? was't not?

Mat. Ay, Sir, *George Down-right*.

Bob. Hang him, rook, he! why, he has no more judgement than a malt-horse. By St *George*, I wonder you'd lose a thought upon such an animal; the most peremptory absurd clown of *Christendom*, this day, he is holden. I protest to you, as I am a gentleman and soldier, I ne'er chang'd words with his like. By his discourse, he should eat nothing but hay. He was born for the menger, pannier, or pack-saddle! he has not so much as a good phrase in his belly, but all old iron and rusty proverbs! a good commodity for some smith to make hob-nails of.

Mat. Ay' and he thinks to carry it away with his manhood still, where he comes. He brags he will gi' me the bastinado, as I hear.

Bob. How! he the bastinado! how came he by that word, trow?

Mat. Nay, indeed he said codgel me; I term'd it so for my more grace.

Bob. That may be; for I was sure, if was none of his word. But when? when said he so?

Mat. Faith, yesterday, they say; a young gallant, a friend of mine told me so.

Bob. By the foot of *Pharoah*, an' 'twere my case now, I
should

should send him a challenge, presently. The bastinado! A most proper, and sufficient dependence, warranted by the great *Caranza*. Come hither, you shall challenge him. I'll shew you a trick or two, you shall kill him with, at pleasure; the first stuccata, if you will by this air.

Mat. Indeed you have absolute knowledge i' the mystery, I have heard, Sir.

Bob. Of whom? of whom ha' you heard it, I beseech you?

Mat. Troth, I have heard it, spoken of by divers, that you have very rare and un-in-one-breath-utterable skill, Sir.

Bob. By heaven, no not I: no skill i' the earth; some small rudiments i' the science, as to know my time distance, or so. I have profest it more for noblemen, and gentlemen's use, than mine own practice, I assure you. I'll give you a lesson. Look you, sir. Exalt not your point above this state, at any hand: so, sir. Come on; O, twine your body more about, that you may fall to a more sweet comely gentleman-like guard. So, indifferent. Hollow your body more sir, thus. Now, stand fast o'your left leg, note your distance, keep your due proportion of time —Oh, you disorder your point most irregularly! Come, put on your cloke; and we'll go to some private place, where you are acquainted, some tavern; or so—and have a ——what money ha' you about you, Mr *Matthew?*

Mat. Faith, I ha' not past two shillings.

Bob. 'Tis somewhat with the least; but come. We will have a bunch of radishes, and salt, to taste our wine: and a pipe of tobacco, to close the orific of the stomach: and then we'll call upon young *Well*-bred. Perhaps we shall meet the *Corydon*, his brother, there; and put him to the question. Come along, Mr *Matthew.*   [*Exeunt.*

ACT. II.   SCENE. I.

A Warehouse belonging, to KITELY.

Enter KITELY, CASH, *and* DOWN-RIGHT.

KITELY.

THOMAS, come hither,
There lies a note within, upon my desk,

Here

Here take my key; it is no matter, neither.
Wh re is the boy ?
    Casb. Within, sir, i' the warehouse.
    Kit. Let him tell over straight that *Spanish* gold,
And weigh it, with th' pieces of eight.   Do you.
See the delivery of those silver stuffs
To Mr *Lucar.*   Tell him, if he will,
He shall ha' the *Grogans* at the rate I told him;
And I wil meet him on the *Exchange,* anon
    Casb. Good, sir.   [*Exit.*
    Kite. Do you see that fellow, brother *Down-right* ?
    Dow. I, what of him :
    Kite. He is a jewel, brother,———.
I took him of a child, up, to my door;
And chris en'd him, give him my own name, *Thomas* ;
Since bred him, at the Hospital ; where proving
A toward imp, I call'd him home, and taught him
So much, as I have made him my cashier,
And find him, in his place, so full of faith,
That I durst trust my life into his hands.
    Dow. So would not I, in any bastard's brother,
As it is like, he is ; although I knew,
Myself his father.   But you said you'd somewhat
To tell me, gentle brother what is't?
    Kite. Faith, I am very loth to utter it;
As fearing it may hurt your patience ;
But, that I know your judgment is of strength,
Against the nearness of affection———
    Dow. What need this circumstance ? Pray you be di-
        rect.
    Kite. I will not say how much I do ascribe
Unto your friendship ; nor, in what regard
I hold your love ; but let my past behaviour,
And usage of your sister, but confirm
How well I've been affected to your———
    Dow. You are too tedious, come to the matter, the
        matter.
    Kite. Then, without further ceremony, thus.
My brother *Well-bred,* Sir, (I know not now)'
Of late, is much declin'd in what he was,
And greatly alter'd in his disposition.
When he came first to lodge here in my house,
Ne'er trust me if I were not proud of him;
                                          Methought

Methough he bare, himself in such a fashion,
So full of man, and sweetness in his carriage,
And, what was chief, it shew'd not borrow'd in him,
But all he did became him as his own,
And seem'd as perfect, proper and possest
As breath with life, or colour with the blood.
But now his course is so irregular,
So loose, affected, and depriv'd of grace,
And he himself withal so fal'n off,
From that first place, as scarce no note remains,
To tell men's judgments where he lately stood.
He's grown a stranger to all due respect,
Forgetful of his friends, and not content
To stale himself in all societies,
He makes my house here common as a *mart*,
A theatre, a public receptacle,
For giddy humour and diseased riot;
And here (as in a tavern or a stew,)
He, and his wild associates, spend their hours,
In repitition of lascivious jests;
Swear, leap, drink, dance, and revel night by night,
Controul my servants; and indeed what not?

Dow. 'Sdains, I know not what I should say to him i'
the whole world! he values me at a crack'd three farthings,
for ought I see; it will never out o' the flesh that's bred i'
the bone! I have told him enough, one would think if
that would serve. Well! he knows what to trust to, for
George. Let him spend and spend, and domineer, till this
heart ake an he think to be relieved by me, when he is got
into one o' your city ponds, the counters, he has the wrong
sow by the ear, i' faith, and claps his dish at a wrong man's
door. I'll lay my hand o' my halfpenny, ere I part with't
to fetch him out, I'll assure him.

Kite. Nay, good brother, let it not trouble you thus.

Dow. 'Sdeath, he mad's me: I could eat my very spur-
leathers, for anger! but, why are you so tame? why do
not you speak to him, and tell him how he disquiets your
house?

Kite. O, there are divers reasons to dissuade, brother:
But, would yourself vouchsafe to travail in it,
(Though but with plain and easy circumstance)
It would, both come much better to his sense,
And savour less of stomach, or of passion,

You

You are his elder brother and that title
Both gives and warrants you authority;
Whereas, if I should intimate the least,
It would but add contempt to his neglect.
Heap worse on ill, make up a pile of hatred,
That, in the rearing would come tott'ring down,
And, in the ruin, bury all our love.
Nay, more than this, brother; if I should speak
He would be ready, from his heat of humour,
And over-flowing of the vapour, in him,
To blow the ears of his familiars,
With the false breath, of telling what disgraces,
And low disparagements I had put upon him.
Whilst they, sir, to relieve him in the fable,
Make their loose comments upon ev'ry word,
Gesture, or look, I use; mock me all over,
And out of their impetuous rioting phant'sies,
Beget some slander, that shall dwell with me.
And what would that be, think you? marry, this,
They would give out (because my wife is fair,
Myself but newly married, and my sister
Here sojourning a virgin in my house)
That I were jealous! nay as sure as death,
That they would say. And how that I had quarrell'd
My brother purposely, thereby to find
An apt pretext to banish them my house.

   Dow. Mass, perhaps so; they're like enough to do it.
   Kite. Brother, they would believe it; so should I
(Like one of these penurious quack-salvers)
But set the bills up to mine own disgrace,
And try experiments upon myself;
Lend scorn and envy opportunity.
To stab my reputation and good name——

Enter MATTHEW *and* BOBADIL.

   Mat. I will speak to him——
   Bob. Speak to him? away, by the foot of *Pharoah*, you
shall not, you shall not do him that grace.
   Kite. What's the matter, sirs?
   Bob. The time of day, to you, gentlemen o' the house.
Is Mr *Well-bred* stirring?
   Dow. How then? what should he do?

Bob.

Bob. Gentleman of the house, it is to you: is he within sir?

Kite. He came not to his lodging to night, sir, I assure you.

Dow. Why do you hear? you.

Bob. The Gentleman-citizen hath satisfy'd me, I'll talk to no scavenger.   *Exeunt* Bobadil *and* Matthew.

Dow. How scavenger? stay, sir, stay?

Kite. Nay brother *Down right*.

Dow. Heart! stand you away, and you love me.

Kite. You shall not follow him now, I pray you brother, good faith you shall not; I will over-rule you.

Dow. Ha! scavenger? well, go to, I say a little; but by this good day (God forgive me I should swear) if I put it up so, say, I am the rankest coward ever liv'd; 'sdains an' I swallow this, I'll ne'er draw my sword in the sight of *Fleet Street* again, while I leave; I'll sit in a barn, with *Mudge Lowlet*, and catch mice first. Scavenger?

Kite. Oh, do not fret yourself thus, never think on't.

Dow. These are my brother's consorts; these! these are his comrades, his walking mates! he's a gallant, a cavaliero too, right hangman cut! Let me not leave, and I could not find in my heart, to swinge the whole gang of 'em, one after another, and begin with him first. I am griev'd it should be said he is my brother, and take these courses. Well, as he brews, so he shall drink, for *George* again. Yet, he shall hear on't, and that tightly too, an' I leave, i' faith.

Kite. But, brother, let your reprehension, then,
Run in an easy current, not o'er high
Carried with rashness, or devouring choler;
But rather use the soft persuading way,
More winning, than enforcing the consent.

Dow. Ay ay, let me alone for that, I warrant you,
                              [*Bell rings.*

Kite. How now? oh, the bell rings to breakfast.
Brother, I pray you go in, and bear my wife
Company till I come; I'll but give order
For some dispatch of business to my servant——

Dow. I will—scavenger, scavenger!—[*Exit* Down-right.

Kite. Well, tho' my troubled spirit's somewhat eas'd,
It is not repos'd in that security
As I could wish: but, I must be content.
Howe'er I set a face on't to the world,
Would I had lost this finger at a venture,

So

So *Well-bred* had ne'er lodg'd within my house.
Why't cannot be, where there is such resort,
Of wanton gallants, and young revellers,
That any woman should be honest long.
Is't like, that factious beauty will preserve
The public weal of chastity unshaken,
When such strong motives muster, and make head
Against her single peace? no, no.   Beware,
When mutual appetite doth meet to treat.
And spirits of one kind and quality,
Come once to parley, in the pride of blood:
It is no slow conspiracy that follows.
Well, to be plain, if I but thought, the time
Had answer'd their affections; all the world
Should not persuade me, but I were a cuckold!
Marry, I hope they ha' not got that start;
For opportunity hath bilkt 'em yet,
And shall do still, while I have eyes and ears
To attend the impositions of my heart.
My pres'nce shall be as an iron-bar,
'Twixt the conspiring motions of desire:
Yea, every look or glance, mine eye ejects,
Shall check occasion, as one doth his slave,
When he forgets the limits of prescription.

Enter Dame KITELY.

Dame. Sister *Bridget*, pray you fetch down the rose-
water above in the closet.   Sweetheart, will you come in
to breakfast?

Kite. An' she have over-heard me now?

Dame. I pray thee, good muss, we stay for you.

Kite. By heav'n I would not for a thousand angels.

Dame. What ail you, sweetheart? are you not well?
speak good muss.

Kite. Troth my head akes extremely, on a sudden.

Dame. Oh, the Lord!

Kite. How now? what?

Dame. Alas, how it burns! muss, keep you warm,
good truth it is this new disease! there's a number are
troubled withal! for love's sake, sweetheart, come in, out
of the air.

Kite. How simple, and how subtle are her answers!

A

A new disease, and many troubied with it !
Why, true: she heard me, all the world to nothing.

Dame. I pray thee, good sweetheart, come in, the air
will do you harm in troth.

Kite. I'll come to you presently ; 'twill away I hope.

Dame. Pray heaven it do.   [*Exit* Dame.

Kite. A new disease ? I know not, new or old.
But it may well be call'd poor mo tals plague;
For, like a pestilence it doth infect
The houses of the brain.   First, it begins
Solely to work upon the phantasy,
Filling her seat with such pestiferous air
As soon corrupts the judgment, and from thence,
Sends like contagion to the memory;
Still each to other giving the infection.
Which, as a subtile vapour, spreads itself,
Confusedly through every sensive part,
Till not a thought, or motion in the mind,
Be free from the black poison of suspect.
Ah, but what misery is it to know this?
Or, knowing it to want the minds direction,
In such extremities? Well, I will once more strive,
(In spite of this black cloud) myself to be,
And shake that fever off, that thus shakes me.   [*Exit.*

S C E N E.   III.

Mori-Fields.

Enter Brain-worm, *disguis'd like a Soldier.*

Brain. 'Slid, I cannot choose but laugh to see myself
translated thus.   Now must I create an intolerable sort of
lies, or my present profession loses the grace ; and yet the
lie to a man of my coat, is as omnious a fruit as the *fico.*
O, sir, it holds for good polity ever, to have that outward-
ly in vilest estimation, that inwardly is most dear to us.   So
much for my borrow'd shape. Well, the truth is, my old
master intends to follow my young, dry foot over *More-
fields,* to *London* this morning; now I knowing of this
hunting match, or rather conspiracy, and to insinuate with
my young master (for so must we that are blue-waiters
and men of hope and service do) have got me afore in
                                                            this

this disguise, determined here to lie in ambuscade, and intercept him in the mid-way. If I can but get his clock, his purse, his hat, nay any thing to cut him of, that is, to stay his journey——*Veni, vidi, vici,* I may say with captain *Cæsar,* I am made for ever, I faith. Well, now I must practise to get the true garb of one of these lanceknights, m arm here, and my——young master! and his cousin Mr *Stephen,* as I am a true counterfeit man of war, and no soldier!　　　　　　　　　　　　[*Retires.*

Enter Ed. KNO'WELL *and* Master STEPHEN.

E. Know. So, sir, and how then coz?

Step. S'foot, I have lost my purse, I think.

E. Know. How? lost your purse! where? when had you it?

Step. I cannot tell, stay.

Brain. 'Slid I am afraid they will know me, would I could get by them.

E. Know. What? ha' you it?

Step. No, I think I was bewitch'd, I——

E. Know. Nay do not weep the loss: hang it, let it go.

Step. Oh, it's here; no, an' it had been lost, I had not car'd, but for a jet-ring mistress *Mary* sent me.

E. Know. A jet-ring? oh, the poesy, the poesy?

Step. Fine i' faith! *Though fancy sleep, my love is deep:* Meaning that though I did not fancy her, yet she loved me dearly.

E. Know. Most excellent!

Step. And then I sent her another and my poesy was; *The deeper, the sweeter, I'll be judg'd by St* Peter.

E. Know. How, by St *Peter?* I do not conceive that.

Step. Marry St *Peter* to make up the metre.

E. Know. Well, there the saint was your good patron, help'd you at your need; thank him, thank him.

Brain. I cannot take leave of 'em so; I will venture come what will. Gentlemen, please you exchange a few crowns, for a very excellent good blade, here. I am a poor gentleman, a soldier; one that, in the better state of my fortunes, scorn'd so mean a refuge, but now it is the humour of necessity to have it so. You seem to be gentlemen, well affected to martial men, else I should rather die with silence, than live with shame, however vouchsafe to re-

　　　　　　　　　　　　　　　　'member

member, it is my want speaks, not myself. This condition agrees not with my spirit.——

E. Kno. Where hast thou serv'd?

Brain. May it please you, sir, in all the late wars of *Bohemia, Hungaria, Dalmatia, Poland*, where not, Sir? I have been a poor servitor by sea and land, any time this fourteen years, and followed the fortunes of the best commanders in *Christendom.* I was twice shot at the taking of *Aleppo*, once at the relief of *Vienna* ; I have been at *Marseilles, Naples*, and the *Adriatic* gulph; a gentleman-slave in the galleys thrice, where I was most dangerously shot in the head, through both the thighs, and yet, being thus maim'd, I am void of maintenance, nothing left me but my scars, the noted marks of my resolution.

Step. How wilt you sell this rapier, friend?

Brain. Generous sir, I refer it to your own judgment ; you are a gentleman, give me what you please.

Step. True, I am a gentleman, I know that, friend : but what though? I pray you say, what would you ask?

Brain. I assure you, the blade may become the side or thigh of the best prince in *Europe.*

E. Kno. Ay, with a velvet scabbard.

Step. Nay, and't be mine, it shall have a velvet scabbard, coz, that's flat: I'd not wear it as 'tis and you would give me an angel.

Brain. At your worship's pleasure, sir ; nay, 'tis a most pure *Toledo.*

Step. I had rather it were a *Spaniard!* but tell me, what shall I give you for it? An' it had a silver hilt——

E. Kno. Come, come, you shall not buy it ; hold, there's a shilling, fellow, take thy rapier.

Step. Why, but I will buy it now, because you say so ; and there's another shilling, fellow, I scorn to be out-bidden. What, shall I walk with a codgel, like a higgin-bottom? and may have a rapier for money?

E. Kno. You may buy one in the city.

Step. Tut, I'll buy this i' the field, so I will ; I have a mind to't because 'tis a field rapier. Tell me your lowest price.

E. Kno. You shall not buy it, I say.

Step. Ay this money but I will, though I give more than 'tis worth.

E. Kno. Come away, you are a fool.

Step. Friend, I am a fool, that's granted: but I'll have
it for that word's sake.   Follow me for your money.

Brain. At your service, sir.   [*Exeunt.*

Enter Kno'well.

Kno. I cannot loss the thought, yet of this letter
Sent to my son : nor leave to admire the change --
Of manners, and the breeding of our youth
Within the kingdom, since myself was one.
When I was young, he liv'd not in the stews
Durst have conceiv'd a scorn, and utter'd it
On a grey head: age was authority
Against a buffoon: and a man had then
A certain reverence paid unto his years,
That had none due unto his life.
But, now, we are all fall'n ; youth, from their fear ;
And age, from that which bred it, good example.
Nay, would ourselves were not the first, even parents,
That did destroy the hopes, in our own children :
Or they not learn'd our vices in their cradles,
And suck'd-in our ill customs with their milk.
Ere all their teeth be born, or they can speak,
We make their pallates cunning! The first words
We from their tongues with, are licenteous jests.
Can it call whore ? cry bastard ? O, then kiss it,
A witty child ! can't swear ! the father's darling !
Give it two piumbs.   Nay, rather than't shall learn
No bawdy song, the mother herself will teach it !
But, this is in the infancy ;
When it puts off all this.   Ay, it is like:
When it is gone into the bone already.
No, no: this die goes deeper than the coat,
Or shirt, or skin.   It stains unto the liver
And heart, in some.   And rather than it should not,
Note, what we fathers do ! Look how we live !
What mistresses we keep ! at what expence,
And teach 'em all bad ways to buy affliction !
Well, I thank heaven, I never yet was he
That travell'd with my son before sixteen,
To shew him the *Venetian* courtezans,
Nor read the grammar of cheating, I had made
To my sharp boy at twelve: repeating still
The rule, *Get money ; still, get money, boy ;*

No

No matter by what means.
These are the trade of fathers, now ! however,
My son, I hope, hath met with in my threshold
None of these household precedents ; which are strong,
And swift, to rape youth to their precipice.
But let the house at home be ne'er so clean
Swept, or kept sweet from filth !
If he will live abroad with his companions,
In dung, and brothels ; it is worth a fear.
Nor is the danger of conversing less
Than all that I have mention'd of example.

Enter BRAIN-WORM.

Brain. My master ? nay faith, have at you : I am flesh'd
now, I have sped so well.   Worshipful sir, I beseech you
respect the state of a poor soldier ; I am asham'd of this
base course of life (God's my comfort) but extremity
provokes me to't: what remedy ?
Kno. I have not for you now.
Brain. By the faith I bear unto truth, gentleman, it is
no ordinary custom in me, but only to preserve manhood.
I protest to you, a man I have been, a man I may be by
your sweet bounty.
Kno. Pr'ythee, good friend, be satisfied.
Brain. Good sir, by that hand, you may do the part of
a kind gentleman, in lending a poor soldier the price of
two cans of beer, a matter of small value ; the king of heaven shall pay you, and I shall rest thankful : sweet worship——
Kno. Nay, an' you be so importunate——
Brain. Oh, tender sir, need will have his course : I was
not made to this vile use ! well, the edge of the enemy
could not have abated me so much : [*he weeps.* [It's hard,
when a man hath served in his prince's cause, and be thus
——Honourable worship, let me derive a small piece of
silver from you, it shall not be given in the course of
time ; by this good ground, I was fain to pawn my rapier
last night for a poor supper ; I had suck'd the hilts long
before, I am a pagan else : sweet honour.
Kno. Believe me, I am taken with some wonder
To think a fellow of thy outward presence
Should in the frame and fashion of his mind,
Be so degenerate, and sordid-base !

H 2

Art

Art thou a man, and sham'st thou not to beg?
To practise such a servile kind of life?
Why, were thy education ne'er so mean,
Having thy limbs, a thousand fairer courses
Offer themselves to thy election.
Either the wars might still supply thy wants,
Or service of some virtuous gentleman,
Or honest labour: nay, what can I name
But would become thee better than to beg?
But men of thy condition feed on sloth,
As doth the beetle on the dung she breeds in,
Not caring how the metal of your minds
Is eaten with the rust of idleness.
Now, afore me, whate'er he be that should
Relieve a person of thy quality,
While thou insists in this loose desperate course,
I would esteem the sin not thine, but his.

Brain. Faith, sir, I would gladly find some other course,
if so——

Kno. Ay, you'ld gladly find it, but you will not seek it.

Brain. Alas! sir, where should a man seek? in *the*
wars, there's no ascent by desert in these days, but——and
for service, would it were as soon purchas'd as wish'd for
(the air's my comfort) I know what I would say——

Kno. What's thy name?

Brain. Pl·ase you, *Fitz-Sword,* sir.

Kno. Fitz-Sword?
Say that a man would entertain thee now,
Would'st thou be honest, humble, just, and true?

Brain. Sir, by the place and honour of a soldier——

Kno. Nay, nay, I like not those affected oaths;
Speak plainly, man; what think'st thou of my words?

Brain. Nothing, sir, but wish my fortunes were as happy, as my service should be honest.

Kno. Well, follow me; I'll prove thee, if thy deeds will
carry a proportion to thy words.

Brain. Yes, sir, straight; I'll but garter my hose. Oh
that belly were hoop'd now, for I am ready to burst with
laughing! Never was bottle or bag-pipe fuller. 'Slid!
was there ever seen such a fox in years to betray himself
thus? Now shall I be possessed of all his counsels; and by
that conduit, my young master. Well, he is resolv'd to
prove my honesty; faith and I am resolv'd to prove his
patience:

patience : Oh, I shall abuse him intolerably. This small piece of service will bring him clean out of love with the soldier for ever. He will never come within the sight of a red coat, or a musket-rest again. It's no matter, let the world think me a bad counterfeit, if I cannot give him the slip at an instant : why, this is better than to have staid his journey ! well, I'll follow him : Oh ! how I long to be employ'd !   *Exit.*]

ACT. III.   SCENE I.

Stocks-market.

Enter MATTHEW, WELL-BRED, *and* BOBADIL.

MATTHEW.

YES, faith, sir ; we were at your lodging to seek. you too.

Well. Oh, I came not there to-night.

Bob. Your brother delivered us as much.

Well. Who ? my brother *Down-right ?*

Bob. He.   Mr *Well-bred*, I know not in what kind you hold me ; but let me say to you this : as sure as honour, I esteem it so much out of the sun-shine of reputation to throw the least beam of regard upon such a ———

Well. Sir, I must hear no ill words of my brother.

Bob. I protest to you, as I have a thing to be saved a-- bout me, I never saw any gentleman-like part———

Well. Good captain [*faces about*] to some other dis- course.

Bob. With your leave, sir, an' there were no more men living upon the face of the earth, I should not fancy him, by St *George*.

Mat. Troth, nor I ; he is of a rustical cut, I know not how : he doth not carry himself like a gentleman of fashi- on———

Well. Oh, Mr *Matthew*, that's a grace peculiar but to a few, *quos æquus amavit Jupiter.*

Mat. I understand you, sir.

Enter Y. Kno'well and STEPHEN.

Well. No question you do, or you do not, sir. *Ned'*
H 3

Kno'well.

Kno'well! by my soul, welcome! how dost thou, sweet spirit, my genius? 'Slid, I shall love *Apollo* and the mad *Thespian* girls the better while I live, for this, my dear fury: now I see there's some love in thee! sirrah, these be the two I writ to thee of: nay, what a drowsy humour is this now? Why dost thou not speak?

E Kno. Oh, you are a fine gallant, you sent me a rare letter.

Well. Why, was't not rare?

E Kno. Yes, I'll be sworn, I was never guilty of reading the like; match it in all *Pliny's* epistles, and I'll have my judgment burn'd in the ear for a rogue: make much of thy vein, for it is inimitable. But I marvel what camel it was that had the carriage of it? for doubtless, he was no ordinary beast that brought it!

Well. Why?

E Kno. Why, sayest thou? why dost thou think that any reasonable creature, especially in the morning (the sober time of the day too) could have mistaken my father for me?

Well. 'Slid, you jest, I hope.

E Kno. Indeed, the best use we can turn it to, is to make a jest on't now: but I'll assure you, my father had the full view o' your flourishing style, before I saw it.

Well. What a dull slave was this? But, sirrah, what said he to it, i' faith?

E Kno. Nay, I know not what he said: but I have a shrewd guess what he thought.

Well. What, what?

E Kno. Marry, thou art some strange, dissolute young fellow, and I not a grain or two better, for keeping thee company.

Well. Tut, that thought is like the moon in her last quarter, 'twill change shortly: but, sirrah, I pray thee be acquainted with my two hangbys here; thou wilt take exceeding pleasure in 'em if thou hear'st 'em once go: my wind-instruments. I'll wind 'em up.—But what strange piece of silence is this? the sign of the dumb man?

E Kno. Oh, sir, a kinsman of mine, one that may make your music the fuller, an' he please, he has his humour, ris.

Well. Oh, what is't, what is t?

E Kno.

E Kno. Nay, I'll neither do your judgment nor his folly that wrong, as to prepare your apprehension.   I'll leave him to the mercy o' your search, if you can take him, so.

Well. Well, captain *Bobadil,* Mr *Matthew,* I pray you know this gentleman here ; he is a friend of mine, and one that will deserve your affection.   I know not your name, sir, but I shall be glad of any occasion to render me more familiar to you.

Step. My name is Mr *Stephen,* sir; I am this gentleman's own cousin, sir ; his father is mine uncle, sir ; I am somewhat melancholy, but you shall command me, sir, in whatsoever is incident to a gentleman.

Bob. Sir, I must tell you this, I am no general man, but for Mr *Well-bred's* sake (you may embrace it at what height of favour you please) I do communicate with you : and conceive you to be a gentleman of some.parts ; I love few words.

E K. And I fewer, sir.   I have scarce enow to thank you.

Mat. But are you indeed, sir, so given to it ?

[*To* Mr Stephen.

Step. Ay, truly, sir, I am mightily given to melancholy.

Mat. Oh, it's your only fine humour, sir; your true melancholy breeds your perfect fine wit, sir : I am melancholy myself divers times, sir ; and then do I no more but take pen and paper presently, and overflow you half a score or a dozen of sonnets, at a sitting.

Step. Cousin, is it well; am I melancholy enough ?

E Kno. Oh, ay, excellent !

Well. Captain *Bobadil,* why muse you so?

E Kno. He is melancholy too.

Bob. Faith, sir, I was thinking of a most honourable piece of service was perform'd to-morrow, being St *Mark's* days shall be some ten years now.

E Kno. In what place, captain ?

Bob. Why, at the beleag'ring of *Strigonium,* where, in less than two hours, seven hundred resolute gentlemen, as any where in *Europe,* lost their lives upon the breach. I'll tell you, gentlemen, it was the first, but the best leagure, that ever I beheld with these eyes, except the taking in of——what do you call it, last year, by the *Geno-ese:* but that (of all other) was the most fatal and dangerous exploit, that ever I was ranged in, since I first bore

arm.

arms before the face of the enemy, as I am a gentleman and soldier.

Step. 'So, I had as lief as an angel, I could swear as well as that gentleman?

E Kno. Then you were a servitor at both, it seems; at *Strigonium?* and what do you call't?

Bob. Oh Lord, sir! by St *George*, I was the first man that enter'd the breach: and, had I not effected it with resolution, I had been slain, if I had had a million of lives.

E Kno. 'Twas pity you had not ten; a cat's, and your own i' faith. But, was it possible?

Mat. Pray you, mark this discourse, sir.

Step. So I do.

Bob. I assure you, upon my reputation, 'tis true, and yourself shall confess.

E Kno. You must bring me to the rack first.

Bob. Observe me judicially, sweet sir: they had planted me three demi-culverings, just in the mouth of the breach: now, sir, as we were to give on, their master gunner (a man of no mean skill and mark, you must think) confronts me with his linstock, ready to give fire: I spying his intendment, discharg'd my petronel in his bosom, and with these single arms, my poor rapier, ran violently upon the *Moors*, that guarded the ordnance, and put 'em all pell-mell to the sword.

Well. To the sword? to the rapier, captain?

E Kno. Oh. it was a good figure observ'd, sir! but did you all this, captain, without hurting your blade?

Bob. Without any impeach o' the earth: you shall perceive, sir. It is the most fortunate weapon, that ever rid on poor gentleman's thigh: shall I tell you, sir? you talk of *Morglay, Excalibur, Durindana,* or so? tut, I lend no credit to that is fabled of 'em, I know the virtue of mine own, and therefore I dare the boldlier maintain it.

Step. I marvel whether it be a *Toledo,* or no?

Bob. A most perfect *Toledo,* I assure you, sir.

Step. I have a countryman of his here.

Mat. Pray you, let's see, sir: yes, faith, it is!

Bob. This is a *Toledo?* pish.

Step. Why do you pish, captain?

Bob. A *Fleming,* by heaven; I'll buy them for a gilder a piece, an' I would have a thousand of them.

E Kno.

E. Kno. How say you, cousin? I told you thus much.

Well. Where bought you it, Mr. *Stephen?*

Step. Of a scurvy rogue soldier, (a hundred of lice go with him) he swore it was a *Toledo.*

Bob. A poor provant rapier, no better.

Mat. Mass, I think it be, indeed! now I look on't better.

E Kno. Nay, the longer you look on't the worse. Put it up, put it up.

Step. Well, I will put it up, but by——(I ha' forgot the captain's oath, I thought to have sworn by it) a'n e'er I meet him——

Well. O, it's past help now, sir, you must ha' patience.

Step. Whorson cony-catching rascal! I cou'd eat the very hilts for anger!

E Kno. A sign of good digestion! you have an ostrich stomach, cousin.

Step. A stomach? I would I had him here, you should see an' I had a stomach.

Well. It's better as 'tis: come, gentlemen, shall we go?

Enter BRAIN-WORM.

E. Kno. A miracle, cousin, look here! look here!

Step. O, god' slid, by your leave, do you know me, sir?

Brain. Ay, sir, I know you by sight.

Step. You sold me a rapier, did you not?

Brain. Yes, marry, did I, sir

Step. You said it was a *Toledo,* ha?

Brain. True, I did so.

Step. But it is none?

Brain. No, sir, I confess it is none.

Step. Do you confess it? Gentlemen, bear witness, he has confest it. By god's will, an' you had not confest it——

E. Kno. Oh, cousin, forbear, forbear.

Step. Nay, I have done, cousin.

Well. Why, you have done like a gentleman, he has confest it, what wou'd you more?

Step. Yet, by his leave, he is a rascal, under his favour, do you see?

E. Kno. Ay, by his leave, he is, and under favour: a pretty piece of civility! sirrah, how dost like him?

Well. O, it's a most precious fool, make much on him:

II 5.   I can

I can compare him to nothing more happily, than a drum: for every-one may play upon him.

E. Kno. No, no, a child's whistle were far the fitter.

Brain. Sir, shall I intreat a word with you?

E. Kno. With me, sir? you have not another *Toledo* to sell ha' you?

Brain. You are conceited, sir; your nsme is Mr. *Know'well,* as I take it.

E. Kno. You are i' the right; you mean not to proceed in the catechism, do you?

Brain. No, sir, I am none of that coat.

E. Kno. Of as bare a coat, though? well, say, sir.

Brain. Faith, sir, I am but servant to the drum extraordinary, and indeed, (this smoky varnish being wash'd off, and three or four patches removed) I appear your worship's in reversion, after the decease of your good father *Brain-worm.*

E. Kno. Brain-worm! Slight, what breath of a conjurer hath blown thee hither in this shape?

Brain. The breath o' your letter, sir, this morning: the same that blew you to the wind mill, and your father after you.

E. Kno. My father.

Brain. Nay, never start, 'tis true, he has followed you over the fields, by the foot, as you would do a hare i' the snow.

E. Kno. Sirrah, *Well-bred,* what shall we do, sirrah? my father is come over after me.

Well. Thy father, where is he?

Brain. At justice *Clement's* house here, in *Coleman-street,* where he but stays my return; and then————

Well. Who's this? *Brain-worm?*

Brain. The same, sir.

Well. Why how, i' the name of wit, eomest thou transmuted thus?

Brain. Faith, a device, a device: nay, for the love of reason, gentlemen, and avoiding the danger, stand not here, withdraw, and I'll tell you all.

E. Kno. Come, cousin.   *Exeunt.*

SCENE

S C E N E.   III.

The Ware-House.

Kite. What says he, *Thomas?* did you speak with him?
Cash. He will expect you, sir, within this half hour.
Kite. Has he the money ready, can you tell?
Cash. Yes, sir, the money was brought in last night.
Kite. O, that's well: fetch me my cloke, my cloke,
Stay, let me see, an hour, to go and come;
Ay, that will be the least: and then it 'twill be
An hour before I can dispatch with him;
Or very near; well, I will stay two hours.
Two hours? ha? things, never dream'd of yet,
May be contriv'd, ay, and effected too,
In two hours absence: well, I will not go.
Two hours; no, fleering opportunity,
I will not give your subtilty that scope.
Who will not judge him worthy to be robb'd
That sets his doors wide open to a thief,
And shews the felon where his treasure lies?
Again, what earthly spirit but will attempt
To taste the fruit of beauty's golden tree,
When leaden sleep seals up the dragon's eyes?
I will not go.   Business go by, for once.
No, beauty, no? you are too precious
To be left so, without a guard, or open!
You must be then kept up, close, and well-watch'd;
For, give you opportunity, no quick-sand
Devours, or swallows swifter! he that lends
His wife (if she be fair) or time, or place,
Compels her to be false.   I will not go.
The dangers are too many.   I am resolv'd for that.
Carry in my cloke again.   Yet, stay.   Yet, do too.
I will defer going, on all occasions.
Cash. Sir, *Snare,* your scrivener, will be there with the
bonds.
Kite. That's true! fall on me! I had clean forgot it;
must go.   What's o' clock?
Cash. Exchange time, sir.
Kite. 'Heart then well *Well-bred* presently be here too,
With one or other of his loose consorts.

H 6

I am

I am a knave, if I know what to say,
What course to take, or which way to resolve.
My brain, methinks, is like an hour-glass,
Wherein my imaginations run, like sands,
Filling up time; but then are turn'd, and turn'd:
So, that I know not what to stay upon,
And less, to put in act.   It shall be so.
Nay I dare build upon his secrecy,
He knows not to deceive me.   *Thomas?*

   Cash. Sir..

   Kite. Yet now, I have bethought too, I will not———
Thomas, is *Cob* within ?

   Cash. I think he be, sir.

   Kite. But he'el prate too, there's no speech of him.
No, there were no man o' the earth to *Thomas,*
If I durst trust him ; there is all the doubt.
But should he have a chink in them, I were gone.
Lost i' my fame for ever : talk for th' Exchange;
The manner he hath stood with 'till this present,
Doth promise no such change ! what should I fear then ?
Well, come what will, I'll tempt my fortune once.
Thomas— you may deceive me, but I hope———
Your love to me is more———

   Cash. Sir, if a servant's
Duty, with faith, may be call'd love, you are
More than in hope, you are possess'd of it.

   Kite. I thank you heartily, *Thomas*; gi' me your hand :
With all my heart, good *Thomas.*   I have, *Thomas,*
A secret to impart unto you—but
When once you have it, I must seal your lips up:
So far I tell you, *Thomas.*

   Cash. Sir, for that———

   Kite. Nay, hear me out.   Think, I esteem you, *Thomas*,
When I will let you in, thus to my private.
It is a thing sits nearer to my crest.
Than thou art aware of, *Thomas.*   If thou shouldst
Reveal it, but ———

   Cash. How ? I reveal it ?

   Kite. Nay,
I do not think thou would'st; but if thou should'st,
'Twere a great weakness.

   Cash. A great treachery.
Give it no other name.

Kite.

Kite. Thou wilt not do't then ?

Casb. Sir, if I do, mankind disclaim me ever.

Kite. He will not swear, he has some reservation.
Some conceal'd purpose, and close meaning, sure :
Else (being urged so much) how should he choose,.
But lend an oath to all this protestation ?
He's no fantic, I have heard him swear.
What should I think of it ? urge him again,
And by some other way ? I will do so.
Well, *Thomas*, thou hast sworn not to disclose ;
Yes, you did swear ?

Casb. Not yet, sir, but I will,.
Please you——

Kite. No, *Thomas*, I dare take thy word.
But if thou wilt swear, do, as thou think'st good ; ·
I am resolv'd without it ; at thy pleasure.

Casb. By my soul's safety then, sir, I protest,
My tongue shall ne'er take knowledge of a word,.
Deliver'd me in nature of your trust.

Kite. It's too much, these ceremonies need not ;.
I know thy faith to be as firm as a rock.
Thomas, come hither, near : we cannot be
Too private in this business. So it is.
(Now he has sworn, I dare the safelier venture)
I have of late, by divers observations——
But whether his oath can bind him, there it is.
I will bethink me e're I do proceed :——
Thomas, it will be now too long to stay,
I'll spy some fitter time soon, or to-morrow..

Casb. Sir, at your pleasure.

Kite. I will think.   Give me my cloke.   And, *Thomas*,
I pray you search the books 'gainst my return,
For the receipts 'twixt me and *Traps*,

Casb. I will, sir.

Kite. And, hear you, if your mistress's brother, *Well-
bred*, Chance to bring hither any gentleman,
Ere I come back ; let one straight bring me word.

Casb. Very well, sir.

Kite. To the exchange ; do you hear ?
Or here in *Coleman-street*, to justice *Clement's*,
Forget it not, nor be out of the way.

Casb. I will not, sir.

Kite. I pray you have a care on't.

Or whether, he come or no, if any other,
Stranger, or else, fail not to send me word.
   Cash. I shall not, sir.
   Kite. Be't your special business
Now to remember it.
   Cash. Sir, I warrant you.
   Kite. But, *Thomas*, this is not the secret, *Thomas,*
I told you of.
   Cash. No, sir, I do suppose it.
   Kite. Believe me, it is not.
   Cash. Sir, I do believe you.
   Kite. By heaven! it is not; that's enough. But *Tho-*
mas, I would not you should utter it, do you see,
To any creature living; yet I care not.
Well I must hence. *Thomas,* conceive thus much;
It was a trial of you, when I meant
So deep a secret to you; I mean not this,
But that I have to tell you; this is nothing, this.
But *Thomas,* keep this from my wife, I charge you.
Lock'd up in silence, midnight, buried here,
No greater hell than to be slave to fear.   [*Exit.*
   Cash. Lock'd up in silence, midnight, buried here.
Whence should this flood of passion, trow, take head? ha?
Best dream no longer of this running humour,
For fear I sink! the violence of the stream
Already hath transported me so far,
That I can feel no ground at all! but soft,
Here is company; now must I——

   Enter WELL-BRED, *Edw.* KNO'WELL, BRAIN-WORM,
       BOBADIL, STEPHEN.

   Well. Beshrew me, but it was an obsolute good jest, and
exceedingly well carried!
   E. Kno. Ay and our ignorance maintained it as well,
did it not?
   Well. Yes, faith, but was't possible thou should'st not
know him? I forgive Mr. *Stephen,* for he is stupidity itself.
   E. Kno. 'Fore heav'n not I. He had so written himself into the habit of one of your poor infantry your de-
cay'd ruinous, worm-eaten gentlemen of the round.
   Well. Why, *Brain-worm,* who would have thought thou
hadst been such an artificer?
   E Know. An artificer? an architect! except a man had
studied begging all his life-time, and been a weaver of lan-
                             guage

guage from his infancy, for the clothing of it ! I never saw
his rival.

Well. Where got'st thou this coat, I marvel?

Brain. Of a *Hounsditch* man, sir; one of the devil's near
kinsmen, a broker.

Enter CASH.

Cash. *Francis! Martin!* ne'er a one to be found now?
what a spite's this?

Well. How now, *Thomas,* is my brother *Kitely* within?

Cash. No, Sir; my master went forth, e'en now: but
master *Down-right* is within, *Cob!* what *Cob?* is he
gone too?

Well. Whither went your master? *Thomas,* can'st thou
tell?

Cash. I know not; to justice *Clement's* I think sir.
Cob!   [*Exit* Cash.

E. Know. Justice *Clement!* what's he?

Well. Why, dost thou not know him? he is a city magistrate, a justice here : an excellent good lawyer, and a
great scholar ; but the only mad merry old fellow in *Europe!* I shew'd him you the other day.

E. Know. Oh, is that he? I remember him now, Good
faith! an he has a very strange presence, methinks; it
shews as if he stood out of the rank from other men.   I
have heard many of these jests i' the university.   They
say he will commit a man for taking the wall of his horse.

Well. Ay, or wearing his cloke of one shoulder, or
serving of God ; any thing indeed, if it come in the way
of his humour.

Enter CASH.

Cash. *Gasper, Martin, Cob!* 'Heart! where should they
be, trow?

Bob. Master *Kitely's* man, pr'ythee vouchsafe us the
lighting of this match,

Cash. Fire on your match, no time but now to vouchsafe? *Francis, Cob.*

Bob. Body of me! here's the remainder of seven pound
since yesterday was seven-night.   'Tis your right *Trinida-
da!* Did you never take any, master *Stephen?*

Step. No, truly, Sir; but I'll learn to take it now,
since you commend it so.

Bob.

Bob. Sir, believe me, upon my relation, for what I tell you the world shall not reprove. I have been in the *In-dies* where this herb grows, where neither myself, nor a dozen gentlemen more, of my knowledge, have received the taste of any other nutriment in the world for the space of one and twenty weeks, but the fume of this simple only. Therefore it cannot be but 'tis most divine, especially you *Trinidado.* Your *Nicotian* is good too: I hold it, and will affirm it before any prince in *Europe,* to be the most sovereign and precious weed that ever the earth tendered to the use of man.

E. Kno. This speech would have done decently in a tobacco-trader's mouth!

Enter CASH *and* COB.

Cash. At justice *Clement's* he is, in the middle of *Cole-man-street.*

Cob. O, ho!

Bob. Where's the match I gave thee? master *Kitely's* man?

Cash. Here it is, sir.

Cob. By God's-me! I marvel what pleasure or felicity they have in taking this roguish tobacco! it's good for no-thing but to choke a man and fill him full of smoke and embers.

[Bob. *beats him with a cudgel;* Mat. *runs away.*

All. Oh, good captain! hold, hold!

Bob. You base scullion, you.

Cash. Come, thou must needs be talking too, thou'rt well enough serv'd.

Cob. Well, it shall be a dear beating, an' I live! I will have justice for this.

Bob. Do you prate? do you murmur?

[Bob *beats him off.*

E. Kno. Nay, good captain, will you regard the humour of a fool?

Bob. A whorson filthy slave, a dung-worm, an excre-ment! body of *Cæsar,* but that I scorn to let forth so mean a spirit, I'd have stabb'd him to the earth.

Well. Marry, the law forbid, sir.

Bob. By *Pharaoh's* foot, I would have done it.   [*Exit.*

Step. Oh, he swears admirably! by *Pharaoh's* foot,

body

body of *Cæsar*; I shall never do it, sure; upon mine hon‑
nour, and by St. *George* ; no I ha'nt the right grace.

Well. But soft, where's Mr. *Matthew ?* gone.

Brain. No, sir; they went in here.

Well. O, let's follow them : master *Matthew* is gone to
salute his mistress in verse. We shall have the happiness
to hear some of this poetry now. He never comes un‑
furnish'd. *Brain-worm ?*

Step. *Brain-worm ;* where ? is this *Brain-worm ?*

E. Kno. Ay, cousin, no words of it, upon your gentil‑
ity.

Step. Not I, body of me ! by this air, St. *George,* and
the foot of *Pharaoh* !

Well. Rare ! your cousin's discourse is simply drawn
out with oaths.

E. Kno. 'Tis larded with 'em. A kind of *French*
dressing, if you love it.   Come, let's in.   Cousin, cousin.

[Exeunt.

S C E N E IV.

A Hall in Justice CLEMENTS *House.*

Enter KITELY *and* COB.

Kite. Ha ! how many are there, say'st thou ?

Cob. Marry, sir, your brother, master *Well-bred*——

Kite. Tut, beside him : what strangers are there, man ?

Cob. Strangers ? let me see ; one, two ; mass, I know
not well, there are so many.

Kite. How ! so many.

Cob. Ay, there's some five or six of them, at the most.

Kite. A swarm, a swarm !
Spite of the devil, how they sting my head
With forked stings, thus wide and large ! But *Cob,*
How long hast thou been coming hither, *Cob ?*

Cob. A little while, sir.

Kite Did'st thou come running ?

Cob. No, sir.

Kite. Nay, then I am familiar with thy hast !
Bane to my fortunes : what meant I to marry ?
I, that before was rank'd in such content,
My mind at rest too in so soft a piece,

Being

Being free master of my own free thoughts,.
And now become a slave? what, never sigh;
Be of good cheer, man, for thou art cuckold:
'Tis done, 'tis done! nay, when such flowing store,
Plenty itself, falls into my wife's lap,
The *Cornucopia* will be mine, I know.   But *Cob,*
What entertainment had they? I am sure
My sister and my wife would bid them welcome! ha?

 Cob. Like enough, sir; yet I heard not a word of it.
 Kite. No; their lips were seal'd with kisses, and the
Drown'd in a flood of joy at their arrival; [voice,
Had lost her motion, state, and faculty.
Cob, which of them was't that kiss'd my wife?
(My sister, I should say) my wife, alas?
I fear not her: ha? who was it, say'st thou?
 Cob. By my troth, sir will you have the truth of it?
 Kite. Ay, good *Cob,* I pray the heartily.
 Cob. Then I am a vagabond, and fitter for *Bridewell,*
than your worship's company, if I saw any body to be
kiss'd, unless they wou'd have kiss'd the post in the mid-
dle of the warehouse; for there I left 'em all, at their tobacco, with a pox!
 Kite. How! were they not gone in then, ere thou
cam'st?
 Cob. O, no, sir!
 Kite. Spite o' the devil! what do I stay here then? *Cob,*
follow me.   [*Exit.*
 Cob. Nay, soft and fair, I have eggs on the spit.   Now
am I for some five and fifty reasons hammering, hammering revenge: nay, an' he had not lain in my house, 'twould
never have griev'd me; but, being my guest, one that I'll be
sworn I lov'd and trusted; and he to turn monster of in-
gratitude, and strike his lawful host! well, I hope to raise
up an host of fury for't. I'll to justice *Clement* for a warrant.   Strike his lawful host!
                [*Exit.*

ACT

ACT. IV.   SCENE. I.

A Roon in KITELY's *House.*

Enter DOWN-RIGHT. *and Dame* KITELY.

DOWN-RIGHT.

WELL, sister, I tell you true: and you'll find it so, in the end.

Dame. Alas, brother, what would you liave me to do? I cannot help it; you see my brother brings 'em in here, they are his friends.

Down. His friends? his friends! 'Slud they do nothing but haunt him up and down, like a sort of unlucky sprites, and tempt him to all manner of villainy, that can be thought of. Well, by this light, a little thing would make me play the devil with some of 'em; and 'twere not more for your husband's sake, than any thing else I'd make the house too hot for the best on 'em; they should say, and swear, hell were broken loose ere they went hence. But, by God's will, 'tis nobody's fault but yours; for an' you had done, as you might have done, they should have been parboil'd and back'd too, every mother's son, ere they should ha' come in e'er a one of 'em.

Dame. God's my life! did ever you hear the like? what a strange man is this! could I keep out all them, think you? I should put myself against half a dozen of men, should I? good faith, you'd mad the patient'st body in the world to hear you talk so without any sense or reason!

Enter Mrs. BRIDGATE, Mr. MATTHEW WELL-BRED, STEPHEN. Ed. KNO'WELL, BOBADIL. *and* CASH.

Bridge. Servant, in troth, you are too prodigal
Of your wit's treasure, thus to pour it fortn,
Upon so mean a subject as my worth.

Mat. You say well, mistress; and I mean as well.

Down. Hay-day, here is stuff!

Well. O, now stand close: pray heav'n she can get him to read; he should do it of his own natural impudence.

Bridge. Servant, what is this same, I pray you?

Mat.

Mat. Marry, an elegy, an elegy, an old to——I'll read it if you please.

Bridge. Pray you do, servant.

Down. O, here's no foppery! death, I can endure the stocks better.

E. Kno. What ails my brother? can he not bear the reading of a ballad.

Well. O, no; rhime to him is worse than cheese, or a bagpipe. But, Mark, you lose the protestation.

Bob. Master *Matthew*, you abuse the expectation of your dear mistress, and her fair sister; fie, while you live, avoid this preplexity.

Mat. I shall, sir.

> *Rare creature, let me speak without offence,*
> *Would heav'n my rude words had the influence*
> *To rule thy thoughts, as thy fair looks do mine,*
> *Then should'st thou be his prisoner, who is thine.*

[Master *Stephen* answers with shaking his head.

E. Kno. 'Slight, he shakes his head like a bottle, to feel an' there be any brain in it!

Well. Sister, what ha' you here? verses? Pray you, let's see. Who made these verses? they are excellent good.

Mat. O, master *Well-bred*, 'tis your disposition to say so, sir. They were good i' the morning, I made 'em *extempore* this morning.

Well. How, *extempore?*

Mat. I would I might be hang'd else: ask captain *Bobadil.* He saw me write them at the——(pox on it) the star yonder.

Step. Cousin, how do you like this gentleman's verses?

E. Kno. O, admirable? the best that ever I heard, coz!

Step. Body o' *Cæsar!* they are admirable!
The best that ever I heard, as I am a soldier.

Down. I am vext, I can hold ne'er a bone of my stile! heart, I think they mean to build and breed here.

Well. Sister *Kitely*, I marvel you get you not a servant than can rhime, and do tricks too.

Down Oh, monster! impudence itself, tricks! come, you might practice your ruffian-tricks somewhere else, and not here, I wuss: this is no tavern, nor drinking-school, to vent your exploits in.

Well.

Well. How now! whose cow was calv'd?

Down. Marry, that has mine, sir.   Nay, boy, never look askance at me for the matter; I'll tell you of it, ay, sir; you and your companions, mend yourselves, when I ha' done.

Well. My companions?

Down. Yes, sir, your companions, so I say, I am not a-fraid of you nor them neither; your hang-bys here.   You must have your poets, and your potlings, your *Soldudos* and *Fooludos*, to follow you up and down the city, and here they must come to domineer and swagger.   Sirrah, you, ballad-singer, and Slops, your fellow there, get you out; get you home : or, by this steel, I'll cut off your ears, and that presently.

Well. 'Slight, stay let's see what he dare do : cut off his ears! cut a whetstone.   You are an ass, do you see ; touch any man here, and by this hand, I'l run my rapier to the hilts in you.

Down. Yea, that I would fain see, boy.

[*They all draw, and they of the house make out to part them.*

Dame. O, Jesu! murder! *Thomas, Gasper!*

Bridg. Help, help, *Thomas.*

E. Kno. Gentlemen, forbear, I pray you.

Bob. Well, sirrah, you, *Holofernes* ; by my hand, I will pink your flesh full of holes with my rapier, for this ; I will by this good heav'n : nay, let him come, gentlemen, by the body of *St. George,* I'll not kill him.

[*They offer to fight again, and are parted.*

Cash. Hold, hold, good gentlemen.

Down. You whorson, bragging coistril!

Enter KITLEY.

Kite. Why, how now? what's the matter? what's the stir here.
Put up your weapons, and put off this rage.
My wife and sister, they are the cause of this :
What *Thomas,* where is the knave ?

Cash. Here, sir.

Well. Come, let's go ; this is one of my brother's anci-ent humours this.   [*Exit.*

Step. I am glad nobody was hurt by his ancient humour.
                                                    [*Exit.*
                                                    Kite

Kite. Why, how now, brother, who inforc'd this brawl?

Down. A sort of leud rake-hells, that care neither for
God, nor the devil: and they must come here to read ballads, and roguery, and trash! I'll mar the knot of 'em ere
I sleep, perhaps; especially *Bob*, there: he that's all manner of shapes! and *songs and sonnets*, his fellow. But I'll
follow 'em.   [*xit.*

Bridge. Brother, indeed, you are too violent,   ·
Too sudden in your humour:
There was one civil gentleman,
And very worthily demean'd himself.

Kite. O, that was some Love of yours, Sister.

Bridge. A love of mine? I would it were no worse,
Brother! You'd pay my portion sooner than you think
for.   -   [*Exit.*

Dame. Indeed, he seem'd to be a gentleman of exceeding fair disposition, and of very excellent good parts.
What a coil and stir is here?   [*Exit.*

Kite. Her love, by heaven! my wife's minion!
Fair disposition, excellent good parts!
Death, these phrases are intolerable!
Well, well, well, well, well, well!
Is it too plain, too clear: *Thomas*, come hither.
What, are they gone!

  - *Cash.* Ay, sir, they went in.
My mistress, and your sister————

Kite. Are any of the gallants within?

Cash. No, sir, they are all gone.

Kite. Art thou sure of it?

Cash. I can assure you, Sir,

Kite. What gentleman was that they prais'd so, *Thomas.*

Cash. One, they call him master *Kno'well*, a handsome
young gentleman, Sir.

Kite. Ay, I thought so: my mind gave me as much.
I'll die, but they have hid him i' the house
Somewhere; I'll go and search: go with me, *Thomas*,
Be true to me, and thou shalt find me a master. [*Exeunt.*

S C E N E II.

More-Fields.

Enter E. Kno'well, Wel-bred, *and* Brain-worm.

E. *Kno.*

E. Kno. Well, *Brain-worm*, perform this business happily, and thou makest a purchase of my love for ever.

Well. I' faith, now let thy spirits use their best faculties;
but at any hand remember the messuage to my brother:
for there's no other means, to start him out of his house.

Brain. I warrant you, sir, fear nothing: I have a nimble soul has wak'd all forces of my phant'sy by this time,
and put 'em in true motion.   What you have possest me
withal, I'll discharge it amply, sir. Make it no question.
[*Exit.*

Well. Forth, and prosper, *Brain-worm.*   Faith, *Ned*
how dost thou approve of my abilities in this advice?

E. Kno. Troth, well, howsoever; but it will come excellent, if it take.

Well. Take, man? why, it cannot chuse but take, if the
circumstances miscarry not; but tell me ingeniously, dost
thou affect my sister *Bridget*, as thou pretend'st?

E. Kno. Friend am I worth belief?

Well. Come do not protest.   In faith, she is a maid, of
good ornament, and much modesty: and, except I conceiv'd very worthily of her, thou should'st not have her.

E. Kno. Nay, that I am afraid will be a question yet
whether I shall have her or no.

Well. 'Slid, thou shalt have her; by this light thou shalt.

E. Kno. Nay, do not swear.

Well. By this hand, thou shalt have her: I'll go fetch
her presently.   Point but where to meet, and as I am an
honest man, i'll bring her.

E. Kno. Hold, hold, be temperate.

Well. Why, by—what shall I swear by? thou shalt have
her, as I am——

E. Kno. Pray thee, be at peace, I am satisfied: and do
believe thou wilt omit no offered occasion, to make my desires compleat.

Well. Thou shalt see and know, I will not.   *Exeunt.*

Enter FORMAL, *and* KNO'WELL.

Form, Was your man a soldier, sir?

Kno. Ay, a knave, I took him begging 'o the way,
This morning, as I came over *More-fields!*

Enter BRAIN-WORM.

O here he is! you have made fair speed, believe me:
Where

Where i' the name of sloth, could you be thus.——

Brain. Marry, peace be my comfort, where I thought I
should have had little comfort of your worship's service,

Kno. How so?

Brain. O, sir, your coming to the city, your entertainment of me, and your sending me to watch—indeed all
the circumstances either of your charge, or my employment, are as open to your son, as to yourself!

Kno. How should that be! unless that villain, *Brain-*
   worm,
Have told him of the letter, and discover'd
All that I strictly charged him to conceal? tis so!

Brain. I am partly o' that faith, 'tis so!

Kno. But how should he know thee to be my man?

Brain. Nay, sir, I cannot tell; unless it be by the black
art! is not your son a scholar, sir?

Kno. Yes, but I hope his soul is not allied
Unto such hellish practice: if it were
I had just cause to weep my part in him,
And curse the time of his creation.
But where didst thou find them, *Fitz-Sword?*

Brain. You should rather ask, where they found me, sir;
for I'll be sworn I was going along in the street, thinking
nothing, when (of a sudden) a voice calls, Mr. *Kno'well's*
man; another cries, soldier; and thus, half a dozen of 'em,
'till they had call'd me within a house, where I no sooner
came, but out flew all their rapiers at my bosom, with some
three or four score oaths to accompany 'em, and all to tell
me, I was a dead man, if I did not confess where you
were, and how I was employed, and about what; which
when they could not get out of me (as I protest they must
have dissected me, and made an anatomy of me first, and
so I told 'em (they lock'd me up into a room i' the top of
a high house, whence, by great miracle, having a light
heart, I slid down by a bottom of packthread into the street,
and so 'scap'd.   But, sir, thus much I can assure you, for
I heard it while I was lock'd up, there were a great many
rich merchants and brave citizens wives with 'em at the
feast, and your son Mr *Edward,* withdrew with one of
'em, and has 'pointed to meet her anon, at one *Cob's* house,
a water-bearer, that dwells by the wall.   Now, there
your worship shall be sure to take him, for there he preys,
and fail he will not.

I

Kno.

Kno. Nor will I fail, to break this match I doubt not.
Go thou along with justice *Clement's* man,
And stay there for me.   At one *Cob's* house, say'st thou?
Brain Ay, sir, there you shall have him. [*Exit* Kno-
    well.]
Yes! invisible? much wench, or much son! 'Slight, when
he has stayed there three or four hours, travelling with the
expectation of wonders, and at length be delivered of air:
O, the sport that I should then take to look on him, if I
durst! but now I mean to appear no more before him in
this shape. I have another trick to act yet.   Sir, I make
you stay somewhat long.
For. Not a whit, sir.
You have been lately in the wars, sir, it seems.
Brain. Marry have I, sir, to my loss; and expence of all,
almost——
Form. Troth, sir, I would be glad to bestow a bottle of.
wine o' you, if it please you to except it——
Bran. O, sir,——
Form. But to hear the manner of your services and your
devices in the wars; they say they be very strange, and
not like those a man reads in the *Roman* histories, or sees
at *Mile end.*
Brain. No, I assure you, sir; why at any time when it
please you, I shall be ready to discourse to you all I know;
and more too, somewhat.
Form. No better time than now sir; we'll go to the
wind mill, there we shall have a cup of neat grist, as we
call it.   I pray you, sir, let me request you, to the *wind-
mill.*
Brain. I'll follow you, sir, and make grist o' you, if I
have good luck.   *[Exeunt.*

Enter MATTHEW, Ed. KNO'WELL, BOBADIL, *and.*

STEPHEN.

Mat. Sir, did your eyes ever taste the like clown of him,
where we were to day, Mr. *Well-bred's* half brother? I
think the whole earth cannot shew his parallel, by this day-
light.
E. Kno. We are now speaking of him: captain *Bobadil*
tells me, he is fall'en foul o' you too.
Mat. O, ay, sir! he threatened me, with the banado

Bob. Ay, but I think I taught you prevention this morning, for that——You shall kill him; beyond question; if you be so generously minded.

Mat. Indeed it is a most excellent trick !

Bob. O, you do not give spirit enough to your motion, you are too tardy, too heavy ! O, it must be done like light'ning hey ?   [*he practises at a post.*

Mat. Rare captain !

Bob. Tut, 'tis nothing, an't be not done in a——*punto!*

E. Kno. Captain, did you ever prove yourself upon any of our masters of defence here ?

Mat. O, good, sirs ! yes I hope he has.

Bob. I will tell you, sir.   They have assaulted me some three, four, five, six of them together, as I have walk'd alone in divers skirts o' the town, where I have driven them before me the whole length of a street, in the open view of all our gallants pitying to hurt them, believe me.   Yet all this lenity will not overcome their spleen; they will be doing with the pismire, raising a hill a man may spurn abroad with his foot, at pleasure.   By myself I could have slain them all, but I delight not in murder.   I am loth to bear any other than this bastinado for 'em : yet I hold it good policy not to go disarm'd, for tho' I be skilful, I may be oppress'd with multitudes.

E. Kno. Ay, believe me, may you ; and, in my conceit, our whole nation should sustain the loss by it, if it were so.

Bob. Alas, no; what's a peculiar man, to a nation ? not seen.

E. Kno. O, but your skill, Sir !

Bob. Indeed, that might be some loss : but who respects it? I will tell you, sir, by the way of private, and under seal ; I am a gentleman, and live here obscure and to myself: but, were I known to his majesty, and the lords (observe me) I would undertake (upon this poor head and life) for the public benefit of the state, not only to spare the entire lives of his subjects in general, but to save the one half nay, three parts of his yearly charge in holding war, and against what enemy soever.   And how would I do it, think you ?

E. Kno. Nay, I know not nor can I conceive.

Bob. Why thus, sir.   I would select nineteen more to myself, throughout the land ; gentlemen they should be, of good spirit, strong and able constitution ; I would choose
them

them by an instinct, a character that I have : and I would
teach these nineteen the special rules, as your *punto,* your
Reverso, your *Stoccata,* your *Imbrocata,* your *Possada,* your
Montanto : till they could all play very near, or altogether
as well as myself.   This done, say the enemy were forty
thousand strong, we twenty would come into the field the
tenth of *March,* or thereabouts ; and we would challenge
twenty of the enemy; they could not, in their honour, refuse us ; well, we would kill them ; challenge twenty more,
kill them ; twenty more, kill them too : and thus would we
kill every man his twenty a day, that's twenty score, tha'ts
two hundred ; two hundred a day, five days a thousand ;
forty thousand ; forty times five, five times forty, two hundred days kills them all up by computation.   And this I
will venture my poor gentlemen-like carcase to perform
(provided there be no treason practis'd upon us) by fair
and discreet manhood, that is, civilly by the sword.

E. Kno. Why, are you so sure of your hand, captain, at
all times?

Bob. Tut, never miss thrust. upon my reputation with
you.

E. Kno. I would not stand in *Down-right's* state then,
an' you meet him, for the wealth of any one street in *London.*

Bob. Why, sir, you mistake ! if he were here now, by
this welkin I would not draw my weapon on him ! let this
gentleman do his mind : but I will bastinado him, by the
bright sun ! wherever I meet him.

Mat. Faith, and I'll have a fling at him at my distance.

Enter Down-right, *walking over the Stage.*

E. Kno. God's so! look you where he is: yonder he
goes.

Down. What peevish luck have I, I cannot meet with
these bragging rascals ?

Bob. It's not he, is it ?

E. Kno. Yes faith ! it is he ?

Mat. I'll be hang'd, then, if I were he.

E. Kno. I assure you, that was he.

Step. Upon my reputation, it was he.

Bob. Had I thought it had been he, he must not have
gone so: but I can hardly be induc'd to believe it was he,
yet.

I 2

E. Kno.

E. Kno. That I think, sir. But see, he is come again?

Down. O, *Pharaoh's* 'oot! have I found you? come draw, to your tools; draw, gipsy, or I'll thresh you.

Bob. Gentleman of valour, I do believe in thee, hear me——

Down. Draw your weapon, then.

Bob. Tall man, I never thought on't till now; body of me! I had a warrant of the peace served on me even now, as I came along, by a water-bearer; this gentleman saw it, Mr. *Matthew*.

[*He beats him, and disarms him.* Matthew *runs away.*

Down. 'Sdeath, you will not draw, then?

Bob. Hold, hold, under thy favour, forbear.

Down. Prate again, as you like this, you whorson foist, you. You'll controul the point, you? your consort is gone; had he staid, he had shar'd with you, sir.

[*Exit* Down-right.

E. Kno. Twenty, and kill 'em; twenty more, kill them too. Ha! ha!

Bob. Well, gentlemen, bear witness, I was bound to the peace, by this good day.

E. Kno. No, faith; it's an ill day, captain, never reckon it other; but say you were bound to the peace, the law allows you to defend yourself: that will prove but a poor excuse

Bob. I cannot tell, sir. I desire good cons'ruction, in fair sort. I never sustain'd the like disgrace, by heaven: sure I was struck with a planet thence, for I had no power to touch my weapon.

E. Kno. Ay, like enough, I have heard of many that have been beaten under a planet; go, get you to a surgeon. 'Slid an' these be your tricks, your *Passado's*, and your Montanto's, I'll none of them.

Bob. I was planet-struck certainly.   [*Exit.*

E. Kno. O, manners! that this age should bring forth such creatures! that nature should be at leisure to make 'em! Come, coz.

Step. Mass, I'll have this cloke.

E. Kno. God's will, 'tis *Down-right's.*

Step. Nay, its mine now; another might have ta'en it up as well as I: I'll wear it it, so I will.

E. Kno. How, an he see it? he'l challenge it, assure yourself.

Step.

step. Ay, but he shall not ha't; I'll say, I bought it.
E. Kno. Take head you buy it not too dear, coz. [*Exit.*

SCENE III.

A Chamber in KITELEY's *house.*

Enter KITLEY *and* CASH.

Kite. Art thou sure, *Thomas*, we have pry'd into all and every part throughout the house? is there no by-place, or dark corner has escap'd our searches?

Cash. Indeed, sir, none; there's not a hole or nook un-search'd by us, from the upper loft into the cellar.

Kite. They have convey'd him then away, or hid him in some privacy of their own——Whilst we were searching of the dark closet by my sister's chamber, did'st thou not think thou heard'st a rustling on the other side, and a soft tread of feet?

Cash. Upon my troth, I did not, sir; or if you did, it might be only the vermin in the wainscot; the house is old and over-run with 'em.

Kite. It is, indeed, *Thomas*—we should bane these rats—dost thou understand me—we will—they shall not harbour here; I'll cleanse my house from 'em, if fire or poison can effect it—I will not be tormented thus——They knaw my brain, and burrow in my heart——I cannot bear it.

Cash. I do not understand you, sir! good now, what is't disturbs you thus? pray, be compos'd; these start of passion have some cause I fear, that touches you more nearly.

Kite. Sorely, sorely, *Thomas*—it cleaves too close to me—Oh me [*Sighs*] Lend me thy arm—so, good *Cash.*

Cash You tremble and look pale! let me call assistance.

Kite. Not for ten thousand worlds—Alas! alas! 'tis not in med'cine to give ease—here, here it lies.

Cash, What, sir?

Kite. Why,—nothing, nothing.—I am not sick, yet more than dead; I have a burning fever in my mind, and long for that, which having, would destroy me.

Cash. Believe me, 'tis your fancy's imposition; shut up your generous mind from such intruders—I'll hazard all my growing favour with you: I'll stake my present, my future welfare, that some base whispering knave (pardon me sir)

I 3   hath

hath in the best and richest soil, sown seeds of rank and e-
vil nature! O, my master, should they take root——
[*Laughing within.*

Kite. Hark! hark! dost thou not hear? what think'st
thou now? are they not laughing at me? they are, they
are: they have deceiv'd the wittol, and thus they triumph
in their infamy—This aggravation is not to be borne.
[*Laughing again.*] Hark again!——*Casb*, do thou unseen
steal in upon 'em, and listen to their wanton conference.

Casb. I shall obey you, tho' against my will.   [*Exit.*

Kite. Against his will? ha! it may be so—-He's young,
and may be brib'd for them—they've various means to
draw the unwary in; if it be so, I'm lost, deceiv'd, betray'd,
and my bosom (my full-fraught bosom) is unlock'd and
open'd to mockery and laughter! heaven forbid! he cannot be that viper; sting the hand that rais'd and cherish'd
him! was this stroke added, I should be curs'd—but it
cannot be—no, it cannot be!

Enter Cash.

Cash. You are musing, sir.

Kite. I ask your pardon, *Casb*,—ask me not why—I
have wrong'd you, and am sorry 'tis gone.

Casb. If you suspect my faith——

Kite. I do not—say no more—and for my sake let it die,
and be forgotten—Have you seen your mistress, and heard
—whence was that noise?

Casb. Your brother master *Well-bred* is with 'em, and I
found 'em throwing out their mirth on a very truly ridiculous subject; it is one *Formal*, as he stiles himself, and
he appertains (so he phrases it) to justice *Clement*, and
would speak with you.

Kite. With me! art thou sure it is the justice's clerk?
Where is he?

Enter Brain-worm (*as* Formal.)

Who are you, friend?

Brain. An appendix to justice *Clement*, vulgarly call'd
his clerk.

Kite. What are your wants with me?

Brain. None.

Kite. Do you not want to speak with me?

Brain. No——but my master does.

Kite.

Kite. What are the justice's commands?

Brain. He doth not command, but intreats master *Kitely*
to be with him directly, having matters of some moment to
communicate unto him.

Kite. What can it be! say, I'll be with him instantly;
and if your legs, friend, go no faster than your tongue, I
shall be there before you.

Brain. I will, *Vale.*

Kite. 'Tis a precious fool indeed !——I must go forth—
But first, come hither, *Thomas*——I have admitted thee
into the close recesses of my heart, and shew'd thee all
my frailties, passions, every thing——
Be careful of thy promise, keep good watch :
Wilt thou be true, my *Thomas?*

Casb. As truth's self, sir——
But be assur'd you're heaping care and trouble
Upon a sandy base ; ill plac'd suspicion
Recoils upon yourself—She's chaste as comely ;
Believe't she is—Let her not note your humour ;
Disperse the gloom upon your brow, and be
As clear as her unsullied honour.   [these

Kite. I will then, *Casb*—thou comfort'st me——I'll drive
Fiend-like fancies from me, and be myself again.
Think'st thou she has perceiv'd my folly ? 'Twere
Happy if he had not—She was not—
They who know no evil will suspect none.

Casb. True, sir; nor has your mind a blemish now.
This change has gladdened me—Here's my mistress.
And the rest, settle your reason to accost 'em.

Kite. I will, *Casb*, I will——

Enter WELL-BRED, Dame KITLEY, *and* BRIDGET.

Well. What are you plotting, brother *Kitely*
That thus of late you muse alone, and bear
Such weighty care upon your pensive brow ?   [*laughs*

Kite. My care is all for you, good sneering brother,
And well I wish you'd take some wholsome counsel,
And curb your headstrong humours ; trust me, brother,
You were to blame to raise commotions here,
And hurt the peace and order of my house.

Well. No harm done, brother, I warrant you,
Since there is no harm done ; anger costs
A man nothing, and a brave man is never

His own man 'till he be angry—to keep
His valour in obscurity, is to keep himself,
As it were, in a cloke-bag: what's a brave
Musician unless he play?
What's a brave man unless he fight?

Dame. Ay, but what harm might have come of it, brother?

Well. What, school'd on both sides! Prithee, *Bridget,*
save-me from the rod and lecture.

       [*Bridget and* Well-bred *retire.*

Kite. With what a decent modesty she rates him!
My heart's at ease, and she shall see it is—
How art thou, wife? thou look'st both gay and comely,
In troth thou dost—I am sent for out, my dear,
But I shall soon return——Indeed, my life,
Business that forces me abroad is irksom,
I cou'd content me with less gain and 'vantage
To have thee more at home, indeed I cou'd.

Dame. Your doubts, as well as love, may breed these
thoughts.

Kite. That jar untunes me.
What dost thou say? doubt thee?   [*Aside.*
I shou'd as soon suspect myself—no, no,
My confidence is rooted in thy merit,
So fixt and settled, that, wer't thou inclin'd
To masks, to sports, and balls, where lusty youth
Leads up the wanton dance, and the rais'd pulse
Beats quicker measures, yet I could with joy,
With heart's ease and security—not but
I had rather thou should'st prefer thy home
And me, to toys and such like vanities.

Dame. But sure, my dear,
A wife may moderately use these pleasures,
Which numbers, and the time give sanction to,
Without the smallest blemish on her name.

Kite. And so she may— And I'll go with thee, child;
I will indeed——I'll lead thee there myself;
And be the foremost reveller.—I'll silence
The sneers of envy, stop the tongue of slander;
Nor will I more be pointed at, as one
Disturb'd with jealousy——

Dame. Why, were you ever so?

Kite. What!—ha! never—ha, ha, ha!

             She

She stabs me home.   (*Aside*)   Jealous of thee?
No, do not believe it—speak low, my love,
Thy brother will overhear us—no, no, my dear,
It cou'd not be, it cou'd not be—for—for—
What is the time now?—I shall be too late—
No, no, thou may'st be satisfy'd.
There's not the smallest spark remaining——
Remaining! what do I say? there never was,
Nor can, nor never shall be—so be satisfy'd—
Is *Cob.* within there?—Give me a kiss,.
My dear, there, there; now we are reconcil'd——
I'll be back immediately—Good-bye, good bye—
Ha, ha, jealous, I shall burst my sides with laughing;
Ha, ha, *Cob*;. where are you, *Cob?* ha, ha——   [*Exit.*
                    [Well-bred *and* Bridget *come forward.*

Well. What have you done to make your husband part
so merry from you?   he has of late been little given to
laughter.

Dame. He laugh'd indeed, but seemingly without mirth:
his behaviour is new and strange: he is much agitated, and
has some whimzy in his head, that puzzles mine to read it.

Well. 'Tis jealousy, good sister, and writ so largely that
the blind may read it; have not you perceiv'd it yet?

Dame. If I have, 'tis not always prudent that my tongue
shou'd betray my eyes, so far my wisdom tends, good brother, and little more I boast—But what makes him ever
calling for *Cob* so? I wonder how he can employ him.

Well. Indeed, sister, to ask how he employs *Cob*, is a
necessary question for you, that are his wife, and a thing not
very easy for you to be satisfy'd in—But this, I'll assure
you, *Cob's* wife is an excellent bawd, sister, and oftentimes
your husband haunts her house; marry to what end, I cannot altogether accuse him: imagine you what you think
convenient.   But I have known fair hides have foul hearts,
ere now, sister.

Dame. Never said you truer than that, brother; so much
I can tell you for your learning.   O, ho! is this the fruit
of's jealousy? I thought some game was in the wind, he
acted so much tenderness but now; but I'll be quit with
him.——*Thomas!*

Enter CASH.

Fetch your hat, and go with me; I'll get my hood, and
I 5,   out

out the back-ward.way. ———I would to fortune I could take him there, I'd return him his own, I warrant him! I'd fit him for his jealousy!   *[Exit.*

Well. Ha, ha! so, e'en let em go; this may make sport anon—What, *Brain-worm?*

Enter BRAIN-WORM.

Brain. I saw the merchant turn the corner, and came back to tell you, all goes well; wind and tide, my master.

Well. But how got'st thou this apparel of the justice's man?

Brain. Marry, sir, my proper fine penman won'd needs bestow the grist 'o me at the *wind-mill*, to hear some martial discourse, where I so marshalled him, that I made him drunk with admiration: and because too much heat was the cause of his distemper, I stript him stark naked, as he lay long asleep, and borrow'd his suit to deliver this counterfeit message in, leaving a rusty armour, and an old brown bill, to watch him 'till my return; which shall be when I have pawn'd his apparel, and spent the better part of his money, perhaps.

Well. Well, thou art a successful merry knave, *Brain-worm*: his absence will be subject for more mirth. I pray thee return to thy young master, and will him to meet me and my sister *Bridget* at the *Tower* instantly; for here, tell him, the house is so stor'd with jealousy, there is no room for love to stand upright in. We must get our fortunes committed to some large prison, say; and then the *Tower*, I know no better air, nor where the liberty of the house may do us more present service. 'Away.

[*Exit* Brain-worm.

Bridg. What, is this the engine that you told me of? What further meaning have you in the plot?

Well. That you may know, fair sister-in-law how happy a thing it is to be fair and beautiful.

Bridg. That touches not me, brother.

Well. That's true; that's ev'n the fault of it; for, indeed beauty stands a woman in no stead, unless it procure her touching——Well, there's a dear and well respected friend of mine, sister, stands very strongly and worthily affected towards you, and have vow'd to inflame whole bone-fires of zeal at his heart, in honour of your perfections, I have already engaged my promise to bring you where you shall

hear

hear him confirm much more. *Ned Kno'well* is the man, sister. There's no conception against the party; you are ripe for a husband, and a minutes loss to such an occasion is a great trespass in a wise beauty.——What say you, sister? On my soul, he loves you. Will you give him the meeting?

Bridg. Faith, I had very little confidence in my own constancy, brother, if I durst not meet a man: but this motion of yours favours an old kinght adventurer's servant, a little too much, methinks.

Well. what's that, sister?

Bridg. Marry, of the go-between.

Well. No matter if I did: I wou'd be such a one for my friend.——But see, who is return'd to hinder us.

Enter KITELY.

Kite. What villainy is this? call'd out on a false message! this was some plot; I was not sent for. *Bridget.* where's your sister?

Bridg. I think she be gone forth, sir.

Kite. How! is my wife gone forth? whither, for heaven's sake?

Bridg. I know not, sir.

Well. I'll tell you, brother, whither I suspect she's gone.

Kite Whither, good brother?

Well. To *Cob's* house, I believe. But keep my counsel.

Kite. I will, I will——To *Cob's* house! Does she haunt there?

She's gone on purpose now to cuckold me
With that lewd rascal who to win her favour,
Hath told her all—Why wou'd you let her go?

Well. Because she's not my wife; if she were, I'd keep her to her tether.

Kite. So, so; now 'tis too plain.—I shall go mad
With my misfortunes; now they pour in torrents:
I am bruted by my wife, betray'd by my servant,
Mock'd at by my relations, pointed at by my neighbours;
Despis'd by myself.——there is nothing left now
But to revenge myself first, next hang myself;
And then—all my cares will be over.   [*Exit.*

Bridg. He storms most loudly; sure you have gone too far in this.

Well. 'Twill all end right, depend upon't.——But let r

lose no time; the coast is clear; away, away; the affair is worth it, and cries haste.

Bridg. I trust me to your guidance, brother; and so fortune for us.   [*Exeunt.*

ACT. V.   SCENE I.

Stocks-markt.

Enter MATTHEW, *and* BOBADIL.

MATTHEW,

I WONDER, captain, what they will say of my going away? ha?

Bob. Why, what should they say? but as of a discreet gentleman? quick, wary, respectful of nature's fair lineaments: and that's all.

Mat. Why so! but what can they say of your beating?

Bob. A rude part, a touch with soft wood, a kind of gross battery us'd, lain on strongly, born most patiently: and that's all. But wherefore do I wake this remembrance? I was fascinated, by *Jupiter!* fascinated: but I will be unwitched and reveng'd by law.

Mat. Do you hear? i'st not best to get a warrant and have him arrested, and brought before justice *Clement?*

Bob. It were not amiss, would we had it!

Mat. Why here comes his man, let's speak to him.

Bob. Agreed: do you speak.

Enter BRAIN-WORM *as* Formal.

Mat. Save you, sir.

Brain. With all my heart, sir.

Mat. Sir, there is one *Down-right*, hath abus'd this gentleman and myself, and we determine to make ourselves amends by law; now, if you would do us the favour to procure a warrant to bring him before your master, you shall be well considered of, I assure you, sir.

Brain. Sir, you know my service is my living, such favours as these, gotten of my master, is his only preferment, and therefore, you must consider me, as I may make benefit of my place.

Mat. How is that, sir?

Brain.

Brain. Faith, sir, the thing is extraordinary, and the gen-tleman may be of great account: yet, be what he will, if you will lay me down a brace of angels in my hand, you shall have it, otherwise not.

Mat. How shall we do, captain? he asks a brace of an-gels, you have no money.

Bob. Not a cross, by fortune.

Mat. Nor I, as I am a gentleman, but two pence left of my two shillings in the morning for wine and raddish; let's find him some pawn.

Bob. Pawn? we have none to the value of his demand.

Mat. O, yes, I can pawn my ring here.

Bob. And harkee, he shall have my trusty *Toledo* too: I believe I shall have no service for it to-day.

Mat. Do you hear, sir? we have no store of money at this time, but you shall have good pawns; look you, sir, I will pledge this ring, and that gentleman his *Toledo*, be-cause we would have it dispatch'd.

Brain. I am content, sir; I will get you the warrant pre-sently. What's his name, say you, *Down-right*?

Mat. Ay, ay, *George Down-right.*

Brain. Well, gentlemen, I'll procure you the warrant presently; but who will you have to serve it?

Mat. That's true, captain, that must be consider'd.

Bob. Body o' me, I know not! 'tis service of danger!

Brain. Why, you were best to get one of the varlets o' the city, a serjeant: I'll appoint you one, if you please.

Mat. Will you sir? why, we can wish no better.

Bob. We'll leave it to you, sir.

　　　　　　　　[*Exeunt* Bobadil *and* Matthew.

Brain. This is rare! now will I go pawn this cloke of the justice's man's, at the brokers for a varlet's suit, and be the varlet myself; and so get money on all sides.　　[*Exit.*

S C E N E. II.

The Street before Cobb's *House.*

Enter Kno'well.

Kno. O, here it is; I have found it now——Hoa, who is within here?　　　　　　[*Tib appears at the window.*

　　　　　　　　　　　　　　　　Tib

Tib. I am within, sir, what is your pleasure ?

Kno. To know who is within besides yourself.

Tib. Why, sir, you are no constable, I hope ?

Kno. O, fear you the constable ? then I doubt not you have some guests within deserve that fear—I'll fetch him straight.

Tib. For heavens sake, sir——

Kno. Go to, come tell me, is not young *Kno'well* here ?

Tib. Young *Kno'well.* I know none such, sir, o' my honesty.

Kno. Your honesty, dame ! it flies too lightly from you : there is no way but fetch the constable.

Tib. The constable ! the man is mad, I think.

Enter CASH *and* Dame KITELY.

Cash. Hoa ! who keeps house here ?

Kno. O, this is the female copesmate of my son. Now shall I meet him straight.   *(Aside.)*

Dame. Knock, *Thomas,,* hard.

Cash. Hoa ! good wife.

Tib. Why, what's the matter with you.

Dame. Why, woman, grieves it you to open the door ! belike, you get something to keep it shut.

Tib. What mean these questions, pray you ?

Dame. So strange you make it, is not my husband here !

Kno. Her husband !   [*Aside.*

Dame. My tried and faithful husband Master *Kitely.*

Tib. I hope he needs not to be tried here.

Dame. Come hither, *Cash*—I see my turtle coming to his haunts ; let us retire.   [*They retire.*

Kno. This must be some device to mock me withal. Soft—who is this ?—Oh ! 'tis my son disguis'd; I'll watch him, and surprise him.

Enter KITELY *muffled in a cloke.*

Kite. 'Tis truth, I see, there she skulks.
But I will fetch her from her hold—I will—
I tremble so, I scarce have power to do the justice
Her infamy demands.

[*As* Kitely *goes forward, Dame* Kitely *and* Kno'well *lay*
    hold of him.

Kno. Have I trapped you, youth ? You can't 'scape me now.

Dame.

Dame. O, sir ! have I forestall'd your honest market ?
Found your closs walks ? you stand amaz'd
Now, do you ? Ah, hide, hide your face for shame !
I' faith, I am glad I have found you yet at last.
What is your jewel, tro ? in, come let's see her; fetch
Forth the wanton dame—If she be fairer
In any honest judgment, than myself,
I'll be content with it; but she is change;
She feeds you fat, she sooths your appetite,
And you are all well. Your wife, an honést woman,
Is meat twice sod to you, sir.   O you treacher !
Kno. What mean you, woman ? let go your hold.
I see the counterfeit—I am his father, and claim him as
       my own.
Kite. [*discovering bimself*] I am your cuckold, and claim
my vengeance.
Dame. What, do you wrong me, and insult me too ?
thou faithless man !
Kite. Out on thy more than strumpet's impudence !
Steal'st thou thus to thy haunts ? and have I taken
Thy bawd, and thee, and thy companion,
This hoary-headed letcher, this old goat,
Close at your villany and would'st thou 'scuse it,
With this stale harlot's jest, accusing me ?
O, old incontinent ! dost thou not shame
To have a mind so hot ? and so entice,
And feed the inticements of a lustful woman ?
Dame. Out, I defy thee, thou dissembling wretch !
Kite. Defy me, strumpet, ask thy pander here,
Can he deny it, or that wicked elder ?
Kno. Why, hear you, sir——
Cash. Master, 'tis in vain to reason, while these passions
blind you—I'm griev'd to see you thus,
Kite. Tut, tut, never speak, I see thro' every
Veil you cast upon your treachery : but I have
Done With you, and root you from my heart for ever.
For you, sir, thus I demand my honour's due ;
Resolv'd to cool your lust, or end my shame.   [*Draws.*
Kno. What lunacy is this ? put up your sword, and un-
deceive yourself—no arm that e'er pois'd weapon can af-
fright me.   But I pity folly, nor cope with madness.
Kite. I will have proofs—I will—so you good wife bawd,
Cob's wife : and you that make your husband such a mon-
                         ster,

ster, and you, young pander, and old cuckold maker, I'll
ha' you every one before the justice—nay, you shall an-
swer it; I charge you go.   Come forth, thou bawd.
                    [*Goes into the house and brings out* Tib.
  Kno. Marry, with all my heart, sir; I go willingly.
Tho' I do taste this as a trick put upon me,
To punish my impertinent search; and justly;
And half forgive my son for the device.
  Kite. Come, will you go?
  Dame. Go, to thy shame believe it.
  Kite. Tho' shame and sorrow both my heart betide,
Come on—I must and will be satisfy'd   [*Exeunt.*

S C E N E.   III.

Stock's-Market.

Enter BRAIN-WORM.

  Brain. Well, of all my disguises yet, now am I most like
myself; being in this serjeant's gown.   A man of my present profession never conterfeits 'till he lays hold upon a
debtor, and says, he rests him! for then he brings him to
all manner of unrest.   A kind of little kings we are, bearing the diminutive of a mace, made like a young artichoke
that always carries pepper and salt in itself.   Well, I know
not what danger I undergo by this exploit   pray heaven I
come well off.

  Enter BOBADIL, *and* Mr. MATTHEW.

  Mat. See, I think, yonder is the varlet, by his gown.
'Save you, friend: are you not here by appointment of ju-
tice *Clement's* man ?
  Brain. Yes, an't please you, sir: he told me two gentlemen had will'd him to procure a warrant from his master
(which I have about me) to be serv'd on one *Down-right.*
  Mat. It is honestly done of you both; and see where
the party come, you must arrest: serve it upon him quickly, before he be aware——

  Enter Mr. STEPHEN *in* DOWN-RIGHT's *Cloke.*

  Bob. Bear back, master *Matthew,*
  Brain. Master *Down-right,* I arrest you in the queen's
                                                            name.

name, and must carry you before a justice, by virtue o^f this warrant.

Step. My friend, I am no *Down-right*, I. I am master *Stephen*, : you do not well to arrest me, I tell you truely : I am in nobody's bonds or books, I would you should know it. A plague on you heartily, for making me thus afraid before my time.

Brain. Why now you are deceiv'd gentlemen.

Bob. He wears such a cloke, and that deceiv'd us; but see, here a comes indeed ! this is the officer.

Enter Down-right.

Down. Why, how now, signior Gull ! are you turn'd filcher of late ? Come, deliver my cloke.

Step. Your cloke, sir? I bought it even now in open market.

Brain. Master *Down right*, I have a warrant I must serve it upon you, procured by these two gentlemen.

Down. These gentlemen ? these rascals?

Brain. Keep the peace, I charge you in her majesty's name.

Down. I obey thee. What must I do, officer?

Brain. Go before master justice *Clement*, to answer what they can object against you, sir. I will use you kindly, sir.

Mat. Come, let's before, and make the justice, captain—

[*Exit.*

Bob. The varlet's a tall man, before heaven !   [*Exit.*

Down. Gull, you'll gi' me my cloke ?

Step. Sir, I bought it, and I'll keep it.

Down. You will ?

Step. Ay, that I will.

Down. Officer, there's thy fee, arrest him.

Brain. Master *Stephen*, I must arrest you.

Step. Arrest me, I scorn it. There take your cloke, I'll have none on't.

Down. Nay, that shall not serve your turn, now, sir. Officer, I'll go with thee to the justice's: bring him along.

Down. Why, is not here your cloke, what would you

Step. I'll ha' you answer it, sir.   [have ?

Brain. Sir, I'll take your word, and this gentleman's too, for his appearance.

Down. I'll ha' no words taken. Bring him along.

Brain. So, so, I have made a fair mash on't,

Step. Must I go ?

Brain.

Brain. I know no remedy, Master *Stephen.*

Down. Come along before me here. I do not love your hanging look behind.

Step. Why, sir, I hope you cannot hang me for it. Can he, fellow?

Brain I think not, sir. It is but a whipping matter, sure!

Step. Why then let him do his worst, I am resolute.

[*Exit.*

SCENE, IV.

A Hall in Justice CLEMENT *'House.*

Enter CLEMENT, KNO'WELL, KITELY, Dame KITELY, TIB, CASH, COB, *and Servants.*

Clem. Nay, but stay, stay, give me leave; my chair, sirrah. You, master *Kno'well,* say you went thither to meet your son.

Kno. Ay, sir.

Clem But who directed you thither?

Kno. That did mine own man, sir.

Clem. Where is he?

Kno. Nay, I know not, now; I left him with your clerk:

Clem. My clerk? about what time was this?

Kno. Marry, between one and two, as I take it.

Clem. And what time came my man with this false message to you, master *Kitely?*

Kite. After two, sir. and appointed him to stay here for me.

Clem. Very good; but, Mrs. *Kitely,* how chance it that you were at *Cob's?* ha?

Dame. An' please you, sir, I'll tell you: my brother *Well-bred* told me, that *Cob's* house was a suspected place.——

Clem. so it appears, methinks: but on.

Dame. and that my husband used thither daily.

Clem. No matter, so he us'd himself well, mistress.

Dame. True, sir, but you know what grows by such haunts, oftentimes.

Clem. I see rank fruits of a jealous brain, mistress *Kitely;* but did you find your husband there, in that case, as you suspected?

Kite. I found her there, sir.

Clem. Did you so? that alters the case. Who gave you knowledge of your wife's being there?

Kite. Marry, that did my brother *Well-bred.*

Clem.

Clem. How, *Well-bred* first tell her, then tell you after ?
where is *Well-bred?*

Kite. Gone with my sister, sir, I know not whither.

Clem. Why, this is a mere trick, a device: you are gul-
led in this most crosly, all! Alas, poor wench, wert thou
suspected for this?

Tib. Yes, and't please you.

Clem. I smell mischief here, plot and contrivance, master
Kitely. However, if you will step into the next room
with your wife, and think cooly of matters, you'll find
some trick has been play'd you—I fear there have been
jealousies on both parts, and the wags have been merry
with you.

Kite. I begin to feel it—I'll take your counsel—will you
go in, *Dame ?*

Dame. I will have justice Mr. *Kitely.*

[*Exit* Kitely *and* Dame.

Clem. You will be a woman, Mr. *Kitely*, that I see——
How now, what's the matter ?

Enter Servant.

Serv. Sir, there's a gentleman i' the court without, desires to speak with your worship.

Clem. A gentleman ! what's he ?

Serv. A soldier, sir, he says.

Clem. A soldier ! my sword, quickly : a soldier speak
with me ! stand by, I will end your matters anon—Let
the soldier enter; now, Sir, what ha' you to say to me ?

Enter Bobadil *and* Matthew.

Bob. By your worship's favour——

Clem. Nay, keep out, sir, I know not your pretence, you
send me word, sir, you are a soldier; why, sir, you shall
be answer'd here. Here be them have been among sol-
diers. Sir your pleasure.

Bob. Faith, sir so it is, this gentleman and myself have
been most uncivilly wrong'd and beaten by one *Down-
right*, a coarse fellow about the town here, and for my own
part, I protest, being a man in no sort given to this filthy
humour of quarrelling, he hath assaulted in the way of my
peace ; despoil'd me of my honour; disarm'd me of my
weapons ; and rudely laid me along in the open streets;
when I not so much as once offer'd to resist him.

Clem. O God's precious ! Is this the soldier ? Lie there,
my

my sword, 'twill make him swoon, I fear; he is not fit to
look on't, that will put up a blow.

Mat. An't please your worship he was bound to the
peace.

Clem. Why, an' he ware, sir, his hands were not
bound; were they?

Serv. There's one of the varlets of the city, sir, has
brought two gentleman here, one upon your worship's
warrant.

Clem. My warrant?

Serv. Yes, sir, the officer says, procur'd by these two.

Clem. Bid him come in. Set by this picture; what
Mr. *Down-right!* are you brought at Mr. *Fresh-water's*
suit here?

[*Enter* Down-right, Stephen, *and* Brain-worm.

Down. I' faith, sir. And here's another brought at my
suit.

Clem. What are you, sir.

Step. A gentleman, sir? O, uncle!

Clem. Uncle? who, master *Kno'well?*

Kno. Ay, sir, this is a wise kinsman of mine.

Step. God's my witness, uncle, I am wronged here mon-
strously; he charges me with stealing of his cloke, and
would I might never stir, if I did not find it in the street by
chance.

Down. O, did you find it, now? you said you bought
it ere-while.

Step. And you said I stole it; nay, now my uncle is
here, I'll do well enough with you.

Clem. Well, let this breathe a while; you that have cause
o complain there, stand forth: had you my warrant for
this gentleman's apprehension?

Bob. Ay, an't please your worship.

Clem. Na, do not speak in passion so: where had you it?

Bob. Of your clerk, sir.

Clem. That's well, an' my clerk can make warrants and
my hand not at 'em! Where's the warrant? Officer, have
you it?

Brain. No, sir, your worship's man, master *Formal*, bid
me do it for these gentlemen, and he would be my discharge.

Clem. Why, master *Down-right*, are you such a novice as be serv'd, and never see the warrant?

Down. Sir, he did not serve it on me.

Clem. No, how then?

Down. Marry, sir, he came to me, and said he must serve it, and he would use me kindly, and so——

Clem. O, God's pity, was it so, sir? He must serve it? give me a warrant, I must serve one too—you knave, you slave, you rogue, do you say you must, sirrah? away with him to the jail, I'll teach you a trick, for your *must*, sir.

Brain. Good sir, I beseech you be good to me.

Clem. Tell him, he shall to the jail, away with him, I say.

Brain. Nay, sir, if you will commit me, it shall be for commiting more than this: I will not lose by my travel any grain of my fame certain.   [*Throws off his disguise.*

Clem. How is this?

Kno. My man, *Brain-worm!*

Step. O yes, uncle, *Brain-worm* has been with my cousin *Edward* and I all this day.

Clem. I told you all there was some device.

Brain. Nay, excellent justice, since I have laid myself thus open to you, now, stand strong for me; both with your sword and your ballance.

Clem. Body o' me, a merry knave! give me a bowl of sack; if he belongs to you, master *Kno'well*, I bespeak your patience.

Brain. That is it I have most need of. Sir, if you'l pardon me only, I'll glory in all the rest of my exploits.

Kno. Sir, you know I love not to have my favours come hard from me. You have your pardon: though I suspect you shroudly for being of councel of my son against me.

Brain. Yes, faith, I have, sir; though you retain'd me doubly this morning for yourself; first, as *Brain-worm*, after as *Fitz-Sword.* I was your reform'd soldier, sir, 'twas I sent you to *Cob's* upon the errand without end.

Kno. Is it possible! or that thou should disguise thyself so as I should not know thee?

Brain. O, sir! this has been the day of my metamorphosis; it is not that shape alone that I have run through to day. I brought master *K tely* a message too, in the form of master Justice's man here, to draw him out o' the way, as well as your worship; while master *Well-bred*

mgiht

might make a conveyance of mistress *Bridget* to my young master.

Kno. My son is not married I hope.

Brain. Faith, sir, they are both, as sure as love, a priest, and three thousand pounds, which is her portion, can make 'em : and by this time are ready to bespeak their wedding supper at the *wind-mill*, except some friend here prevent 'em, and invite 'em home.

Clem. Marry that will I. I thank thee for putting me in mind on't. Sirrah, go you and fetch them hither upon my warrant. Neither's friends have cause to be sorry, if I know the young couple aright. But I pray thee, what hast thou done with my man, *Formal?*

Brain. Faith, sir, after some ceremony past, as making him drunk, first with story, and then with wine (but all in kindness) and the stripping him to his shirt ; I left him in that cool vein, departed, sold your worship's warrant to these two, pawned his livery for that varlet's gown to serve it in : and thus have brought myself, by my activity, to your worship's consideration.

Clem. And I will consider thee in a cup of sack. Here's to thee, which having drank off, this is my sentence. Pledge me. Thou hast done, or assisted to nothing, in my judgment, but deserves to be pardon'd for the wit o' the offence. Go into the next room ; let master *Kitely* into this whimsical business, and if he does not forgive thee, he has less mirth in him, than an honest man ought to have. How now, who are these ?

Enter Ed. KNO'WELL, WELL-BRED, *and* BRIDGET.

O, the young company. Welcome, welcome, Give you joy. Nay, Mrs. *Bridget*, Blush not ; you are not so fresh a bride, but the news of it is come hither before your Master Bridegroom, I have made your peace, give me your hand : so will I for all the rest ere you forsake my roof.

All. We are the more bound to your humanity, sir.

Clem. Only these two have so little of man in 'em, they are no part of my care.

Step. And what shall I do ?

Clem. O ! I had lost a sheep, an' he had not blated. Why, sir you shall give Mr. *Down-right* his cloke : and I will intreat him to take it. A trencher and a napkin you
shall

shall have in the buttery, and keep *Cob* and his wife company here; whom I will intreat first to be reconciled; and you to endeavour with your wit to keep 'em so.

Step. I'll do my best,

Clem. Call master *Kitely* and his wife there.

Enter Mr. KITELY *and* Dame KITELY.

Did I not tell you there was a plot against you? did I not smell it out, as a wise magistrate ought? have not you trac'd, have not you found it, eh! master *Kitely?*

Kite. I have.——I confess my folly, and own I have deserved what I have suffer'd for it. The trial has been severe, but it is past. - All I have to ask now, is, that as my folly is cur'd, and my persecutors forgiven, my shame may be forgotten.

Clem. That will depend upon yourself, master *Kitely;* do not you yourself create the food for mischief, and the mischievous will not play upon you.—But come, let a general reconciliation go round, and let all discontents be laid aside.—You Mr. *Down-right*, put off your anger.—You Mr. *Kno'well*, your cares.—And do you, master *Kitely* and your wife, put off your jealousies.

Kite. Sir, thus they go from me; kiss me, my wife.
See, what a drove of horns fly in the air,
Wing'd with my cleansed, and my credulous breath!
Watch 'em suspicious eyes, watch where they fall.
See, see! on heads, that think they've none at all!
O, what a plenteous world of this will come,
When air rains horns, all may be sure of some!

Clem. 'Tis well, 'tis well! This night we'll dedicate to friendship, love, and laughter. Master Bridegroom, take your bride and lead; every one a fellow. Here is my mistress——*Brain-worm*.! to whom all my addresses of courtship shall have their reference; whose adventures this day, when our grand-children shall hear to be made a fable, I doubt not but it shall find both spectators and applause.

THE END.

THE FAIRIES.

DRAMATIS PERSONÆ.

THESEUS, Duke of *Athens* Mr. *Beard.*
EGEUS, an *Athenian* Lord, Mr *Chamnys.*
LYSANDER, in Love with HERMIA, Sig. *Curioni.*
DEMETRIUS, in Love with HERMIA, Mr. *Atkins.*
HIPPOLITA, Princes of the *Amazons*, betrothed to THESEUS, Mrs. *Jefferson.*
HERMIA, Daughter to EGEUS in Iove with LYSANDER, Sig. *Passerini.*
HELENA, in love with DEME-
TRIUS Mrs. *Vernon.*
OBERON, King of the *Fairies*, Master *Reinbolt.*
TITANIA, Queen of the *Fairies,* Miss *Young.*
PUCK, or ROBIN GOODFELLOW, a *Fairy.* Master *Moore.*
A FAIRY, Master *Evans.*
Other Fairies *attending the King and Queen.*
The SCENE *lies in Athens, and in a Wood not far from it.*

ACT I.   SCENE I.

Enter THESEUS *and* HIPPOLITA *with Attendants.*

Theseus.

NOW fair *Hippolita*, our nuptial hour
Draws on apace, four happv days bring
Another moon: but oh, methinks, how slow
This old moon wanes! she lingers mv desires.
Awake the pert and nimble spirit of mirth:
Turn melancholy forth to funerals;
The pale companion is not or our pomp.
Hippolita I woo'd thee with mv sword,
But I will wed thee in another kev,
With pomp, wth triumph, and with revelling.

AIR.

AIR.

Pierce the air with sounds of joy,
Come, Hymen, with the winged boy, .
Bring song and dance and revelry.
From this our great solemnity,
Drive care and sorrow far away;
Let all be mirth and holiday!

SCENE. II.

Enter EGEUS, HERMIA, LYSANDER, *and* DEMETRIUS.
EGEUS.

Happy be *Theseus,* our renowned Duke.
Thes. Thanks, good *Egeus.*
Egeus. Full of vexation, come I with complaint
Against my child, my daughter *Hermia.*
Stand Forth, *Demetrius;* my noble lord,
This man hath my consent to marry her.
Stand forth, *Lysander :* and my gracious duke,
This man hath witch'd the bosom of my child;
With cunning hath he filch'd my daughter's heart,
Turn'd her obedience, to stubborn harshness.
Therefore do I claim the *Athenian* law. ·
As she is mine I may dispose of her:
Which shall be either, to *Demetrius,*
Or to her grave.
  Thes. What say you, *Hermia?* be advis'd, fair maid,
To you your father should be as a God;
One that compos'd your beauties.
  Her. I would my father look'd but with my eyes.
  Thes. Rather your eyes must with his judgment look.
  Her. I do beseech your grace, that I may know
The worst of it if I refuse *Demetrius.*
  Thes. Either to die the death, or to abjure
For ever the society of men.
For aye to be in shady cloister mew'd, ·
To live a barren sister all your life.
Chanting faint hymns to the cold fruitless moon.
Thrice blessed they that master so their blood,
To undergo such maiden pilgrimage!
But Earthlier happy is the rose distill'd,
Than that, which, withering on the virgin thorn,

Grows, lives, and dies, in single blessedness.

Her. So will I grow, so live, so die, my Lord,
Ere I will yield my virgin patient up
Unto his lordship, to whose unwish'd yoke
My soul consents not to give sovereignty.

A I R.

With mean disguise let others nature bide,
    And mimick virtue with the paint of art :
I scorn the cheat, of reason's foolish pride,
    And boast the graceful weakness of my heart :
The more I think, the more I feel my pain,
    And learn the more each heav'nly charm to prize,
While fools, too light for passion, safe remain,
    And dull sensation keeps the stupid wise.

Thes. Take time to pause, and by the next new moon
The sealing day betwixt my love and me,
Upon that day either prepare to die,
For disobedience to your father's will;
Or else to wed *Demetrius,* as he would;
Or on *Diana's* altar to protest,
For aye, austerity and single life.
  Egeus. Hermia is mine, and all my right ot her
Do estate unto *Demetrius.*
  Lys. Demetrius (I'll avouch it to his head,)
Made love to *Nedar's* daughter *Helena,*
And won her soul, and she, sweet lady, doats,
Devoutly doats, doats in idolatry,
Upon this spotted and inconstant man.
  Thes. I must confess that I have heard so much
But come, *Egeus,* and *Demetrius* come,
I have some private schooling for you both :
Of this no more—Let not these jars untune
Our hearts, high-strung to harmony and love.

A I R *and* C H O R U S.

Joy alone shall employ us
No griefs shall annoy us,
No sighs the sad heart shall betray ;
Let the vaulted roof ring,
Let the full chorus sing,
Blest Theseus *and* Hippolita !

[Exeunt.
SCENE

SCENE III.

Manent Lysander *and* Hermia.

Lysander.

How now, my love? why is your cheek so pale?
How chance the roses there do fade so fast?
Her. Belike for want of rain, which I could well
Beteem them from the tempest of mine eyes.
  Lys. Hermia, for ought that ever I could read,
Could ever hear by tale or history,
The course of true love never did run smooth,
But either it was different in blood,
Strangely misgrafted in respect of years,
Or else it stood upon the choice of friends,
Or if there were a sympathy of choice;
War, death, or sickness, did lay siege to it:
Making it momentary as a sound,
Swift as a shadow, short as is a dream.
  Her. If then true lovers have been ever crost,
It stands as an edict in destiny;
Then let us teach our trial patience;
Because it is a customary cross,
As due to love, as thoughts and dreams and sighs,
Wishes and tears, poor *Fancy's* followers!
  Lys. A good persuasion, therefore hear me, *Hermia:*
Steal forth thy fathers house to-morrow night,
And in the wood, a league without the town,
There will I stay for thee, there marry thee,
And fly from *Athens* and her rigorous laws.
Thou know'st the place, where I did meet thee once
To do observance to the morn of May.

AIR.

When that gay season did us lead
To the tann'd hay-cock in the mead,
When the merry bells rung round,
And the rebecks brisk did sound,
When young and old came forth to play
On a sunshine holyday.

Let

Let us wander far away
Where the nibbling flocks do stray
O'er the mountains barren breast,
Where labouring clouds do often.rest,
O'er the meads with duizies py'd.
Shallow brooks and rivers wide.

Her. My good *Lysander,*
I swear to thee, by *Cupid's* strongest bow,
By his best arrow with the golden head.
By the simplicity of *Venus'* doves,
By that which knitteth souls, and prospers loves,
By all the vows that men have ever broke,
In number more than ever women spoke,
Hermia to-morrow in the depth of night
Will meet *Lysander,* and attempt her flight.

SCENE. IV.

Enter HELENA.

Her, Good speed, fair *Helena,* whither away?
Hel. Call you me fair? that fair again unsay,
Demetrius loves you,

AIR.

O Hermia fair, O happy, happy fair,
Your eyes are load-stars, and your tongue's sweet air ;
More tuneable than lark to shepherd's ear,
When wheat is green, when hawthorn buds appear :
O teach me how you look, and with what art
You sway the motion of your lover's heart.

Her. I frown upon him, yet he loves me still.
Hel. Oh that your frowns would teach my smiles such
    skill !
Her. Take comfort; he no more shall see my face,
Lysander and myself will fly this place.

AIR.

Before the time I did Lysander *see,*
Seem'd Athens *like a paradise to me :*

O then

O then, what graces in my love do dwell,
That he hath turn'd a heaven into a hell!

Lys. *Helen*, to you our minds we will unfold:
To-morrow night, when *Phoebe* doth behold
Her silver visage in the wa'try glass,
Decking with liquid pearl the bladed grass,
(A time that lovers flights doth still conceal)
Through *Athens* gate have we devis'd to steal.
Her. And in the wood, where often you and I
Upon faint primrose beds were wont to lie,
Emptying our bosoms of their counsels sweet;
There my *Lysander* and myself shall meet,
And thence from *Athens* turn away our eyes,
To seek new friends and strange companions.
Farewell, sweet play-fellow.
Lys. *Helen*, adieu,
As you on him, *Demetrius* doat on you.

[*Exeunt Lys. and Her.*

S C E N E V.

HELENA,

I'll tell *Demetrius* of fair *Hermia's* flight;
Then to the wood will he to-morrow night
Pursue her; I'll at distance steal behind,
His sight alone will ease my tortur'd mind.
How happy some o'er other some can be?
Through *Athens* I am thought as fair as she.
But what of that, *Demetrius* thinks not so.

A I R.

Love looks not with the eyes but with the mind,
And therefore is wing'd Cupid painted blind :
Nor hath love's mind of any judgment taste ;
Wings, and no eyes, figure unheedy haste,
And therefore is love said to be a child
Because in choice he often is beguil'd.

                          SCENE

SCENE VI.

Changes to a Forest.

Enter a FAIRY *at one Door, and* PUCK *at another.*

Puck. How now, spirit, whither wander you?
Fair. Over hill, over dale,
Through bush, through briar,
Over park, over pale,
Through flood, through fire,
I do wander every where,
Swifter than the moon's sphere;
And I serve the *Fairy* Queen,
To dew her orbs upon the green.
  Puck. I must go seek some dew drops-here,
And hang a pearl in every cowslip's ear.

AIR.

Where the bee sucks, there lurk I,
In a cowslip's bell I lie,
There I couch when owls do cry:
On the bat's back I do fly
After sun-set merrily,
Merrily, merrily, shall I live now,
Under the blossom that hangs on the bough.

The king doth keep his revels here to night,
Take heed the queen come not within his sight,
For *Oberon* is passing fell and wrath,
Because that she, as her attendant, hath
A lovely boy, and he would have the child V
Knight of his train, to trace the forests wild.
But make room, *Fairy*, here comes *Oberon*.
  Fair. And here my mistress; would that we were gone.

SCENE VII.

Enter OBERON *and his Train at one door.* QUEEN *and her
Train at another.*

OBERON.

I'll meet by moon-light, proud *Titania*.

Queen.

Queen. What, jealous *Oberon?* *Fairies,* skip hence,
I have forsworn his bed and company.
    Ober. Why should *Titania* cross her *Oberon ?*
I do but beg a little changeling boy.
    Queen. The *Fairy land* buys not the child of me;
His mother was a votress of my order,
And in the spiced *Indian* air by night
Full often she hath gossipt by my side;
But she being mortal, of that boy did die,
And for her sake I do rear up her child,
And for her sake I will not part with him.
    Ober. How long within this wood intend you stay
    Queen. Perchance, 'till after *Theseus'* wedding-day.
If you will patiently dance in our round,
And see our moon-light revels go-with us :
If not, shun me, and I will spare your haunts.
    Ober. Give me that boy, and I will go with thee.
    Queen. Not for thy *Fairy* kingdom.   Elves away.

AIR.

O'er the smooth enamell'd green,
Where no print of step hath been,
Follow me as I sing,
And touch the warbled string.

                    [*Exeunt Queen and train.*

    Ober. Well, go thy way; thou shalt not from this grove
Till I torment thee for this injury—
My gentle *Puck,* come hither; thou remember'st
I shew'd thee once a flower, fetch me that herb.
The juice of it on sleeping eye-lids laid,
Will make a man or woman madly doat
Upon the next live creature that it sees.
    Puck. I'll put a girdle round about the earth
In forty minutes.

                    [*Exit Puck.*

    Ober. Having once this juice,
I'll watch *Titania* when she is asleep,
And drop the liquor of it in her eyes :
The next thing which she waking looks upon,
She shall pursue it with the soul of love ;
(And ere I take this charm from off her sight
(As I can take it with another herb)
I'll make her render up her page to me.

K 4   AIR.

AIR.

Come follow, follow me
Ye fairy elves that be,
O'er tops of dewy grass,
So nimbly do we pass,
The young and tender stalk
Ne'er bends where we do walk.

ACT II. SCENE I.

An open plain bordered with wood.

Enter OBERON.

OBERON.

WHO comes here ? I am invisible,
And I will hear their conference.

Enter DEMETRIUS, HELENA *following him.*

DEMETRIUS.

Hence, get thee gone, and follow me no more.
You do impeach your modesty too much,
To leave the city, and commit yourself
Into the hands of one that loves you not,
To trust the opportunity of night,
And the ill counsel of a desart place,
　Helen. It is not night when I do see your face,
Nor doth this wood lack worlds of company,
For you, in my respect, are all the World.
　Deme. I'll run from thee and hide me in the brakes,
And leave thee to the mercy of wild beasts.
　Helen. The wildest hath not such a heart as you ;
Run when you will the story shall be chang'd ;
Apollo flies, and *Daphne* holds the chase.
　Deme. I will not stay thy questions, let me go,
Or if you follow me, do not believe
But I shall do thee mischief in the wood.

AIR,

AIR.

HELENA.

Love made the lovely Venus burn,
In vain, and for the cold youth mourn;
A youth as cold as you, but he
At least pursued no other she.
So have I seen the lost Clouds pour,
Into the sea a useless shower,
And the vexed sailors curse the rain,
For which poor shepherds pray'd in vain.

[Exeunt Dem, and Hel.

Ober. Fare thee well, nymph, ere he doth leave this
    grove,
Thou shalt fly him, and he shall seek thy love.

SCENE II.

Enter PUCK.

Welcome wanderer, hast thou the flower there?
Puck. Ay, there it is.
  Ober. I pray thee give it me;
I know a bank whereon the wild thyme blows,
Th re sleeps *Titania*, some time of the night;
I with the juice of this will streak her eyes,
And make her full of hateful fantasies,
Take thou some of it, and seek thro' this grove;
A sweet *Athenian* lady is in love
With a disdainful youth; anoint his eyes,
But do it when the next thing he espies
May be the lady.   Thou shalt know the man,
By the *Athenian* garments he hath on,
Effect it with some care, that he may prove
More fond of her, than she upon her love.

[Exit.
SCENE

K 5

SCENE III.

Enter QUEEN *with her Train.*

QUEEN.

Come, now a roundel, and a *Fairy* song:
Then for a third part of a minute hence,
Some to kill cankers in the musk-rose-buds,
Some war with rear-mice for their leathern wings,
To make my small elves coats : And some keep back
The clamorous owl, that nightly hoots, and wonders
At our queint spirits.

AIR.

You spotted snakes with double-tongue,
 Thorny hedghogs, be not seen,
Newts and blind worms do no wrong,
 Come not near the Fairy *Queen.*
 Philomel with melody,
 Sing in your sweet lullaby :
Lulla, lulla, lullaby, lulla, lulla, lullaby,
 Never harm, nor spell nor charm,
Come the Fairy's *pillow nigh,*
 So good night with lullaby.

Weaving spiders come not here ;
 Hence, you long-legg'd spinners, hence :
Beetles black approach not near,
 Worm nor snail do no offence.
 Philomel with melody
 Sing in your sweet lullaby.
Lulla, lulla, lullaby, lulla, lulla, lullaby,
 Never harm, nor spell nor charm
Come the Fairy's *pillow nigh,*
 So good night with lullaby.

Exeunt Fairies.

Enter OBERON.

Ober. What thou seest when thou dost wake
 It for thy true love take ;

         Love

Love and languish for his sake :
Be it ounce, or cat, or bear,
Pard, or boar, with bristled hair,
In thy eye what shall appear,
When thou wak'st it is thy dear;
Wake when some vile thing is near.

      [OBERON *squeezes the juice on her eyes and Exit*

SCENE IV.

Enter LYSANDER *and* HERMIA.

[LYSANDER,

Fair love, you're faint with wandering in the wood ;
   And, to speak truth, I have forgot our way :
We'll rest us, *Hermia,* if thou think it good,
   And tarry for the comfort of the day.
   Her. Be't so, *Lysander;* find you out a bed,
For I upon this bank will rest my head,
   Lys. One turf shall serve as pillow for us both,
One heart, one bed, two bosoms, and one troth.

D U E T T E.

   Not the silver doves that fly,
     Yoak'd in Cytherea's car ;
   Are so beauteous to the eye,
     Are so choicely match'd by far.
   Not the wings that bear aloft
     The gay sportive God of love,
   Are so lovely bright and soft.
     Or with more consent do move.

Lys. There will I lie ; sleep give thee all his rest.
Her. With half that wish, the wisher's eyes be prest.
                  [*They sleep.*

SEENE V.

Enter PUCK.

PUCK.

Through the forest have I gone.
But *Athenian* find I none
On whose eyes I might approve,
This flower's force in stirring love;
Night and silence ! who is here ?
Weeds of *Athens* he doth wear;
This is he my Master said,
Despised the *Athenian* maid !
And here the maiden sleeping sound
On the damp and dirty ground.
Churl, upon thy eyes I throw,
All the power this charm doth owe
When thou wak'st, let love forbid,
Sleep his seat on thy eye-lid:
So awake when I am gone,
For I must now to *Oberon,*   *[Exit Puck.*

SCENE VI.

Enter DEMETRIUS, *and* HELENA *following.*

HELENA

Stay, tho' thou kill me, sweet *Demetrius !*
  Deme. I charge thee hence, and do not haunt me thus.
  Helen. O wilt thou, darling, leave me ? do not so.
  Deme, Stay, on thy peril, I alone will go.   *[Exit Demetrius.*
  Helen. Happy is *Hermia.* wheresoe'er she lies;
For she hath blessed and attractive eyes.
How came her eyes so bright ? not with salt tears,
If so, my eyes are oftener wash'd than hers.
But who is here ? *Lysander,* on the ground ;
Dead or asleep, I see no blood no wound:
Lysander if you live, good Sir, awake.

                                   Say,

AIR.

LYSANDER.

Say, lovely dream, where could'st thou find
Shades to counterfeit that face;
Colours of this glorious kind,
Come not from any mortal place;
In heaven itself thou sure wert drest,
With that angel-like disguise,
Thus deluded am I blest,
And see my joy with closed eyes.

Transparent *Helen*, nature here shews art,
That through thy bosom makes me see thy heart:
Where is *Demetrius?* Oh, how fit a word
Is that vile name, to perish on my sword?
  Hel. Do not say so, *Lysander*, say not so?
What tho' he loves your *Hermia*, yet you know,
That *Hermia* still loves you; then be content.
  Lys. Content with *Hermia?* no, I do repent
The tedious minutes I with her have spent;
Not *Hermia*, but *Helena* now I love:
Who will not change a raven for a dove?
  Hel. Wherefore was I to this keen mock'ry born?
When at your hands did I deserve this scorn?
But fare you well. Perforce I must confess,
I thought you lord of more true gentleness.
                  [Exit HELENA.

  Lys. She sees not *Hermia, Hermia* sleep thou there,
Helen is now *Lysander's* only Care.
                  [Exit LYSANDER.

SCENE VI.

HERMIA.

  Help me, *Lysander*, help me, do thy best,
To pluck this crawling serpent from my breast:
Ay me, for pity, what a dream was here?
Lysander, speak, I almost swoon with fear;
Methought a serpent eat my heart away,
And you sat smiling at his cruel prey:
Lysander, what remov'd? *Lysander*, lord!
What out of hearing, gone? no sound, no word?

                        Where

Where are you, speak? alas! he is not near.

AIR.

Sweet soothing hope, whose magic-art,
　Transforms our nights to day,
Dispel the clouds, that wrap my heart,
　With thy enliv'ning ray:
Thus when the sky, with noxious steams
　Has been obscur'd a-while,
The sun darts forth his piercing beams,
　And makes all nature smile.

[*Exit* Hermia.

SCENE VII.

Enter Oberon *and train, meeting* Puck.

Puck.

Hail, and welcome, gracious king,
And all the *Fairies* that you bring;
But wherefore do you thus delay?
The gentle night is prest to pay
The usury of long delights,
She owes to our protracted rites.
　Obe. My fairy sprights, brief be your sports to night,
Much business we have yet to do ere light.
The queen in slumber wrapt near yonder brake,
At cautious distance watch her till she wake;
Then know, what 'tis that first comes in her eye,
That she must doat on in extremity:
Her new-born flame will all her thoughts employ,
Than I for asking, get her *Indian* boy.
This done, I will her charmed eye release
From vision gross, and all things shall be peace.

AIR.

But you must not long delay,
　Nor be weary yet,
There's no time to cast away,
　Or for Fairies to forget
The virtue of their feet;
Knotty legs and plants of clay.
Seek for ease, and love delay:

But

But with you it still should fare,
As with the air, of which you are.

By the stars glimmering light
Aided by the glow-worm's fire,
Every elf and fairy spright,
Hop as light as bird from briar.
Now, now, begin to set
Your spirits in an active heat;
Instruct your nimble feet,
The velvet ground to beat:
To-morrow be it seen
Where we to-night have been.
Sing and dance around this place,
Hand in hand, with *Fairy* grace.

Dance.

AIR.

Now until the break of day,
Through this wood each Fairy stray,
And your night-sports celebrate:
Every Fairy take his gait,
Trip away, make no stay,
Meet me all by break of day.

Exeunt.

ACT III.   SCENE I.

A FOREST.

Enter OBERON *and* PUCK.

OBERON.

HOW now, mad spright,
　　What night-rule now about this haunted grove?
Puck. My Mistress with a patch'd fool, is in love.
Near to her close and consecrated bower,
This clown with others had rehears'd a play
Intended for great *Theseus'* nuptial day.
When, starting from her bank of mossy-down,
Titania wak'd, and straightway lov'd the clown.
　Obe. This falls out better than I could devise.
But hast thou latched the *Athenian's* eyes?

Puck.

Puck. That is finish'd too; I took him sleeping;
And the *Albenian* woman by his side,
That when he wakes, of force she must be ey'd.

SCENE II.

Enter DEMETRIUS *and* HERMIA,.

OBERON.

Stand close this is the same *Albenian*.
   Puck This is the woman, but not this the man.
   Deme. O, why rebuke you him that loves you so?
   Her. If thou hast slain *Lysander* In his sleep,.
Then kill me too—
The sun was not so true unto the day,
As he to me. Would he have stolen away
From sleeping *Hermia?*
It cannot be but thou hast murder'd him,
So should a murderer look, so dread, so grim—
   Deme. So should the murder'd look, and so should I
Pierc'd thro' the heart, with your stern cruelty:
Yet you, the murderer, Look as bright and clear,
As yonder *Venus* in her glimmering sphere.

AIR.

HERMIA.

How calm's the sky, how undisturb'd the deep,
Nature is hush't the very tempests sleep;
The drowsy winds breathe gently thro' the trees,
And silent on the beach repose the seas:
Love only wakes, the storm that tears my breast
For ever rages and distracts my rest.
O love, relentless love, tyrant accurst,
In desarts bred, by cruel tygers nurst.

                                         [*Exit* HERMIA.

Deme. There is no following her in this fierce vein,
Here, brooding o'er my thoughts, I will remain,
                                       [*Lies down.*

SCENE III.

OBERON.

What hast thou done? thou hast mistaken quite,
And laid thy love-juice on some true love's sight,

                                       About

About the wood go swifter than the wind,
And *Helena* of *Athens* see thou find.
By some illusion, see thou bring her here;
I'll charm his eyes against she doth appear.
 Puck Swifter than arrow from the *Tartar's* bow,
I go, I go, look how I go.   [*Exit* PUCK.
 Obe. Let soothing sound, his senses chain,
And spread oblivion o'er his brain.
       Anoints DEMETRIUS's *eye.*

A I R.

Flower of this purple dye,
Hit with Cupids *archery,*
Sink in apple of his eye; .
When his love he doth espy,
Let her shine as gloriously
As the Venus *of the sky.*
When thou wak'st if she be by,
Beg of her for remedy.

     Enter PUCK.

 Puck Captain of our *Fairy* band,
Helena is near at hand
And the youth, mistook by me,
Pleading for a lover's fee.
 Obe. Stand aside : the noise they make
Will cause *Demetrius* to awake.

S C E N E IV.

   Enter LYSANDER *and* HELENA.

LYSANDER.

Why should you think that I should woo in scorn ?
Scorn and derision never came in tears.
Look, when I vow I weep ; and vows so born,
In their nativity all truth appears.
 Hel. These vows are *Hermia's.*

             AIR.

AIR.

LYSANDER.

Do not call it sin in me,
That I am forsworn for thee
Thou for whom even Jove *would swear,*
Juno *but an Æthiop were,*
And deny himself for Jove,
Turning mortal for thy love.

DEMETRIUS. *(awaking.)*

O *Helen*, goddess ! nymph, perfect, divine,
To what my love, shall I compare thine eyne?
Crystal is muddy ; O how ripe in show
Thy lips, those kissing cherries tempting grow !
Hel. Can you not hate me, as I know you do,
But you must join in flouts to mock me too ?
Lys. You love *Hermia*, therefore with all my heart,
In *Hermia's* love, I yield you up my part ;
And yours in *Helena* to me bequeath.
Hel. Never did mockers waste more idle breath.
Deme. Lysander, keep thy *Hermia*, I will none,
If e'er I lov'd her, all that love is gone.
And now *Helen*, it is home returned.

SCENE V.

Enter HERMIA.

Her. Dark night, that from the eye his function take
The ear more quick of apprehension makes : -
Mine ear, I thank it, brought me to thy sound.
But why unkindly didst thou leave me so ?
Lys. Why should he stay, whom love doth press to go
Her. What love could press *Lysander* from my side ?
Lys. Lysander's love, fair *Helena.*
Her. You speak not as you think: it cannot be.
Hel. Injurious *Hermia*, most ungrateful maid,
Have you conspir'd, have you with these contriv'd
To bait me with this foul derision ?
Is all the counsel that we two have shar'd,
The sisters vows, the hours that we have spent,

When

When we have chid the hasty footed time,
For parting us: O! and is all forgot.
But fare ye well, 'tis partly mine own fault,
Which death or absence soon shall remedy.

A I R.

Since Hermia neglects me,
And He thus rejects me,
My pride with my heart shall contend,
I'll quit love for ever,
Our friendship dissever,
Adieu to my lover and friend.

My easy believing,
Your guiles and deceiving,
No more my fond heart shall betray ;
I'll roam desart places,
I'll fly human faces,
From friendship and love fly far away.
                    [*Exit* HELENA.

Lys. Stay, gentle *Helena,* hear my excuse ;
My love, my life, my soul, fair *Helena.*
Deme. I say I love her more than thou, *Lysander.*
Lys. If thou say so, withdraw, and prove it too.
Deme. Quick, come.
Her. *Lysander,* whereto tends all this ?
Am not I *Hermia ?* are not you *Lysander ?*
Lys. Therefore be out of hope, for it is true,
That I do hate thee, and love *Helena.*
                    [*Exeunt* DEM. *and* LYS.

A I R.

Come pride, love-disdaining,
Hence sighs and complaining,
Affection is banish'd my breast—
By nature tho' tender,
To rage I surrender
That heart which soft passion possest.
Fury, revenge, and slighted love,
Have to a serpent chang'd the dove.

                    [*Exit.*

                    SCENE

S C E N E VI.

Enter OBERON *and* PUCK.

A I R

OBERON.

Sigh no more, ladies, sigh no more,
   Men were deceivers ever ;
One foot on sea, and one on shore,
   To one thing constant never.

This is thy negligence: still thou mistak'st:
Or else commit'st thy knaveries willingly.
Thou seest these lovers seek a place to fight;
Hie therefore, *Fairy*, over-cast the night,
Then crush this herb into *Lysander's* eye,
Whose liquor hath this virtuous property,
To take from thence all error with its might,
And make his eye-balls rowl with wonted sight.
   Puck. Where is our *Fairy Queen*, my high-grac'd lord?
   Obe. Within the wood there, on a daisy bank
Sleeping she lies, her patch'd fool by her side;
Her dotage now I do begin to pity,
And with this herb will take the charm away:
When next she wakes, all this derision
'Shall seem a dream and fruitless vision.
     This, this I'll infuse,
     Whose sovereign dews
Shall clear each film that cloud her sight;
And you her crystal humours bright,
From noxious vapours purg'd and free,
     Shall be as you were wont to be.

                  [*Exit* OBERON.

A I R.

PUCK.

Up and down, up and down,
I will lead them up and down:
I am fear'd in field and town,
Goblin, lead them up and down.

                      [*Exit*.
SCENE

SCENE VII.

Enter OBERON, and QUEEN from the wood.

QUEEN.

My *Oberon!* what visions have I seen!
Ober. Silence a-while ;
Titania, musick call, and strike more dead
Than sleep, the sense of all these lovers.
Queen. Musick, ho, musick ; such as charmeth sleep.

AIR.

Orpheus with his lute made trees,
And the mountain tops that freeze
Bow themselves when he did sing ;
To his musick, plants and flowers
Ever spring, as sun and showers
There had made a lasting spring.

Obe. Sound, musick ; come, my *Queen,* take hand with me
And rock the ground whereon these sleepers be
       [*Dance, and Exeunt.*

SCENE -VIII.

Enter THESEUS, HIPPOLITA, EGEUS, *and Train.*

THESEUS.

Go one of you, find out the forester,
For now our observation is perform'd;
And since we have the vaward of the day,
My love shall hear the musick of my hounds :
Uncouple in the western valley, go
Dispatch I say ; but soft, what nymphs are these

EGEUS (*looking out.*)

My lord, this is my daughter here asleep,
And this *Lysander* ; this *Demetrius* is,
I wonder at their being here together.
Thes. No doubt they rose up early to observe
The rite of *May,* and hearing our intent,

           Com-

Come here in grace of our solemnity.
But speak *Egeus*, is not this the day
That *Hermia* should give answer of her choice ?

Egeus. It is, my lord.

Thes. Go bid the huntsmen wake them with their horns

AIR.

Hark, ba.k, how the hounds and horn,
Chearly rouse the slumb'ring morn :
From the side of yon boar hill,
Thro' the high wood echoing shrill.

[They wake.

Thes. Good-morrow friends ; saint *Valentine* is past.
Begin these wood-birds but to couple now ?
How comes this concord in the world
That hatred is so far from jealousy,
To sleep by hate, and not fear enmity ?

Lys. My lord, I shall reply amazedly
Half sleep, half waking ; but, as I do think,
I came with *Hermia* hither. Our intent
Was to be gone from *Athens*, where we might be
Free from the peril of th' *Athenian* law.

Egeus. Enough, enough, my lord, you have enough
I beg the law, the law upon his head :
They would have stoll'n away, they would, *Demetrius*,
Thereby to have defeated you and me.

Deme. My lord, the joy and pleasure of mine eye,
Is only *Helena.* To her, my lord,
Was I betrothed ere I *Hermia* saw;
But like a sickness did I loath this food ;
But now in health come to my natural taste.

Thes. *Egeus*, I will overbear your will,
For in the temple, by and by with us,
These couples shall eternally be knit;
And, for the morning now is something worn,
Our purpos'd hunting shall be set aside.

Deme. These things seem small and undistinguishable,
Like far-off mountains turned into clouds.

AIR.

AIR.

HELENA.

Love's a tempest, life's the ocean,
*   Passion crost, the deep deform ;*
Rude and raging tho' the motion,
*   Virtue fearless, braves the storm :*
Storms and tempests may blow over
*   And subside to gentle gales ;*
So the poor despairing lover,
*   When least hoping, oft prevails.*

Thes. Come now (to Love and *Hymen,* let us pay
Our vows, and then with mirth conclude the day)
A fortnight hold we this solemnity,
In nightly revel, and new jollity.

CHORUS.

Hail to love, and welcome joy
Hail to the delicious boy !
See the sun from love returning,
Love's the flame in which he's burning :
Hail to love, the softest pleasure ;
Love and beauty reign for ever.

[*Exeunt.*

FINIS.

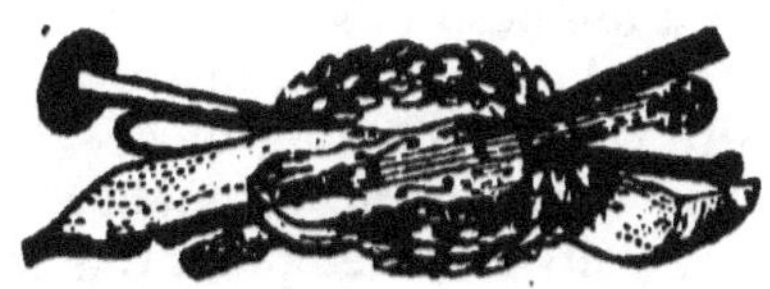

FLORIZEL

AND

PERDITA.

DRAMATIS PERSONÆ.

Leontes Mr. *Garrick.*
Polixenes Mr. *Havard.*
Camillo Mr. *Davies.*
Old Shepherd Mr. *Berry.*
Clown Mr. *Woodward.*
Autolicus Mr. *Yates.*
Cleomines Mr. *Jefferson.*
Florizel Mr. *Holland.*

Gent. Mr. *Blakes.*
Servant Mr. *Beard.*
Rogero Mr. *Walker.*
Perdita Mrs. *Cibber.*
Paulina Mis *Bennet.*
Dorcas Miss *Minors.*
Mopsa Mrs. *Bradshaw.*
Hermione Mrs. *Pritchard.*

SCENE I.

The Court of BOHEMIA.

Enter CAMILLO *and a* GENTLEMAN.

CAMILLO.

THE Gods send him safe passage to us, for he seems embarked in a tempestuous season.

Gent. I pray thee, lord *Camillo,* instruct me, what concealed matter there is in the coming of *Leontes* to *Bohemia,* shou'd so wrap our king in astonishment?

Cam. Good sign your knowledge in the court is young if you make that your question.

Gent. I wou'd not be thought too curious, but I prithee, be my tutor in this matter.

Cam. To be short then——Give it thy hearing, for my tale is well worthy of it; these two kings, *Leontes* of *Sicily,* and

Polixenes

Polixenes went to repay *Sicily* the visitation that he justly ow'd him.——Most royally, and with the utmost freedom of society, was he entertain'd both by *Leontes*, and his queen *Hermione;* a lady, whose bodily accomplishments were un-parellel'd, but by those of her own mind. The free strokes of youth and gaiety, in her extended civility to *Polixenes* (pleas'd as she was to see her lord delighted) bred in him suspicion of her conduct.

Gent. And that is an evil weed, that once taking root, needs no manure.

Cam. I then waited about the person of *Leontes*, and was alone thought worthy the participation of his jealousy. In-to my bosom he disgorg'd his monstrous secret, with no tenderer an injunction than to take off his innocent, abused guest, by poison.

Gent. To kill *Polixenes!*

Cath. Even so.——What cou'd I do? What ran evenest with the grain of my honesty I did, and have not since re-pented me ;——whisper'd *Polixenes* of the matter—left my large fortunes, and my larger hopes in *Sicily*, and on the very wing of occasion flew with him hither, no richer than my honour; and have since been ever of his bosom.

Gent. I tremble for the poor queen, left to the injuries of a powerful king, and jealous husband.

Cam. Left too in her condition! for she had some while promis'd an heir to *Sicily*, and now, mark me,—for the occasion.——

Gent. Cannot surpass my attention.——

Cam. Scarcely settled in *Bohemia* here, we are alarm'd with the arrival of *Paulina* (that excellent matron, and true friend of her unhappy queen) from whom we too soon learn how sad a tragedy had been acted in *Sicily*—the dis-honor'd *Hermione* clapp'd up in prison, where she gave the king a princess—the child (the innocent milk yet in her innocent mouth) by the king's command, expos'd; ex-pos'd even on the desarts of the kingdom ;——our *Polix-enes* being falsly deemed the father.

Gent. Poor babe; unhappy queen! tyrant *Leontes!*

Cam. what blacker title will you fix upon him, when you shall hear that *Hermione*, in her weak condition (the childbed privilege deny'd, which belongs to women of all fashion) was haul'd out to an open mockery of trial; that on this inhuman outrage (her fame being kill'd before) she

died;—in the very prison where she was deliver'd, died;
and that on her decease, *Paulina* (whose free tongue was
the king's living scourge, and perpetual remembrancer to
him of his dead queen) fled with her effects, for safety of
her life, to *Bobemia;* here——I tire you.

Gent. My king concern'd, I am too deeply interested in
the event, to be indifferent to the relation.

Cam. All this did *Leontes*, in defiance of the plain answer
of the oracle, by him consulted at *Delphi;* which now, after sixteen years occurring to his more sober thoughts, he
first thinks it probable, then finds it true, and his penitence
thereupon is as extreme, as his suspicions had been fatal.
In the course of his sorrows, as we are inform'd, twice at-
tempted on his life; and this is now his goad to the present
expedition; to make all possible atonement to his injur'd
brother *Bobemia*, and to us the fellow-sufferers in his
wrongs:—we must break off——the king and good *Paulina*——

Enter POLIXINES *and* PAULINA.

Polix. Weep not now, *Paulina*, so long-gone-by my
fortunes; this strange and unexpected visit, from *Leontes*
calls all your sorrows up a-new: but good *Paulina*, be satisfied that heav'n has will'd it so. That sixteen years absence shou'd pass unnotic'd by this king, without exchange
or gifts, letters, or embassies: and now!——I am amaz'd
as thou art; but not griev'd——

Paul. Grudge me not a tear to the memory of my queen,
my royal mistress; and there dies my resentment; now,
Leontes, welcome.

Polix. Nobody resolv'd: of him think we no more of
'till he arrives.

Cath. Hail, royal sir. If the king of *Sicily* escape this
dreadful tempest, I shall esteem him a favourite of the gods,
and his penitence effectual.

Polix. Of that fatal country *Sicily*, and of its penitent
(as we must think him) and reconcil'd king, my brother,
(whose loss of his most precious queen and child are even
now a-fresh lamented) I prithee, speak no more;—say to
me, when saw'st thou prince *Florizel*, my son? Fathers
are no less unhappy their issue not being gracious, than
they are in losing 'em, when they have approv'd their virtues.   *Cam.*

Cam. Sir, it is three days since I saw the prince; what his happier affairs may be, are to me unknown; but I have musingly noted, he is of late much retir'd from court, and is less frequent to his princely exercises than formerly he hath appear'd.

Polix. I have consider'd so much *Camillo*, and with some care; so far, that I have eyes under my service, which look upon his removedness; from whom I have this intelligence, that he is seldom from the house of a most homely shepherd—A man, they say, that from very nothing, is grown rich beyond the imagination of his neighbours.

Paul. I have heard too of such a man, who hath a daughter of most rare note; the report of her is extended more than can be thought to begin from such a cottage.

Polix. That's likewise part of my intelligence; and, I fear, the angel that plucks our son thither. Thou, *Camillo*, shalt accompany us to the place, where we will (not appearing what we are) have some questions with the shepherd; from whose simplicity I think it not uneasy to get the cause of my son's resort thither.

Cam. I willingly obey your command.

Polix. My best *Camillo!*—we must disguise ourselves.

Paul. Lest your royalty be discover'd by the attendance of any of your own train; my steward, *Dion*, shall provide disguises, and accompany your design with all secrecy.

Polix. It is well advis'd—I will make choice of some few to attend us, who shall wait at a distance from the cottage—you instruct *Dion* in the matter, while we prepare ourselves.

[*Exit* Pollixenes *and* Camillo.

Paul. (*sola.*) What fire is in my ears! can it be so?
Or are my senses cheated with a dream?
Leontes in *Bohemia!*— O most welcome,
My penitent leige—my tears were those of joy
—*Paulina*, for her royal mistress' sake,
Shall give thee welcome to this injur'd coast:
Such as the riches of two mighty kingdoms,
Bohemia join'd with fruitful *Sicily*,
Wou'd not avail to buy—*Leontes*, welcome,
Let thy stout vessel but the beating stand
Of this chaf'd sea, and thou art whole on land.

[*Exit* Paulina.

L 2   SCENE

SCENE II.

The Country by the Sea-Side. A Storm.

Enter an OLD SHEPHERD.

I would there were no age between thirteen and three and twenty; or that youth wou'd sleep out the rest: for there is nothing in the between, but getting wenches with child, wronging the ancientry, stealing, fighting——Hark you now! wou'd any but these boil'd brains of two and twenty hunt this weather! they have scar'd away two of my best sheep, which, I fear, the wolf will sooner find than the master; if any where I have 'em, 'tis by the sea-side, browzing of ivy——Yet I'll tarry till my son come: he hollow'd but even now——Whoa! ho—hoa——

Enter CLOWN.

Clown. Hoilloa! hoa!

Old Shep. What, art so near? What ail'st thou man?

Clown. I have seen such a sight!

Old Shep. Why, boy, how is it?

Clown. I wou'd you did but see how the sea chafes, how it rages, how it rakes up the shore——But I am not to say it is a sea, for it is now the sky; betwixt the firmament and it you cannot thrust a bodkin's point.——But O the most, piteous cry of the poor souls, sometimes to see 'em, and not to see 'em——But then, the ship—to see how the sea flapdragon'd it—but first how the poor souls roar'd, and the sea mock'd 'em——Then the ship, now boring the moon with her main mast, and anon swallow'd with yest and froth, as you'd thurst a cork into a hogshead.

Old Shep. Name of mercy! when was this, boy?

Clown. Now, now, I have not wink'd since I saw it! the men are not yet cold under water.

Old Shep. Wou'd I had been by the ship-side to have help'd em.

Clown. There your charity wou'd have lak'd footing.

Old Shep. Heavy matters! heavy matters!

Clown. Look! look, father—there are two of 'em cast ashore, and crawling up the rock—now they are down again—poor souls, they have no strength to keep their hold;——I will go help them.

Old Shep.

Old Shep. Run, run, boy ! thy legs are youngest.

Clown. Stay, they have found the road to the beach, and come towards us.

Old Shep. Some rich men, I warrant 'em ; that are poorer than we now.

Clown. Lord, father ! look—they are out-landish-folk, their fine clothes are shrunk in the wetting.

Enter LEONTES, *supported by* CLEOMINES.

Cleom. Bear up, my liege ;—again welcome on shore.

Leon. Flatter me not—— In death distinctions cease—
Am I on shore ; walk I on land, firm land,
Or ride I yet upon the billows backs ?
Methinks I feel the motion—who art thou ?

Cleom. Know you me not ?——Your friend *Cleomhus*.

Leon. Where are my other friends ?—What, perish'd all,

Cleom. Not a soul sav'd ! ourselves are all our crew,
Pilot, shipmaster, boatswain, sailors, all.

Leon. Land we the Gods ! Yet wherefore perish'd they.
Innocent souls ! and I, with all my guilt,
Live yet to load the earth ?——O righteous Gods !
Your ways are past the line of man to fathom.

Cleom. Waste not your small remaining strength of body
In warring with your mind. This desart waste
Has some inhabitants——Here's help at hand——
Good day, old man——

Old Shep. Never said in worse time—a better to both
your worships—command us, Sir.

Clown. You have been sweetly soak'd ; give the Gods
thanks that you are alive to feel it.

Leon. We are most thankful, Sir.

Cleom. What desarts are these same ?

Old Shep. The desarts of *Bohemia*.

Leon. Say'st thou *Bohemia* ? ye Gods *Bohemia!*
In ev'ry act your judgements are sent forth
Against *Leontes!*——Here to be wreck'd and sav'd !
Upon this coast !—— All the wrongs I have done,
Stir now afresh within me ——Did I not
Upon this coast expose my harmless infant——
Bid *Polixenes* (falsly deem'd the father)
To take this child——O hell born jealousy !
All but myself most innocent—and now
Upon this coast——Pardon, *Hermione!*

L 3

'Twas

'Twas this that sped thee to thy proper heav'n;
If from thy sainted seat above the clouds,
Thou seest my weary pilgrimage thro' life,
Loath'd, hated life, 'cause unenjoy'd with thee——
Look down, and pity me.

Cleom. Good Sir, be calm:
What's gone, and what's past help, should be past grief;
You do repent these things too sorely.

Leon. I cant repent these things, for they arc heavier
Than all my woes can stir: I must betake me
To nothing but despair—a thousand knees
Ten thousand years together, naked, fasting,
Upon a barren mountain, and still winter,
In storms perpetual, could not move the Gods
To look this way upon me.

Clown. What says he, pray? The sea has quite wash'd
away the poor gentleman's brains. Come, bring him along
to our farm; and we'll give you both a warm bed, and dry
cloathing.

Cleom. Friends, we accept your offer'd courtesy.
Come, Sir—bear up—be calm—compose your mind;
If still the tempest rages there, in vain
The Gods have sav'd you from the deep.

Leon. I'll take thy council, friend;—lend me thy arm——
Oh, *Hermoine!*   [*Leans on him.*

Cleom. Good shepherd, shew us to the cottage.

Old Shep. This way, this way——

Clown. And now the storm's blown over, father; we'll
send down *Nicholas* and his fellow to pick up the dead bodies, if any may be thrown ashore, and bury them.

Old Shep. 'Tis a good deed, boy——Help the gentlemen,
and bring them after me.   [*Exeunt.*

S C E N E. III.

Another Part of the Country.

Enter AUTOLICUS (*Singing.*

S O N G.

When daffodils begin to peere
  With hey the doxy over the dale,
Why then comes in the sweet o' th' year,
  For the red blood reigns o'er the winter's pale.

The

The white sheet bleaching on the hedge ;
With hey the sweet birds, O bow they sing !
Doth set my progging tooth on edge ;
For a quart of ale is a dish for a king.

I once serv'd prince *Florizel,* and in my time wore three-pile ; but now am out of service.

SONG.

But shall I go mourn for that my dear ?
The pale moon shines by night ;
And when I wander here and there,
I then do go most right.

My traffic is sheets ; when the kite builds, look to lesser linen.   My father nam'd me *Autolicus,* being litter'd under *Mercury ;* who, as I am, was like a snapper-up of un-considered trifles : with dice and drab I purchas'd this caparison, and my revenue is the sily cheat—for the life to come, I sleep out of the thought of it—a prize! a prize !

Enter CLOWN.

Clown. Let me see, every eleven weather tods—every tod yields pound; and odd shilling ; fifteen hundred shorn—what comes the wool to ?

Autol. If the sprindge hold, the cock's mine.   [*Aside.*

Clown. I can't do't without counters——Let me see, what am I to buy for our sheep-shearing-feast ?——Three pounds of sugar, five pounds of eurrants, rice.——What will this sister of mine do with rice ? But my father hath made her mistress of the feast, and she lays it on.——She hath made me four and twenty nosegays for the shearers—I must have saffron to colour the warden pies—mace—dates—none—that's out of my note; nutmegs, seven ; a race or two of ginger, but that I may beg ; four pound of prunes, and as many raisins o' th' sun.

Autol. (*grovelling on the ground*) Oh! that ever I was born !

Clown. In the name of me——

Autol. O help me, help me : pluck but off these rags, and then death, dea h——

Clown. Alack, poor soul, thou hast need of more rags to lay on thee, rather than to have these off.

Autol. Oh, Sir, the loathsomeness of 'em offend me, more

L 4

than

than the stripes I have received; which are mighty ones, and millions——

Clown. Alas, poor man ! a million of beating may come to a great matter.

Autol. I am robb'd; Sir, and beaten ; my money and apparel ta'en from me, and these detestable things put upon me.

Clown. What, by a horseman or a footman ?

Autol. A footman, sweet Sir; a footman.

Clown. Indeed he should be a footman, by the garments he has left with thee. If this be a horseman's coat, it hath seen very hot service.——Lend me thy hand, I'll help thee: Come, lend me thy hand.   [*Helps him up.*

Autol. Oh, good Sir; tenderly——Oh !

Clown. Alas, poor soul !

Autol. O ! good Sir; softly, good Sir; I fear, Sir my shoulder blade is out.

Clown. How now, can'st stand ?

Autol. Softly, dear Sir; good Sir, softly; you ha' done me a charitable office.   [*Picks his pocket.*

Clown. Dost lack any money ? I have a little money for thee.

Autol. No good, sweet Sir; no, I beseech you, Sir; I have a kinsman not past three-quarters of a mile hence, unto whom I was going ; I shall there have money, or any thing I want——Offer me no money, I pray you, that kills my heart.

Clown. What manner of fellow was he that robb'd you ?

Autol. A fellow, Sir, that I have known to go about with trol-my-dames: I knew him once a servant of the prince ; I cannot tell, good Sir, for which of his virtues it was ; but he was certainly whipt out of the court.

Clown. His vices, you wou'd say ; there is no virtue whipp'd out of the court; they cherish it to make it stay there, and yet it will do no more but abide.

Autol. Vices, I would say, Sir.——I know this man well, he hath been since an ape-bearer, then a process-server, a bailiff; then he compast a motion of the prodigal son, and married a tinker's wife within a mile where my land and living lies ; and having flown over many knavish professions, he settled only in rogue ; some call him *Autolicus.*

Clown. Out upon him, prig ! for my life, prig ; he——haunts wakes, fairs, and bear-beatings.

Autol

Autol. Very true, Sir; he, Sir, he; that's the rogue that put me into this apparel.

Clown. Not a more cowardly rogue in all *Bohemia*; if you had but look'd big, and spit at him, he'd have run.

Autol. I must confess to you, Sir, I am no fighter; I am false of heart that way; and that he knew, I warrant him.

Clown. How do you do now?

Autol. Sweet Sir, much better than I was; I can stand and walk; I will e'en take my leave of you; and pace soft-ly towards my kinsman's.

Clown. Shall I bring thee on thy way?

Autol. No good fac'd Sir; no good Sir; no, sweet Sir.

Clown. Then farewel——I must go buy spices for our sheep-shearing.

Autol. Prosper you, sweet Sir. Your purse is not hot e-nough to purchase your spice. I'll be with you at your sheep-shearing too——If I make not this cheat bring out another, and the shearers prove sheep, let me be unrol'd and my name put into the book of virtue.

S O N G.

Jog on, jog on, the foot-path way,
And merrily bent the stile—a—
A-merry heart goes all the day,
Your sad tires in a mile—a   [*Exit.*

A C T II.   S C E N E. I.

A Prospect of a Shepherd's Cottage.

Enter FLORIZEL *and* PERDITA.

FLORIZEL.

THESE your unusual weeds, to each part of you
Do go a life; no shepherdess but *Flora*.
Peering it *April's* front, this your sheep-shearing
Is a meeting of the petty gods,
And you the queen on't.

Perd. Sir, my gracious lord.
To chide at your extremes it not becomes me:
O pardon that I name 'em; your high self,
The gracious mark o' th' land; you have obscur'd
With a swain's wearing; and me, poor lowly maid,

L 5   Most

Most goddess-like prank'd up: but that our feasts
In every mess have folly, and the feeders
Digest it with a custom, I shou'd blush
To see you so attired; sworn, I think,
To shew myself a glass.
   Flor. I bless the time,
When my good faulcon made her flight across
Thy father's ground.
   Perd. Now *Jove* afford you cause!
To me the difference forges dread: your greatness
Hath not been us'd to fear; ev'n now I tremble
To think your father, by some accident,
Shou'd pass this way, as you did: O the fates!
How wou'd he look, to see his work, so noble,
Vilely bound up! What wou'd he say! or how
Shou'd I, in these my borrow'd flaunts, behold
The sterness of his presence?
   Flor. Apprehend.
Nothing but jollity: the Gods themselves,
Humbling their deities to love, have taken
The shapes of beasts upon 'em——*Jupiter*
Become a bull, and bellow'd; the green *Neptune*
A ram, and bleated; and the fire rob'd God,
Golden *Apollo*, a poor humble swain,
As I seem now—their transformations
Were never for a piece of beauty rarer,
Nor in a way so chaste: since my desires
Run not before mine honour, nor my lusts
Burn hotter than my faith.
   Perd. Oh, but dear Sir,
Your resolution cannot hold, when 'tis
Oppos'd, as it must be, by th' power o' th' king:
One of these two must be necessities,
Which then will speak, that thou must change this purpose
Or I my life.
   Flor. Thou dearest *Perdita*;
With these forc'd thoughts, I prithee, darken not
The mirth o' th' feast; or I'll be thine my fair,
Or not my father's; for I cannot be
Mine own, nor any thing to any, if
I be not thine. To this, I am most constant,
Tho' destiny say, no. Be merry, gentlest,
Strangle such thoughts as these, with any thing

That

That you behold the while. Your guests are coming:
Lift up your countenance; as 'twere the day
Of celebration of that nuptial, which
We two have sworn shall come.

Perd. O lady fortune,
Stand thou auspicious!

Enter OLD SHEPHERD, CLOWN, MOPSA, DORCAS; *with*
 POLIXENES, CAMILLO, *and servants.* POLIXENES, *and*
 CAMILLO, *disguised.*

Flor. See your guests approach;
Address yourself to entertain 'em sprightly,——
And let's be red with mirth.

Old Shep. Fie, daughter, when my old wife liv'd, upon
This day, she was both pantler, butler, cook,
Both dame and servant; welcom'd all, serv'd all;
Wou'd sing her song, and dance her turn; now here,
At upper end o' th' table; now i' th' middle;
On his shoulder, and his; her face o' fire,
With labour; and the thing she took to quench it,
She wou'd to each one sip: you are retir'd,
As if you were a feasted one, and not
The hostess of the meeting: pray you, bid
These unknown friend's to's welcome; for it is
A way to make us better friends, more known.
Come, quench your blushes, and present yourself,
That which you are, mistress o' th' feast: come on,
And bid us welcome to your sheep-shearing,
As your good flock shall prosper.

Perd. Sir's welcome.
It is my father's will, I shou'd take on me
The hostess-ship o' th' day; you're welcome, sirs.
Give me these flowers there, *Dorcas*; reverend sirs.
For you, there's rosemary, and rue; these keep
Seeming and savour all the winter long:
Grace and remembrance be unto you both,
                              [*To* Polixenes *and* Camillo.
And welcome to our shearing.

Polix. Shepherdess,
A fair one are you; well you fit our ages
With flowers of winter.

Perd. Here are flowers for you;   [*To others.*
Hot lavendar, mint, savoury, marjoram,

The mary-gold, that goes to bed with the sun,
And with him rises weeping: these are flowers
Of middle summer; and I think are given
To men of middle age   You're very welcome.
    Cam. I shou'd leave grazing were I of your flock,
And only live by gazing.
    Perd. Out alas!
You'd be so clean, that blasts of *January*,
Wou'd blow you thro' and thro'—now my fairest friend,
I wou'd I had some flowers o' th' spring, that might
Become your time of day; and yours, and yours,
That wear upon your virgin-branches, yet
Your maiden honours growing, daffodils,
That come before the swallow dares; and take
The winds of *March* with beauty; vi'lets dim,
But sweeter 'than the lids of *Juno's* eyes,
Or *Cytberea's* breath; pale primroses,
That die unmarried, ere they can behold
Bright *Phœbus* in his strength; gold oxlips and
The crown imperial; lillies of all kinds
The flower-de-lis being one; o' these I lack
To make your garland of, and my sweet friend,
                                              [*To* Florizel.
To strow him o'er and o'er.
    Flor. What? like a coarse?
    Perd. [*apart to* Florizel.] No, like a bank, for love to lie
        and play on.
Not like a coarse—come, come, take your flowers
Methinks, I play, as I have seen them do
In *Whitsun* pastorals: sure this robe of mine
Does change my disposition.
    Flor. What you do,
Still betters what is done—when you speak, sweet,
I'd have you do it ever; when you sing,
I'd have you buy and sell so; give alms;
Pray, so; and for the ordering your affairs,
To sing them to. When you do dance, I wish you
A wave o' th' sea, and you might ever do
Nothing but that; move still, still so,
And own no other function.   Each your doing,
So singular in each particular,
Crowns what you're doing in the present deeds,
That all your acts are queens,
                                              Perd.

Perd. O *Doricles,*
Your praises are too large ; but that your youth
And the true blood, which peeps forth fairly thro' it,
Do plainly give you out an unstained shepherd ;
With wisdom, I might fear, my *Doricles,*
You woo'd me the false way.

   Flor. I think, you have
As little skill to fear, as I have purpose
To put you to't.   But come ; our dance I pray ;
Your hand my *Perdita ;* so turtles pair
That never mean to part.

   Perd. I'll swear for 'em.

   Old Shep. Come, come, daughter. leave for a while these
private dalliances, and love-whisperings, clear up your pipes
and call, as custom is, our neighbours to our shearing.

   Perd. I will obey you.

S O N G.

I.

Come, come, my good shepherds, our flocks we must shear,
In your holy-day suits, with your lasses appear ;
The happiest of folk, are the giltless and free
And who are so giltless so happy as we ?

II.

We harbour no passions, by luxury taught,
We practise no arts, with hypocrisy fraught ;
What we think in our hearts, you may read in our eyes ;
For knowing no falshood, we need no disguise.

III.

By mode and caprice are the city dames led,
But we, as the children of nature are bred ;
By her hand alone, we are painted and dress'd
For the roses will bloom, when there's peace in the breast.

IV.

That giant, ambition we never can dread ;
Our roofs are too low, for so lofty a head ;
Content and sweet chearfulness open our door,
They smile with the simple, and feed with the poor.

V.

When love has posses'd us, that love we reveal :
Like the flocks that we feed, are the passions we feel ;

So

So harmless and simple we sport, and we play,
And leave to fine folks to deceive and betray.

Polix. This is the prettiest low born lass that ever
Ran on the green-sord; nothing she does, or seems,
But smacks of something greater than herself,
Too noble for this place.

Cam. He tells her something,
That makes her blood look out: good sooth, she is
The queen of curds and cream.

Clown. Come on—our dance—strike up.

Dorc. Mopsa must be our mistress, marry, buy some gar-
lick to mend her kissing with.

Mops. Now, in good time, musk, will not mend thine.

Dorc. Thou art a false man; did'st not thou swear, (it
was but yesternight in the tallet, over the dove house) how
that at your shearing, you wou'd this day shame *Mopsa,*—
and——

Clown. Hold ye, maidens, hold ye——not a word—we
stand upon our manners here,—come strike up.

Mops. Here's to do; marry I'll swear he promis'd me
long enough afore that in the hay-field—by the token, our
curate, came by; and whereof all our folk were gone further a field; he advis'd us to get up, and go home quickly,
for that the dew fell apace and the ground was dank, and
unhealsome; more nor that, you promis'd me gloves, and
ribbands, and kiracks at the fair,————and more nor
that——

Clown. Not a word; not a word more, wenches.

Dorc. Marry, come up! others have had promises, as well
as some ;—but I have heard old folks in the parish say, that
some folks have been proud and courtly, and falshearted
ever since some folks father found a pot of money by the
sea-side here.——But I say nothing.

Clown. Come, come' strike up.
　　　A Dance of Shepherds and Shepherdesses.

Polix. I pray good shepherd, what fair swain is this,
Who dances with your daughter.

Old Shep. They call him *Doricles;* and he boasts himself
To have a worthy breeding; but I have it.
Upon his own report, and I believe it:
He looks like sooth; he says, he loves my daughter;
I think so too; for never gaz'd the moon

Upon

Upon the water, as he'll stand and read
As 'twere my daughter's eyes; and to be plain,
I think there's not half a kiss to chuse,
Who loves the other best.

Polix. She dances featly.

Old Shep. So she does any thing, tho' I report it
Thou shou'd be silent: if young *Doricles,*
Do light upon her, she shall bring him that,
Which he not dreams of.

(POLIXINES *and* OLD SHEPHERD *talk apart*)

Enter a Servant.

O, master, if you did but hear the pedlar at the door,
you wou'd never dance again after a tabor and pipe; no,
the bagpipe cou'd not move you; he sings several tunes
faster than you'll tell money; he utters them, as he had eat-
en ballads, and all men's ears grow to his tunes.

Clown. He cou'd never come better; he shall come in:
I love a ballad but even too well; if it be doleful matter merrily set down; or a very pleasant thing indeed, and sung
lamentably.

Serv. He hath songs for man or woman of all sizes; no
milliner can fit her customers with gloves; he has the prettiest love-songs for maids, so without bawdry (which is
strange) for such delicate burthens of *jump her and thump
her:* and where some stretch-moth'd rascal wou'd, as it
were, mean mischief, and break a full gap into the matter,
he makes the maid to answer—*Whoop, do me no harm,
good man*—puts him off, slights him, with—*Whoop, do me no
harm good man.*

Polix. This is a brave fellow.

Clown. Believe me, thou talk'd of an admirable conceited
fellow; has he any unbraided wares?

Serv. He hath ribbands of all colours i' th' rainbow; points
more than all the lawyers in *Bohemia* can learnedly handle,
though they came to him by the gross; inkles, caddisses,
cambricks, lawns; why, he sings them over, as they were
Gods and Goddesses; you wou'd think a smock a she-angel
he so chants to the sleeve-hand, and the work about the
square on't.

Clown. Prithee, bring him in, and let him approach singing.

Perd.

Perd. Forewarn him that he use no scurrilous words in's songs.

Clown. You have of these pedlars, that have more in 'em than you think, sister.

Perd. Ay, good brother, or go about to think.

Enter AUTOLICUS *singing.*

Lawn, as white as driven snow,
Cyprus, black as e'er was crow ;
Gloves, as sweet as damask roses,
Mask, for faces, and for noses :
Bugle bracelets, necklace amber,
Perfume for a lady's chamber,
Golden coifs, and stomachers,
For my lads to give their dears :
Pins, and packing-sticks of steel,
What maids lack from head to heel :
Come buy of me, come ; come buy, come buy ;
Buy lads, or else your lasses cry,
  Come buy, etc.

Clown. If I were not in love with *Mopsa,* thou shou'd'st take no money of me; but being enthralled as I am, it will also be the bondage of certain ribbands and gloves.

Mops. I was promised them against the feast; but they come not too late now.

Dorc. He hath promis'd you ; more than that or there be liars.

Mops. He hath paid you all he promis'd you ; may be, he hath paid you more, which will shame you to give him again.

Clown. Is there no manners left among you maids ? Is there no milking time when yon are going to bed, or killhole, to whistle of those secreets, but you mnst be tittle-tattle before all our guests ? 'ti s well they are whispering, clamour your tongues, and not a word more.

Mops. I have done : come, you promis'd me a tawdry lace and a pair of sweet gloves.

Clown. Have I not told thee how I was cozen'd by the way, and lost all my money.

Autol. and, indeed, Sir, there are cozeners abroad; therefore it behoves men to be wary.

Clown. Fear not, thou, man——thou shalt lose nothing here.

Autol.

Autol. I hope so, Sir; for I have about me many parcels of charge.

Clown. What hast here? ballads?

Mops. Pray now buy some; I love a ballad in print, Or a life, for then we are sure they are true.

Autol. Here's one to a very doleful tune; how a usurer's wife was brought to bed with twenty money bags at a burthen, and how she long'd to eat adder's heads, and toads carbonado'd.

Mops. Is it true, think you?

Autol. Very true, and but a month old,

Dorc. Bless me, from marrying a usurer!

Antol. Here's the midwife's name to it; and five or six honest wives that were present. Why shou'd I carry lies abroad?

Mops. Pray, you now, buy it.

Clown. Come on: lay it buy; let's first see more ballads; we'll buy the other things anon.

Autol. Here's another ballad of a fish, that appear'd upon the coast on *Wednesday* the fourscore of *April*, forty thousand fathom above water, and sung this ballad, against the hard hearts of maids: it was thought she was a woman, and turn'd into a cold fish, for she wou'd not exchange flesh with one that lov'd her: the ballad is very pitiful, and as true.

Dorc. Is it true, too, think you?

Autol. Five justices hands at it; and witnesses more than my pack will hold.

Clown. Lay it by too.——Another.

Autol. This is a merry ballad, but a very pretty one.

Mops Let's have some merry ones.

Antol. Why, this is a passing merry one, and goes to the tune of *two maids wooing a man:* there's scaice a maid westward but she sings it; 'tis in request, I can tell you.

Clown. *Nicholas, Dorcas,* and *Mopsa* can sing that; we had the tune on't a month ago.——Come *Nicholas,* strike up.

S O N G.

Man. *Get you hence, for I must go,*
  Whither it fits not you to know,
Dor. *Whither?* Mop. *O Whither?* Dor. *Whither?*
           Mop.

Mop. *It becomes thy oath full well,*
        Thou to me thy secrets tell.
Dor. *Me, to let me go thither:*
Mop. *Or thou go'st to the grange, or mill,*
Dor. *If to either thou do'st ill,*
Man. *Neither.* Dor. *What neither?* Man. *Neither,*
Dor. *Thou hast sworn my love to be;*
Mop. *Thou hast sworn it more to me;*
Both. *Then, whither go'st? Say whither?*

    Clown. We'll have this song out anon by ourselves;
My father and the gentlemen are in sad talk;
And we'll not trouble them; come, bring away
The pack after me. Wenches, I'll buy for you both:
Pedlar, let's have the first choice. Follow me girls.
    Autol. And you shall pay well for 'em.   [*Aside.*

SONG.

Will you buy any tape, or lace for your cap?
    My dainty buck my dear-a——?
Any silk and thread? any toys for your head,
    f the new'st and fin'st, fin'st wear-a——?
Come to the pedlar; money's a Medlar,
    That doth utter all men's ware-a——?
            [*Ex.* Autolicus, Clown, Dorcass, *and* Mopsa.

Enter LEONTES *and* CLEOMINES, *from the Farm-House.*

    Cleom. Why will you not repose you, Sir? these sports,
The idle merriments of hearts at ease,
But ill will suit the colour of your mind,
    Leon. Peace—I enjoy them in a better sort——
Cleomines, look on this pretty damsel;
            [*Pointing to* PERDITA.
Haply such age, such innocence and beauty,
Had our dear daughter own'd, had not my hand——
O had I not the course of nature stop'd
On weak surmise——I would not think that way——
And yet I must, always, and ever must.
    Cleom. No more, my liege——
    Leon. Nay, I will gaze upon her; each salt dropt
That trickles down my cheek, relieves my heart,
Which else wou'd burst with anguish.

                        Polix.

Polix (to *Camil.*) Is it not too far gone? 'tis time to
    part 'em;
He's simple, and tells much—how now, fair shepherd,
                     [*To* Florizel.

Your heart is full of something that does take
Your mind from feasting. Sooth, when I was young,
And handed love as you do, I was wont
To load my she with knacks; I would have ransack'd
The pedlar's silken treasury, and have pour'd it
To her acceptance: you have let him go,
And noth,ng marted with him. If your lass
Interpretation should abuse, and call this
Your lack of love or bounty, you were straited
For a reply, at least, if you make care
Of happy holding her.

   Flor. Old Sir, I know;
She prizes not such trifles as these are:
The gifts she looks from me, are pact and lockt
Up in my heart; which I have given already,
But not deliver'd. O hear me breathe my love
Before this ancient Sir; who, it should seem,
Hath sometime lov'd. I take thy hand, this hand,
As soft as dove's down, and as white as it,
Or *Ethiopian's* tooth, or the fann'd snow,
That's bolted by the northern blast twice o'er.

   Polix. What follow's this?

   Leon. How prettily the young swaim seems to wash
The hand was fair before?

   Polix. You've put him out;
Come to your protestation: let me hear
What you profess.

   Flor. Do, and be witness to't.

   Polix. And this my neigbbour too.

   Flor. And he, and more
Than he, and men; the earth; and heav'ns, and all;
That were I crown'd the most imperial monarch,
Thereof most worthy: were I the fairest youth
That ever made eye swerve, had force and knowledge,
More than was ever man's I would not prize 'em
Without her love; for her employ them all;
Commend them, and condemn them, to her service,
Or to their own perdition.

   Polix. Fairly offer'd.

                                Leo

Leon. This shews a sound affection.

Old Shep. But, my daughter
Say you like to him?

Perd. I cannot speak
So well; nothing so well, no, nor mean better
By the pattern of my own thoughts, I cut out.
The purity of his.

Old Shep. Take hand's——a bargain;
And friends, unknown, you shall bear witness to't,
I give my daughter to him, and will make
Her portion equal his.

Flor: O, that must be
I' th' virtue of your daughter; and being dead,
I shall have more than you can dream of yet;
Enough then, for your wonder: come on;
Contract us 'fore these witnesses.

Old Shep. Come, your hand;
And, daughter, yours.

Polix. Soft, swain, a while; 'beseech you,
Have you a father?

Flor. I have; but what of him?

Polix. Knows he of this?

Flor. He neither does, nor shall.

Polix. Methinks a father
Is, at the nuptial of his son, a guest
The best becomes the table: 'pray you, once more;
Is not your father grown incapable
Of reasonable affairs? is he not stupid
With age, and alt'ring rheums? can he speak? hear!
Know man for man? dispute his own estate?
Lies he not bed-rid, and again, does nothing
But what he did, being childish!

Flor. No, good Sir;
He has his health, and ampler strength indeed,
Than most have of his age?

Leon. By my white beard,
You offer him, if this be so, a wrong
Something unfilial: reason my son
Shou'd chuse himself a wife; but as good reason,
The father (all whose joy is nothing else
But fair posterity) shou'd hold some council
In such a business.

Flor. I yield all this.

But

But for some other reasons, my grave Sirs,
Which 'tis not fit you know; I not aquaint
My father of this business.
      Polix. Let him know't.
      Flor. He shall not.
      Polix. Prithee, let him.
      Leon. O let him.
      Flor. No; he must not.
      Old Shep. Let him, my son, he shall not heed to grieve
At knowing of thy choice.
      Flor. Come, come, he must not:
Mark our contract.
      Polix. (Discovering himself.) Mark your divorce, young
            Sir;
Whom son I dare not call; thou art too base
To be acknowledg'd.   Thou a scepter's heir,
That thus affect'st a sheep-hook !
      Leon. (Amaz'd.) How ! *Polixenes* ! what mystery is this
I want the power to throw me at his feet,
Nor can I bear his eyes——
                  [*Leans on* Cleomines, *and they go apart.*
      Polix. And thou, old traitor,   [*To the* Old Shepherd.
I'm sorry, that by hanging thee, I can but
Shorten thy life one week : and thou, fresh piece
Of excellent witchcraft, who of force must know
The royal fool thou cop'st with——
      Old Shep. O my heart !
      Polix. I'll have thy beauty scratch'd with briars, and made
More homely than my state.   For thee, fond boy,
If I may ever know thou dost but sigh,
That thou no more shalt see this knack as never
I mean thou shalt, we'll bar thee from succession ;
Not hold thee of our blood, no, not our kin ;
Far than our deucation off : mark thou my words ;
Follow us to the court—thou churl ; for this time
Tho' full of our displeasure, yet we free thee
From the dead blow of it ; and new enchantment,
Worthy enough a herdsman ; yea, him too,
That makes himself, but for your honour therein,
Unworthy thee ; if ever henceforth, thou
These rural latches to his entrance open,
Or hoop his body more with thy embraces,
I will devise a death as cruel for thee,

                                          As

As thou art tender to it.   [*Exit* Polixenes *and* Camillo.
    Perd. Ev'n here undone!
I was not much afraid; for once or twice,
I was about to speak, and tell him plainly,
The self-same sun, that shines upon his court,
Hides not his visage from our cottage, but
Looks on all alike—wil't please you, Sir, be gone?
                                        [*To* Florizel.

I told you what woul'd hap'—this dream of mine
Being now awake, I'll queen it no inch farther,
But milk my ewes, and weep.
    Leon. (*Coming forward.*) How now, old father?
Good shepherd, speak.
    Old Shep. I cannot speak nor think,
Nor dare to know, that which I know—O Sir,
                                        [*To* Florizel.

You have undone a man of fourscore three,
That thought to fill his grave in quiet; yea,
To die upon the bed my father dy'd,
To lie close by his honest bones; but now
Some hangman must put on my shroud, and lay me
Where no priest shovels in dust—O cursed wretch
                                        [*To* Perdita.

Thou knew'st this was the prince, and would'st adventure
To mingle faith with him——Undone! undone!
If I might die this hour, I have liv'd
To die when I desire.   [*Exit.*
    Perd. O my poor father!
    Leon. (*To* Cleomines.) The honest wretch, he helps us at
        our need——
I will no longer vail me in this cloud,
But plead unmask's, this good old shepherds cause
Before my own; ev'n at *Bohemia's* knees.
    Flor. (*To* Perdita.) Why look you so upon me?
I am but too sorry, not afraid; delay'd,
But nothing alter'd! what I was, I am,
And ever shall be thine, my *Perdita!*
    Perd. Alas, alas! my lord; these hopes are fled
How often have I told you 'twou'd be thus?
How often said, my dignity wou'd last
But 'till 'twere known!
    Flor. It cannot fail, but by
The violation of my faith; and then

Let nature crush the sides o' th' earth together,
And mar the seeds within!—lift up thy looks!——
From my succession, wipe me, father; I
Am heir to my affection.

   Leon. Be advis'd——

   Flor' I am, and by my fancy; if my reason
Will thereto be obedient, I have reason;
If not, my senses, better pleas'd with madness,
Did bid it welcome.

   Leon. This is desp'rate, Sir!

   Flor. So call it; but it does fulfil my vow;
I needs must think it honesty; my heart
Is anchor'd here, as rooted as the rocks,
Who stand the raging of the roaring deep,
Immoveable, and fix'd—let it come on——
I'll brave the tempest!

   Perd. Be patient. *Doricles.*

   Leon. Passion transports you, prince; be calm a while,
Nor scorn my ear's and council, but attend;——
My lowly seeming, and this outward garment,
But ill denote my quality and office——
Trust to my words, tho' myst'ry obscures 'em——
I know the king your father, and if time,
And many accidents (cease foolish tears)
Have not effac'd my image from his breast,
Perhaps he'll listen to me—I am sorry,
Most sorry, you have broken from his liking,
Where you were ty'd in duty; and as sorry
Your choise is not so rich in worth as beauty,
That you might well enjoy her—Prince, you know
Prosperity's the very bond of love,
Whose fresh complexion, and whose heart together,
Affliction alters.

   Perd. One of these is true;
I think affliction may subdue the cheek,
But not take in the mind.

   Leon. Yea, say you so?
There shall not at your father's house, these sev'n years,
Be born another such.

   Flor. O reverend Sir!
As you wou'd wish a child of your own youth
To meet his happiness in love, speak for me;
Remember, since you ow'd no more to time

                          Than

Than I do now; and with thought of like affectionss,
Step forth my advocate.

Leon. You touch me deep,
Deep, to the quick, sweet prince; alas! alas!
I lost a daughter, that 'twixt heav'n and earth
Might thus have stood begetting wonder, as
You lovely maiden does—of that no more;——
I'll to the king your father—this our compact
Your honour not o'erthrown by your desires,
I am a friend to them and you.

[*Exit* Leontes *and* Cleomines.

Flor. Dear, look up;
Tho' fortune, visible an enemy,
Shou'd chase us with my father; power, no jot
Hath she to change our loves.

Perd, Alas, my lord,
Bethink yourself as I do me.   Heav'n knows,
All faults I make, when I do come to know 'em
I do repent—Alas! I've shewn too much
A maiden's simpleness; I have betray'd,
Unwittingly divorc'd a noble prince
From a dear father's love; have caus'd him sell
His present honour, aud his hop'd reversion.
For a poor sheep-hook, and its lowly mistress,
Of lesser price than that—beseech you, Sir,
Of your own state take care, drown the remembrance
Of me; my father's cott; and these poor beauties
Wroug'd by your praise too often.

Flor. My *Perd'ta,*
How sweetly dost thou plead against thyself?
Let us retire, my love—again I swear,
Not for *Bohemia,* nor the pomp that may
Be there out-glean'd; for all the sun sees, or
The close earth wombs, or the profound seas hide
In unknown fathoms, will I break my oath,
To thee, my fair betroth'd—with thee I'll fly
From stormy regions and a low'ring sky;
Where no base views our purer minds shall move;
And all our wealth be innocence and love.

ACT

A C T III.

Another Part of the Country.

Enter AUTOLICUS in rich Cloaths.

AUTOLICUS.

HOW fortune drops into the mouth of the diligent man ?—see, if I be not transform'd courtier again—four silken gamesters, who attended the king; and were revelling by themselves, at some distance from the shepherd's, have drank so plenteously, that their weak brains are turn'd topsy turvy—I have found one of 'em, an old court comrade of mine, retir'd from the rest, sobering himself with sleep under the shade of a hawthorn ; I made use of our antient familiarity to exchange garments with him ; the pedlar's cloaths are on his back, and the pack by his side, as empty as his pockets, for I have sold all my trumpery ; not a counterfeit stone, nor a ribband, glass, pomander, browch, table-book, ballad, knife, tape, glove, shoe-tie, bracelet, horn ; they throng'd who shou'd buy first, as if my trinkets had been hallow'd, and brought a benediction to the buyer ; by which means, I saw whose purse was best in picture ; and what I saw to my good use I remember'd—my good *Clown* (who wants but something to be a reasonable man) grew so in love with the wenches song, that he wou'd not stir his pettitoes till he had tune and words, which so drew the rest of the herd to me, that all their other senses stuck in ears : no hearing, no feeling, but my Sir's song, and admiring the nothing of it. I pick'd and cut most of their festival purses ; and had not the old man come in with a whoo-bub against his daughter and the king's son, and scar'd my choughs from the chaff, had not left a purse alive in the whole army ;—ha, ha, ha, what a fool honesty is ! and trust, his sworn brother, a very simple gentleman ! I see this is the time the unjust man doth thrive ; the gods do this year connive at us; and we may do any thing extempore—aside, aside here is more matter for a hot brain. Ev'ry lane's end, ev'ry shop, church, session, hanging, yields a careful man a work.

M*Enter*

Enter CLOWN *and* OLD SHEPHERD.

Clown. See, see, what a man you are now—there is no other way, but to tell the king she is a changeling, and none of your flesh and blood.

Old Shep. Nay, but hear me.

Clown. Nay, but hear me.

Old Shep. Go to, then.——

Clown. Let him know the truth of the matter; how you found her by the sea-side some eighteen years agone; that there was this bundle with her, with the things and trinkets contained therein; but there was some money too, which being spent in nursing her, you need say nothing about it, together with all the circumstances of the whole affair; do it, I say.

Old Shep. And what then, think'st thou?

Clown. Why then, she being none of your flesh and blood, your flesh and blood has not offended the king, and so your flesh and blood is not to be punish'd by him: shew those things—I say, you found about her, those secret things: this being done, let the law go whistle—I warrant you.

Old Shep. I will tell the king all, every word; yea, and his son's pranks too; who, I may say, is no honest man, neither to his father nor to me, to go about to make me the king's brother-in-law.

Clown. Indeed brother-in-law was the farthest off you cou'd have been to him; and then your blood had been the dearer, by I know not how much an ounce.

Autol. (*Aside.*) Very wisely puppies.

Old Shep. Well, let us to the king; there is that in this fardel, will make him scratch his beard.

Clown. Pray heartily he be at the palace.

Autol. (*Coming forward.*) How now, rusticks, whither are you bound?

Old Shep. To th' palace an' it like your worship.

Autol. Your affairs there? what? with whom? the condition of that fardel, the place of your dwelling, your names, your age, of what having, breeding, and any thing that is fitting to be known, discover.

Clown. We are but plain fellows, Sir,

Autol. A lye—you are but rough and hairy; let me have no lying, it becomes none but tradesmen.

Old Shep. Are you a courtier, an' like you, Sir?

Autol.

Autol. Whether it like me or no, I am a courtier—seest thou not the air of the court in these enfoldings ? hath not my gait in it the measure of the court ? reflect not I on thy baseness, court-contempt ? think'st thou of that I insinuate or toze from thee thy business, I am therefore no courtier ? cap-a-pee ; and one that will either push on, or push back thy business there ; whereupon, I command thee to open thy affair.

Old Shep. My business, Sir, is to the king.

Autol. What advocate hast thou to him ?

Old Shep. I know not, and't like you.——Advocate !
[*Aside to* Clown.

Clown. Advocate's the court word for a pheasant ; say you have none.   [*Apart.*

Old Shep. None, Sir ; I have no pheasant, cock, nor hen.

Autol. How blest are we that are not simple men !
Yet nature might have made me as these are,
Therefore I will not disdain.   [*Aside.*

Clown. (to *Old Shep.*) This cannot be but a great courtier.

Old Shep. (To *Clown.*) His garments are rich, but he wears 'em not handsomely.

Clown. He seems to be more noble in being fantas'ical ; a great man I'll warrant ; I know by the picking one's teeth.

Autol. The fardel there, what's in the fardel ? Wherefore that box ?

Old Shep. Sir, there lies such secrets in this fardel and box, which none must know but the king : and which he shall know within this hour, if I may come to th' speech of him.

Autol. Age, thou hast lost thy labour.

Old Shep. Why, Sir ?

Autol. The king is not at the palace, he's gone aboard a new ship to purge melancholy, and air himself ; for if thou be'st capable of things serious, thou must know the king is full of grief.

Old Shep. So, 'tis said, Sir ; about his son that shou'd have marry'd a shepherd's daughter.

Autol. If that shepherd be not in hand fast, let him fly ; the curses he shall have, the tortures he shall feel, will break the heart of man, the back of monster.

Old Shep. Think you so, Sir ?

Autol. Not he, alone, shall suffer what wit can make hea-

M 2
vy,

vy, and vengeance bitter ; but those that are germain to him, tho' remov'd fifty times, shall all come under the hangman ; which tho' it be great pity, yet it is necessary ; an old sheep-whistling rogue, a ram tender, to offer to have his daughter come into grace!—Some say he shall be ston'd ; but that death is too soft for him, say I : draw our throne into a sheep-cot! all death's are too few, the sharpest too easy.

Clown. Has the old man e'er a son, Sir ; do you hear an't like you, Sir ?

Autol. He has a son, who shall be flay'd alive, then 'nointed over with money, set on the head of a wasp's nest ; then stand till he be three quarters and a dram dead ; then recover'd again with aqua-vita, or some other hot infusion ; then (raw as he is, and in the hottest day prognostication proclaims,) shall he be set against a brick wall, the sun looking with a southward eye upon him, where he is to behold him with flies, blown to death : but what talk we of these traitorly rascals, whose miseries are to be smil'd at, their offences being so capital ? Tell me, (for you seem to be honest, plain men) what you have to the king; being something gently consider'd I'll bring you where he is, tender your persons to his presence, whisper him in your behalf, and if it be in man, besides the king, to effect your suits, here is a man shall do it.

Clown. He seems to be of great authority, close with him, give him gold ; tho' authority be a stubborn bear, yet he is often led by the nose with gold ; shew the inside of your purse to the outside of his hand, and no more ado ; remember ston'd and flay'd alive.   [*Aside to* Old Shepherd.

Old Shep. And't please you, Sir, undertake the business for us, here is that gold I have ; I'll make it as much more, and leave this young man in pawn, 'till I bring it you.

Autol. After I have done what I promis'd——

Clown. Ay, Sir.

Autol. Well, give me the moiety—are you a party in this business ?

Clown. In some sort, Sir : but tho' my case be a pitiful one, I hope I shall not be flay'd out of it.

Autol. O, that's the case of the shepherd's son ; hang him, he'll be made an example.

Clown. (to *Shep.*) Comfort! good comfort! we must to the king, and shew our strange sights ; he must know 'tis

none

none of your daughter, nor my sister; we are gone else—
Sir, I will give you as much as this old man does, when the
business is perform'd, and remain, as he says, your pawn,
'till it be brought you.

Autol. I will trust you; walk before toward the sea-side;
go on the right hand, I will but look upon the hedge, and
follow it.

Clown. We are blest in this man, as I may say, ev'n blest

Old Shep. Let's before as he bids us; he was provided to
do us good.   [*Exeunt.* Shepherd *and* Clown.

Autol. If I had a mind to be honest, I see fortune wou'd
not suffer me; she drops booties in my mouth—I am courted now, with a double occasion: gold, and a means to do
the king good; which, who knows how that may turn to
my advancement! I will bring these two moles, these blind
ones before him; if that the complaint they have to the king
concerns him nothing, let him call me rogue for being so
far officious; I am proof against that title, and what shame
else belongs to it: to him will I present them; there may
be better in it.   [*Exit.*

S C E N E, PAULINA's *House.*

Enter PAULINA *and a* GENTLEMAN.

Paul. Beseech you, Sir, now that my first burst of joy is
over, and my ebbing spirits no longer bear down my attention, give my ear again the circumstances of this strange
story: *Leontes* arriv'd! escap'd from the fury of the sea!
vail'd in the semblance of a poor shepherd! and has now
thrown himself into the arms of *Polixenes!* 'tis a chain of
wonders!

Gent. Yet the tale is not more wonderful than true; I
was present at the interview.

Paul. Speak, Sir, speak; tell me all.

Gent. Soon as our king return'd from the palace, he retir'd with the good *Camillo,* to lament the unhappy and ill-
plac'd affection of his son: yet, as gleams of sunshine oft
break in upon a storm, so, thro' all his indignation, there
burst out by intervals paternal love and sorrow; 'twas
brought him that a person of no great seeming intreated ad-
mittance; a refusal was return'd to his bold request; but
the stranger, unaw'd by this discouragement, advanc'd to
the king's presence; his boldness had met with an equal pu-

                                        nishment

nishment, had he not on the sudden assum'd a majesty of mien and feature, that threw a kind of radiance over his peasant garb, and fixt all who saw him with silent wonder and admiration.

Paul. Well, but *Polixenes!*

Gent. He stept forth to the stranger; but 'ere he cou'd enquire the reasons of his presumption—behold, said *Leontes* bursting into grief, behold unhappy king, that much hath wrong'd you—behold *Leontes!*——On this the king started from him—true, I have wrong'd you, cry'd *Leontes;* but if penitence can atone for guilt, behold these eyes, wept dry with honest sorrow; this breast, rent with honest anguish; and if you can suspect that my heart yet harbours these passions which once infested it here, I offer it to your sword; lay it upon to the day!

Paul. O, the force, the charm, of returning virtue;

Gent. Its charm was felt, indeed, by the generous king; for at once forgetting that fatal enmity that had so long divided them, he embrac'd the penitent *Leontes*, with the unfeign'd warmth of one who had found a long lost friend return'd beyond hope from banishment or death; while *Leontes,* overwhelm'd with such unlook'd for goodness, fell on his neck, and wept: thus they stood embracing and embrac'd, in dumb and noble sorrow! Their old friendship being thus renew'd, *Leontes* began his intercession for prince *Florizel:* but *Polixenes*—break we off—here comes the good *Camillo;* speak, thou bear'st thy tidings in thy looks.

Enter CAMILLO.

Cam. Nothing but bonfires—the oracle is fulfill'd,
O, *Paulina,* the beatings of my heart, will scarce
Permit my tongue to tell thee what it bears.

Paul. I know it all, my friend; the king of *Sicily* is arriv'd.

Cam. Not only the king of *Sicily* is arriv'd, but his daughter; his long-lost daughter is found.

Paul. Gracious God support me! his daughter found! can it be? how was she sav'd? and where has she been conceal'd?

Cam. That shepherdess, our prince has so long and so secretly affected, proves *Sicilia's* heiress: the old shepherd, her suppos'd father, deliver'd the manner how he found

her

her upon the coast, produced a fardel, in which are incon-
test: d proofs of every circumstance.

Paul. Can this be true?

Cam. Most true, if ever the truth were pregnant by circumstance that which you hear, you'll swear you see, there
is such unity in the proofs. The mantle of queen *Hermi-
-one*, her jewel about the neck of it, the letters (pardon me
the mention of them) of our lord *Antigonus*, found with it
which I know to be his characters: the majesty of the creature in resemblance of the mother; the affection of noble-
ness, which nature shews above her breeding, and many
other evidences, proclaim her with all certainty to be the
king's daughter.

Paul. Praised be the God's wou'd I had beheld the behaviour of the two kings at the unravelling of this story.

Cam. Ay, *Paulina*, for you have lost a sight, which was
to be seen—cannot be spoken of. There might you have
beheld one joy crown another, so, and in such a manner,
that it seem'd sorrow wept to take leave of 'em for their
joy waded in tears: there was casting up of eyes, holding
up of hands, with countenance of such distraction, that they
were to be known by garment, not by favour. *Sicily*, being ready to leap out of himself for joy of his found daughter, lifted the princess from the earth, and so lock'd her in
embracing, as if he would pin her to his heart, that she
might no more be in danger of losing: then, as if that joy
had now become a loss, cries—Oh, thy mother! thy mother! now he thanks the *Old Shepherd*, who stands by like
a weather-beaten conduit of many kings reigns; then asks
Bohemia forgiveness; then embraces his son-in-law; then
again worries his daughter with clipping her.——I never
heard of such another encounter, which lames report to
follow it, and undoes description to draw it.

Paul. The dignity of this act was worth the audience of
kings and princes, for by such was it acted.

Cam. One of the prettiest touches of all, and that which
angled for my eyes, was, at the relation of the queen's
death, with the manner how she came by it (bravely confess'd and lamented by the king;) how attentiveness wounded his daughter, 'till from one sign of dolor to another, she
with an, *Alas!* I wou'd fain say, blend tears——I am sure
my heart wept blood. Who was most marble, there chang'd

M 4

colour;

colour; some swooned, all sorrow'd; if the world cou'd have seen't, the woe had been universal.

Paul. Are they return'd to court?

Cam. Not yet. They were proceeding with due ceremony, and the clamorous joy of the multitude, when I took advantage of their delay, to recount to you this rhapsody of wonders.   [*Trumpets.*

Paul. Camillo, haste thee; this royal assembly is entering now the city. Haste thee, with *Paulina's* greeting to the double majesty, and our new found princess; give them to know I have in my keeping a statue of *Hermione*, perform'd by the most rare master in *Italy*; who, had he himself eternity, and cou'd put breath into his work, wou'd beguile nature of her custom, so perfectly he is her ape. He, so near to *Hermione*, has done *Hermione*, that they will speak to her, and stand in hope of answer. Invite them to the sight of it, put thy message into what circumstance of compliment the time and sudden occasion may admit, and return with best speed to prepare for their unprovided entertainment.   [*Exit.*

Cam. I obey you, madam.   [*Exeunt severally.*

SCENE, the Court.

Enter AUTOLICUS.

Now had I not the dash of my former life in me, wou'd preferment fall upon my head. I brought the old man and his son to the king's and told them, I heard them talk of a fardel, and I know not what—but 'tis all one to me; for had I been the finder out of his secret, it wou'd not have relish'd among my other discredits—here come those I have done good to against my will, and already appearing in the blossoms of their fortune.

Enter OLD SHEPHERD *and* CLOWN, *fantastically dress'd.*

Old Shep. Come, boy; I am past more children; but thy sons and daughters will be all gentlemen born.

Clown. (to *Autolicus*.) You are all well met, Sir; you denied that I was a gentleman born: see these cloath's! say you see them not, and think me still no gentleman born—give me the lye, do—and try whether I am now no gentleman born.

Autol. I know you are now, Sir, a gentleman born.

Clown.

Clown. Ay, and have been so, for any time this half hour.

Old Shep. And so have I, boy.

Clown. So you have; but I was a gentleman born before my father; for the king's son took me by the hand and call'd me brother; and then the two kings call'd my father brother; and then, the prince, my brother, and the princess, my sister (that is, that was my sister) call'd my father, father; and so we all wept; and there was the first gentleman-like tears that ever we shed.

Old Shep. We may live, son, to shed many more.

Clown. Ay, or else 'twere hard luck, being in so preposterous estate as we are.

Autol. I humbly beseech you, Sir, to pardon all the faults I have committed to your worship; and to give me your good report to the prince my master.

Old Shep. Prithee, son, do; for we must be gentle, now we are gentlemen.

Clown. Thou wilt amend thy life?

Autol. Ay, an't like your good worship.

Clown. No, it does not like my worship now; but it is like it may like my worship when it is amended; therefore have heed that thou do'st amend it.

Autol. I will, an't like you.

Clown. Give me thy hand; hast nothing in't? am not I a gentleman? I must be gently consider'd—am not I a courtier? Seest thou not the air of the court in these enfoldings? Hath not my gait in it the measure of the court?

Autol. Here is what gold I have, Sir;—so, I have brib'd him with his own money.   [*Aside.*

Clown. And when am I to have the other moiety? and the young man in pawn till you bring it me?

Autol. After you have done the business, Sir.

Clown. Well, I swear to the prince, thou art as honest a tall fellow as any in *Bohemia.*

M 5

Catharine and Petruchio.

DRAMATIS PERSONÆ.

Petruchio Mr. Woodward.
Baptista Mr. Burton.
Hortensio Mr. Mozeen.
Grumio Mr. Yates.
Music-Master Mr. Jefferson.
Biondello Mr. Blakes.
Pedro Mr. Clough.
Taylor Mr. H. Vaughan.
Nathaniel Mr. W. Vaughan.

Peter Mr. Ackman.
Nicholas Mr. Atkins.
Philip Mr. Marr.
Joseph Mr. Lewis.

Catharine Mrs. Clive.
Bianca Mrs. Bennet.
Curtis Mrs. Bradshaw.

ACT I.

SCENE, BAPTISTA's *House.*

Enter BAPTISTA, PETRUCHIO, *and* GRUMIO,

BAPTISTA.

THUS have I, 'gainst my own self-interest,
    Repeated all the worst you are t' expect
From my shrewd daughter, *Cath'rine*; if you'll venture,
Maugre my plan and honest declaration,
You have my free consent, win her, and wed her.
  Pet. Signior *Baptista*, thus it stands with me.
Anthonio, my father, is deceased;
You knew him well, and knowing him, know me,
Left solely heir to all his lands and goods,
Which I have better'd rather than decreas'd,
And I have thrust myself into the world,
Haply to wive and thrive as best I may ;
My business asketh haste, old Signior,
And ev'ry day I cannot come to wooe.
Let specialties be therefore drawn between us,
That cov'nants may be kept on either hand,
  Bapt. Yes, when the special thing is well obtain'd,

My

My daughter's love, for that is all in all.

Pet. Why, that is nothing ; for I tell you, father,
I am as peremptory, as she proud-minded ;
And where two raging fires meet together,
They do consume the thing that feeds their fury,
Tho' little fire grows great with little wind,
Yet extreme gusts will blow out fire and all ;
So I to her, and so she yields to me ;
For I am rough, and wooe not like a babe.

Grum. Nay, look you, Sir, he tells you flatly what his
mind is ; why give him gold enough and marry him to a
puppet, or an old trot with ne'er a tooth in her head.
Tho' she had as many diseases as two and fifty horses ; why
nothing comes amiss, so money comes withal.

Bapt. As I have shew'd you, Sir, the coarser side,
Now let me tell you she is young and beauteous,
Brought up as best becomes a gentlewoman ;
Her only fault (and that is fault enough)
Is that she is intolerably froward ;
If that you can away with, she is yours.

Grum. I pray you, Sir let her see him while thhe umour
lasts. O' my word an' she knew him as well as I do, she
would think scolding would do little good upon him. She
may perhaps call him half a score knaves, or so ; why,
that's nothing; an' he begin once, she'll find her match,
I'll tell you what, Sir, an' she stands him but a little, he
will throw a figure in her face, and so disfigure her with
it, that she shall have no more eyes to see withal than a
cat—You know him not, Sir,

Bapt. And you will wooe her, Sir ?

Pet. Why came I hither but to that intent
Think you a little din can daunt my ears ?
Have I not, in my time, heard lions roar?
Have I not heard the sea puff'd up with winds ?
Have I not heard great ord'nance in the field ?
And heav'n's artillery thunder in the skies ?
Have I not in a pitched battle heard
Loud 'larums, neighing steeds, and trumpets clangue
And do you tell me of a woman's tongue ;
That gives not half so great a blow to hear,
As will a chesnut in a farmer's fire ?
Tush, tush ! scare boys with bugs.

Bapt. Then thou'rt the man,

                              The

The man of *Cath'rine*, and her father too:
That shall she know, and know my mind at once
I'll portion her above her gentler sister,
New-married to *Hortensio* :
And if with scurral taunt, and squeamish pride,
She make a mouth, and will not taste her fortune,
I'll turn her forth to seek it in the world ;
Nor henceforth shall she know her father's doors.

   Pet. Sayest thou me so ? then as your daughter, Signior,
Is rich enough to be *Petruchio's* wife;
Be she as crust as *Socrates' Xantippe*,
She moves me not a whit—were she as rough,
As are the swelling *Adriatic* seas,
I come to wive it wealthily in *Padua* ;
If wealthily, then happily in *Padua.*

   Bapt. Well may'st thou wooe, and happy be thy speed ;
But be thou arm'd for some unhappy words.

   Pet. Aye, to the proof as mountains are for winds,
That shake not, tho' they blow perpetually.
CATHARINE *and the* Music-master *make a noise within.*

   Music-mast. [*within*] Help! help!

   Cath. [*within*] Out of the house, you scraping fool

   Pet. What noise is that ?

   Bapt. Oh, nothing ; that is nothing——
My daughter *Cathrine*, and her Music-master ;
This is the third I've had within this month :
She is an enemy to harmony.

Enter MUSIC-MASTER.

How now, friend, why dost thou look so pale ?

   Music-mast. For fear, I promise you, if I do look pale.

   Bapt. What, will my daughter prove a good musician ?

   Music-mast. I think she'll sooner prove a soldier;
Iron may hold with her, but never lutes.

   Bapt. Why, then, thou canst not break her to the lute ?

   Music-mast. Why, no ; for she hath broke the lute to me.
I did but tell her she mistook her frets,
And bow'd her hand, to teach her fingering,
When with a most impatient devilish spirit,
Frets call you them ? quoth she, I'll fret your fools cap :
And with that word, she struck me on the head,
And through the instrument my pate made way,
And there I stood amazed for a while,

As on a pillory, looking through the lute:
While she did call me rascal-fidler,
And twagling Jack, with twenty such vile terms,
As she hath studied to misuse me so.
    Pet. Now by the world, it is lusty wench,
I love her ten-times more than e'er I did,
Oh how I long to have a grapple with her!
    Music-mast. I wou'd not make another trial with her,
To purchase *Padua:* for what is past,
I'm paid sufficiently: if at your leisure,
You think my broken fortunes, head and lute
Deserve some reparation, you know where
T'enquire for me; and so good gentlemen,
I am your much disorder'd humble servant.   [*Exit.*
    Bapt. Not yet mov'd, *Petruchio!* do you flinch?
    Pet. I am more and more impatient, Sir; and long
To be a part'ner in these favourite pleasures.
    Bapt. O, by all means, Sir;—will you go with me;
Or shall I send my daughter *Kate* to you?
    Pet. I pray you do, I will attend her here.   [*Exit* Bapt.
Grumio, retire, and wait my call within.   [*Exit* Grum.
Since that her father is so resolute,
I'll wooe her with some spirit when she comes;
Say that she rail, why then, I'll tell her plain
She sings as sweetly as a nightingale;
Say that she frown, I'll say she looks as clear
As morning roses, newly wash'd with dew;
Say she be mute, and will not speak a word,
Then I'll commend her volubility,
And say she utter'th piercing eloquence:
If she do bid me pack, I'll give her thanks.
As tho' she bid me stay by her a week;
If she deny to wed, I'll crave the day
When I shall ask the banes, and when be married:
But here she comes, and now *Petruchio,* speak.

Enter CATHARINE.

    Cath. How! turn'd adrift, nor know my fathers house!
Reduc'd to this, or none, the maids last prayer;
Sent to be woo'd like bear unto the stake?
Trim wooing like to be!——and he the bear,
For I shall bait him—yet the man's a man.
    Pet. Kate in a calm!—maids must not be wooers.

Good-

Good-morrow, *Kate*, for that's your name I hear,

  Cath. Well have you heard, but impudently said,
They call me *Catharine*, that do talk of me.

  Pet. You lie in faith, for you are call'd plain *Kate*,
And bonny *Kate*, and sometimes *Kate* the curst:
But *Kate*— the prettiest *Kate* in *Christendom*,
Take this of me, *Kate* of my consolation!
Hearing thy mildness prais'd in ev'ry town,
Thy virtues spoke of, and thy beauty sounded,
Thy affability, and bashful modesty,
(Yet not so deeply as to thee belongs,)
Myself am mov'd to wooe thee for my wife.

  Cath. Mov'd in good time; let him that mov'd you hi-
    ther,
Remove you hence! I know you at the first,
You were a moveable.

  Pet. A moveable? why, what's that?

  Cath. A joint-stool.

  Pet. Thou hast hit it; come, sit on me.

  Cath. Asses are made to bear, and so are you.

  Pet. Women are made to bear, and so are you.
Alas, good *Kate*, I will not burthen thee,
For knowing thee to be but young and light.——

  Cath. Too light for such a swain as you to catch;
                           [*Going.*

  Pet. Come, come you wasp; i'faith you are too angry.

  Cath. If I be waspish, 'best beware my sting.

  Pet. My remedy, then is to pluck it out.

  Cath. Ay, if the fool cou'd find it where it lies.

  Pet. The fool knows where the honey is, sweet *Kate*.
                       [*Offers to kiss her.*

  Cath. 'Tis not for drones to taste.

  Pet. That will I try.   *she strikes him.*
I swear I'll cuff you, if you strike again.——
Nay, come; *Kate*, come; you must not look so sour.

  Cath. How can I help it, when I see that face;
But I'll be shock'd no longer with the sight.

  Pet. Nay, hear you, *Kate*, in sooth you 'scape not so.

  Cath. I chafe you, If I tarry, let me go.

  Pet. No, not a whit, I find you passing gentle;
'Twas told me you were rough, and coy, and sullen,
And now I find report a very liar,
For thou art pleasant, gamesome, passing courteous,

                             But

But slow in speech, yet sweet as spring-time flowers;
Thou can'st not frown, thou can'st not look ascance,
Nor bite the lip as angry wenches will,
Nor hast thou pleasure to be cross in talk:
But then with mildness entertain'st thy wooers,
With gentle conf'rence, soft and affable.
 Catb. This is beyond all patience; don't provoke me.
 Pet. Why doth the world report that *Kate* doth limp?
Oh sland'rous world! *Kate*, like the hazle twig,
Is strait, and slender, and as brown in hue
As hazle nuts, and sweeter than the kernels.
O let me see thee walk, thou do'st not halt.
 Catb. Go, fool, and whom thou keep'st command.
 Pet. Did ever *Dian'* so become a grove,
As *Kate* this chamber, with her princely gaite?
Oh be thou Dian', and let her be *Kate*,
And then let *Kate* be chaste, and *Dian'* sportful.
 Catb. Where did you study all this goodly speech?
 Pet. It is *extempore*, from my mother-wit
 Catb. A witty mother, witless else her son.
 Pet. Am I not wise?
 Catb. Yes, in your own conceit;
Keep yourself warm with that, or else you'll freeze,
 Pet. Or rather warm me in thy arms, my *Kate!*
And therefore setting all this chat aside,
Thus in plain terms; your father hath consented
That you shall be my wife; your dowry 'greed on,
And will you, nill you, I will marry you.
 Catb. Whether I will or no!—O fortune's spite!
 Pet. Nay, *Kate*, I am a husband for your turn;
For by this light, whereby I see thy beauty,
(Thy beauty that doth make me like thee well)
Thou must be married to no man but me;
For I am he am born to tame you, *Kate.*
 Catb. That will admit dispute, my saucy groom,
 Pet. here comes your father; never make denial,
I must and will have *Cathrine* to my wife.

Enter BAPTISTA.

 Bap. Now, Signior, now; how speed you with my
  daughter?
 Pet. How shou'd I speed but well, Sir? how but well?
It were impossible I should speed amiss.
Bapt.

Bapt. Why how, now, daughter *Catharine,* in your dumps?

Cath. Call me daughter? Now I promise you,
You've shew'd a tender fatherly regard,
To wish me wed to one halflunatic;
A mad cap ruffian and a swearing jack,
That thinks with oaths to face the matter out.

Bapt. Better this jack than starve, and that's your por-
        tion——

Pet. Father, 'tis thus; yourself and all the world
That talk'd of her, have talk'd amiss of her;
If she be curst, it is for policy;
For she's not froward but modest as the dove;
She is not hot, but temperate as the morn;
For patience she will prove a second *Grissel,*
And *Roman Lucrece,* for her chastity:
And, to conclude, we've 'greed so well together,
We have fix'd to-morrow for the wedding-day.

Cath. I'll see thee hang'd to-morrow, first—to-morrow?

Bapt. Petruchio, hark; she says she'll see thee hang'd first!
Is this your speeding?

Pet. Oh! be patient, Sir;
If she and I be pleas'd, what's that to you;
'Tis bargain'd 'twixt us twain, being alone,
That she shall still be curs'd in company.

Cath. A plague upon his impudence! I'm vex'd—
I'll marry my revenge, but I will tame him.   [*Aside.*

Pet. I will tell you, 'tis incredible to believe
How much she loves me; Oh! the kindest *Kate!*
She hung about my neck, and kiss on kiss.
She vy'd so fast, protesting oath on oath,
That in a twink she won me to her love.
Oh! you are novices; tis a world to see.
How tame, when men and women are alone——
Give me thy hand, *Kate,* I will now away
To buy apparel for my gentle bride:
Father, provide, the feast, and bid the guests.

Bapt. What dost thou say, my *Catharine?* Give thy hand.

Cath. Never no man shall *Cath'rine* give her hand'
Here 'tis and let him take it, an' he dare.

Pet. Were it the sore-foot of an angry bear.
I'd shake it off; but as it is *Kate's* I kiss it.

Cath. You'll kiss it closer, e'er our moon be wain'd.

Bapt. Heav'n send you joy, *Petruchio*—'tis a match.

                                              Pet.

Pet. Father, and wife, adieu.
Unto my country-house, and stir my grooms,
Scower their country-rust, and make 'em fine,
For the reception of my *Catharine*.
We will have rings, and things, and fine array;
To-morrow, *Kate*, shall be our wedding-day.
                                        [*Exit* Petruchio.

Bapt. Well, daughter, tho' the man be somewhat wild,
And thereto frantic, yet his means are great;
Thou hast done well to seize the first kind offer,
For by thy mother's soul 'twill be the last.
   Cath. My duty, Sir, hath followed your command.
   Bapt. Art thou in earnest? hast no trick behind?
I'll take thee at thy word, and send t'invite
My son-in-law, *Hortensio*, and thy sister;
And all our friends to grace thy nuptials, *Kate*.
                                        [*Exit* Baptista.

   Cath: Why, yes: sister *Bianca* now shall see
The poor abandon'd *Cath'rine*, as she calls me.
Can hold her head as high, and be as proud,
And make her husband stoop unto her lure,
As she, or e'er a wife in *Padua*.
As double as my portion be my scorn;
Look to your seat, *Petruchio*, or I throw you.
Cath'rine shall tame this haggard;—or if she fails,
Shall tye her tongue up, and pair down her nails,
                                        [*Exit* Catharine.

A C T II.

Enter BAPTISTA, HORTENSIO, CATHARINE, BIANCA,
            and Attendants.

BAPTISTA.

SIGNIOR *Hortensio*, this is th' appointed day,
That *Cath'rine* and *Petruchio* shall be married;
And yet we hear not of our son-in-law.
What will be said? what mockery will it be,
To want the bridegroom when the pries: attends
To speak the ceremonial rites of marriage?
What says *Hortensio* to th's shame of ours?
   Cath. No shame but mine; I must, forsooth'd, be forc'd
To give my hand oppos'd against my heart,
Unto a mad brain rudesby, full of spleen,
Who woo'd in haste, and means to wed at leisure.
                                        I told

I told you, I, he was a frantic fool,
Hiding his better jests in blunt behaviour:
And to be noted for a merry man.
He'll woo a thousand, 'point the day or marriage,
Make friends, invite; yea, and proclaim the banes.
Yet never means to wed where he hath woo'd
Now must the world point at poor *Catharine*,
And say, lo! there is mad *Petrucbio's* wife,
If it please him come and marry her.

 Bian. Such hasty matches seldom end in good.

 Hort. Patience. good *Catb'rine*, and *Bianca* too;
Upon my life, *Petrucbio* means but well,
Whatever fortune stays him from his world;
Tho' he be blunt, I know him passing wise;
Tho' he be merry, yet withal he's honest.

 Catb. Wou'd I had never seen his honesty.——
Oh! I could tear my flesh for very madness.

[Exit. Catharine.

 Bapt. Follow your sister, girl, and comfort her.

[Exit Bianca.

I cannot blame thee now to weep and rage,
For such an injury would vex a saint;
Much more a shrew of thy impatient humour.

 Hort. Was ever match clapt up so suddenly!

 Bapt. Hortensio: faith I play a merchant's part.
And venture madly on a desp'rate mart.

 Hort. 'Twas a commodity lay fretting by you;
'Twill bring you gain, or parish on the seas,

 Bapt. The gain I seek is quiet in the match.

 Hort. No doubt *Petrucbio's* got a quiet catch.

Enter BIONDELLO.

 Bion. Master, master, news; and such news as you never heard of.

 Bapt. Is *Petrucbio* come?

 Bion. Why no, Sir.

 Bapt. What then!

 Bion. He is coming; but how? why in a new hat, and
an old Jerkin; a pair of old breeches, thrice turn'd; a pair
of boots that have been candle cases, one buckled, another lac'd; an old rusty sword, ta'en out of the town armo-
ry, with a broken hilt, and chapeless, with two broken
points; his horse hip'd with an old mothy saddle; the stir-
rups of no kindred; besides posses'd with the glanders, and
like

like to mose in the chine; troubled with the lampasse, in-
fected with the farcy, full of windgalls, sped with spavins,
raied with the yallows, past cure of the fives, stark spoiled
with the staggers, be-gnawn with the bots, waid in the back,
and shoulder-shotten, near legg'd before, and with a half-
chec'd bit; and a head-stall of sheep-leather, which being
restrained, to keep him from stumbling, hath been often
burst, and now repaired with knots, one girt six times piec'd,
and a woman's cruppure of velure, which hath two letters
for her name, fairly set down in studs, and here and there
piec'd with pack-thread.

 Bapt. Who comes with him?

 Bion. O Sir, his laquey, for all the world comparison'd
like the horse with a linen stock on one leg, and a kersey
boot hose on the other, gartered with a red and blue list,
an old hat, and the humour of forty fancies prick'd upon
it for a feather; a monster! a very monster in apparel, and
not like a christian foot-boy, or a gentleman's lacquey.

 Bapt. I am glad he's come, howsoever he comes.

 Enter PETRUCHIO *and* GRUMIO, *fantastically habited.*

 Pet. Come, where be these gallants? who is at home?

 Bapt. You're welcome, Sir.

 Pet. Well am I come then, Sir.

 Bapt. Not so well 'parell'd as I wish you were.

 Pet. Why were it better, I should rush in thus:
But where is *Kate?* where is my lovely bride?
How does my father? Gentles, methinks you frown;
And wherefore gaze this goodly company?
As if they saw some wond'rous monument,
Some comet, or unusual prodigy?

 Bapt. Why, Sir, you know this is your wedding-day.
First we were sad, fearing you would not come;
Now sadder, that you come so unprovided,
Fy! doff this habit, shame to your estate;
And eye-sore to our solemn festival.

 Hort. And tell us what occasion of import
Hath all so long detained you from your wife,
And sent you hither so unlike yourself?

 Pet. Tedious it were to tell, and harsh to hear,
Let it suffice, I'm come to keep my word;
But where is *Kate?* I stay too long from her
The morning wears; 'tis time we were at church.

 Hort. See not the bride in these unrev'rent robes;

Go

Go to my bed-chamber, put on cloaths of mine.
Pet. Not I, believe me, thus I'll visit her.
Bapt. But thus I trust you and will not marry her.
Pet. Good sooth, even thus; therefore ha' done with
      words;
To me she's m.rried, not unto my cloaths:
Could I repair what she could wear in me,
As I could change these poor accoutrements,
'Twere well for *Kate,* and better for myself.
But what a fool am I to chat with you,
When I should bid good-morrow to my bride,
And seal the title with a lovely kiss ?
What ho! my *Kate!* my *Kate!*   [*Exit* Petruchio.
Hort. He hath some meaning in this mad attire:
We will persuade him be it possible;
To put on better e'er he go to church.
Bapt. I'll after him, and see the event of this.
                              [*Exeunt all but* Grumio,
Grum. He's gone to church with her. I wou'd sooner
have led her to the gallows. If he can but hold it, 'tis
well——and if I know any thing of myself and master, no
two men were ever born with such qualities to tame women.——When madam goes home, we must look for ano-
ther-guise master then we have had. We shall see old coil
between 'em.——If I can spy into futurity a little, there
will be much clatter among the moveables, and some practice for the surgeons. By this the parson has given 'em
his licence to fall together by the ears.
                    Enter PEDRO.
Ped. Grumio, your master bid me find you out, and speed
you to his country-house, to prepare for his reception, and
if he finds not things as he expects 'em, according to his di-
rections that he gave you, you know, he says, what follows: this message he delivered before his bride, ev'n in
her way to church, and shook his whip in token of his love.
Grum. I understand it, Sir, and will convey the same token to my horse immediately, that he may take to his heels
in order to save my bones, and his own ribs.
                              [*Exit* Grumio.

Ped. So odd a master, and so fit a man,
Were never seen in *Padua* before.
                    Enter BIONDELLO.
Now, *Biondello,* came you from the church ?

                                        B*on*.

Bion. As willingly as e'er I came from school.
Ped. And is the bride or bridegroom coming home?
Bion. A bridegroom say you? 'tis a groom indeed;
A grumbling groom, and that the girl shall find.
Ped. Curster than she; why 'tis impossible.
Bion. Why, he's a devil; a devil! a very fiend!
Ped. Why, she's a devil; a devil! the devils dam.
Bion. Tut! she's a lamb, a dove, a fool to him:
I'll tell you, brother *Pedro*, when the priest
Should ask if *Catharine* should be his wife?
Ay, by gogs-wounds, quoth he, and swore so loud,
That all amaz'd the priest let fall his book:
And as he stoop'd again to take it up,
This mad-brain'd bridegroom took him such a cuff,
That down fell priest and book, and book on priest,
Now take them up, quoth he, if any list.
    Ped. What said the wench, when he rose up again?
    Bion. Trembled and shook; for why, he stamp'd and
        swore,
As if the Vicar went to cozen him.
But after many ceremonies done,
He calls for wine; a health, quoth he, as if
Ha'd been abroad carousing to his mates
After a storm; quafft of the muscadel
And threw the sops all in the sexton's face;
Having no other cause, but that his beard
Grew thin and hungerly, and seem'd to ask
His sops, as he was drinking. This done, he took
The bride about the neck, and kiss'd her lips
With such a clamarous smack, that at the parting
All the church echo'd; and I seeing this,
Came thence for very shame; and after me
I know the rout is coming:
Such a mad marriage never was before——   *Music.*
Hark, hark, I hear the minstrels play.
    Enter PETRUCHIO *(singing)* CATHARINE, BIANCA,
        HORTENSIO *and* BAPTISTA.
    Pet. Gentlemen and friends, I thank you for your pains;
I know you think to dine with me to-day,
And have prepar'd good store of wedding cheer;
But so it is, my haste doth call me hence;
And therefore, here I mean to take my leave.
    Bapt. Is't possible you will away to-night?

Pet. I must away to-day, before night come.
Make it no wonder ; if you knew my business,
You would intreat me rather go than stay ;
And honest company, I thank you all,
That have beheld me give away myself
To this most patient, sweet, and virtuous wife :
Dine with my father, drink a health to me,
For I must hence, and farewel you all.

   Hort. Let me intreat you, stay till after dinner.

   Pet. It may not be.

   Bion. Let me intreat you, that my sister stay ;
I come on purpose to attend the wedding ;
And pass this day in mirth and festival.

   Pet. It cannot be.

   Cath. Let me intreat you.

   Pet. I am content.——

   Cath. Are you content to stay ?

   Pet. I am content, you shall intreat my stay ;
But yet not stay, intreat me how you can.

   Cath Now, if you love me stay.

   Pet. My horses, there ; what ho, my horses there——

   Cath. Nay then,
Do what thou can'st, I will not go to-day ;
No, nor to-morrow, nor till I please myself ;
The door is open, Sir, their lies your way ;
You may be jogging, while your boots are green.-
For me, I'll not go, 'till I please myself ;
'Tis like you'll prove a jolly surly groom,
To take it on you at the first so roundly.

   Bapt. O *Kate* content thee ; pr'ythee be not angry.

   Cath. I will be angry ; what hast thou to do ;
Father be quiet, he shall stay my leisure.

   Hort. Ay marry, Sir ; now it begins to work.

   Cath. Gentlemen, forward to the bridal dinner.
I see a woman may be made a fool,
If she had not a spirit to resist.

   Pet. They shall go forward, *Kate*, at thy command.
Obey the bride, you that attend on her :
Go to the feast, revel and domineer ;
Carouse full measure to her maidenhead ;
Be mad and merry, or go hang yourselves,
But for my bonny *Kate*, she must with me.
Nay, look not big, nor stamp, nor stare, nor fret

I will

I will be master of what is mine own;
She is my goods, my chattles; she is my house,
My houshold-stuff, my field, my barn,
My horse, my ox, my ass, my any-thing;
And here she stands, touch her whoever dare
I'll bring my action on the proudest he,
That stops my way in *Padua*: *Petruchio*,
Draw forth thy weapon, thou'rt beset with thieves;
Rescue thy wife then, if thou be a man;
Fear not sweet wench, they shall not touch thee, *Kate*;
I'll buckler thee against a million, *Kate*.

> [*Exeunt* Pet. *and* Cath.

Bapt. Nay, let them go, a couple of quiet ones.

Hort. Of all mad matches never was the like
What's your opinion of your gentle sister?

Bion. That being mad herself, she's madly matched.

Bapt. Neighbours and friends, tho' bride and bridegroom
want
For to supply the places at the table;
You know there wants no junkets at the feast:
Hortensio, you'll supply the bridegroom's place,
And let *Bianca* take her sister's room.

Bian. My sister's room! were I in her's indeed,
This swaggerer shou'd repent his insolence. [*Exeunt omnes.*

Enter GRUMIO.

Grum. Fie, fie on all jades, and all mad master's, and all
foul ways! Was ever man so beaten? was ever man so
raide! was ever man so weary? I am sent before to make a
fire, and they are coming after to warn them: now, were I
not a little pot, and soon hot, my very lips might freeze to
my teeth, my tongue to the roof of my mouth, my heart in
my belly, ere I should come by a fire, to thaw me, but I
with blowing the fire shall warm myself, for considering the
weather, a taller man than I will take cold; holloa, hoa,
Curtis!

Enter CURTIS.

Curt. Who is it that calls so coldly?

Grum. A piece of ice   If thou doubt it, thou may'st slide
from my should to my heel with no greater a run but my
head and my neck.   A fire, good *Curtis*.

Curt. Is my master and his wife coming, *Grumio!*

> *Grum.*

Grum. Oh, ay, *Curtis,* ay, and therefore, fire, fire; cast on no water.

Curt. Is she so hot a shrew as she's reported?

Grum. She was, good *Curtis,* before the frost; but thou know'st Winter tames men, woman, and beast, for it hath tam'd my old master, and my new mistress, and myself, fellow *Curtis.*

Curt. Away you thick-pated-fool, I am no beast.

Grum. Where's the cock? Is supper ready, the house trim'd rushes strew'd, cobwebs swept, the serving-men in their new fustain, their white stockings, and every officer his wedding garments on? Be the *Jack's* fair within, the *Jill's* fair without, carpets laid, and every thing in order?

Curt. All ready: and therefore, I pray thee, what news?

Grum. First know my horse is tired, my master and mistress fall'n out.

Curt. How.

Grum. Out of their saddles into the dirt: and thereby hangs a tale.

Curt. Let's ha't, good *Grumio.*

Grum. Lend thine ear.

Curt. Here.

Grum. There.   [*Strikes him.*

Curt. This is to feel a tale, not to hear a tale.

Grum. And therefore is call'd a sensible tale: and this cuff was but to knock at your ear, and beseech listning. Now I begin: *imprimis,* we came down a foul hill, my master riding behind my mistress ——

Curt. Both on one horse!

Grum. What's that to thee? tell thou the tale. But ha'lst thou not crost me, thou should'st have heard how her horse fell, and she under her horse; thou shouldst have heard in how merry a place, how she was bemoild, how he left her with her horse upon her, how he beat me because her horse stumbled, how she waded through the dirt to pluck him off me; how he swore, how she pray'd, that never pray'd before, how I cry'd. how the horses ran away, how her bridle was burst, how I lost my crupper; how my mistress lost her slippers, tore and bemir'd her garments, limp'd to the farm-house, put on *Rebecca's* old shoes and petticoat; with many things worthy of memory, which now shall die, in oblivion, and thou return unexperienc'd to thy grave.

Curt. By this reckoning he is more shrew than she.

Grum.

Grum. Ay, for the nonce—and that, thou and the proudest of you all shall find, when he comes home.—But what talk I of this? call forth *Nathaniel, Joseph, Nicholas, Philip, Walter, Sugarsop,* and the rest: let their heads be sleek-com'd, their blue coats brush'd, and their garters of an indifferent knit; let them curt'sy with their left legs, and not presume to touch a hair of my master's horse tail, till they kiss their hands.   Are they all ready?

Curt. They are.

Grum. Call them forth.

Curt. Do you hear, ho! *Nathaniel, Joseph, Nicholas,* etc. Where are you?

Enter NATHANIEL, PHILIP, *etc.*

Nath. Welcome home, *Grumio.*

Phil. How now, *Grumio?*

Pet. What, *Grumio!*

Nich. Fellow *Grumio!*

Nath. How now, old lad!

Grum. Welcome you; how now, you; what you; fellow you; and thus much for greeting.   Now, my spruce companions, is all ready, and all things neat?

Nath All thing are ready, how near is our master?

Grum. E'en at hand, alighted by this; and therefore be not cock's passion! Silence, I hear my master.

Enter PETRUCHIO *and* CATHARINE.

Pet. Where are these knaves? What, no man at door to hold my stirrup, nor to take my horse? where is *Nathaniel, Gregory. Philip?*

All-Servants. Here, here, Sir; here, Sir.

Pet. Here, Sir; here, Sir; here, Sir; here, Sir;
You loggerheaded, and unpolish'd grooms:
What no attendance, no regard, no duty?
Where is the foolish knave I sent before?

Grum. Here, Sir, as foolish as I was before.

Pet. You peasant swain, you whoreson malt-horse drudge,
i d — not bid thee meet me in the park,
And bring along these rascal knaves with thee?

Grum. *Nathaniel's* coat, Sir, was not fully made:
And *Gabriel's* pumps were all unpink i' th' heel:
There was no link to colour *Peter's* hat,
And *Walter's* dagger was not come from sheathing:

There were none fine but *Adam*, *Ralph*, and *Gregory*;
The rest were ragged, old, and beggarly:
Yet as they are, here are they come to meet you.
   Pet. Go, rascals, go, and fetch my supper in.
[*Exeunt servants.*
(*Sings.*)

  " Where is the life that late I led ?
  " Where are those"——Sit down, *Kate*,
And welcome. " Soud, soud, soud, soud."

Enter servants with Supper.

Why, when, I say ? Nay, good sweet *Kate*, be merry.
Off with my boots you rogue: you villains, when !——

(*Sings.*)

  " It was a fryar of orders grey
  " As he forth walked on his way."
Out, out, you rogue: you pluck my foot awry.
Take that, and mind the plucking of the other.
[*Strikes him.*

Be merry, *Kate;* some water here. What hoa !
Where's my spaniel *Troilus ?* Sirrah, get you hence,
And bid my cousin *Ferdinand* come hither:
One, *Kate*, that you must kiss and be acquainted with.
Where are my slippers ?—Shall I have some water ?

Enter a Servant with Water.

Come, *Kate*, and wash, and welcome heartily.
[*Servants lets fall the water.*

You whoreson villain, will you let it fall ?
  Cath. Patience, I pray you, 'twas a fault unwilling.
  Pet. A whoreson, beetle-headed, flap-ear'd knave ?
Come, *Kate*, sit down ; I know you have a stomach.
  Cath. Indeed I have :
And never was repast so welcome to me.
  Pet. Will you give thanks, sweet *Kate*, or else shall I ?
What's this, mutton ?
  Serv. Yes.
  Pet. Who brought it ?
  Serv. I.
  Pet. 'Tis burnt, and so is all the meat——
What dogs are these ! Where is the rascal cook ?
How durst you, villain, bring it from the dresser,

And serve it thus to me, that love it not?
There; take it to you, trenchers, cups, and all.
                         [*Throws the meat*, etc. *about.*
You heedless jolt heads, and unmanner'd slaves.
What, do you grumble? I'll be with you straight.
                         [*Exeunt all the servants.*

    Cath. I pray you, husband, be not so disquiet,
The meat was well, and well I could have eat,
If you were so disposed; I'm sick with fasting.
    Pet. I tell thee, *Kate*, 'twas burnt and dry'd away,
And I expressly am forbid to touch it:
For it engenders choler, planteth anger;
And better it were that both of us did fast,
Since of ourselves, ourselves are choleric,
Than feed it with such over-roasted flesh——
Be patient; to-morrow it shall be mended,
And for this night, we'll fast for company.
Come, I will bring thee to thy bridal-chamber.   [*Exeunt.*

    Enter NATHANIEL *and* PETER.

    Nath. Peter, didst thou ever see the like?
    Pet. He kills her in his own humour. I did not think
so good and kind a master cou'd have put on so resolute a
bearing.
    Grum. Where is he?

    Enter CURTIS.

    Curt. In her chamber, making a sermon of continency to
her, and rails, and swears, and rates; and she, poor soul
knows not which way to stand, to speak; and sits as one
new risen from a dream. Away, away, for he is coming
hither.   *Exeunt.*

    Enter PETRUCHIO.

    Thus have I, politickly, begun my reign;
And 'tis my hope to end successfully:
My falcon now is sharp, and passing empty;
And 'till she stoop, she must not be full gorg'd,
For then she never looks upon her lure.
Another way I have to man my haggard,
To make her come, and keep her keeper's all:
That is, to watch her, as we watch these kites,
That bit and beat, and will not be obedient.
She eat no meat to-day, nor none shall eat:
Last night she slept not, nor to-night shall not;

N 2

A

As with the meat, some undeserved fault
I'll find about the making of the bed;
And here I'll fling the pillow, there the bolster,
This way the coverlet; that way the sheets;
Aye, and amid' this hurly, I'll pretend
That all is done in rev'rent care of her;
And in conclusion she shall watch all night:
And if she chance to nod, I'll rail and brawl,
And with the clamour keep her still awake.
This is a way to kill a wife with kindness,
And thus I'll curb her mad and head-strong humour—
He that knows better how to tame a shrew,
Now let him speak; 'tis charity to shew.   [*Exit.*

A C T III.

Enter CATHARINE *and* GRUMIO.

GRUMIO.

NO, no, forsooth, I dare not for my life,   [pears;
    Cath. The more my wrong, the more his spite ap-
What! did he marry me to famish me?
Beggars that come unto my father's door,
Upon intreaty have a present alms;
If not, elsewhere they meet with charity:
But I who never knew how to intreat,
Nor ever needed that I should intreat,
Am starv'd for meat, giddy for lack of sleep;
With oaths kept waking, and with brawling fed;
And that which spights me more than all these wants,
He does it under name of perfect love:
As who would say, if I should sleep or eat
'Twere deadly sickness or else present death!
I pr'ythee go and get me some repast;
I care not what, so it be wholesome food.
  Grum. What say you to a neat's foot?
  Cath. 'Tis passing good; I pr'ythee let me have it.
  Grum. I fear, it is too flegmatic a meat;
How say you to a fat tripe, finely boil'd?
  Cath. I like it well; good *Grumio*, fetch it me.
  Grum. I cannot tell;—I fear, its choleric:
What say you to a piece of beef and mustard?
  Cath. A dish that I do love to feed upon.
  Grum. Aye, but the mustard is too hot a little.

                                             Cath.

Catb. Why then the beef, and let the mustard rest.

Grum. Nay, that I will not, you shall have the mustard,
Or else you get no beef of *Grumio.*

Catb. Then both, or one, or any thing thou wilt,

Grum. Why then, the mustard, dame, without the beef.

Catb. Go, get thee gone, thou false deluding slave,
[Beats him.

That feed'st me only with the name of meat·
Sorrow on thee, and all the pack of you,
That triumph thus upon my misery,
Go, get thee gone, I say.

Enter PETRUCHIO.

Pet. How fares my *Kate ?*
What, sweeting, all amort? Mistress, what cheer ?

Catb. 'Faith as cold as can be.

Pet. Pluck up thy spirits, look chearful upon me.
For now my honey-love we are refresh'd——

Catb. Refresh'd ! with what?

Pet. We will return unto thy father's house,
And revel as bravely as the best,
With silken coats, and caps, and golden rings,
With ruffs, and cuffs, and fardingals, and things :
With scarfs, and fans, and double change of brav'ry,
Now thou hast eat, the taylor stays thy leisure,
To deck thy body with his rustling treasure.

Enter Taylor.

Come, taylor, let us see these ornaments.

Enter Haberdasher.

Lay forth the gown—What news with you, Sir ?

Hab. Here is the cap your worship did bespeak.

Pet. Why this was moulded on a porringer ;
A velvet dish : fye, fye ; 'tis lewd and filthy :
Why 'tis a cockle, or a walnut-shell,
A knack, a toy, a trick, a baby's cap.
Away with it, come let me have a bigger.

Catb. I'll have no bigger, this doth fit the time,
And gentlewomen wear such caps as these.

Pet. When you are gentle, you shall have one too,
And not till then.

Catb. Why, Sir; I trust I may have leave to speak,
N 3
And

And speak I will; I am no child, no babe;
Your betters have endur'd me to say my mind;
And if you cannot, best you stop your ears;
My tongue will tell the anger of my heart,
Or else my heart concealing it, will break:
And rather than it shall, I will be free,
Ev'n to the utmost as I please in words.

    Pet. Thou say'st true, *Kate*; it is a paultry cap,
A custard coffin, bauble silken pie.
I love thee well, in that thou lik'st it not.

    Cath. Love me, or love me not, I like the cap;
And I will have it, or I will have none.

    Pet. Thy gown? why aye; come, taylor, let me see't.
O mercy, heav'n! what masking stuff is here?
What's this, a sleeve? 'Tis like a demi-canon;
What up and down, carv'd like an apple-tart!
Here's snip, and nip, and cut, and slish, and slash,
Like a censer in a barber's shop,
Why, what the devil's name, taylor, call'st thou this?

    Grum. I see she's like to've neither cap nor gown.

    Tay. You bid me make it orderly and well,
According to the fashion of the time.

    Pet. Mary and did: but if you be remember'd,
I did not bid you marr it to the time.
Go, hop me over every kennel home;
For you shall hop without my custom, Sir;
I'll none of it; hence, make your best of it.

    Cath. I never saw a better fashioned gown,
More quaint, more pleasing, nor more commendable;
Belike you mean to make a puppet of me.

    Pet. Why, true; he means to make a puppet of thee.

    Tay. She says your worship means to make a puppet of
      her.

    Pet. Oh! most monstrous arrogance!
Thou lyest, thou thread, thou thimble,
Thou yard, three-quarters, half-yard, quarter, nail.
Thou flea, thou nit, thou winter-cricket, thou!
Brav'd in mine own house, with a skein of thread!
Away thou rag! thou quantity, thou remnant,
Or I shall so be-mete thee with thy yard,
As thou shall think on prating whilst thou liv'st;
I tell thee, I, that thou hast marr'd the gown.

    Tay. Your worship is deceiv'd, the gown is made just as
                              my

my master had direction; *Grumio* gave orders how it should
be done.

Grum. I gave him no order, I gave him the stuff.

Tay. But how did you desire it should be made?

Grum. Marry, Sir, with a needle and thread.

Tay. But did you not request to have it cut!

Grum. Tho' thou hast fac'd many things face not me; I
say unto thee, I bid thy master cut the gown, but I did not
bid him cut it to pieces. *Ergo*, thou liest.

Tay. Why, here is the note of the fashion to testify.

Pet. Read it.

Tay. Imprimis, a loose-bodied gown.

Grum. Master, if ever I said a loose-bodied gown, sew
me up in the skirts of it, and beat me to death with a bottom of brown thread : I said a gown.

Pet. Proceed.

Tay. With a small compass cape.

Grum. I confess the cape.

Tay. With a trunk sleeve.

Grum. I confess two sleeves.

Tay. The sleeves curiously cut.

Pet. Ay, there's the villainy.

Grum. Error i' th' bill, Sir; error i' th' bill; I command-
ed the sleeves should be cut out, and sow'd up again, and
that I'll prove upon thee, tho' thy little finger be arm'd in
a thimble.

Tay. This is true that I say ; an' I had thee in a place
thou should'st know it.

Grum. I am for thee, straight: come on you parchment
shred !   [*They fight.*

Pet. What, chickens sparr in presence of the kite !
I'll swoop upon you both : out, out, ye vermin——
                                           [*Beats 'em off.*

Cath. For heav'n's sake, Sir, have patience ! how you
fright me !   [*Cryng.*

Pet. Well, come my *Kate ;* we will unto your father's.
Even in these honest, mean habiliments :
Our purses shall be proud, our garments poor
For 'tis the mind that makes the body rich ;
And as the sun breaks through the darkest cloud,
So honour peereth in the meanest habit.
What is, the jay more precious than the lark,
Because feathers are more beautiful?

Or is the adder better than the eel,
Because his painted skin contents the eye?
Oh no, good *Kate*; neither art thou the worse
For this poor furniture, and mean array.
If thou accounts't it shame, lay it on me;
And therefore; frolic we will hence, forthwith,
To feast and sport us at thy father's house :
Go call my men, and bring our horses out.

   Cath. O happy hearing! Let us strait be gone;
I cannot tarry here another day.

   Pet. Cannot, my *Kate!* O fie! indeed you can——
Besides, on second thoughts, 'tis now too late ;
For, look, how bright and goodly shines the moon.

   Cath. the moon! the sun; it is not moon-light now.

   Pet. I say it is the moon that shines so bright.

   Cath. I say it is the sun that shines so bright.

   Pet. Now, by my mother's son, and that's myself;
It shall be moon, or star; or what a list,
Or e'er I journey to your father's house :
Go on and fetch our horses back again :
Evermore crost, and crost ; nothing but crost !

   Grum. Say as he says, or we shall never go.

   Cath. I see 'tis vain to struggle with my bonds ;
So be it moon, or sun, or what you please ;
And if you please to call it a rush candle,
Henceforth I vow, it shall be so for me.

   Pet. I say it is the moon.

   Cath. I know it is the moon.

   Pet. Nay, then you lie ; it is the blessed sun.

   Cath. Just as you please, it is the blessed sun ;
But sun it is not, when you say it is not ;
And the moon changes, even as your mind ;
What you will have it nam'd, even that it is,
And so it shall be for your *Catharine*.

   Pet. Well, forward, forward, thus the bowl shall run,
And not unluckily, against the biass :
But soft, some company is coming here,
And stops our journey.

Enter BAPTISTA, HORTENSIO, *and* BIANCA.

Good-morrow, gentle mistress, where away ?
Tell me, sweet *Kate*, and tell me truly too
Hast thou beheld a fresher gentlewoman

Such

Such war of white and red within her cheeks!
What stars do spangle heav'n with such beauty,
As those two eyes become that heav'nly face?
Fair lovely maid once more good day to thee;
Sweet *Kate*, embrace her for her beauty's sake.
    Bapt. What's all this?
    Catb. Young budding virgin, fair, and fresh, and sweet,
Whither away, or where is thy abode?
Happy the parents of so fair a child;
Happier the man whom favourable stars
Allot thee, for his lovely bed-fellow.
    Bian. What mummery is this?
    Pet. Why, how now, *Kate*; I hope thou art not mad!
This is *Baptista*, our old reverent father;
And not a maiden, as thou say'st he is.
    Catb. Pardon, dear father, my mistaken eyes,
That have been so bedazled with the sun,
That every thing I look on seemeth green;
Now I perceive thou art my reverent father;
Pardon, I pray thee, for my mad mistaking.   [*kneels.*
    Bapt. Rise, rise, my child; what strange vigary's this?
I came to see thee with my son and daughter.
How lik'st thou wedlock? Ar't not alter'd, *Kate*?
    Catb. Indeed I am.   I am transform'd to stone.
    Pet. Chang'd for the better much; ar't not my *Kate*?
    Catb. So good a master, cannot chuse to mend me.
    Hprt. Here is a wonder, if you talk of wonders.
    Bapt. And so it is; I wonder what it bodes?
    Pet. Marry, peace it bodes, and love, and life,
And awful rule, and right supremacy;
And to be short, what not, that's sweet and happy.
    Bian. Was ever woman's spirit broke so soon!
What is the matter, *Kate*? hold up thy head,
Nor lose our sex's best prerogative,
To wish and have our will.——
    Pet. Peace, brawler, peace,
Or I will give the meek *Hortensio*,
Your husband, there, my taming recipe.
    Bian. Lord, never let me have a cause to sigh,
'Till I be brought to such a silly pass.
    Grum. (*to Bapt.*) Did I not promise you, Sir, my ma-
ster's discipline wou'd work miracles?
    Bapt. I scarce believe my eyes and ears.

                                            Bian.

Bian. His eyes and ears had felt these fingers e'er
He shou'd have moap'd me so.

Catb. Alas ! my sist: r———

Pet. Calbarine, I charge thee tell this headstrong woman,
What duty 'tis she owes her lord and husband.

Bian. Come, come, you're mocking, we will have no
telling.

Pet, Come, on, I say.

Bian. She shall not.

Hort. Let us hear for both our sakes, good wife.

Pet. Catbarine, begin.

Catb. Fie, fie, unknit that threatning, unkind brow,
And dart not scornful glances from those eyes ;
To wound thy lord, thy king, thy governor,
It blots thy beauty, as frost bite the meads,
Confounds thy fame, as whirlwinds shake fair buds,
And in no sense is meet or amiable.

Pet. Why, well said *Kate.*

Catb. A woman mov'd is like a fountain troubled,
Muddy, ill-seeming, thick, bereft of beauty ;
And while it is so, none so dry or thirsty
Will dain to sip, or touch a drop of it.

Bian. Sister, be quiet———

Pet. Nay, learn thou that lesson———On, on, I say,

Catb. Thy husband is thy lord, thy life, thy keeper,
Thy head, thy sovereign : one that cares for thee,
And for thy maintainance : commits his body
To painful labour, both by sea and land,
To watch the night in storms, the day in cold,
While thou ly'st warm at home, secure and safe;
And craves no other tribute at thy hands,
But love, fair looks, and true obedience ;
Too little payment for so great a debt.

Bapt. Now fair befal thee, son *Petrucbio,*
The battle's won, and thou cans't keep the field.

Pet. Oh ! fear me not———

Bapt. Then, my new gentle *Catbarine,*
Go home with me along, and I will add
Another dowry to another daughter,
For thou are changed as thou hadst never been.

Pet. My fortune is sufficient. Her's my wealth
Kiss me, my *Kate ;* and since thou art become
So prudent, kind, and dutiful a wife,

Petru-

*P*etruchio here shall doff the lordly husband;
An honest mask, which I throw off with pleasure.
Far hence all rudeness, wilfulness, and noise,
And be our future lives one gentle stream
Of mutual love, compliance, and regard.

 Cath. Nay, then I'm all unworthy of thy love,
And look with blushes on my former self.

 Pet. Good *Kate*, no more—this is beyond my hopes—
    [*Goes forward with* Catharine *in his hand.*
Such duty as the subject owes the prince,
Even such a woman oweth to her husband:
And when she's froward, peevish, sullen, sower,
And not obedient to his honest will;
What is she but a foul contending rebel,
And graceless traitor to her loving lord?
How shameful 'tis when women are so simple
To offer war where they should kneel for peace;
Or seek for rule, supremacy, and sway,
Where bound to love, to honour and obey.

THE END OF VOLUME FIRST.

www.ingramcontent.com/pod-product-compliance
Lightning Source LLC
Chambersburg PA
CBHW031938130726
47905CB00008BA/2545